THREE DEAD IN STARBUCKS

A Tom Wallace Novel

Dave Tevelin

D1509035

In memory of

Caity Mahoney

Emory Evans

Aaron Goodrich

Washington, D.C.

July 7, 1997

Jamie yawned again as she moved into the right lane of Wisconsin Avenue without bothering to look in the rear-view mirror or flick her turn signal. At 5:25 on the Monday morning of the July 4th weekend, no one was heading to Georgetown except her and the few other miserable souls who had to open their shops dark and early, and she was going to conserve every atom of her energy until the second she could get back home and fall into a coma.

Her mind drifted back to Rehoboth, but it was all a blur of beer, sand, hot bodies on the beach, and one particularly hot body in her bed. A fresh steaming Venti Pike Place Roast would give her the clarity she wasn't sure she really wanted, but as she turned into the parking lot next to her Starbucks, her jumble of thoughts turned into one simple question.

Why was Caity's car still in the lot?

Caity Mahoney was the night manager, but the doors closed at 8 and the crew would've been done by 9, so she should've been long gone. Jamie pulled around the passenger side of her silver '94 Saturn and saw the front tire was flat. So that explained it: She couldn't drive home so she called a cab or someone to pick her up. Mystery solved. She pressed her head to the side window just to be sure and smiled to see that all that was in there was her usual array of dog stuff – a chew toy, a brush, and a mangy red towel.

She turned the corner to the front entrance and found the door key just as her assistant manager's large body hurtled out the door and knocked her to the sidewalk. She laid there and watched Stacy run into the middle of Wisconsin, screaming words she couldn't understand, her arms waving at cars that weren't there. "Stacy!" she yelled. "What are you doing? What's wrong?"

1

"Don't go in there, Jamie! Do *not* go in there!" She threw her hands to her chest. "Oh, my good God Jesus Christ! Do you have a car phone?"

"No," Jamie said, pushing herself up off the pavement. "Why do you need a phone?" she asked, but Stacy was running up Wisconsin, waving her hands frantically. "Stop! Stop!" she heard her yell, then saw the lights of a Metrobus cresting the hill she'd just come down. Jamie took off after her.

"Stacy! Stop! He can't see you! He'll kill you!"

But she kept running until the bus caught her in his headlights and screeched to a stop twenty feet in front of her. Jamie reached her side at the door. The driver pulled it open, the bewildered look on his face matching how she felt. "What's –" he got out before Stacy screamed at him "There's a dead body in the Starbucks!"

"What?" Jamie yelled. The driver's mouth opened but no words came out.

"You got a phone in there, don't you?" Stacy asked him, gulping for air. "Yeah," he said, pointing a shaky finger at its perch on the dash. "Then call 9-1-1 and tell 'em to get down to the Starbucks at 1810 Wisconsin *now*! There's a dead girl in there, blood all over. You get them down there now!"

The driver's eyes bugged before his hand lurched to the phone. Stacy didn't wait for him to pick it up and started running back down Wisconsin before Jamie caught up with her and tugged her onto the sidewalk. Stacy buried her face in her shoulder and moaned a dark muffled howl before pulling her head back, tears spilling down her cheeks.

"Oh my Lord!" she said. "Oh my Lord! I can't stop seeing her, I can't! I can't go back in there. Don't make me, Jamie, please!"

"Neither one of us is going in there till the police show up, I promise you," Jamie said. She let the bus roar past them before she asked the question she couldn't put off any longer.

"Stacy, was it Caity? Is that who you saw?"

Stacy nodded and bawled. Jamie held her close and tried to remember what little she knew about the night manager other than what was obvious to anyone who was in her company for more than a second: Caity Mahoney was a trim pretty redhead full of life. They'd chatted at some staff things, but all she could remember now was that she'd graduated from Towson State and started working at Starbucks maybe a year ago. Someone told her she had an internship at the White House after Clinton got re-elected, but that was it. Stacy finally caught her breath enough to talk.

"I came in to open up like usual but even before I got to the door, I knew somethin' was off. The lights were on, and so was the music, and that wasn't like Caity at all, you know that. Every day we came in, that place was tight and ready."

Jaime stiffened before she realized why, then pulled her head back and held Stacy's shoulders tight. "How about her crew?" she asked. "Did you see any of them?"

Stacy slapped her hands to her eyes. "Oh my God, no! Oh Lord, maybe they left before she –"

They heard the police car before they saw it, the wail of its siren shattering the stillness of the rising dawn.

"We need to get down there," Jamie said. They locked hands and hurried back down the sidewalk. Two police cars, sirens wailing and beacons flashing, humped over the hill in front of them, then made quick ueys and pulled to a stop in front of the shop. Jamie and Stacy picked up the pace to meet them at the door. A uniformed white officer blocked the sidewalk and held up his hands.

"Ladies, this is a crime scene," he said. "You'll have to get your coffee somewhere else today."

"No," Jamie said, "we work here. We're the ones who got the bus driver to call you."

"Hold on, stay right there," he said and walked back to a large black man in a dark blue sport jacket getting out of the back seat of the car closest to them. They talked for a second, then the man in the jacket approached them and extended his hand to Jamie.

"Good morning, I'm Tom Wallace. I'm a detective with the Metropolitan Police Department. And you are?"

"Jamie Starr," she said, shaking his hand tightly. "I'm the morning manager here. Stacy Johnson's my assistant."

"I'm sorry to meet you like this," Wallace said, looking over their shoulders. They turned to follow his eyes and saw two uniformed officers enter the store slowly, guns drawn.

"Were either of you in there this morning?"

"I was," Stacy said. "It was horrible."

"What'd you see?"

"The first thing was the lights on and the music playin' and the place was still dirty from the night before, stuff the night shift never ever left me, but okay, shit happens, so I go back to the employees' office to get my smock and there she was, dead on the floor, blood everywhere, and I just lost it and ran back out the door and banged straight into Jamie comin' in and then we got the bus to stop, and he called you all."

4

Wallace pulled a pen and pad out of the breast pocket of his jacket. The sound of sirens over his shoulder was growing louder. "You know her name?" he asked.

Jamie spelled it out, loudly. "You see anyone else?" he asked Stacy. She shook her head and he turned to Jamie. "You?"

"I haven't been in there."

The sirens grew louder still and they turned to see a cruiser's twirling lights coming down the hill, then a line of headlights bursting into view. Wallace put the pen and pad back in his jacket.

"Okay," he said, "I'm going to go in and check it out, then I'm going to come back out here and continue our conversation, okay?" Wallace pointed to the patrolman who stopped them and waved him over. "Officer, please keep these folks safe and out of the way till I get back. Ladies, I'll be back as soon as I can."

He stepped into the store and took a look around. The counter where people ordered and picked up their coffee was to the left, in between two doors to the street. Shelves stocked with packaged coffee, mugs, steel thermoses, plastic thermoses, and things he wouldn't even try to name were on the wall to his right. Tables and chairs were straight ahead, an open door just past them. A police technician standing in the doorway crouched down, giving Wallace a view of a woman in a white shirt lying on her back, her legs pointing in his direction. Another tech was kneeling at her head.

Wallace took his time heading back to them, more to take in anything of possible interest than to avoid seeing one more corpse in a career and a city full of them. Just past the pastry counter, he saw a slice of a white-iced muffin sitting on a piece of wax paper on top of a clipboard holding a sheet of paper. He twisted his head to see it was a weekly schedule and kept walking. A spray cleaner and a rag sat on the tabletop next to the doorway. The tech in the doorway

5

stood up and backed away to give him the full view of Caity Mahoney.

She laid between a hand truck and stacks of green plastic carriers to his left and metal shelves of brown cardboard boxes to the right. Her head was turned toward the carriers, pale green eyes open wide, long dark red hair matted with even darker blood. Two streaks of caked blood stretched from her forehead down her left cheek to join a third streak coming from behind her ear. Bloody lines ran from her left shoulder past the collar of her white T-shirt. Her green shorts and white stockings were unremarkable, but Wallace caught a flash of metal peeking out from under her left calf. He knelt down to get a better look and saw two keys attached to a small brown wrist coil. He looked around for a safe or a locked cabinet they might fit into, but saw nothing.

He stood up and bumped into someone standing close behind him. "Excuse me," they both said and Wallace turned to look up at Bob Mueller, someone he'd only seen in a courtroom before, and not even there very often. Mueller was Chief of the Homicide Section of the U.S. Attorney's Office, a position that would've been a crowning achievement for most criminal lawyers, but not for someone who'd already been the Assistant Attorney General of DOJ's Criminal Division under President Bush. Almost as puzzling was why he'd show up at a murder scene before dawn.

"Mr. Mueller," he said, extending his hand. "I'm Tom Wallace, a homicide detective with MPD. I'm a little surprised to see you here."

Mueller shook his hand but couldn't take his eyes off Caity. "This one hits close to home," he said. "I've got a daughter her age." Wallace turned back to Caity and took her in again.

"So what do we know?" Mueller asked.

"Not much yet," Wallace said and recounted what Stacy and Jamie had told him. A shaggy head of brown hair popped around a corner and Wallace turned to see Jim Trainum, one of his detectives, waving him to come closer. When Mueller started to follow him, Trainum held up a palm. "Sir, I don't know who you are, but you need to stay out here. There are two dead bodies back there."

"He's the head of homicide at the USA's," Wallace said and turned to Mueller. "He can come back, if he wants."

Mueller nodded and followed Wallace around the corner to a supply area. The body of a young black man with a shaved head lay closest to them, eyes closed and face turned towards more metal shelving stacked with boxes. He wore a black T-shirt and white shorts. A broomstick was pinned between his body and the floor. Wallace stepped over the stick and saw a thick layer of blood coating the floor to the right of the body, stopping just short of a white man's body lying face down, his legs lying over the other man's right leg. His black T-shirt was tucked into blue pants that stretched over shiny blue work boots.

Wallace turned to see Mueller shaking his head, then squeezed past him out of the room. "The forensics guys been in there yet?" he asked Trainum.

"No, they're just wrapping up the gir –." A piercing cry from the front door cut him off. Wallace looked up to see one of the uniforms holding a young black woman tight to him. He threaded through the aisle to reach them, then softly laid a hand on her shoulder. Two anguished eyes filled with tears looked back at him.

"Caity's dead? Is that for real?"

"I'm afraid so," Wallace said. The girl screamed like she'd been speared. "No, no, oh God no!"

"I am so sorry," he said and rubbed his hand across her back. "But I'm afraid there are more."

Her eyes dilated. "Who? Oh Lord, who?"

"Two young men –"

"Oh my God! Emory? Baby?"

"We don't know their names. One's black, young, with a shaved –"

"Oh Lord! That's Emory. He sometimes works the early shift with me. What's the other guy look like?"

"All I can tell you right now is he's white, thin, maybe a little taller, it's hard –"

"Oh no, no, no, oh Baby!" She buried her scream in the uniform's shoulder and they held each other tight. Wallace dipped into his jacket pocket and pulled out his pen and pad.

"Miss, can you give me their names? Take your time."

She lifted her head. "Emory Evans, and Aaron – hold on – Goodrich! He's Baby. Oh, that poor sweet child. And he just started here too."

"And your name?" Wallace asked. "Wanda Wells. I'm a barista." Wallace squinted at her. "I work the counter," she said.

Wallace looked for someone he could trust, hoping Trainum was somewhere in sight. In the four years since he came to MPD from Arlington County's PD, Trainum had earned a reputation for being smart, fearless, and happy to buck the system when it needed to be bucked. His first assignment at the department was the midnight shift in the 3rd District, where the main job was to round up the same hookers every night on 14th Street. It took him about a week of that bullshit to complain to the higher-ups about what a fucking waste of

8

time it was, and one more day for his supervisor to start "losing" his nightly reports just to let him know he should keep his opinions to himself. When Trainum started looking for somewhere, anywhere, to get out of there, Wallace had the good fortune to be looking for someone. It took him no time to see that Trainum was a guy who played it by the book but thought outside the lines, so when a Detective 2 opening came up in January, Wallace gave him the job before he even put his papers in.

Trainum caught his wave and met him out of Wanda's earshot. "I want you to talk to Wanda Wells back there," Wallace said. "She works the counter in the morning and can give you some information about the victims. Also, see if there's anyone else we ought to talk to, suspicious customers, crazy locals, anyone who might've had any possible reason to do this shit. There're two other employees out there you should ask too, Jamie and Stacy."

Trainum nodded and pulled out his own pad. Wallace saw the forensic guys comparing notes at the doorway to Caity's body and went back to hear what they found. She was now lying face down, and the blood spattered across the left shoulder of her shirt told him that was where the bullet went in. He pointed to it.

"She shot anywhere else?"

"No," the older tech said. He pointed to the pool of blood sticking to the floor under her original position. "You saw the blood coming down the front of her shirt from her left shoulder, right?" He didn't wait for Wallace to answer. "You combine that with the blood-on-blood pattern on the floor, that means she was upright when the fucker shot her."

"Standing?"

"Most likely sitting, judging from her legs and where the splatter is." Wallace looked over to the shelves of packaging. The red dots

9

speckling the cardboard and plastic wrap were bigger closer to the ground. "But we'll run some tests just to be sure."

"One shot?"

"One shot. But she's got other marks – cuts, abrasions – so there was probably some kind of struggle between her and that asshole." Wallace pointed to the keys next to her leg. "Maybe trying to get those," he said. "Got an extra pair of gloves?" The tech fished a pair out of his box.

"You done here?" Wallace asked. "Take your pictures?"

"We're done. Poor kid."

Wallace slipped on the gloves and picked up the key coil. "You see a safe in here?"

"No, it's all shelves and supplies and shit." Wallace nodded and headed for the other room. He asked the tech at the door the same question. "Yeah, over there," he said, pointing to the wall past Baby's head. "On the other side of the file cabinet."

Wallace sidestepped down Evans' body, planted a foot between his legs, and took one long stride over Baby. He knelt down but saw no place to put a key, just a push pad of letters, numbers, and symbols. He got back to his feet, threaded his way back out of the room, and snaked his way through the growing crowd of cops, techs, and EMTs back to the street. The sun was up now and the heat rising. Jamie and Stacy were talking to Trainum by the parking lot. Wallace made a beeline for Jamie and held up the keys.

"What are these for?"

"They unlock the doors to the back rooms."

"And you need a code for the safe?"

"Right."

"Is there money anywhere else?"

"No."

"I don't mean is it supposed to be anywhere else. I mean would Caity have kept some somewhere else for some reason?"

"No, never."

"Okay, give me the code." Wallace scribbled it on his pad and made his way back to the safe. He knelt down, entered the code, heard a buzz, and pulled the handle down. The door pulled back to reveal plastic bags full of cash, filled coin wrappers, and a white box stacked with credit card receipts. He shook his head. *Three people killed for absolutely nothing*, he thought, and looked over to see a tech gently turning Evans over onto his back. His shirt had a huge tear in it, just to the left of his heart. The tech started swabbing his skin.

"How many?" Wallace asked.

"Three. This one here's a contact wound," he said, gesturing at his chest, "and there's two more in the head."

"Contact too?" Wallace asked.

"No, and his head was definitely down. You come around here, you'll see. Took one right through the top and another one in the back of his head, like he was pitching forward after the first one. One thing I can tell you about the guy who did this? He was a fucking coward."

Wallace pointed at Goodrich. "And him?"

"Haven't gotten over there yet, but the way his legs are on top, the black guy got it before he did."

11

Wallace grunted his way up to his feet and took a look down at Goodrich. No blood was visible on his back or on the floor. He started to leave but turned back when he saw a piece of paper with handwriting on it lying on the desktop above Goodrich's head. He stepped closer and bent down to read it. The heading said "List Of Things To Do," but the only thing listed was "Apologize to Chad". Wallace wrote that on his pad and patted the tech on the shoulder on his way past. A cop he didn't recognize was waiting for him, standing next to a middle-aged white guy with thinning dark hair he didn't recognize either.

"Detective," the cop said, "this is Jim Mauro. He lives in the neighborhood and says he noticed something unusual here last night."

"Okay," Wallace said. "What'd you see?"

"Like I was telling him, I was taking a walk last night with my two girls. It was so beautiful and cool by then, we just wanted to get out, you know, so anyhow we wind up coming by here around ten o'clock or so and the little one, she's ten, she needs to go to the bathroom and I see the lights are on – and I think, that's strange, the place is usually dark after eight, closing time, you know, but, hey, maybe's someone around, so I go to the door – the one down there, closest to S Street – but it was locked so I didn't even try the other one, which was probably a good thing, huh? Anyhow, we hustled on home, but then this morning, when I saw all the police cars and commotion here, I thought maybe I ought to tell someone all that, so that's it. What happened anyhow?"

Wallace scribbled 'Lights on at 10' in his pad. "Spell your name please, sir." Mauro did.

"I'm sorry, but I can't talk now," Wallace said and steered him back to the sidewalk. When he turned to go back in, he saw Stacy and

12

Jamie where he left them, still talking to Trainum, now with Wanda alongside. He walked over to Stacy.

"Excuse me, I have another question for you. Were you the first one here this morning?"

"Yeah."

"And which door did you come in?"

"The one away from us, towards S."

"And was it locked?"

"Yeah."

"And which door did you come out?"

"The other one, this one."

"Was it locked too?"

"Yeah, I had to flip that thingy to get out. Took me three, four times, I was so nervous!"

"Is there another way in here? Maybe through the back?"

"Yeah, there's a supply door back there, but it's always locked unless a delivery guy tells us he's here, and on a Sunday, especially July Fourth weekend Sunday, there wouldn't be no deliveries."

"And Caity would've checked to make sure it was locked, I guarantee you," Jamie said.

"Either of you have a key to the back?"

"I do," she said and led him around back of the building. She fished into her pocketbook and pulled out a ring full of keys, put one in the door, and turned it. Wallace heard the bolt move.

"Caity had two keys on a coil," Wallace said. "You know what they were for?"

"The back rooms. We keep them behind the counter until we need them."

"So where would she keep the keys to the doors, or does one key unlock them both?"

"No, one key opens the front doors and another one opens the back." She held up her key ring. "If she was like me, she probably kept them with all her other ones."

Wallace stared at the keys, lost in thought. "So what are you trying to figure out?" Jamie asked. "How he got in?"

"Yeah," he said, "but mostly out." Wallace walked her back out front, pulled Trainum past the door, and told him about the locked doors. "So, any ideas?" he asked.

Trainum mulled it over, then said "I can come up with some guesses how he might've gotten in. Maybe he came in before they locked up on some kind of ruse, or maybe he came in through the back while they were taking out the trash or something, or maybe there's a window – but I have no idea how he got out and locked the doors behind him, unless –"

Wallace finished the sentence for him. "Unless he had a set of keys too."

"So how's that happen? You're thinkin' this is an inside job?"

Wallace pulled the note he copied from the desk in the supply room and showed it to him.

"Apologize to Chad," Trainum read. "Who's Chad?"

"I got no idea," Wallace said. "But maybe the ladies do."

They turned to head back, then stopped to watch a black Ford LTD pull to the curb just past them. The back door opened and Wallace knew who it was even before he got out. Larry Soulsby, Chief of Police, tugged his cap tight to his head and walked around the back of the car, giving Wallace a quick nod that he did not return. The sight of Soulsby reminded him that the weekend was a complete disaster even before the murders. On July 4, the jackass yanked about sixty of the detectives Wallace worked with every day out of headquarters and strewed them across MPD's seven districts. Soulsby said he was doing it to put more boots on the street, but these guys were more valuable for their brains, not their feet. Wallace was grateful he somehow made the cut, but the whole mess reeked of consultants, politics, and desperation, like everything else under the guy.

Soulsby pulled open the back door on the other side and helped a woman out of the car. She was wearing a dark gold kerchief over lighter hair, sunglasses, a black zippered jacket, and black slacks. Soulsby led her over to Wallace.

"Detective, this is Mrs. Annenberg, Miss Mahoney's mother. She asked to see the body."

"I just need to –" she began, then faltered and held Wallace's forearm.

"I understand," he said. "Follow me." He led them back to the doorway, the crowd parting to let them through. Inside, he turned to her, blocking the view of Caity's body. Her sunglasses were still on. "Mrs. Annenberg," he said, "the body is on the floor right in front of us. There's a lot of blood, I just want to let you know."

She took off the glasses with both hands, revealing eyes filled with heartbreak, and took a deep breath. "Let me see her, please," she said. Wallace moved to the side and looked at Caity so he didn't have to look at her mother until he heard a sharp intake of breath and

15

turned back to see her bury her head in Soulsby's chest. Wallace waited for her to lift it before he brought himself to ask the question.

"Is that Caity, Mrs. Annenberg?" Her face sunk back into Soulsby's chest but Wallace could still hear her "Yes".

"Okay then," Soulsby said, "we're done here. Let's go outside." Wallace followed them back through the silent still crowd. Back on the sidewalk, Mrs. Annenberg turned to the sun and closed her eyes for a good while before she put her sunglasses back on. Wallace put a hand on her elbow as Soulsby walked her back to the car.

"Ma'am," Wallace said, "I'm truly very sorry to do this, but if I could, I'd like to ask you just a few questions."

"Detective –" Soulsby started before she cut him off. "Of course. I'll help any way I can."

"Thank you. This looks like a robbery gone very bad, but just to make sure we're not missing anything, do you know any reason anyone would have wanted to – do this to her?"

"Oh, Lord, no. She never lost a friend. That's what we always said about her. Everyone loved her and she loved everyone. That's the honest truth."

"Did she have a husband or a boyfriend? Anyone she lived with?"

"No, she lived alone, in an efficiency apartment," she said and took a deep breath. "And if she lived with anyone, it would not have been a man." Wallace pondered that for a second before she confirmed what he was thinking. "She came out – I think that's the correct expression – to me and my husband – her stepfather – just this past year. But there was absolutely no one in her life, man or woman, who would have done something to her like this, I can assure you of that."

"Can't this wait, Detective?" a clearly uncomfortable Soulsby asked.

"No, please," Mrs. Annenberg said. "I want to help." But Wallace took the hint. He wanted to stay downtown and stay on the case. "Just one more question, ma'am," he said. "Can you give me her address so we can see if there's anything there that might help us figure this thing out?"

"Yes, it's in the Adams Morgan neighborhood, which, again, she just loved. Hold on one minute, it's in my book." Soulsby gave Wallace another look that he ignored again while she got it. She read him the exact address and tucked the book back in her pocketbook before a look of concern crossed her face. "Oh my, that reminds me. I'll have to get Marlu."

"Who is Marlu?" Wallace asked.

"Her dog. Oh, that poor baby will be heartbroken too."

Wallace felt a tap on his shoulder and turned to see one of the techs' gloved hands holding two shell casings.

"Detective, we found these back there, near the girl," he said. "And there's a slug in the ceiling above her – ". He stopped at the sight of Wallace's hot glare even before he saw Mrs. Annenberg's face lose all its color. "Okay, we'll talk later," he said and headed back deep into the shop as fast as he could without actually running. Soulsby wrapped an arm around Mrs. Annenberg and led her back to the LTD. Once he closed the door, he took four heavy strides back to Wallace.

"Detective, do we have a problem? Something you want to tell me?"

"About what, Chief?" Wallace said blankly.

Soulsby's pale white skin turned crimson. "I don't know about what, but you know what? I don't give a shit either. Keep your eye on the fucking ball and get this lady some fucking justice, all right?" He spun around and strode back to the car before Wallace could answer, which was probably a good thing for both of them.

Wallace turned to see Trainum looking at him, shaking his head. Wallace rolled his eyes, then led him back to Wanda, Jamie, and Stacy in front of the parking lot. Stacy flicked the burning butt of a cigarette into the street. Wallace held up his pad.

"Any of you know who Chad is or why Caity thought she had to apologize to him?" They all read the paper. "He worked here, mostly on the weekends," Wanda said, "but I got no idea why she would've owed him an apology." The others' faces told him the same thing.

"Anybody else who worked here you think would've had a reason or been crazy enough to do something like this?" Trainum asked.

Stacy looked at Wanda, then Jamie. "Go on, tell him," Jamie said to her. "They'll check it out and if it's nothing, then that's it, but – "

"There was a guy named Walter that used to work here," Stacy said, "but he got fired a little while back because he stole a couple of hundred bucks from the safe."

"You know his last name?" Trainum asked. Stacy sighed and said "Worrell" and spelled it out.

"You know where he might be now?"

"No idea," Stacy said. "We don't run with the same crowd."

"Did he work the night shift with Caity?" Wallace asked Jamie.

18

"He kind of did swing work, sometimes for her, sometimes for me, maybe in the afternoons too, that I don't know."

"Okay," Wallace said. "Anyone else you think we ought to talk to?"

"There was a guy named Yasmin who used to work at the Starbucks down on M Street, until he got fired for stealing too."

"Any reason to think he'd do anything up here as payback or something?"

"I don't know that either," Jamie shrugged.

"Anyone else?" Trainum asked. The women looked at each other and shook their heads.

"Anything else you think might be suspicious," Wallace asked, "even if it might be totally off the wall?" He got the same response, then looked at his watch. 7:27. A little girl holding her mother's hand laid a bouquet of daisies next to the door behind him. He pulled his hand down over his eyes, let it linger on his face long enough to cover a giant yawn, then turned to Trainum. "So let's go find Chad and these other two guys and see if we can do some fucking justice here, okay?"

September 29, 1997

1

Wallace let the *Post* fall from his armpit onto his desk, laid his half-smoke and coffee next to it, and fell into his swivel chair to the usual accompaniment of the chair's squeak and his grunt. He pried the lid off the coffee and took a long draw before he yanked the Style section out of the paper, turned to the last funnies page, and found his horoscope. *Make a list of all the good things in your life and carry it with you all day. You'll be amazed at the happiness it brings you.* He snorted his reaction to that and slapped the paper shut, but couldn't keep his brain from starting to making the list. It ended at one, and even that had a big asterisk next to it.

The one ostensibly good thing in his life was that he was now a Detective Commander in the Operations Command section at MPD headquarters. That job didn't even exist on the first reorganization chart Soulsby threw together the weekend of the Starbucks murders, but it did after the re-reorganization the clown came up with less than two weeks ago, immediately known across the department as the September 18 Massacre. This time around, the Chief reassigned not only the guy he'd just appointed to head the Detectives unit, but every one of the seventeen supervisors who reported to him too. He told the newspapers he did it because he was totally committed to getting MPD's rate of solved homicides up to the national average within a year, which was not only a pipe dream, since D.C. had a higher murder rate than any other city in the country, but also a sick joke to every detective in the department because he'd showed them all – twice – that he didn't believe in any of them.

That also meant that none of them was going to do anything to make Soulsby's job one iota easier – or Wallace's, because now he was playing for the Chief's team. He could have told them what Soulsby told him when he gave him the job – "I'm like the Godfather, man: I hold my friends close, but my enemies closer" – but they wouldn't have believed him anyhow.

He ripped off a bite of the half-smoke and let his mind drift back, way back, to try to think of when he really did have more than one good thing in his life. His career at MPD'd been a long and winding road, sometimes one step forward, but mostly two back, especially early on. He still felt the twin shocks of his gun going off during a fight with a guy he was trying to arrest and the bullet going through the brain of his partner Marcus Morris over thirty years ago. That stalled his career, but his drinking trying to cope with it put it in a long slow reverse.

He could see clearly now that he hadn't always made the smartest decisions either, like the time he decided all on his own to go to Memphis to follow a lead in the murder of Brenda Queen on the stage of the Howard Theatre the night Martin Luther King was murdered in 1968. That fuckup – and his abiding taste for alcohol – kept him squirreled away filing reports and working cold cases for way too long until he finally got a chance to show he could still be a good detective during Hamaas Khaalis' takeover of three buildings downtown in '77. He swore off the booze and got the rest of himself together almost ten years ago, but now, he couldn't help but remember an expression he'd heard from somebody somewhere: Be careful what you wish for, because you just might get it.

Even if MPD had a Chief he could respect, this was a tough time to be in Homicide. It was bad enough that after three years of falling, the murder rate was spiking in D.C. at the same time it was still dipping everywhere else in the country, but ever since someone leaked that the Division got paid $2 million for overtime last year without anything to show for it, the pressure had ratcheted up even more. A knock on the door mercifully interrupted his reverie. He spun around to see Trainum.

"Morning, boss," he said. "You hear about the call that came in last night?"

"No. About what?"

"Starbucks."

So much for mercy. The Starbucks investigation got his constant attention, the way a bear trap tends to get the bear's attention. It had dominated both their lives from the moment they pulled to the curb on Wisconsin that July morning, and despite all the attention they paid it, it was going absolutely nowhere. His brain regurgitated the last twelve weeks in a split-second.

The bodies, the two shell casings, and the slug in the ceiling were the only physical evidence they found. The casings came from two different guns, a .38 revolver and a .380 pistol, which meant there could have been two shooters, but, without any living eyewitnesses, that was still only a supposition. All in all, they'd questioned forty people but were no closer to solving the murders than they were the day it happened. All they'd managed to do in almost three months was eliminate every lead, and Wallace's head started to pound all over again thinking about how the department managed to screw that up too.

They brought in Walter, the employee who got caught stealing, right away. As soon as Soulsby heard that a tech saw blood on his shoes, he told the press they had "a number one suspect." Walter agreed to take a polygraph to back up his alibi, but when he read what Soulsby said, he changed his mind – and refused to let Wallace into his apartment to pick up the shoes. His alibi later checked out, but all the press reported was how MPD screwed up by not getting the shoes. When an aunt of Caity's called Wallace to let him know how pissed the family was, he explained that when they did eventually get them, it turned out there was no blood on them after all, but that didn't calm her down. "Jesus Christ, Detective! Even I know he could've cleaned them or swapped them out before you guys finally

23

got there!" was etched in his memory forever, even before she slammed down the phone.

The Yasmin Tabet lead was a loser too. Wallace thought they were onto something when he left town right after the murders, and his heart skipped a beat when they found him in California, but his polygraph came back clean. It also turned out that Yasmin was pissed because MPD tore up his D.C. apartment so bad that his landlord wouldn't give him back his security deposit. After the department stiffed him, Wallace, Trainum, and Brad Garrett, an FBI agent Trainum persuaded to help them out on the case, paid him back out of their own pockets.

Chad was another dead end. When Wallace came to his apartment and showed him Caity's reminder to apologize to him, he broke down crying. "It was so nothing," he finally got out. "Right in the middle of the crush that morning, we ran out of Pike Place Decaf bags up on the shelf and she kind of barked at me to go get more up there. I just went and got them, I wasn't pissed about it, but I am so sorry it was even on her mind, especially –" He couldn't finish and Wallace just patted him on the back and let himself out.

As far as how the shooter, or shooters, got out, Trainum told him that the guy who made the early morning bakery deliveries that day found the door unlocked, but didn't notice anything strange, so he just locked it behind him with his own key to the place. And they never did find out why her tire was flat, but it didn't matter anyway because no one was able to concoct any tale that connected a flat tire outside to three dead bodies inside.

"No," Wallace said when his synapses finally stopped flaring. "What call?"

"Tipster," Trainum said. "Saw the thing on AMW."

Wallace didn't think his head could throb any worse, but he was wrong. America's Most Wanted ran a blurb right after the shootings, giving a number to call at MPD if anyone knew anything about the case. Nearly everyone who called in gave them a false lead they could debunk immediately, and after Starbucks raised the reward from $50,000 to $100,000, the flow of bullshit doubled too.

"What's special about this one?" he asked.

Trainum reached inside a manila folder and handed him a copy of the call sheet. The ID number was 234. Wallace skimmed through it while Trainum summarized it for him.

"Guy said he knows who did it. Two guys, one named Carl who lives with his mom and his wife and kids on Gallatin Street Northeast. Described him as short, medium brown skin, mid-20s, around 140 pounds, has a beard, sometimes a mustache, and drives some kind of purple car. Said he meant to just rob the place with a buddy of his, a barber who works somewhere on Bladensburg Road, but wound up killing the girl because she wouldn't give up the safe. Also said he killed his last partner because he gave up his name. Our guy on the call said the dude came across like he was real sure of himself. Said 'my information is gold'."

Wallace threw the sheets on top of his paper. "That right there sets off my b.s. detector. He say he knows this firsthand?"

"No," Trainum said, "said he got it from someone else, and no, he did not say who."

"Did he say who he was?"

"Hell, no. And AMW guarantees their callers anonymity, at least until there's a reward, so they're not going to give him up."

"He say why he's doing it? He got a beef with Carl? Or is he just a fine upstanding God-fearing man doing the right thing?"

25

"Told our guy he's got a hundred thousand reasons."

Wallace shook his head and reached for his coffee. "Okay, check it out" he sighed. "Can't be too many Carls on Gallatin Street toolin' around in a purple – "

"Already did," Trainum said, and handed him another sheet, this one from the D.C. Department of Motor Vehicles. "DMV shows one Carl Derick Cooper, aka Carl Derek Havord Cooper, living on Gallatin Street, with two cars registered in his name, a blue '94 Plymouth Eagle and a two-tone gray '85 Chevy Caprice, and one in his wife's name." He locked eyes with Wallace. "A purple '94 Honda Civic." Wallace sat up and took a sheaf of papers from him.

"So I went through the criminal information systems – Fed and local – and found our Mr. Cooper's been arrested seven times, convicted once. Armed robbery in '90, served two years."

"Got any details on that?" Wallace asked.

"Yeah. Cooper and a guy named Vontae" – he spelled it out – "Kincaid held up 7-11s in Prince Georges twice in '89. The second time, a witness saw the car and took down the tag, which turned out to be Kincaid's, and he gave it all up, including naming Cooper as the gunman and the brains of the operation."

"Any idea where Vontae is now?"

"Yeah," Trainum said, looking back down at his file, "Lincoln Memorial Cemetery. Been there since July 21, 1993."

"Carl have something to do with that?"

"No charges were ever filed, but the fact that Mr. Kincaid would up dead in a parking lot somewhere in Prince Georges with two bullets lodged in the back of his head tells my keen detecting mind there may be a connection."

26

"Did PG ever talk to him?"

"They did, but they spent more time investigating a guy named Teddy Thigpen aka 'Man'. I guess they decided Man wasn't the man though, because no one ever got charged."

"Anyone else around who might know something about Carl and Vontae?"

"Vontae's mother still living. She's out in Bladensburg, and there's a Roberta Rawlins who used to be his girlfriend out there too." Wallace tried hard to find a reason to believe this Carl wasn't worth pursuing, but he couldn't.

"Okay, better than anything else we got," he finally said, then thought about how nothing stays secret anymore at MPD, especially on cases like this. "You tell anyone else here about any of this?"

"No. The only other guy that knows anything about it is the guy who took the call and I let him know if I heard anyone else talking about it, I'd know who told them. He got the message." Wallace nodded.

"Okay, so let's just keep diggin' quietly so Carl doesn't get his antenna up. How about if you follow up with the jail here and PG, and I'll run him through city records, school records, employment, the whole nine yards. Let's keep each other posted, face to face, nothing in writing, and keep your folder there under lock and key. How's that sound?"

Trainum threw him a salute and headed out the door before sticking his head back in.

"Hey, can I let Garrett in too? So far, Mueller's kept him just dealing with the families till we develop something the Feebies can actually help us with. Is this it?"

27

Wallace had to think that over a second. He was paranoid about anything getting out, but Mueller and the Bureau knew how to keep things in the vault, and the Feds had some tools they didn't. And there was one more thing.

"Tell him everything," he said. "We need all the help we can get."

2

At nine on the dot two days later, Trainum and Wallace rolled up to the FBI's Washington Field Office a few blocks away on 4th Street Northwest.

"There he is," Trainum pointed and Wallace followed his wave to a guy who could have been posing for a GQ shoot in front of the building. He was maybe in his late forties, salt and pepper hair cut close to his head in the usual G-man style, but handsome enough to be straight out of Law & Order. He flashed a small quick smile and picked up his definitely non-Government Issue black leather briefcase. As he came closer, even Wallace could tell that charcoal pinstriped suit never decorated a rack at the Men's Wearhouse. Garrett pulled open the back door on the passenger side and patted Trainum on the back before reaching his hand over the seat to Wallace.

"I've heard nothing but good things," he said. "Same here," Wallace said, then took in Trainum with new eyes as he pulled away from the curb, most specifically his blotchy beard and the long tangles of brown hair spilling over the collar of his ripped black leather jacket. *How did this Odd Couple ever connect?* he asked himself, then looked back at Garrett in the rear-view mirror.

"Jim tells me you guys go back, but I don't know the whole story, so fill me in." He saw them lock eyes in the mirror. "I'll give you the Reader's Digest version," Garrett said. "About four, five years ago, I was kind of the go-between guy for local law enforcement around here whenever anyone wanted help from the crew that works violent crime cases for us at Quantico. Jim wound up talking to me to see if we could do anything on a case that had them stymied."

"Which one?" Wallace asked him, but Trainum answered.

"Lawrence O'Connell."

"Why do I know that name? And why do I remember it was a total fuckup?"

"Great memory," Trainum said. "Because it was, courtesy of yours truly."

"Don't be so hard on yourself," Garrett said. "We gave you a lot of help." Trainum sighed and refreshed Wallace's recollection.

"He worked for the Voice Of America, in Southwest, and he left work early one day to pick up his son from school, but he never made it. A couple days later, a guy walking his dog finds him outside RFK Stadium, bloody, beat to shit, and dead. We check out all the local security cameras and the banks and we see that maybe twenty minutes after he left, a woman used his card at an ATM up on Capitol Hill, about ten blocks from where he worked. Then a few hours later, the same card's used at a couple places in Maryland, then a little later at a liquor store back on the Hill. So we're looking and we're looking and we're finding nothing, okay? But then –"

"Then," Garrett said, "is when we do our part. One of our guys has an informant who tells him he has solid info on who did it, a homeless woman – shit, she was practically a girl, twenty-one – so Jim and one of our guys pick her up and talk to her and, lo and behold, she confesses. Hooray, case solved, except for one little thing. She didn't do it."

"Okay, now I remember," Wallace said, then looked to Trainum, "but I didn't remember you were on it."

"It's not on my resume," Trainum said. "To Jim's credit," Garrett said, "he was also the one who figured out she couldn't have done it." Trainum shook his head at the still bitter memory.

"I got gulled into thinking she had to be the one from all the crap info I was given, so I leaned on her till she gave me what I wanted.

It was a good lesson, Commander, that's all I can tell you. You got no worries with me – now."

"So now we use Jim to train our guys and the locals on what *not* to do," Garrett said, "even more than what to do. We've been helping each other out ever since."

"All right, good to know," Wallace said, turning in his seat to look at him. "So how much you know about Starbucks?"

"The only thing I had anything to do with was helping hunt down the guy who went to California, but Jim's been keeping me filled in."

"And he walked through the place with me when it was still shuttered," Trainum said, "so he knows the scene."

Wallace saw they were on New York Avenue heading for Bladensburg Road. They'd be at Vontae Kincaid's mother's place in less than fifteen minutes, so he changed the subject. "And what do you know about Cooper's connection to Vontae Kincaid?"

"Just what Jim told me about them doing some business together and Mr. Kincaid winding up dead." Wallace caught his look at Trainum in the mirror and Trainum's nod back. "But I think we're all going to learn a lot more real soon."

Wallace threw him a puzzled look. "Today?"

"Absolutely," Garrett said, reaching into his briefcase and pulling out a CD-ROM disk, "and after we do a little digging into this." He handed it to Wallace. "What's this?" he asked.

"A lot of stuff on Mr. Cooper, both legit and not so legit."

"Jim told me about the not legit part. There's a legit?"

31

"He works as a security officer at Wang in Virginia, out around Tysons Corner somewhere. Also's got a wife, Cissy. She works at a Best Buy in Laurel. And they've got a two-year-old son."

"An All-American family man," Wallace said. "What else?"

"That's where the digging's going to start," Garrett said. "We need to chase down a lot of the names and numbers we got from his phone."

Wallace sat up straight. "You tapped his line? Who said you had probable cause to put up a wire?"

"No one," Garrett said. "We didn't get this off a tap. We got it off a pen register. You *capisce* pen registers?" Wallace did *capisce*, but there was only one case he ever worked on that used them. "I remember you guys using them on Rayful Edmond, but that was a giant cocaine conspiracy case. I thought that's all you could use 'em on."

"Oh no, sir," Garrett said. "All we need to do to is swear to God to a judge that what we're looking for is relevant to a – quote unquote – ongoing criminal investigation, which, you know, would pretty much cover anything at the *Federal Bureau of Investigation*."

Wallace looked at Trainum, dumbfucked. "Ain't that some shit," he said. "We're playing for the wrong team."

"Not really," Garrett said. "It's a Federal law, but D.C. or any state can use it too." "God bless America," Trainum said. Garrett laughed.

"Don't get too carried away. You can't listen in to what they're saying. It just gives you the numbers the calls are going to or coming from." "Right," Wallace said, "which gives you the names of the people you can visit and say 'I think we have somethin' to talk about. You first'."

Trainum turned a corner off Bladensburg. "This is it, gentlemen. We're here." Wallace held up the CD. "Do I get to keep this?"

"Sorry," Garrett said, reaching for it, "but no. I want to get our guys to go through the calls and see who he talks to the most, then they'll burn me a clone so we can both keep score. What I know, you'll know, I promise."

"Can one of our techs sit in with your guys while they go through it?" Trainum asked, pulling up to the house. "We might know some numbers and names you don't. Save everybody time."

"Let me talk to my boss, see if he'll bring it up to Mueller." Garrett tucked the disk back into his briefcase. "So now that we're here, who exactly are we talking to?"

"Vontae's mother, Albertha," Trainum said, "and his girlfriend's brother Jaysonn – with a 'y' and two 'n's, if you're going to run him. We really wanted to talk to the girlfriend – Roberta – but she's working, and the mother wanted him there, and I didn't want to argue about it, so long story short, he's there. I don't know what we'll get out of him."

"And what do you expect from mom?"

"Not real sure about that either," Wallace said, "but this is the first time we've had something to go on, and somethin's better than nothin', so let's all find out."

They got out of the car and walked through a chain link fence towards a three-story brown brick garden apartment building that looked a lot like the ones next to it and behind it. A chipped concrete sidewalk ran from the gap in the fence where a gate should have been to a stoop at the front entrance of a structure that had probably been up since the '60s, when public housing first became all the rage. The ground was as brown as the buildings with no sign of grass, only a few thin bushes randomly dotting the landscape. Trainum looked into one of his manila folders and opened the door. "They're in 1-C, gentlemen. After you."

The hall was thin and dark, the nearest working light bulb about ten yards down. It was tough to tell the color of the walls, but more light would have only made them more depressing. Wallace settled at Maybe Green Sometime and watched Trainum knock on the third door on the right.

"Hello?" a woman's voice said.

"Good morning, Mrs. Kincaid. This is Jim Trainum. I'm here for the meeting we talked about?" In a few seconds, Wallace heard a bolt slide and a doorknob turn before the door popped open an inch. A dark brown eye peered over a chain at Trainum, then at him. "And you are?"

"I'm Tom Wallace, ma'am. Mr. Trainum and I work together at the police department." He stepped aside so she could peer at Garrett. "And this is Brad Garrett from the FBI."

"Is everything okay, mama?" he heard a young man's voice call out. "I guess so," she said, then unlatched the chain and pulled the door open wide enough that Wallace could see a tall black man, maybe in his thirties, looking back at him from under a ragged 'fro, more than a little suspicion in his eyes.

"And you're Jaysonn?" he asked.

"I am."

"Are we cool, bro?" Wallace asked him. "You need to see a badge?" Jaysonn put his game face on. "No, we cool. Let 'em in, 'Bertha."

She closed the door behind them and led them down a short hallway past the tiny kitchen to a metal folding table with three plastic chairs crammed together on one side. She took one of the two wooden ones on the other side and Jaysonn took the one next to her. Wallace squeezed into the far chair and waited for Garrett and Trainum to get into theirs, then nodded to Trainum to get to it.

"Roberta's still not able to join us?" he asked.

"No," Albertha said, "her shift don't end till half past three. She definitely wanted to be here though, I will tell you that. That girl has got a lot of pain still, what's this now, four years since my baby left us?"

"It is," Trainum said, "and we're all sorry for your loss, Mrs. Kincaid. Please know that." She lifted a crinkled napkin to dab her eyes. Jaysonn planted his forearms on the table and leaned in. "I'll tell you whatever you want to know about that motherfucker, so shoot. Axe me anything you want."

They all pulled out their pads. "First of all," Trainum said, "let's make sure we're all talking about the same motherfucker. Carl Cooper? Is that right?"

"Yeah," Jaysonn said. "'L'il Cooper,' the runt." Trainum turned to Albertha. "Is that the Carl Cooper you know too?"

"I never heard anyone call him that," she said, "but if you're talking about the Carl Cooper Vontae knew, he's the only one I knew."

"He's the one," Trainum said. "So how did Vontae know him?"

She shook her head and took a deep breath before she forced the words out. "They did some stuff together is all I know, some bad stuff, but Carl was the one who got him into all of it. Vontae would've never done any of it, hadn't been for him."

35

"I'm sure," Trainum said. "Do you know what kind of stuff Carl had him do?"

"No, and I didn't want to know neither. I was just happy my boy came home safe and sound every night they went out somewhere together – until he didn't."

"Were they out together that night?"

"They wasn't supposed to be far as I know. Vontae said he was just going out to get some smokes and I went to bed until I hear some hammerin' on the door and it's the police, tellin' me he'd been shot dead."

"What do you think happened that night, Mrs. Kincaid?"

"I have no earthly idea, even now, and I think about it every day. It's a misery that don't stop."

"Do you know someone named Teddy Thigpen?"

"I know him," Jaysonn said. "'Man'". Trainum ignored him and repeated the question to Albertha. "I know who he is," she said, "but only from hearin' Vontae talk about him sometimes. If I ever saw him, I don't know it."

Trainum turned back to Jaysonn. "And how do you know him?"

"See him around. Everyone knows Man."

"Do you think he had anything to do with Vontae's death?"

"I heard he might've, but if he did, it was because Carl put him up to it. Too big a punk to take care of it his self, so he went and got Man to do it for him."

"And why do you think that?"

Jaysonn shook his head and shot a sideways glance at Albertha before he answered. "'Cause he *thought* Vontae ratted him out for some things they did, supposedly."

"How do you know that's what he thought?" Jayson shrugged.

"Just stuff you hear, you know, and it made perfect sense to me. It's exactly what the little fucker woulda done, even if he didn't really know."

"How well did your sister Roberta know Vontae?" Wallace asked.

"Real well. They were like together all the time, like man and wife together."

"But they weren't married, right?"

"Right, but they might as well've been. Only thing they didn't have was the license."

"And is that how you got to know Mrs. Kincaid, through Roberta?"

"Yeah," he said. "We keep in touch. I try to help her out with this and that, you know."

"You got a work number for Roberta so we can talk to her?" He did and Wallace wrote it down. "Anyone else either of you think we ought to talk to about Carl, or Starbucks, or Vontae?"

Albertha shook her head, but Jaysonn said "Yeah, there is. There's a cat Carl runs with who'd know everything about everything. Name's Leon. They tight."

"Leon got a last name?"

"That's all I know him by. Cuts hair somewhere 'round here."

Wallace's pen lurched to a halt. He turned to look at Trainum, who was already looking at him. He knew exactly what he was thinking because he was thinking it too: *Caller 234. Carl did Starbucks with a barber who worked on Bladensburg Road.*

"Got a name or address for him? Or the shop?" Wallace asked.

"Naw," Jaysonn said. "I can get 'em though." Wallace didn't need word getting out about anyone trying to track somebody down about Starbucks. "Don't bother," he said. "We'll get it. Anything else either of you think we ought to know?"

They looked at each other and shook their heads. Trainum thanked them for their time and none of them said a word till they were back in the car.

"What he said about a barber being involved," Trainum said to Garrett, "we got that from an informant too."

"Think he was the informant?" Garrett asked.

"Guy was anonymous, on a tip line," Wallace said, then saw Trainum look at him and tilt his head "What?"

"Looks like you could use a haircut," Trainum said.

3

Two days later, Wallace picked up his phone to hear Garrett say his name, followed by a lilting female voice saying "would like to invite you to a conference call. Please say yes to accept." Wallace did as he was asked and, in a second, caught Garrett and Trainum in mid-conversation.

"I don't know, I haven't seen him," Trainum said. "Let's ask him."

"Detective Wallace, are you on?" Garrett asked.

"I am. Ask me what?"

"Have you got your hair cut yet?"

"No, but I'm fixing to. I spent some time yesterday cruising all the Bladensburg barber shops I could find in the yellow pages. I didn't want to go in and start asking for Leon somebody for obvious reasons, but I just wanted to get a count and maybe, just maybe, see if Carl's car was at one of 'em."

"And was it?" Garrett asked.

"Of course not. Why would we get any kind of goddamn break in this case? But there's only four shops, so that at least narrows it down. Between us and PG, maybe we can send some undercovers in to see which one he's at."

"Funny you should mention that," Garrett said, "because I was trying to see if *I* could make a connection to Leon on the pen register – which also reminds me, Mueller said your guys can sit in with us to go over the call lists. He's happy to have the help."

"Excellent," Trainum said. "Did you find his number?" Wallace asked.

"So it seems there were a lot of calls between Cooper's phone and a phone billed to a lady named Chantay Ellis," Garrett said. "We went through all the CJIS databases and came up with a hit for an Ellis with a matching number. First name Leon, her husband."

"Well, well, well," Wallace said. "The good Lord finally did smile upon us. What was the hit?"

"Robbery. Convicted in '95 for holding up a 7-11 in Beltsville in '94." Wallace remembered that's what Vontae Kincaid used to do with Cooper before his career came to a sudden stop in '93. "Cooper have anything to do with it?" he asked.

"Wasn't charged," Garrett said, "but that doesn't mean he didn't."

"Anything else in there?" Trainum asked.

"Nope. Just the personal stuff. He's African-American, 26 years old, and lives in Cheverly. His current law enforcement status is he was paroled for the robbery, in '95."

"And since then?" Wallace asked. "His parole agent told me he's been gainfully employed." He paused another second and Wallace could've sworn he heard him stifle a chuckle. "As a barber. At the – let me make sure I get this right – One World Unisex Hair Salon. On Bladensburg Road."

"All right!" Trainum crowed.

"I know exactly where that is," Wallace said. "Drove past it yesterday. When was the last time he and Cooper talked?"

"Shit, when didn't they? Hold on a second." Wallace heard pages riffle before Garrett came back on the line. "Twelve times just this week, at home and the shop. Every day but one."

40

"You got Leon's home address? "Yeah," Garrett said, "3554 55th Avenue in Hyattsville. It's another project."

"Want to take a ride tonight, Commander?" Trainum asked. "See if Carl might be there? Maybe we're on a fucking roll for a change." Wallace still had his doubts, but he heard himself say "Seeing that purple car'd be enough for me. Come get me around 10:30."

At twenty-five to eleven, he saw a rusty brown Oldsmobile sitting outside the gate to his condo community just across from Fort McNair, lights off, engine idling. He bent down to see Trainum salute him in the driver's seat and got in. Trainum handed him a green hanging file before he pulled away from the curb. Wallace opened it and saw two mug shots. He flicked the overhead light on.

"Who's who?" he asked.

"Guy in the green sweatshirt's Cooper." Wallace looked at the face. Decent-looking guy, medium dark complexion, neat mustache and beard, close-cropped Afro, maybe receding a little. The letter board in front of him showed his DOB as 5-6-69, Ht. 5'7", Wt. 166. He looked at Ellis' picture. He was bigger and heavier with a lighter complexion, a tight shiny natural, and a beard that ran down his neck. DOB 8-3-71. 5'11", 232.

"Barber's got good hair," he said, and pulled a binder clip full of printouts and photos out of the folder.

"That's the stuff on Cooper's cars, all three of 'em," Trainum said. "The pictures are car models I found on the Internet, not his. I tried, but I couldn't find a purple Civic. He might have the only one."

"What kind of criminal drives a purple car?" Wallace asked. "You see it, you'll remember it."

"Yeah, if it was me," Trainum said, "I'd go with the gray Chevy. Much more professional. Discreet, right?"

41

"But harder to see at night," Wallace said. "Here's hoping he took the Civic." He flicked the overhead light off. The stretch of Route 50 they were on was usually pretty quiet this time of night but streams of headlights filled all three lanes heading back into the District. "What's with all the traffic tonight?" he asked. Trainum thought about that a second before the light went on.

"You know what? I bet that's the crowd leaving the Stones show, out where the Redskins play, Jack Kent Cooke?"

"The Stones?" Wallace said. "The Rolling Stones? I thought those guys would be dead by now." Trainum laughed. "Well, at least one of them is, but they're still out there touring, man. Mick's still got it, I tell you."

"Man, I picked the wrong line of work. How old is he, seventy? Eighty?"

"Maybe. I'll tell you though, I saw them once at the Capital Centre and it was wild. In the middle of one of the songs, this giant inflatable dick came out of the stage and got bigger and bigger until all this confetti and stuff came exploding out the top all over the crowd in front. It was unbelievable."

"Sounds great," Wallace said.

Trainum headed north on the Baltimore-Washington Parkway and got onto 450 in about a mile, then cut his way through the neighborhood to 55th Avenue. Brick three-story apartment buildings lined the street, cars filling every space on both sides. "This is the block," he said.

"You look on your side, I'll look on mine," Wallace said. Trainum slowed down like anyone looking for a space would. Wallace saw nothing that looked like any of Cooper's cars. They passed a dark basketball court that looked empty until he saw puffs of cold breath

42

coming from a few dim figures bundled up under the hoop closest to them. They came to a corner with a street that looked like it curved back behind the nest of buildings they just passed.

"Turn here," he said. Trainum made the right and they crept on in silence, no one in sight now. At the end of the block, he made a right onto Newton Street to finish the loop around the complex. Wallace saw taillights fire up on a car on his side about twenty yards ahead. A guy on the sidewalk tapped the car's roof, then walked back towards the buildings. When their headlights reached the car, Wallace stopped breathing. It was small and purple. He didn't recognize the make but as the driver turned to watch them go by, he recognized the face.

"That was him, man! Cooper, I swear!" he said. "It was! I saw him too," Trainum said.

Wallace scrambled to make sense of the day. *We are on a roll!* was his first thought, but it quickly gave way to a second: *We still don't have a shred of evidence. Even if the guy in the car was Cooper and even if he and Ellis did do the murders at Starbucks, unless one of them confessed, they had no case.* He shook his head. *In this damned thing, even the good times are bad.*

4

Five days later, Trainum knocked on Wallace's open door and shook a handful of papers at him. "Got a minute?" he asked. "Garrett just sent over the latest calls from the register." Wallace waved him in and Trainum circled behind his chair before he laid the stack in front of him so they could go through it together. "That's a lotta calls," Wallace said.

"Yeah, the circle's getting wider. You remember we added Roberta, Vontae Kincaid's ex-squeeze, right?"

"And?"

"And we got her talking to Leon. A lot."

"How do you know it's Leon and not the wife?"

"Because the wife's not the one working at the One World Unisex Hair Salon. Garrett added that too."

"How 'bout Carl? Is he callin' the salon?"

"Oh yeah," Trainum said. "They're still talkin' every day, sometimes every hour."

"Roberta and Carl talk?"

"That I haven't seen."

"Okay," Wallace said. "Then let's pay her a visit and see if we can find out what – or who – she and Leon are talking about."

"I will give her a call." Wallace expected Trainum to split, but when he didn't, he spun his chair around. "Anything else?"

"Just – and you can tell me it's none of my business, but can I ask you a question?"

"Shoot."

"Are you letting you-know-who know about what we're doing, what we're finding?"

"Soulsby? Hell, no! I haven't told anyone anything except you and Garrett."

"Yeah, that's sorta what I figured. You think maybe you ought to, now that something's actually happening?"

"What is actually happening, Detective? We have a couple of potential leads, that's all, emphasis on the potential. This is nothin' I would ever even think of running past you-know-fucking-who in any other case."

"I was just thinking –" Wallace cut him off. "And why would I do it in this case of all cases? Remember Walter Worrell and his goddamn shoes? We tell him about Carl Cooper, he'll tell the papers and kill the case on him before it even gets started. Come on, man, get serious!"

"I just think it wouldn't hurt to let him know we're making some progress. Keep him from doing something stupid again, like reassigning someone else to the case, or –"

"Re-re-reorganizing? No, man. That is not a good idea, not yet. He'd only blab something he shouldn't to the press – or to the Mayor, who'd do the same thing, only worse."

He'd tried not to let himself think about Marion Barry ever since his fellow citizens bestowed a second term on him in 1995, apparently figuring he'd been totally rehabilitated during the five months he spent in prison after being caught on video smoking a crack pipe at a D.C. hotel, but now he remembered all over again that if you threw out the four years Sharon Kelly held the job, the Not So Honorable Marion Barry had been D.C.'s only mayor since 1979 – "Mayor for

Life," one of the local papers called him. The only consolation this time around was that because he let the city's debt grow so out of control, Congress created a D.C. Financial Control Board that was in charge of pretty much everything of consequence. This Barry was just a figurehead, but Wallace knew he still had a lot of power to make mischief, if nothing else.

"Let me know what you hear from Roberta," he said, and spun back to his computer to let Trainum know the conversation was over, only to hear a knock on the door frame a second later.

"C'mon, Jim, what –" he got out before he saw it wasn't Trainum, but Melvin Ruffin, another one of his detectives. "I can come back," he said.

"No, come on in. What's up?"

"I got someone you may want to talk to. A guy named Eric Butera."

"Who's Eric Butera?"

"He just got out of jail for violating probation for robbing a cab driver a few years ago. That was all tied up with him being a cokehead, but bottom line is he says he got clean in jail and was calling me because he's got some information about Starbucks."

"Where'd he get it? In jail?"

"No, it was before he went in, back in July, right after the murders. He said he was buying some cocaine somewhere in Southwest and heard someone talking about it."

"And what did this someone say?"

"'Starbucks' is pretty much the only thing he remembers." Ruffin looked down at his notes. "That, and when the guy saw him looking

46

at him, he said something like 'Hey, white boy, mind your own fuckin' business.' That's pretty much it."

"Not a whole lot, is it?"

"No," Ruffin said, "but we've busted a few places down there since then. Maybe if we bring him in, show him some pictures of the guys we brought in, it'll jog his memory – or not. It's your call."

Ruffin was not someone who ordinarily gave the words of a cokehead – especially a white one – much credence. He'd been one of the first black detectives who'd been promoted on Wallace's recommendation, and Wallace had been reminded of that ever since, mainly by white detectives who did not enjoy his constant carping about their skills, their ignorance of the "ghet-to," and most of all, their promotions before his. "The color of his skin's more important to him than the color of his uniform" was the way one of them put it. Because Wallace knew exactly why Ruffin felt that way more than any of them ever would, he dealt with it, but it wasn't always easy. Plus, they had even less reason to talk to Vontae Kincaid's mother, but even that gave them something to follow up on.

"Okay," he said. "Bring him in."

The next morning, Wallace watched a heavy-set white man maybe in his early thirties, with thick eyebrows and a hairline gaining on his combed-back dark brown hair, walk into his office, followed by Ruffin carrying a black binder of mug shots. "Detective Wallace," he said, "Eric Butera." Wallace shook his hand and invited him to take a seat. Ruffin laid the book on Wallace's desk and pulled up a chair beside Butera.

"Thank you for coming in," Wallace said. "We appreciate your willingness to help us out." Butera shrugged. "I just felt I had an obligation to, you know. That thing was so terrible."

47

"Has he looked at the pictures yet?" Ruffin shook his head. "No, I thought you'd want to be in on it." Wallace turned to Butera. "I do, but before you go through them, I want to ask you a few things. First, why'd you go to that particular place to get your stuff?"

"Greenleaf Gardens? I'd been there before, man, a lot of times, like for years."

"Same place every time?"

"Yep. 1015 Delaware."

"You know whose place it is?"

"No, and I don't want to know either. Get in and get out, that's the drill."

"But you were there long enough to hear somebody talking about Starbucks, right?"

"Right." Butera turned to Ruffin. "And it hit me after we talked on the phone that it was actually two different times I heard somebody talk about it."

"The same night?" Ruffin asked.

"No, two different times in like the same week."

"Okay, what do you remember about the first time? Who said what?"

"I just heard 'Starbucks', but it was just a word in a conversation somewhere across the room, and I didn't look up to see who said it. I just did my thing and split. The second time though, I did look up because, you know, it was the second time."

"And what did you hear?" Wallace asked.

48

"What I told him before, just this one guy leaning against a wall talking, you know, pretty quiet with another guy, and I heard him say 'the Starbucks thing', you know, like he wasn't talking about the coffee."

"Either one of them say anything else?"

"Yeah. The other guy sees me looking at them and goes like 'yo, white guy, mind your own fuckin' business.'"

"And what did you do?"

"Minded my fuckin' business and got the hell out of there. Both of 'em had guns, man."

"Did you see what kind of guns?" Ruffin asked. Butera shook his head. "Just hand guns, that's all I can tell you – I'm no expert, man. That shit's out of my league."

"These guys black or white?" Wallace asked.

"Black. If there was another white guy there, I didn't see him, but I wasn't lookin' either. I just made my score and beat it."

"Can you describe either of them?"

"The guy that talked was bigger than I was, thicker, a lot more muscular. He had some kind of cloth cap on and it was dark, so I'm really not sure about anything else, except the look on his face. He scared the shit out of me."

"And the other guy?"

"Nothing really. He was kinda facing away from me, so I didn't really get a good look. Smaller than the other guy, that's about it. Like I said, it was dark and quick and I wasn't looking too hard, you know? Maybe the pictures'll spark something, I don't know. I hope." Ruffin opened the cover and pushed the book in front of Butera

"Just one more question," Wallace said. "Why'd you decide to come forward now?"

"Because I had a lot of time to think about it in jail and I'm seeing things a lot clearer now than when I went in, let's put it like that. I'm just tryin' to do the right thing, hope I can help you guys find whoever did it, that's it, really." Wallace nodded and pointed to the mug book.

"Okay, we'll get out of your face for a while," he said and flipped a small yellow note pad across the desk. "You see anyone you think you might remember, slip some paper in there. Take your time. We'll be out in the hallway."

Butera nodded and they left him alone. At the elevator, Ruffin asked "So? What do you think?"

"I think he *wants* to help. Whether he can, I got my doubts. Even if he thinks he recognizes someone in there, it's been months. It was dark. It was short. We may need to run it past someone in Mueller's office, see if we got probable cause to pick up anyone, assuming he even thinks he sees one of them."

"How about a stakeout? Send some plainclothes guys down the Gardens to look for whoever he fingers."

Wallace shook his head. "There are so many places down there and way too much of a chance at least one of those guys'd make us."

"Okay, so we go in and make a buy," Ruffin said.

"No," Wallace said, "same risk, only worse. Guy gets trapped in there, he's toast."

"So what then? Send him in? Do nothing?"

Wallace saw Butera's head pop into the hall and look his way. "Hey," he called out. "I think I recognize one of 'em."

"Let's see what he says first," Wallace said. When they got back to the room, Butera pointed to the photo in front of him. "That's the guy. I'm 99% sure of it." Wallace and Ruffin leaned in closer to take in a picture of a black man maybe in his late 20s, darkly complected, with a scar running down his left cheek. Wallace didn't bother to look at the perp's name.

"That ain't Carl or Leon," he muttered to Ruffin, who hacked a hard laugh. "You really thought we'd be that lucky, Commander?"

"Which guy? What time?" Wallace asked Butera anyhow.

"The guy the second time, the one who told me to mind my own business. I couldn't mistake that face."

"No one else? From either time?" Ruffin asked.

"No, just him, but I swear that's him."

Wallace stood up and looked at Ruffin. 'Anything else?' he mouthed. When Ruffin shook his head no, Wallace reached a hand out to Butera. "Thank you very much for coming in, sir. We need to give this some thought for a little while. If we can use you, Detective Ruffin'll let you know how."

Butera shook his hand, thanked him, and left. When Wallace sat back in his chair, he immediately pictured the face of the man who came to mind every time he thought about sending an informant into a crack house: Andy Scheingold.

Schein was an informant during Rayful Edmond's heyday, but he was a lot more than that. They'd met about 20 years earlier, when

51

Wallace had saved him and his friend Jake Katz from a beating at a Smokey Robinson show at the D.C. Coliseum, but neither of them made the connection until Wallace was questioning Schein after he'd bought dope from a DEA agent somewhere out in the Virginia burbs. When he told him they'd let him walk if he wore a wire, Schein agreed before the words were out of his mouth, but a year later, Wallace had to listen to the horror of Edmond's crowd yanking the wire from his chest, then puked his guts out when he discovered Schein's body, his head practically severed from the rest of it. Wallace never did get over the guilt of sending him to his grave and vowed it would never happen again. He finally got the guts to tell Katz – most of – what happened and it took years for them to restore – most of – a friendship they'd shared for thirty years. He'd never forget Katz salvaging his career during Hamaas Khaalis' siege of the city in '77 any more than he knew Katz would ever forget Wallace scraping him off the floor at the Coliseum. Even now, long after Katz had left the USA's office and started representing bad guys for a living, Wallace's next thought was *I owe him a call.*

He made himself refocus on Butera and turned to Ruffin in the chair across from him. "So?" he asked.

"So, I think we need to do *something.* Him seeing a gun is what's stickin' with me. That might be just the physical evidence we need. We have to get lucky in this thing for real sometime, don't we?"

Wallace rolled his eyes. "You remember 'Born Under A Bad Sign'? Albert King? 'If it wasn't for bad luck, I wouldn't have no luck at all'? That's us, man."

"We can't do nothin', Commander, that's all I'm sayin'."

Wallace knew he'd be risking Butera's life on a very slim chance. But he also knew Ruffin was right. Something trumped nothing, especially now. He made himself focus on how to reduce the risks first. "Okay," he said, "but if we send this guy in there, we got to have eyes on him at all times, at least goin' in and goin' out. "

"And ears?"

Schein's death mask flitted through Wallace's synapses one more time. He knew wearing a wire was not going to increase Butera's odds of coming out alive of whatever this turned out to be. "No, that's way too risky," he said, and drummed his fingers on the table for more than a few seconds before looking back up at Ruffin.

"Okay, how's this? He knows he needs to keep it short, so even if he takes a couple of seconds to scan the room to see if he can spot one of those guys, he'll be in and out quick enough. If he sees them, he gives us a sign when he comes out and we roll in, scoop everybody out, and fish out whoever he saw for a chat after they're booked. If he doesn't, we pick him up down the street and everyone goes home in one piece. How's that?"

"Works for me," Ruffin said.

"All right," Wallace said. *Let's see if it works for you-know-fucking-who*, he thought.

5

A week later, Soulsby approved the plan. A week after that,
Christmas came two days before Thanksgiving, over lunch at the
FOP. Wallace was scarfing down a sausage when Trainum suddenly
pointed to the TV over the bar and yelled "Hey! Turn it up!"
Wallace turned to see Soulsby standing behind a microphone, tears
running down his cheeks. The place went dead quiet. The TV grew
louder.

"I cannot allow another controversy to impact my officers and
detract from their accomplishments," Soulsby said, his voice
trembling. "My concern for the welfare of my officers and the
people they serve transcends my own personal welfare." Wallace
turned to Trainum to see if he had a clue about what they were
hearing. The look on his face confirmed neither of them did. "I
have therefore decided on my own accord to step down as chief of
police," Soulsby quivered on, "but not because I feel I have done
anything wrong. Though I seem somewhat emotional, this is the
happiest day I've had in two years."

"Brother, that makes two of us," Wallace said loud enough to get
hacks of laughter from the table next to them. "You got that right," a
heavy white Sergeant said. "Guy and his little butt buddy Stowe,
they're gettin' what they deserve." Wallace's quizzical look
prompted the Sergeant to fill him in. "Him and Stowe, he's a
Lieutenant somewhere? They live together, which is bad enough,
but then it turns out they got some kind of sweetheart deal on the
rent, payin' like six hundred or somethin' for an apartment that's
supposed to go for like two thousand a month."

Wallace turned back to hear Soulsby say "No one can dispute the
fact I have always cared for the people, and for the men and women
sworn to protect them. But the accusations day in and day out have

really detracted from the department. Now we have officers and sergeants who enjoy coming to work every day."

"Fuckin' A! We will now!" he heard behind him before a peal of laughter and a bubbling buzz all around him swallowed up whatever else Soulsby was saying. The Sergeant leaned close to him. "Stowe was already in the deep shit 'cause he blackmailed some married guy he caught down at one of the queer joints in Southeast. And this is fucking Soulsby's roommate? They deserve each other's all I can say."

"So who's taking his place?" Wallace asked over the din.

"I'm out of that loop," the Sergeant said, "but I'm guessin' it'll be Proctor till they hire somebody."

Proctor was Sonya Proctor. She joined MPD about ten years after Wallace but climbed the ladder a lot quicker than he did, due not only to his penchant for moving down the rungs almost as fast as she moved up, but also to her wisdom in tying herself to Maurice Turner when he was Chief back in the eighties. Soulsby made her his Assistant Chief in February and now here she was: The first black woman, permanent or acting, to become the Chief of the Metropolitan Police Department. Wallace was almost as happy to see her make it as he was to hear Soulsby's ass hit the pavement.

On the walk back to headquarters, Trainum asked him "Is she in the loop on Starbucks?"

"I'll find out," Wallace said, "and I'll fill her in on Butera once we know exactly what we're doing. Got any ideas on who else ought to be down there with him besides Ruffin?"

Trainum didn't have to give that much thought. "Carlo Cimino. He knows the streets better than anyone in the Division, black or white."

Wallace nodded his approval. Cimino had come up through the ranks and always let Ruffin's b.s. roll off his back, so he'd be perfect. That left just one item on his agenda. "One more thing," he said. "It's my ass on the line so I need to be there, but you don't."

Trainum stopped walking. "Are you effing serious? Why not?"

"Because I need someone back here I know I can count on just in case something goes south, which you and me both know it will." He planted a finger on Trainum's chest. "That's you."

"Shit, I got to start fucking up more," Trainum muttered.

By the afternoon of December 4, all the parts were in place. Wallace, Ruffin, and Cimino would be on the scene, Wallace in one unmarked car, Ruffin in another, and Cimino and Butera in a third. Cimino would drop Butera off out of sight from the townhouse, then wait down Delaware Avenue a block away. Ruffin would wait around the corner on K Street. Wallace would circle the block every few minutes in a different direction to monitor the house as close as he could, and buzz Trainum's pager to get help as fast as he could. The other two would post far enough from the townhouse to keep anyone heading in or out from suspecting that Butera was anyone other than just another junkie getting his shit.

Just like he did every other time he'd been there, Butera would go in through the back door of number 1015, and stay no more than 15 minutes. He'd pay 80 dollars for the drugs with marked 20s. While he was in there, he'd keep his eyes and ears open to pick up something that'd give them a reason to go in – one of the two guys was there, someone said 'Starbucks,' someone had a handgun – or anything else they could say with a straight face was probable cause. The only difference from his usual drill would be he'd leave out the front door rather than the back so that Ruffin could pick him up a block away down K. When Proctor signed off on it just before close of business, Wallace needed just one more approval to make it go.

56

He watched Ruffin dial up Butera, heard him say "It's on tonight. You ready?" and exhaled only when Melvin gave him the thumbs up.

6

At 9 that night, Cimino pulled his civilian black Jeep to the front of St. Peter's Catholic Church on 10th St. N.W. and edged down the left curb. He'd started picking up his informants at churches a few years back as a way to get God's blessing on their mission, but lately he'd started focusing Him on the task at hand by looking for churches named for the patron saint of something that was tied to the specific crime involved, like the time he recruited a guy who was going to meet a hit man over drinks in Shaw. He put the wire on him in a men's room at St. Stephen's because Stephen was the patron saint of coffin makers. Last Sunday, his priest's sermon was all about Pope John Paul II canonizing a monk named Maxmilian Kolbe who volunteered to be gassed at a concentration camp during World War II. The Germans took him up on his offer, and the Church for some reason made him the patron saint of drug addicts. He was hoping to put that nugget of information to use tonight, but no church in D.C. was named St. Maxmilian's, so he settled for St. Peter's, trying and failing ever since he got in the car to come up with a connection between tonight's enterprise and the patron saint of fishermen. Seeing Butera sitting on the top step under the big arch, he crossed himself and hoped Jesus would forgive him.

Per the plan, he rolled down his window, looked at Butera, then rolled it back up. When Butera got up, Cimino unlocked the doors and waited for him to cross in front and get into the passenger seat before he checked his rear-view mirror, saw just a few pedestrians crossing the intersection behind them, and pulled away slowly. He looked over to Butera and saw a face etched with tension. "You okay?" Cimino asked. "Not really," Butera said, looking straight ahead.

"Hey, look at me," Cimino said. When Butera did, he saw nothing but fear. "C'm'on," he told him, "you been down there dozens of times, right? You know the drill. Just do your business like you always do and get the hell out of there."

Butera ran his hands through his hair and turned away from him. "I know that," he said, "it's just the first time I been down there doin' it for you, you know?" Cimino punched him lightly on the shoulder.

"That's a good thing, man," he said. "We got your back, right? You never had that before, did you?" Butera shook his head no, but he looked way short of convinced. Cimino made a left on Pennsylvania and saw it was practically empty. He got over to the right-hand lane and turned down 4th. They'd be there in less than ten minutes.

"You want to go through it one more time?" he asked. "No," Butera said. "I just want it to be over."

Cimino weighed his options. One: Do one last review anyhow just to make sure he knew what he was doing, or Two: Don't, hope he calms down, and pray for the best. Another glance at Butera told him Two was the only option. He silently called on his Lord and Savior for help and mercy one more time and made his way to K. He rolled slowly past the front of a couple of sets of rowhouses. When he got to the stop sign at the corner with Delaware, he heard Butera say "This is it. I'll get out here."

"Is that your usual deal?"

"That's it," Butera said, "third door down from the alley." He pushed the door open and was out and around the corner before Cimino could say a word. When he found one, it was "Godspeed".

He looked at the clock on the dash. 9:21. He forced himself to count to ten before he made a right onto Delaware. About twenty yards down, he turned to see Butera walking down a concrete sidewalk through a courtyard behind the townhouses, head down. Cimino could make out a few forms near the third door from the

59

alley, but when he rolled past and looked in the mirror, he couldn't see anyone. He made a U-turn just past the corner at L, pulled into an open space on the other side of the street, and grabbed his walkie-talkie from its perch.

"All right, he's there," he said. "I'm parked just down the block. I can get to him in ten seconds if he comes out that way. Where you at, Commander?"

"Down the block across K, in front of the church," Wallace said. "You facing my way or the other way?" "Your way," Cimino said.

"You see him go in?"

"No, he was walking through the courtyard heading for the door when I passed him. A couple of customers were out there so I didn't want to hang around too long. What do you hear from Ruffin?"

"He's out front. I'm going to wait a few minutes, then drive over his way." The line clicked off.

Cimino squinted to see if he could detect any motion down the sidewalk on the other side. Nothing. He looked at his watch and made himself wait the 33 seconds till the second hand swept past the 12 before looking up again. Still no one in sight until he saw two people framed in headlights that pulled off the curb onto Delaware a block in front of him. He watched them hustle across the street heading away from the townhouses, then saw the car with the lights stop at the corner before it crept past the back of the townhouses, its headlights growing bigger and brighter. In a few seconds, a black Chevy pulled to a stop at the intersection in front of him before making a right onto L. Cimino pressed the button on his walkie-talkie.

"Was that you just turned on to L?" he asked.

"Yeah," Wallace said.

60

"You see him?"

"No, just a couple guys crossin' the street, but no one in the yard. Let me know if you see anything. I'm going to spin back up." The line went dead again.

Cimino peered back down Delaware. Nothing. He looked back at the dash. 9:26. He listened to a call squawk in. A B&E in a liquor store up 14th Northwest. He waited in the dark silence, the only sounds the low hum of the engine and the static from the police radio. He strained to look down the block one more time just in case Butera decided to take his usual route out the back, but saw no one. Ruffin's voice nearly made his head hit the roof.

"Carlo, you see anything?"

"No! Shit! I was hoping you did. You talk to Wallace?"

"Yeah, he turned around to circle the block from the other direction. You ain't seen him?"

"No, man, I ain't seen nothin'," he said before a pair of headlights made a turn onto Delaware behind him. "Wait a minute, this might be him." The black Chevy pulled up alongside and Cimino watched the passenger side window slide down. Wallace looked as worried as he felt. He lowered his own window. "Anything?" Wallace asked.

"Nothing."

Wallace looked down at his watch. 9:32. "I'm going to take another tour," he said and started to pull away, but stopped when he saw the tension in Cimino's face. He tried to lighten him up. "And keep your window down, in case we hear any gun shots. Or screaming." It didn't help.

"Dude should've been out by now, right?"

"You'd think. You see or hear anything, get up there pronto."
Cimino nodded and watched Wallace cross L, then take his time
heading past the townhouses until his brakes flashed at the stop sign
at K.

"See him?" he said into the walkie-talkie. "No," Wallace said. "I'm
going to turn around up ahead and park back near the church so
whether he comes out the front or the back, one of us has got to see
him." Cimino decided not to remind him that was the plan all along
and it wasn't working.

He released the button and let his head fall back against the headrest.
He closed his eyes, but a sudden glare of light popped them open. A
pair of headlights topped by spinning red beacons shone down at
him from the other end of Delaware. He popped the door open and
double-timed down the street before he broke into a run. A few
yards short of the courtyard, he saw Wallace run into it and followed
him to a uniformed cop huddling over someone next to the fourth
door from the corner. They watched the cop turn the body over. It
was Butera, his head battered and bloody front and back, eyes puffy
and closed.

"Is he dead?" Wallace asked, his color heading towards green. The
cop spun his head back and took them both in, then moved a hand to
his holster. "Who the fuck are you?"

"MPD," Wallace said and put his hands up in the air, then glanced
down to his sports jacket. "The badge's in my wallet. You can get it
if you want." The cop stood up, pulled the gun out of his holster,
and pointed it at Wallace. "You get it," he said. Wallace reached in,
pulled the wallet out, and flipped it open. The cop leaned in to take
a look at the badge, then cocked his head.

"The fuck're you doing here?"

"He's an informant. We were waiting for him to come out."

"Jesus Christ!" the cop muttered. He holstered his gun and knelt back down. He shook Butera's shoulder softly but got no response, then put a finger to his carotid artery for a few seconds before he reached for his phone and quickly pushed three buttons. "Yeah, this is Patrolman Brady with MPD," he said. "We need an ambulance asap at Delaware and K Southwest. Guy's got a pulse, but it's weak." He clicked off the phone and stood up. "They're on the way," he said and looked down at Butera. "But I'm not sure your boy's gonna make it."

A door behind them creaked and they all spun around. Wallace was the first to get to his gun. He gripped it tight with both hands and pointed it at the door.

"Don't shoot!" a voice from somewhere behind it cried out.

"Get down on your knees!" Brady yelled, his gun now levelled at the door.

"I'm down! I'm down!" the voice yelled back.

"Open it slow!" Wallace called out, staring down the barrel of his Glock 9. "Wide enough so we can see you, then put your hands up!" The door swung open slowly to reveal a young white man in a gray hoodie and dark pants kneeling in the darkness, his hands waving in the air. "Keep them up there," Wallace said, "and stand up!"

He watched him grab the door jamb and get to his feet, then waved him to come closer until he held up his free hand to stop him about ten feet away. The face he saw was more a boy's than a man's, thin and rimmed with a sparse blond beard. When he looked down at Butera, his eyes filled with tears. "Oh man! Oh fuck!" he got out. Wallace heard a siren coming their way.

"What's your name?" he asked.

"Jerome. McNally. I'm the guy that called 9-1-1."

63

"Okay, Jerome, you see what happened out here?"

"Yeah, well, some of it," Jerome said. "He knocked on the door," tilting his head to the one he just came out, "and I went to get it, but when I pulled it open, I saw some dudes shoving him over here, so I pushed it closed enough so, you know, I could see them, but they couldn't see me."

"How many dudes?" Wallace asked.

"Two at first, then a third guy." "They black? White?" "Black." "Okay, then what?"

"One of the first two guys, he punches him right in the face and he goes down. They're yellin' at him to give 'em his money, cocking their fists and shit, but then this other guy – Bruiser, they call him, a big guy – he comes down the walk and starts kickin' him while he's still lyin' there, you know, defenseless, in the stomach, his head, his balls – and the other guys are just watching, laughing, you know? It was fucking sick! I couldn't watch it any more so I just closed the door and went downstairs and I was freaking out, so I found a phone and called you guys, and then I locked myself in the bathroom and cried, man. I never seen anything like that! By the time I come back up, the place is empty, and I look out the window back there and I see the lights flashing, so I thought I oughta come out and tell you what I saw. I still can't fucking believe it!"

"How do you know this Bruiser?" Wallace asked.

"I've seen him here before, a couple of times."

"You know his real name?"

"No, I only heard people call him Bruiser."

"Think you could pick him out of a lineup?" Jerome shrugged. "Maybe."

64

"You recognize either of the other guys?" "No."

The siren whined up K Street and Cimino ran back up to the sidewalk and down to the corner. In a few seconds, a red DC EMS van pulled to the curb and two paramedics ran to Butera. Wallace pulled Jerome off to the side. Cimino joined them, followed a few seconds later by a wide-eyed Ruffin running in from the street.

"No," he panted. "Don't tell me!" None of them did but they didn't have to. He looked from one stricken face to another. "No one saw what happened to him?"

"The kid did," Wallace said. "Some guys grabbed him at the door. He never made it in."

"Oh my Jesus Fucking Christ!" Ruffin said. They all gave the paramedics a wide berth until one of them ran back to the van.

"Is he going to make it?" Wallace asked the other one.

"Hard to say. Pressure's low, heart's slow. He went to see who can take him. The closer they are, the better. Do you know if he was on anything before he got the beating?"

"No," Cimino said, "he was sober, completely normal."

The other paramedic ran back down carrying a flat metal stretcher with a long orange pad tucked under his arm. He pulled a lever on the stretcher that popped it into the full upright position, then pumped a pedal on the wheels to keep it from rolling. When they rolled Butera onto it, Wallace saw his wallet on the ground and walked around them to pick it up. He opened the billfold and shook his head, then looked at Ruffin.

"Empty," he said. "Kill a guy for what, eighty fucking dollars? Jesus!"

"He's still got a chance," the paramedic at Butera's feet said, "but we need to go now."

Wallace laid the wallet on Butera's chest. "Go, go," he said, then called after them. "Where's he going? "GW!" he heard before they slid him in the back. One of them hopped in behind him, the other ran to the driver's side and jumped in, and then they were gone.

"There he goes, man," Ruffin said to Wallace, "one more fucking Starbucks victim." But Wallace wasn't thinking of Butera. He was thinking of Schein and feeling the same guilt he prayed he'd never have to feel again.

"Godspeed," Cimino said.

7

Butera died just before midnight. At 8:15 the next morning, Jerome was poring through the nickname database in the D.C. area law enforcement system. By 9:30, they found mug shots of a few Bruisers to show him. By 10, detectives were out the door looking for a Renaldo Antonio Mathis of no fixed address. At 8:45 two nights later, he was arraigned for murder in the second degree.

That was the good news. The bad news was everything else. The killing refocused the press on the Starbucks murders, spurred more AMW callers to send MPD on more wild goose chases, and ratcheted up the pressure from the families, especially over the holidays, to finally find who killed Caity, Baby, and Emory. When the new year dawned, MPD had spent six months investigating the case with nothing to show for it but Butera's dead body. It wasn't till a few weeks later that Trainum gave Wallace a new reason for hope. Maybe.

Wallace had just hit the sidewalk on Indiana Avenue heading for lunch when he heard Trainum call his name. He turned to see him skipping down the steps, a look on his face he hadn't seen for a long time. He remembered it was called a smile.

"What's up?" he asked. "You got a new job?"

"No," Trainum said, "I just got a call from Brad."

It had been a long time since either one of them had heard from Garrett. Wallace figured the FBI had finally decided it had its own messes to deal with, it didn't need MPD's too. "I thought he'd lost the number," he said.

"He wants us to come over there tomorrow morning. He said they found something that may be interesting on the pen registers." The fact that Garrett wanted them to meet at the Bureau was interesting enough. That would be a first. "All right," Wallace said. "Let's do it."

At ten the next morning, they were escorted through security, down to the basement, and into a room in the data center. Garrett greeted them there and led them back to a room with three computers showing the same screen arrayed next to each other on a conference table. Garrett took the middle seat, Wallace the right, Trainum the left. Garrett pointed to his screen.

"So this is a list of the calls our friend Carl has made and received over the past month." He scrolled down the screen slowly until it showed three highlighted numbers, one yellow, one red, one green. They were all in the Maryland 301 area code. "The yellow number's Leon's barber shop, the red's his home, and the green one's Roberta's, Vontae's girlfriend. You remember I told you Carl and Leon were talking ten, twelve times a week, and we thought that was a lot?"

Wallace nodded. "Well, check this out." Garrett scrolled down the screen a little quicker. It looked like a Christmas tree with a lot of gold tinsel. "They're all talking all the time now, but here's what else is interesting. Hit the toggle switch up at the left." They both did and saw a new list of numbers and a new color.

"That's Roberta's line, showing her calls, in and out. The yellow and red ones are Leon's, the green ones are Carl's home number, and the purple are his work number." There were more of every color lately.

"Any idea why all the chatter? Or why they're talking to her?" Trainum asked. "Nope," Garrett said. "But there's two ways we can find out. One is a warrant to start listening to the calls, but our legal shop says we don't have probable cause yet. The other is to pay Roberta a visit."

"And what do we tell her about why we're there?" Wallace asked. "Bringing up Starbucks might just give 'em all a good reason to *stop* talking to each other." Garrett spun his chair to him.

"You guys have a cold case unit, don't you?" Wallace nodded, beating back the memory of his own time in that frigid zone. "Then tell her you're following up on a new lead you just got on Vontae's murder."

At eleven o'clock sharp on an uncharacteristically balmy January morning two days later, Wallace and Garrett watched Trainum knock on the same door of the apartment they'd been to   last October. This time though, Vontae's mother didn't answer the door. When it swung open, Wallace caught eyes with a pretty young woman with light brown skin and a bushy natural. He fought the urge to check out the rest of her.

"Miss Rawlins?" he asked.

"C'm'on in." She shut the door behind them and led them back to the same cramped table they squeezed around last time. "I'd offer you something, but Albertha ain't got nothin' to spare," she said, then took a seat at the far end of the table and waited for them to take their seats

"Is she going to be joining us today?" Wallace asked. Roberta shook her head. "No, she's here, but just thinkin' about Vontae wears her down, so she's back in the bedroom watchin' The Price Is Right. That's one of her shows, you know, so unless you really need her, I'd just as soon let her be."

"That's fine," Wallace said, then pulled his pad out of his jacket pocket and clicked his ballpoint. "So, should I call you Roberta or –" He stopped short when she held up her hands.

"Wow! Listen," she said, "ain't nobody called me that for a long, long time. Roberta's on my birth certificate because my momma named me for Roberta Flack, who she *loved*. But when it turned out I couldn't even carry a tune for shit, she took to calling me Robbie and it stuck, so just call me that, okay? So, what's the new evidence? What're we talkin' about?"

"Mr. Garrett here's with the FBI. He called Mr. Trainum a few days ago to tell him they'd just got a statement from somebody involved in a different case about a car that supposedly was in the area where Vontae was when he died. We just want to see if the car rings a bell to you."

"What is it?"

Wallace looked down at his blank pad. "A purple car, small, looked like a Toyota or a Honda," he said, "D.C. plates, but he didn't get the number." He looked up at her, his face just as blank. Her eyes fired back before she leaned forward and smacked the table with both hands.

"I don't need no plate number to know whose car that is – that's motherfucking Carl Cooper's car!"

"And who is Carl Cooper?" Garrett asked. She fell back in her chair. "Jesus motherfucking Christ! I *knew* that little bastard had somethin' to do with it! Carl Cooper is a psycho who used to drag Vontae into all his shit."

"What kind of shit?" Wallace asked.

"Robberies mostly, armed robberies," she said. "One or another of 'em would get picked up from time to time, but they always managed to beat it until Carl got put away for real. He always thought Vontae snitched on him, you know, but that wasn't Vontae's way. He never ratted anyone out." Her eyes welled up and Wallace

70

waited a few seconds before he asked "Do you think Carl Cooper might've had a reason to want Vontae dead?"

She banged the table again. "Hell yes he did! And I can tell you *exactly* what happened. Sometime after that fucker got out, Vontae started hangin' with him again, and one night they were with a few other guys outside his house on Gallatin Street, in D.C. One of them was a drug dealer Vontae had a beef with, so when Cooper goes inside, Vontae and one of the other dudes stick him up and take his cash, and bail. The guy bangs on Cooper's door and gives him all kinds of shit for setting him up, so little Cooper, he's too much of a pussy to do anything himself, he gets Man to do it, tells him 'get Vontae's attention', okay? And Man gets his attention, all right, he fucking shoots him dead – with a gun Cooper gave him!"

"And how do you know all this?" Wallace asked.

"You mean 'Do I have proof?'" Robbie said. "No, I ain't got no proof – but I don't need none either. I *know* what happened and so does everyone else around here. This is how he do. And now you got his car? That's all the proof I need. I *knew* that little fucker was behind it!"

She fell back into her seat, shaking her head and muttering, tears of rage filling her eyes. Wallace let her cool, pretending to read his notes, then saw a walker coming around the corner, followed by Albertha, her face filled with concern.

"Is everything okay?" she asked. "I heard some yellin'."

Robbie reached back to pat her arm. "It's okay, mama," she said. "It's all good." But the tears on her cheek betrayed her and Albertha started crying too, gripping the handles of her walker so tight Wallace could see her veins bulge. "It's a trial," she finally said, "a trial that never ends, the devil's trial." She laid a shaking hand on

71

Robbie's shoulder. "She loved him as much as I did, still do."
Robbie brought her free hand up to wipe her face.

"You show 'em the box?" Albertha asked her. Robbie shook her
head, then got up, walked three steps to the kitchen, reached up into
a cabinet over the range to pull out a small beat-up dark wood box
with a curved top, and brought it back to the table.

"That's all we got left of him now," Albertha said. Robbie opened it
and pushed it to Wallace. "May I?" he asked Albertha. "Go 'head,"
she said.

He pulled out a driver's license, a set of keys, and a black do-rag
before seeing what looked like a lime green greeting card envelope.
He pushed it to the side before Robbie said "Yo, let me see that."
He handed it to her and watched her slip it from the envelope, then
well up again.

"Wow," she said, "I haven't thought about this for a long time."

"Read it to me," Albertha said. Robbie cleared her throat and tried
to pull herself together. "'Happy birthday to the one I love. Yours
forever, Vontae.'"

"That's the kind of child he was," Albertha said, "just a sweet boy
always." Robbie took one more look at the front of the card, then
tucked it back in the envelope, kissed where he'd written his return
address, and handed it back to Wallace. "Last birthday he was with
us," she said. Wallace took it from her, then noticed the postmark.
February 25, 1993. He turned the envelope to her and pointed to it.

"Your birthday in February?" he asked. "Yep," she said, "the 23rd
though. He wasn't too good rememberin' things like that."

"Huh," Wallace said, "Mine's the 24th." Her face brightened for the
first time since she greeted them at the door. "Then we're both
Aquarians," she said. "Smart and sarcastic, right?"

"Right on the money. You too?"

"What, you couldn't tell?" They exchanged smiles and Wallace looked to Garrett, then Trainum. "Anything else we need to ask these ladies now?" They both shook their heads no. Wallace got up first and extended his hand to Robbie. She took it and gave it a short squeeze. They said their goodbyes to Albertha and headed for the door. When Robbie opened it to let them out, Wallace let Trainum and Garrett go first.

"So you going to arrest him now?" she asked. Wallace shook his head. "Not yet. We need to do a little more digging to make sure we can convince a judge we've got enough probable cause to arrest him. I will keep you posted."

"You promise?" she smiled.

"I promise," he said and followed the others back to the car. When they got in, he turned to Trainum in the back seat. "Let's plan on coming back to help her celebrate her birthday."

"Yours too," Trainum said. "How weird was that, born a day apart?"

"It really would be," Wallace said, "if I wasn't born September 15th."

8

Wallace studied his reflection in the bathroom mirror, something he didn't ordinarily waste time on. He knew what his face looked like and, until ten days ago, he hadn't cared what anyone else might think about it for a very long time. But this morning, he'd trimmed his mustache, shaved off his soul patch, and, once he found the container buried at the back of the drawer, flossed. He even ironed a white shirt and took the time to find a tie that matched his brown Harris Tweed sport jacket. If there was anything else a man did to get ready to see a woman these days, he didn't want to know. It had been a long time since he'd thought about a woman as anything but a victim or a suspect, and it had been a much longer time since he'd actually been with one.

But now that he was back in the attic of his mind, he remembered that once upon a time, he'd been with a lot of them, too many to count, much less remember. It was only when the memories started seeping back through his synapses that he remembered why he didn't want to remember. Lovemaking was not a thing in his home. His father's idea of sex was to beat his mother, sometimes in front of him, then push her into the bedroom and slam the door behind them. The first time it happened, Wallace heard the bed creak and bounce and his father grunt and curse, but never heard a sound from his mother. The next time and every time after that, he ran to his own room and threw a pillow over his head.

Because love had nothing to do with whatever was happening in his parents' bedroom, it had nothing to do with what happened in his own. Once he became a star running back in high school, finding women to screw was never a problem, there or at Alcorn A&M. The faces and the bodies were all a blur now, but what he did was always the same, always what he imagined his dad did to his mom. His dick was a bayonet and he would ram it into anyone who'd spread her legs for him and even more unmercifully into anyone who wouldn't.

Sex was another way to hate, not love, and he had a lot of hate to pass around.

It was only years later, after he came to D.C., where no one knew or cared who he was on a football field, that he realized not every man treated their women like the Wallace men did. But between the job and the booze, he didn't have the time or the inclination to change his ways, so he just took himself out of the game. The last memory he beat back was the stunned realization that it had been more than ten years since he'd had sex with anything but his own fist.

He rooted back through the drawer and found a half-empty bottle of Old Spice Leather. He unscrewed the cap, smelled the contents without wincing, and rubbed some on his neck before he took a last look at the finished product looking back at him and headed for the door. Two stops and two hours later, he followed Trainum and Garrett down the hallway to Albertha's apartment.

"Robbie get the day off from work?" Trainum asked.

"She just told me any time was good," Wallace shrugged. At 1-C, Trainum knocked on the door and backed away so Wallace was front and center. When Robbie pulled it open, he held up the cake box.

"Happy Birthday!" they sang out, but the look on her face was anything but happy. She pointed at the box. "You got a job in there?" Before Wallace could answer, she waved them inside and closed the door behind them. Wallace nodded at a solemn Albertha sitting at the table, laid the box on the table, and turned to see Robbie fall back against the refrigerator and cross her arms.

"I got laid off," she said. "Yesterday. Nice present, huh?"

"Wow," Wallace said, "what happened?"

"Tell you the truth, I don't even know. I stopped listenin' after 'let you go'. It was a shit job anyway, but at least it put somethin' in my pockets. Now I don't know what I'll do, where I'll go. Can't afford no rent now, that's for damn sure."

"I told you –" Albertha started, but Robbie raised a hand to her. "I know, momma, and that sofa just might be where I wind up, but I told you I need to think on it a little, all right?" Albertha raised her own hand back and the room fell quiet until Robbie pointed at the box.

"So if it ain't a job, what is it?"

He opened the lid and she walked over to check it out. They both read the yellow "Happy Birthday, Robbie!" written on the chocolate frosting. "It's angel cake inside," Wallace said. "Safeway lady said they baked it this morning."

"Well, I'm ready to eat it this morning," Robbie said and headed back to the kitchen. In a minute, she was back with five paper plates, five plastic forks, five sheets of Bounty, and a steak knife. Two minutes later, Wallace wiped the remnants of a bite off his lips and turned to her.

"So can I ask you something else about Carl Cooper?"

Robbie downed the last of her slice and turned to Albertha. "I told you they wasn't comin' here just to celebrate my birthday, didn't I?" Albertha held up both hands this time. "So," she said to Wallace, "what more you need to know about that piece of shit?"

"We heard something else about him that we're checking out. You ever hear he might've had something to do with the Starbucks murders last summer?" She stared at him a second before she answered.

"Yes, I did."

"From who?"

She shrugged her shoulders. "Shit, I don't remember. It was just, you know, out on the street somewhere. Been a long time since I heard anything though, I can tell you that."

"How about someone named Leon Ellis?" Garrett asked. "Ever hear anything about him and Starbucks?"

Robbie gave that more than a second before she shook her head. "No. Now, I did hear that him and Cooper did some things from time to time, you know, but no, I never heard anything about him having anything to do with Starbucks."

"You know I just saw something on the TV about that Starbucks," Albertha said. Wallace and Trainum exchanged curious glances. "What was it?" Wallace asked.

"They're finally opening it up again," she said. "First time since those poor people were killed there. And there's a plaque up there now, listing all their names. It's amazing the police ain't found who did it yet, isn't it?"

Robbie patted her hand and looked at Wallace. "She thinks you guys are PG cops. She didn't mean nothin' by it."

"It is amazing, Mrs. Kincaid. I agree with you," Wallace said and turned back to Robbie. "Do you know Mr. Ellis?"

"Yeah, I know who he is, through Vontae, but I don't know anything about him or what he did or didn't do with that piss-ant Cooper."

Wallace nodded and scribbled "Knows 0 re Leon" in his pad. "Okay, let's get back to Cooper. You know when we came here the first time, you told us that purple car was his. You think of anything else that might tie him to Vontae, or Starbucks, for that matter?"

She thought on that so long that Wallace was going to ask if she heard him when she said "The only other thing I can remember is

77

Vontae telling me how he got his guns. He said he'd have his wife buy 'em, so there wouldn't be any connection – what do you call it, a paper trail – between him and what they'd use to pull off shit. How 'bout that, huh? Set up his own wife to take the fall if anything went wrong. What a miserable fucker!" Trainum and Garrett pulled out their pads.

"His wife is Cissy?" Trainum asked. "Yeah," Robbie said. "Is that her real name?" "Only one I know her by."

"Do you know where she bought them?" Garrett asked.

"You mean like Maryland or D.C.?"

"That'd be a start," he said, "or maybe the gun shop she goes to?" Robbie shook her head. "No, sorry, but you know, I can try and find out."

"How?" Wallace asked.

"I talk to her from time to time. Carl too." Wallace stopped writing.

"But you hate him. You think he killed Vontae. Why –"

"Correction. I *know* he killed Vontae, and that's *why* I stay in touch. Because one day, one glorious day, he'll slip up, want me to forgive him, whatever. And then, I will have the wonderful joy of tellin' you all he did it and be there to watch you take him away. Praise Jesus!"

"How often do you talk to him?"

"Often as I can stand it. Sometimes we do shit together, weed, whatever – but no sex, oh no, I don't need Cissy comin' after me. But I tell you, if it'd put that motherfucker away, I would grit my teeth, steel my spine, and smile all the while."

Wallace looked at Trainum, then Garrett, both looking as dumbfounded as he felt. "Gentlemen, anything else we ought to be asking her? Or Mrs. Kincaid?" When they both managed to shake their heads, Wallace turned back to Robbie.

"Anything else we ought to be asking?" he asked.

"Not that I can think of," she said, "but I'd be happy to make stuff up if it'd put his ass in jail forever – or the chair, even better."

He stood up and nodded to her and Albertha. "We greatly appreciate the help. If we need to follow up on anything after we check out Cissy's gun records, we'll be back in touch." He followed Garrett and Trainum back up the hallway, but stopped when he felt a light hand on his elbow. He turned to see Robbie flash the smile he hadn't seen today, but couldn't help but remember from their first meeting. Her hand stayed on his elbow.

"That could take a while, couldn't it?" she asked. He felt a twitch he hadn't felt for a long, long time.

"What could?" he asked.

"Checking out Cissy's gun records." she said. He started to answer before he knew what he'd say, but she wasn't finished. "You know, you don't have to wait till then to come back for a piece." The power of speech eluded him again, but she knew what was going through his brain. "Piece of cake, Detective. It ain't gonna to last forever."

He managed to flip open his wallet and dig out a card. "If you don't hear from me in the next week or so," he finally got out, "give me a call and we'll work something out."

She lifted her hand from his elbow and took the card. "That would be nice too," she smiled and walked him to the door. He saw Trainum and Garrett talking inside the doorway to the building, turned and nodded to her, and made his way to them, his step a little quicker than it was coming in. When he got to them, Trainum said "Brad and I were just saying she could be a real key to nailing his ass."

"How's that?" Wallace said. Trainum was goggle-eyed. Wallace heard him say something about Cissy and guns and phones, but the only thing on his mind was cake.

9

A run through D.C.'s Vital Records Department showed that Cissy's real name was Selene Lee Joiner, so at least Trainum knew what name to look for. But after three-and-a-half hours of futility trying to find what shop sold her the guns, figuring out where else to look had overtaken the Oldsmobile's lumpy car seat as the primary source of the pain in his ass.

He knew when he started that the only way to find out who sold them to her was to go to every gun shop in the tristate area, if not further, until he found the one that had a record of the sale. Bitter experience had taught him that no Federal, state, or local agency in the District, Maryland, or Virginia required a store to provide its records to the Bureau of Alcohol, Tobacco, and Firearms or anywhere else. All ATF required a handgun seller to do was write down the buyer's name and contact information and the gun's model name, caliber number, and serial number, and the only time it had to send even that to anyone was when it went out of business, which meant that by the time the Feds got it and got around to turning it into electronic data, it was almost guaranteed to be useless to law enforcement or anyone else.

His day began with a trip to the first place any cop looking for a firearm used in a crime in the DMV would go: Realco, a tiny shop out in District Heights, Maryland that had an outsized share of the action in that market. When that didn't pan out, he headed for Silver Spring, where he could hit United Guns on Randolph, the Dick's on Viers Mill, and Atlantic Guns on Bonifant. By the time he'd struck out at the first two, it was time for lunch, so he stopped for a Double Supreme at Burger King before heading to Atlantic. He caught every light, of course, which only gave him more time to consider what faced him if he found nothing there: a last gasp in Maryland at Atlantic's shop in Rockville, then D.C., and then, God forbid, the dozens of stores arrayed across Northern Virginia. He prayed that Carl and Cissy weren't that diabolical.

He pulled into a No Parking space on Bonifant right in front of Atlantic at 1:20. At 3:52, he stopped cursing his life when he finally found the name he was looking for in a folder deep in the back of the bottom drawer. A wrinkled pink copy of a sales slip showed that on June 28, 1996, Selene Lee Joiner bought a 9 mm handgun using a Maryland driver's license and a College Park address. A voice deep in the numb recesses of his brain called to him, but he paid it no heed as he sprinted up the steps and dialed Wallace from a phone booth down the sidewalk. "Commander," he said. "I got the record in my hand."

"Outstanding," Wallace said. "What's it say?" As Trainum read it to him, he felt that gnawing seed of doubt blossom into a fully grown stink weed. When Wallace's silence confirmed what was now front and center in his mind, Trainum said what they both were thinking.

"Shit, the Starbucks shells were from a .38 and a .380."

"Yeah," Wallace said. "Date works though. Good job on that."

Trainum looked at his watch. 3:56. He looked at the shop's door. Open till 6. "I'll talk to you later," he said and hung up. At 3:57, he jerked the bottom file drawer open and resumed hating life.

Wallace put the phone back in its cradle and stared at Cooper's face staring vacantly back at him from the mug shot pinned to the bulletin board across the room. As much as he wanted to believe he was their man, he knew that even if Trainum did find a record tying Cissy to guns that fired the right-sized bullets, they still wouldn't have nearly enough proof to tie Cooper to the murders. No prints. No weapons. No eyewitnesses. Not even a clue from anyone other than anonymous tipsters and the vengeful girlfriend of a murder victim who couldn't even provide hard evidence of Cooper's hand in that crime. It was like the face looking back at him was a jigsaw puzzle with so many pieces missing, it could be anyone's face. He wasn't sure if the chill down his spine was caused by the fear that after six long months, he still didn't have probable cause to pick him up, or the realization that if wasn't him, he had no earthly idea who killed those people.

10

The arrival of spring did little to heat up the investigation, but one development offered Wallace at least some hope, even if Mayor Barry was responsible for it. Although Congress had stripped His Dishonor of any control over the Department's day-to-day operations, he did keep the authority to name a new Chief to replace Soulsby, and on April 21, he picked Charles Ramsey, the number two cop in Chicago, to be the Chief of MPD.

At ten a.m. on the Monday after Ramsey took the job, Sonya Proctor led Wallace, Trainum, and Ruffin into his office and introduced them to him. Wallace took the seat Proctor pointed him to directly across the conference table from the Chief's shiny new gold and walnut nameplate and watched Ramsey finish his meet and greets with the others. He was a little on the stout side, black, medium complected, maybe in his late 40s, with dark-rimmed pie plate glasses, a salt-and-pepper mustache, and a broad smile. Wallace hoped they'd both be smiling when the meeting was over.

Trainum and Ruffin took the seats next to him. Ramsey waited for Proctor to sit in the one to his left before he spoke. "So, as you can probably guess, the Mayor and the folks who vetted me brought the Starbucks investigation up more than once. It was the first thing I asked Assistant Chief Proctor to update me on the day I took the job, and this is the first meeting I put on my calendar, so I want you all to know that finding whoever did this thing is my top priority, and will be until the day we grab him or them, okay?"

He waited for Wallace to nod before he looked to Trainum, then Ruffin, to make sure they understood him too. They did. "And you will have all the resources you need to get the job done, no questions asked, okay?" When they showed him they understood that too, he turned back to Wallace.

84

"Detective, you have an open door policy at all times here, both with me and, if I'm not in, Chief Proctor too."

"I appreciate that, sir, ma'am."

"All right. So what do you need from me right now?"

"Nothing from you, sir. What we need is someone to give us enough information that'll let us get a warrant to start tapping our prime suspect's phone."

"That still Carl Cooper?"

"It is," Wallace said, and summed up what he hoped Ramsey already knew about the AMW tip and Robbie. When he finished, he watched Ramsey sink back into his chair and think for a bit before he spoke.

"That America's Most Wanted part reminded me of a case we had in Chicago when I was Deputy Chief of the Patrol Division about four, five years ago. A woman named Catherine Suh got her brother to kill her boyfriend so she could cash in on his $250,000 life insurance policy, then she ran off to Hawaii and changed her name. We had even less to go on than you have with this Cooper, but one night, a couple of years later, that show ran a bit on her – and she saw it and totally freaked out and disappeared, for weeks, until one day she shows up at the FBI office in Honolulu – totally paranoid, wanting to kill herself, the whole nine yards – and turns herself in. And now, she's spending the rest of her life, with no possibility of parole, at the Women's Correctional Center. So those blurbs sometimes really do work."

"Good to hear, sir," Wallace said.

"The reason I brought that up is I got to know some of the folks running the show, so if you think it might be worth another shot in this case, I'd be happy to call them and see if they'd run something on it again. Maybe our man Carl'd freak out too, or someone'd finally give you something you could use. You never know."

"You never do," Wallace said. "It's definitely worth a shot."

"All right then, I'll give them a call. Anything else I can do for you now?" When Wallace shook his head no, Ramsey stood up and stretched his arm across the table and shook his hand. "Then I will see you tomorrow, hopefully with some good news. You free around five o'clock?"

Wallace laughed. "If I'm not, I'll cancel whatever's on my calendar, Chief, believe me."

At five the next afternoon, Wallace and Trainum were back and Ramsey was waiting for them.

"So I got some good news from the America Most Wanted folks," he said. "They're happy to run it again."

"That's great!" Wallace said, even as the image of him chasing wild geese flashed through his skull.

"Now, they told me not to expect it to show up this week," Ramsey said. "They said they have to 'package' it, which I think means a lot of editing and updating and whatnot, but they promised me they'd do it and I will hold them to it, don't you worry about that."

"I have no worries, sir. Thank you for making that happen."

"So, any developments since yesterday?"

"Do you know who Eric Butera was, sir?" Trainum asked.

"He was the young man who got killed at a crack house, wasn't he?"

"That's him, sir. There was a preliminary hearing this morning on Renaldo Mathis, the guy who killed him, allegedly."

86

"How'd it go?" Ramsey asked.

"Pretty routine. He'll get arraigned next week. Second degree murder while armed."

"All right, that's good. What else?"

"That's pretty much it, sir," Wallace said.

"All right," Ramsey said, "I will see you tomorrow." He stood up, threw them a salute, and turned to leave but stopped at the sound of Wallace's voice.

"Sir, we greatly appreciate you doing this, but some days – a lot of days – nothing happens, and I don't want –"

"Then that's what you'll tell me and we'll move on," Ramsey said. "And if you or Detective Trainum just want to call me and tell me that, that'll be fine too. I just want to us to least touch base every day so that if there's anything I can do for you, I know what it is, and I can do it as soon as possible. That's it. Period. Okay?" He turned to leave, then turned back. "Oh, and by the way, you can drop the 'sir', both of you. 'Chief' will do or 'Hey you', I don't really care. We're all in this together."

Now Wallace chased Chief Soulsby's face out of his brain forever. "Okay, Chief, see you tomorrow."

The tomorrows crept on at a petty pace, with not much to report for weeks at a time. That changed when the phone rang in Wallace's condo a few minutes after ten on a Saturday night in late June. He eyes sprung open before his brain told him he'd been sleeping. He saw Brady Anderson hit a single to left and heard Mike Flanagan tell him that made it 10-3 Orioles before the phone sitting a foot from his head went off again. He forced himself to a sitting position, found the remote, and muted the TV, but it didn't do a thing for the phone. He grabbed it on the third ring and barked into it.

87

"Who is this?"

"Chief Ramsey. Did you see it?" Wallace's mind cleared instantly. "Chief, I'm sorry, I must've fallen asleep. See what?"

"America's Most Wanted. Starbucks was just on there!"

Wallace heard the Call Waiting click. "Chief, can you hold on just a second?" he asked. "That might be Trainum." He clicked off and said "Hello?" before he realized he'd put his boss on hold and cursed himself.

"Hey, did you just see that?" Trainum said. "No, but I got Ramsey on the other line." "Call me back." Wallace clicked over to Ramsey but all he heard was a dial tone. He cursed himself louder and called Trainum back, but got his voice mail. He got out "Jim, this is –" when the real Trainum clicked in. "Tom, can I put you on hold?" he said.

"Are you talking to Ramsey?" Wallace asked. "No, Melvin. He says the phones are ringin' off the hook already. I'll call you right back." Wallace put the receiver back in its cradle, fell back onto the couch, and laid his hands over his eyes.

The phone blared again. He picked it up before the first ring faded. "Chief?"

"No, it's me again," Trainum said. "Melvin said he got a uniform walking by to help him field the calls so everything's cool now."

Wallace rubbed his free hand across his face. "You got any plans tomorrow morning?" he asked. "After you go to church and get yourself right with the Lord, of course."

"Too late for that," Trainum said. "What time you want to meet?"

11

At nine sharp on Sunday morning, they met Ruffin inside the phone center. He pointed at his yellow pad on the table. "Fifty-three calls by midnight," he said. "That's when I left. Don't know how many more came in since."

"Anything interesting?" Wallace said. Ruffin raised an index finger. "One," he said and looked at his pad. "A woman named Angela. Didn't give me her last name, but said her boyfriend Donnell knew the killer." He looked up. "Guy named Carl Cooper."

"I'm listening," Wallace said. Ruffin read what he wrote. "Said he knew him because they grew up on the same block. The boyfriend's nephew Malcolm told him that Carl said he robbed it and shot the white girl because she wouldn't open the safe. Then he shot the black kid because he was trying to help her, and he shot the white kid last." He picked his head up. "That's it."

"No last names on the boyfriend or the nephew?"

"Nope."

"You get her phone number?" Trainum asked. "Yep, and her address."

"Okay, then why don't you give her a call and tell her we'd like to come by." Wallace said. "But before you do that, give me the address so I can post a couple of plainclothes up there in case she has second thoughts and decides to bail before we get there. Jim, see if you can find anything on an Angela or anyone else at that address or any Malcolms or Donnells of interest too."

At 11:30, they approached a dirty black Ford Taurus sitting at the curb on the other side of Oglethorpe Street, a few blocks off the D.C. side of Eastern Avenue. When Ruffin rolled down the driver's side window, the bearded cop in a T-shirt behind the wheel of the Taurus did the same. Wallace leaned across Ruffin from the passenger seat.

"Anyone come in or out?" he asked. "No," the driver said, "and not 'round back either. I think you're good." Wallace threw him a salute and Ruffin backed into a space a half-block up before they walked up the steps to a two-story brown brick house with a rusty corrugated white shade over the front door. Trainum knocked on the metal storm door, then stepped back so Wallace was the first person Angela saw. When she opened the door, Wallace pressed his badge to the glass and she let them in, pointing to a small living room to the right.

"Y'all can sit wherever you like," she said and took the chair closest to the door. Wallace and Ruffin sat on the brown and white striped sofa across from her. Trainum took the yellow plastic chair to their left. Angela was a heavy-set black woman who looked to be in her mid-thirties, with straight hair that was jet black down to its blonde tips. She wore a sleeveless jean jacket over a short-sleeved white shirt and black jeans. Wallace watched her cross her legs and clench her hands tight. He tried to put her at ease.

"First, we want to thank you very much for calling in last night, and for agreeing to see us so quickly. It's greatly appreciated."

She released a hand and held it to her chest. "I just – it's been weighin' on my mind for so long, you know, and I just was waitin' for someone to come forward, or get caught or somethin', but when I saw that bit on the TV last night, I just prayed on it and felt I had to say what I knew, you know?"

Wallace pulled out his pad and pen. "I'm glad you did," he said. "So let's just start with the basics. Can I get your last name?" When she hesitated, he told her "No one'll know but us. You have my word."

90

She thought on that a minute before she asked "How 'bout the reward people though? You'll tell them, right?" Wallace felt the twin high beams of Trainum and Ruffin's stares.

"If you give us information that helps get whoever did this behind bars, you bet," he said.

"All right," she said. "Corrothers. Angela Rae – R–a–e – Corrothers."

"All right, Miss Corrothers. Why don't you tell us what you know?"

"Well, first off, let me just tell you that all I know is what my boyfriend told me Carl Cooper told his nephew."

Wallace raised his hand. "Hold on a second. Your boyfriend's Donnell, right?"

"Right."

"And what's his last name?"

"Do I have to tell you that?" she said. "I don't want him to get in any trouble." Trainum leaned forward and answered before Wallace could. "But you want the reward people to know, don't you? So he can get his share if this leads to something, right?"

If she sensed that all of their bullshit detectors were on high alert, she hid it well. "Well, sure then. It's Leland." Wallace heard Trainum clear his throat and Ruffin pop the latch on his briefcase.

"And Malcolm's last name?" Wallace asked.

"Leland too, Malcolm Leland." Ruffin pulled some papers from a manila folder and slid them under his notepad.

"Okay, so what Donnell told you is what Malcolm told him Carl said. Do I have it right?"

91

"Right," she said. Wallace knew that hearsay wasn't admissible in court and when he counted them up, including her telling them, four hearsays separated him from Carl. He felt his heart grow heavy and his brain spring a migraine. On the other hand, he was here, and she was talking, so he prayed she'd get around to something they could actually use. When she asked if she should go on, he made himself nod yes.

"Okay, so Donnell grew up with Carl, they lived like two doors apart in D.C. and no, I don't know either one of their addresses back then neither."

"We'll get back to that. Just tell us what you told Detective Ruffin last night about what Malcolm told his uncle that Carl said."

"Like I told him, he told Donnell that Carl went in there to rob it and he shot the white girl because she wouldn't open the safe."

"Hold it right there," Wallace said. "Did Donnell say anything about Carl actually robbing the place?"

"As opposed to what?"

"As opposed to not robbing it because he couldn't get his hands on the money."

"Well, he didn't get nothin' is what Donnell told me, because the girl wouldn't open the safe."

"Wouldn't or couldn't?" Trainum asked. She thought for a second. "I remember him sayin' she 'wouldn't' like, you know, she was trying to keep him from gettin' it."

"All right, what else did Donnell say Malcolm told him?" Wallace asked.

"That he shot the black kid next because he was trying to help her."

"Help her do what?" Ruffin asked. Angela shrugged her shoulders and threw up her hands.

"I don't know, maybe help her, you know, fight Carl off or somethin', I really don't know. He didn't explain it and I didn't ask."

"Then what happened?" Wallace asked.

"Then he shot the black guy."

"For any particular reason?"

"I don't know. What I just told you is all that Donnell told me."

"Do you know Carl Cooper?" Trainum asked. "Nope," she said. "Just know of him from what Donnell and now Malcolm say about him."

"Do you and Donnell live together?" Wallace asked.

"No."

"Can you tell us where he lives?" Her eyes grew wet.

"Listen, I'm really sorry I gave you his name. I don't want to get him involved in this, okay? I told you what Malcolm told him and that's all he told me about Carl Cooper and Starbucks *ever*, okay? We got a thing goin' on that I don't want to fuck up, all right? He had nothin' to do with those people getting' killed and I don't need him thinkin' I gave up his name for anything that's got anything to do with that thing or Cooper at all. You all can give me that, can't you?"

"How well do you know Malcolm?" Wallace asked.

"Some, but this ain't what we usually talk about."

"What do you talk about?" She took her time before answering, then shrugged. "This and that, you know, but not nobody gettin' killed."

Ruffin looked to Wallace, got a quick nod, and slid the papers from the back of his pad. He handed them to Angela. "What's this?" she said.

"Malcolm's rap sheet," Wallace said. "You don't have to read it all, but you ought to know it shows a lot of 'this and that', including three warrants out on him for FTAs –"

"FT what now?"

"Failure to appear. In court. We could pick him up on those right now, but I think Donnell'd probably appreciate it if you kept his nephew out of jail, just like you want to keep Donnell out of all this."

It didn't take long for Angela to figure out what he was really saying. Her eyes flashed and narrowed. "So what now? You blackmailin' me? That's how you do me for tryin' to help you all? That ain't right!"

"All we want you to do is get Malcolm to tell you what he knows about what might have happened at Starbucks," Wallace said. "Period."

"So what are you going to do? Make me wear a wire? Snitch him out and get myself killed too? Is that the deal?"

"Doesn't have to be on you," Wallace said. "We could put a tap on your phone. You talk to him right there from your chair, he won't know a thing. You got nothing to worry about."

She lowered her head and crossed her arms tight across her chest, rocking from side to side. "I don't know, Lord, I just don't know," she muttered.

"And," Trainum said, "he wouldn't have any claim on that reward money. He wouldn't even know he had anything to do with it."

She kept rocking and squeezed her eyes tight. "Well now, just let me pray on it a bit."

12

A few minutes before ten the next night, Wallace called Angela and put the phone on speaker. On the fourth ring, he threw Trainum a glance across his desk. Trainum slumped back in his chair, looked somewhere over Wallace's head, and muttered "Why am I not surprised?" He sat back upright when he heard "Hello?" on the other end.

"Hi, Angela. This is Detective Wallace. You ready to go?" They both heard her sigh deeply before she spoke. "I guess, and I don't have to do nothin' with this thing under the table, right? It'll just do what it do, right?"

After their meeting yesterday, Wallace had the Electronic Surveillance unit send a team over to install the tap on her phone. The tap worked and so did the tape recorder in Wallace's office, so nothing was going to go wrong technologically. D.C. was a one-person consent jurisdiction, so Mueller's shop told him he was okay legally. The only issue left was whether Angela was going to run the whole thing off the rails.

"All the equipment is working just fine," he said. "You just need to do your thing, okay? Keep it light. You just have a normal conversation and get around to the Starbucks stuff in your own way, it'll all work out."

"Angela," Trainum said, "do you have any ideas about how you're going to get to it? You want to bounce anything off us?" Another sigh, then "No, I'm good. I know how he rolls. I hope I give you what you want is all."

Trainum looked at Wallace, rubbed his fingers against his thumb, and mouthed "Money, honey."

Wallace said "You're going to do fine, okay? So we're going to let you go now. Soon as you pick up the phone, we'll be on, listening to everything. Don't worry, you're just chatting with a friend, that's all, all right?" They heard her hang up without another word and looked at each other. "Worst comes to worst," Wallace said, "she gets nothing and we move on, that's all."

"Move on?" Trainum asked. "Move on where?"

Wallace didn't have to answer when the recorder clicked on and the reels started turning slowly. The phone rang just once before someone picked up.

"Yo," a male voice said.

"Yo. That you, Malcolm?"

"Who's this?"

"It's Angela."

"Hey, girl. How you? If you lookin' for Donnell, he ain't here."

"Naw, I'm lookin' for you."

"Oh yeah? What for?"

"You ever deal with any of them Jamaican boys sellin' stuff?"

Trainum threw a puzzled look Wallace's way. "You know what she's talking about?" Wallace turned his palms to the ceiling. "No clue."

"No," Malcolm said. "Why?"

"I'm lookin' for someone to go hard against them," Angela said. Malcolm laughed.

"What you talkin' about, go hard? What'd they do?"

"They sold me and some other folks some bad shit nearly killed me! It wasn't no stuff, man, it was poison! So a few of us are thinkin' they need to pay for that, you know what I'm saying?"

"I know what you're sayin', I just can't believe you're saying it. You high now or what?"

"No, damn it, Malcolm, I'm lookin' for someone who'll do these fuckers and clean 'em out."

Wallace watched Trainum's eyes bug out and put his hands over his face. Malcolm couldn't keep from chuckling.

"So what? You think I'm going to go down wherever they are and go all gangsta on them? Are you for real?"

"No, I don't want you to do it. You told me one time you knew somebody who would, someone you trusted would do the job right." Malcolm stayed quiet. "You know, you told me this person done a couple of robberies? Got some bodies?" Wallace pulled his hands down and leaned closer to the recorder. Trainum sat dead still.

After an eternity, they heard Malcolm say "You talkin' about Carl?"

"Yeah, that's his name," Angela said. "Didn't he pull off somethin' big a while back?"

"Yeah," Malcolm said, "he did the Starbucks thing."

"That's right! But hey, didn't you tell me he didn't get no money out of that thing? I want somebody who's going to make those fuckers pay."

"The only reason he didn't get the money was 'cause the lady wouldn't give up the safe."

"Is that what he told you?"

Malcolm didn't answer for a while, then said "Hey, you know what, this is gettin' a little too weird for me."

"Why? You the one that told me his name. I don't have anyone else to call about this sorta thing, you know? I thought you'd be cool."

"Oh, I'm cool. You just movin' a little too fast for me, okay? You tell Donnell you was going to call me?"

"No, baby, and don't you tell him neither. He don't need to be in this, so don't you drag him into it. This is just between me and you, okay?" Malcolm was quiet again, but Angela didn't wait for him to talk. "All right then, I gotta go. You just let me know, okay? Bye." When she hung up, the line went dead.

Trainum looked at Wallace but held his tongue until Wallace finally looked back at him, his face somewhere between resigned and beaten. "You know, that 'lady wouldn't give up the safe' part was just the way that 234 put it last year," he said.

"So, what? You think Malcolm's 234?"

"I don't know. Maybe the guy that told Malcolm is 234."

Wallace sat back and crossed his arms. "Or maybe the guy who told the guy who told Malcolm that is 234." He shook his head. "If you think we're one inch closer to the end zone after that call, man, you tell me what I'm missin'."

Now Trainum shook his head. "You're not missing anything. But maybe we should follow up with him face to face just to see what he really knows and how he knows it. Maybe we can squeeze him a little with the FTAs?"

"No, man," Wallace said. "He already thinks Angela's trying to get some shit on Cooper. If we come down from out of nowhere to screw with him on missin' his court dates, that's only gonna make him think something's up even more."

"Maybe that'll make him cooperate."

"And maybe it'll make him tell Cooper the cops are onto him and let him cover his tracks even more than he has already. Man, we don't need more people telling us they think Carl Cooper maybe mighta had something to do with Starbucks, we need someone or something who can *prove* he did."

"So we just let him be?"

"Unless you've got a better idea."

Trainum shook his head slowly, resigned to their fate again. "So what do we tell Angela?" he asked.

"Nothing," Wallace said, "but if she calls? You tell her that's exactly that's how much reward money she's getting too. One of them's going to have to do better."

They stared vacantly into their own private worlds. Wallace watched an evil magician flick a deck of playing cards into the void, one by one, and glimpsed their faces as they zipped by. Chad. Walter Burrell. Yasmin. 234. Carl Cooper. Albertha. Robbie. Leon Ellis. Eric Butera. Cissy Joiner. Angela. And then there were none.

Now he had his answer to Trainum's question. Now where? Nowhere.

13

No one in MPD had forgotten about the Starbucks murders since the day they happened, but if anyone in the public had, the press did a great job of reminding them on their first anniversary. The *Post* and the *Washington Times* reported on the candlelight vigil held at the site. "It's still very much on all of our minds," the store manager told the *Times*. "We will never forget."

The *Post* cited police sources saying privately that two or three people were involved, two guns were used, and the motive was robbery. The article noted that officials were saying little publicly, pointedly noting that was in stark contrast to the days after the shootings when information about evidence and suspects "flowed from detectives." They also quoted Caity's mother as saying the more time passes, the more doubtful she is that the killers would ever be caught. "We gave the police six months and didn't hear a word from them. We're not sure they even have anyone in mind." A Deputy Chief told the paper that two homicide detectives, two homicide supervisors, and an FBI agent were working on the case full time, and others were added as needed.

One of the supervisors tossed the paper down and waited for one of the detectives to finish reading his. When Trainum did, Wallace said "Finding the assholes who leak this shit would almost make me as happy as finding whoever did Starbucks. It never stops."

"And it never will," Trainum said, "even when we do catch him. That'll just let more assholes who don't know a goddamned thing run their mouths, just like with the fucking guns."

Wallace rolled his eyes. The memory of that fiasco was a few weeks old now, but it still glowed red-hot in his memory. Citing a "source familiar with the ballistics unit," the *Post* reported that MPD had a backlog of 2,500 bullets and shell casings, including ones that came from weapons of the same caliber as the ones used at Starbucks, which meant that a year after the murders, they still couldn't tell if any of them led back to the guns used in the killings.

"At least we don't have to worry about Barry leaking anything," Trainum said. The esteemed Mayor For Life had just stunned everyone in the city by announcing he would not run for a fifth term. He said it was because he could do more from the outside than the inside to fight the Republican-led Congress that had taken away huge chunks of D.C's home rule, but most of the city thought he'd finally just grown tired of the fight altogether. Whatever the reason, nobody was going to believe him anyhow until the filing deadline passed in late August.

Late one night in the middle of August, Trainum took a call passing on some information that was so out of the blue and so complicated, he had a hard time believing it was true even as he prayed it was. He took his time organizing his notes and anticipating every question he imagined Wallace could fire at him before he knocked on his door early the next morning.

"Yo, Commander, you got a few minutes?" Wallace waved him in. "What's up?"

"I got a call yesterday from a detective in Prince Georges. About Carl Cooper." Wallace pointed him to the chair in front of the desk. "Why?" he asked.

"Said he was a suspect in shooting one of their cops, back in '96."

Wallace took that in for a few seconds. "They didn't know that till now?"

"They did – well, the detective working the case did, but he left sometime in '97, and it just kind of fell through the cracks, the guy said." Wallace resisted pulling his hands down his face.

"Kind of a big crack, isn't it, shooting a cop? How'd it happen?"

"I don't have the whole story, just that the guy got shot in the back while he was off-duty and wound up going back to work."

"And why didn't they let us know till now? They didn't look Cooper up in the regional database, see we maybe had a little interest in him?"

"I asked the same thing and I'm just going to tell you what they told me, so don't shoot the messenger. The guy said they only checked it after they got a fresh tip on Cooper and the cop. When he saw Cooper's name as a possible perp in Starbucks, he decided to call us."

"And who gave them the tip?"

"He doesn't know. The guy wouldn't give his name and they couldn't trace the call. But it turns out this wasn't the first time they got a tip on him shooting the guy. They went back over the detective's files and saw that a woman named Joannie Lee Green gave him Cooper's name in late '96."

"And who's she?" Wallace asked as Angela Corrothers' face flashed through his mind. "Another God-fearin' woman looking to score a hundred grand?"

"Hard to know. She's in the pen. In Pennsylvania. Muncy, wherever that is."

"For what?"

"A lot of shit, most of it having to do with coke and robberies – and Teddy Thigpen. Name ring a bell?"

It did. "He's 'Man,' right? The guy who Robbie said killed Vontae Kincaid?"

"Yep."

"And what did this Joannie have to do with him?"

"Again, I don't have it all, but it seems a mutual taste for crack was the main attraction."

Now Wallace did pull his hands down his face, slowly, then laid them on the desk. "All right," he said, "call him back and find out where she is, and we'll get a writ to bring her down here asap." When Trainum stayed in his seat, Wallace turned his palms up and waited for him to say why.

"There's one more thing," Trainum said.

"Of course there is. There always is in this thing. What's this one?"

"The guy didn't give me his name."

Wallace stared at him. "Let me get this straight. The guy with the tip didn't tell the cop his name, and the cop didn't tell you his own name."

"That is correct."

"Well, just for openers then, how do you know the cop's a cop?"

Trainum held up his hands. "Just hear me out. He told me he was calling me from his house because he didn't want his higher-ups to know we were talking."

Wallace clapped his hands and shook a fist in delight. "All right! How great is this!" he said before his smile turned sour. "Now, not only do we not know if he really is a cop, but if he is or even if he's not, he's leakin' shit too! Outstanding!"

Trainum waited to hear if there was more before he went on. "He said that after he got the tip and saw Cooper's name show up in the database on Starbucks, the brass told him 'fuck that, it's not our case, go pick him up for shooting the cop'. He said he finally got

104

them to hold off by telling them they'd all be better off if PG could take some credit for bringing in the Starbucks killer, but he's afraid that if we don't pick him up quick, they'll tell him to get him, so he called me."

Wallace spun his chair around to face the back wall. His eyes stared at an MPD organization chart that was at least two versions old, but his mind was focused on what Trainum had just laid on him. He took a long minute to weigh what they should or shouldn't do before he spun back.

"Okay, let's not risk blowing this guy's help down the road by calling him back and giving his higher-ups a trail to follow. I'll call Ramsey and let him know we're taking a road trip. You call the prison people up there and find out where Man's woman is, and get a car." On his way out the door, Trainum heard "And a map."

14

By the time they got to Harrisburg, the chit-chat had been over for an hour. By the time they pulled to a dead stop in the only traffic jam at 1:44 on a Tuesday afternoon in the history of Hummels Wharf, Pennsylvania, Wallace threw the map on the floor. Trainum saw no motion in either lane ahead, so he flicked the ignition off.

"So near and yet so far," he said. "Isn't that how it goes?"

Wallace rolled his window down and motioned to Trainum to do the same. When he did, they both felt a breeze too small to matter until it picked up when a semi roared past heading south. *That's where we ought to be*, they each thought but neither said. After another thirty seconds of staring out the windshield, Wallace reached into the well behind Trainum's seat and came back with his briefcase. He parked it on his lap and pulled out a thin black binder. Trainum knew what was in it: the file the State Correctional Institution at Muncy faxed him yesterday on Joannie Lee.

"I don't want to spoil it for you," he said, "but it doesn't have a happy ending."

Wallace flipped the pages until he came to a black and white Xeroxed photograph of an attractive but very unhappy female with a placard reading OW5335 hanging cockeyed around her neck. He snapped his head back in amazement.

"This is her?" he asked. "This is Joannie Lee Green?"

Trainum laughed. "I was so looking forward to you seeing her in the flesh."

"This chick is white!"

"And that's why you are a Detective Commander," Trainum said.

She could have been green the way Wallace focused on the picture. "Oh man, I did not see that comin'. How in the hell did she get together with Man?"

"Coke's the easy answer, but her trip was definitely longer and stranger than his. It seems she came from a very well-to-do family in Uniontown PA, some burg almost in West Virginia. Her daddy was a surgeon of something I can't even pronounce. Anyhow, she met Man somewhere up here and he took her down to D.C. and introduced her to his buddy Carl. Pretty soon, she became their getaway driver and – I gave up counting – but they must've stolen like fifty cars and pulled off twelve, fifteen robberies before her and Man decided to come back to Pennsylvania and do the same shit, only without Carl."

Trainum saw the line ahead of them starting to move and turned the car on. They rolled up the windows and he put the air on high.

"Did they have a falling out?" Wallace asked.

"I don't know, we'll have to ask her that, but just to bring you up to today, they were holding up gas stations and 7-11s all over the northeast part of the state, but when they decided to try their hand at a bank in Wilkes-Barre, they showed up crisp and clear on a whole lot of security cameras, which is what brings us to lovely –" he watched a road sign roll past – "Sunbury this fine afternoon."

In another minute, they passed a Northumberland County Sheriff talking to a driver of a red pickup with a front fender hanging onto the shoulder just behind a yellow Camaro with a crumpled trunk, and a minute after that they were doing 65 heading up PA 147 to Muncy. Half an hour later, they pulled gray plastic chairs out from under one side of a gray metal table in a gray cement conference room just behind security at SCI Muncy and started setting up shop. A white female guard brought in a black styrofoam cup of coffee for Wallace and a bottle of water for Trainum, then left to fetch Joannie Lee.

When the door opened ten minutes later, she came through, paused just a second to check them both out, and took a seat across the table.

The guard in the doorway looked at her watch. "She's supposed to be back in her cell in an hour, but if you need her a little longer, you can let me know when I come back and we'll work something out, all right?"

"Appreciate that," Wallace said and waited for her to close the door, then turned to Joannie Lee. Too thin, and taller than he expected, gaunt was the first word that came to mind. Pretty was the second. Her light brown hair was tied in a long tight braid that only people with a lot of time to kill would weave, and her pale skin made her ice blue eyes sparkle even more. Wallace figured she was around thirty-five, but if drugs had something to do with how brittle and bony she looked, maybe younger. He gave her the mandatory smile.

"Thank you for agreeing to see us, Ms. Green."

"You can call me Joannie," she said, leaning in and crossing her arms on the table. "This is about Man, I suppose?"

"Yeah, sort of, and also about a friend of his, Carl Cooper."

She sat back and stared at him warily. "What about Carl Cooper?"

"Do you remember talking to a policeman from Prince Georges County last year about a PG cop who got shot?" Trainum asked.

"I do, but I told him everything I knew."

"I'm sure," Wallace said, "but just in case he didn't ask about something we want to know, we just want to see if you can fill in a few holes for us."

Joannie thought that over a few seconds. then leaned back in. "And if I can, will you tell the D.A. and the judge up here that I helped you

108

out? Because I am looking at another four years, ten months, and twelve days in this place even with good behavior, man, so if there's anything I can do to knock that down even a little bit, believe me: I will."

"All you have to do is tell us the truth. You do that, we'll tell anyone you want."

"All right then. Tell me what you want to know."

"Let's start with what you know about him shooting the cop," Trainum said. Joannie put her hands up.

"First of all, all I know is what Carl told me and Man. I didn't have nothin' to do with that."

"Then just tell us what he told you."

"He called me late one night —"

"When was this?"

"Had to be '96 sometime, probably the summer, 'cause Man and me were up here by September or October. So he tells me he just tried to rob someone but it went real wrong, and when I ask him what do you mean, he says he was walking through a park looking to find a car parked somewhere, which meant whoever was in it were probably fucking, which meant he could grab the guy's wallet and get out of there before he could even pull his pants up. I know, man, but this is how he thinks. So anyhow, he comes on to a car, and he pulls his gun out and throws open the door, and they freak out, but he gets twenty bucks out of the lady and then the guy starts fighting with him, so Carl shoots him. The girl screams 'Bruce!' and Carl, he tells me he says 'Goodbye, Bruce' — I'm tellin' you, this is how he is — and he shoots him *again*, then takes off, with her twenty bucks."

She shook her head and waited for Trainum to stop writing. "Then the next day, he and Man are over my house watchin' TV and the news comes on and the guy says this PG cop named *Bruce* somethin' got shot off duty in a *park*. Me and Man both look at Carl, 'cause he must've told him the story too, and Carl doesn't move, keeps watchin' the TV, and he says 'He better die,' flat just like that. That's Carl Cooper, man, that's all you need to know about him. He is one cold-blooded motherfucker. And they never did nail him for that, right?"

"Nope," Trainum said. "Apparently never even talked to him."

"Yeah, and that reminds me, a week or so later, I saw one of those drawings on TV that the cops make when a witness tells them what a guy looked like? Didn't look a thing like Carl. That cat has nine lives or somethin', I'll tell you that. But it wasn't just luck or karma or whatever, he was good at what he did."

"Like how?" Wallace asked.

"Like he was what you would call a master criminal. Very resourceful, smart, charming when he needed to be, but always willing to go hard, just like with that cop. And you know about the security guard he did in D.C., right?"

No I don't, Wallace thought. "Tell us what you know about it," he said.

She shook her head. "All I know's what Leon Ellis told me. You know who he is?"

Trainum's pen hand froze. He locked eyes with Wallace, then turned back to her. "The barber, right?"

"Right," she said. "He told me that one night they were driving around D.C. and Cooper told him he could use another gun –"

110

"Did he tell you when this was?"

"I don't know, he told me a while back, so maybe like four or five years ago?" She waited for another question that didn't come before going on. "So they go do this job, like at a pizza place somewhere downtown, and they're heading back to Carl's place and this is like an hour or so after Carl mentioned needing the gun and he tells Leon to pull over to the curb quick and then bolts out of the car. Leon watches him go to this apartment building and sees there's a security guy, you know, one of those rent-a-cops, just standing outside the door and Carl pulls out his gun and shoots the dude right in his chest, blood spurting out everywhere, and the guy goes down and Carl bends down and pulls his gun out of his holster and runs back to the car and tells Leon to hit it, which he didn't have to tell him, and he floors it out of there. He killed the guy in cold blood for his gun! Just like that! Unbelievable, right? Except it's true, it's always true with him. Leon told me he just carried on like nothing happened, flickin' the radio dial, lightin' up a cigarette, chit-chatting, but that's who he is, man, for real."

Wallace waited for Trainum to look back up from his pad before he looked back to Joannie Lee.

"Did you ever drive him and Carl anywhere?"

"A lot of places, but I never saw anything like that. Jesus, if I did, that would've been the last time, I guarantee you. Still gives me the shivers today," she said, then gave them one to prove the point.

"Tell me more about him being a 'master criminal'. How'd that play out? Did he always use some foolproof M.O.?"

"Not always the same, kinda depended on the situation, but he was very cautious, very deliberate every time he planned a robbery, and if something he didn't plan on happened, he was always, like I said, resourceful. He always came up with some way to deal with shit."

111

"Give me an example."

She didn't have to think about it. "The one I'll always remember was the time I was driving him and Man back from this pizza place we did somewhere in Silver Spring and the fucking car just broke down on me – like *quit* – right at a light. I'm freaking out, cranking the key, bangin' on the dashboard, but he jumps out and goes down a line of cars at this strip mall till he finds one he can jimmy open, then he hotwires it and steals it on the spot. Like I said, resourceful."

Trainum held up his hand until he finished writing, then said "Tell us more about the cautious and deliberate part."

"Like, whenever we were going out on a job, he handed out latex gloves so no one left a print. And he always carried two guns, just in case."

Trainum's hand lurched to a stop again. Wallace held up one of his. "Hold it right there a minute," he said. "Any particular kinds of guns?"

Joannie shrugged. "I have no idea. I'd be lying to you if I told you anything about them."

Wallace rubbed his cheek before he went on. "You've told us plenty about him being a cold motherfucker. Was he that way to you and Man? Is that why you two came back up to Pennsylvania?"

Joannie shook her head no. "Not really," she said. "I had a husband back here who was bugging me to come back, telling me how much he loved me, missed me, blah, blah, blah. He knew what I was into and he was into his own shit so I shoulda had my doubts, but, for whatever reason – I wasn't thinking too straight at the time – I thought I'd try and see if I could make it all work." She paused and lifted her head long enough for Wallace to see the pain well up in her

112

eyes one more time. "But I couldn't, and then I got busted and then he passed after I got in here, man, so that's where things are. That's all I know."

"Let me just circle back to the guns a minute," Trainum said. "We've looked through a bunch of records looking for Carl buying one, but we didn't find any. We did find one, though, for a Selene Lee Joiner, who I believe is his wife, right?"

"That's right. Cissy."

"It was for a 9-millimeter handgun. I know you said you didn't know, but does that ring any –"

"Dude, it could be 900 millimeters and I wouldn't be able to tell you a thing about it. Sorry."

Trainum flipped the pad shut and looked at Wallace. Wallace looked back at Joannie.

"I think we're through here then, at least for now. If there's some reason we need you down the road, like to appear at a grand jury or a trial, I'll be back in touch."

"Okay, but you're gonna talk to my lawyer now, right, let him know I'm cooperating with you so he can tell whoever else needs to know, right?"

Wallace got up, dug his card out of his wallet, and slid it across the table to her. "Tell him to call me any time. I'd be happy to help any way I can."

They shook her hand and left. When they got back on 147, Trainum said "So? What are you thinking?"

"I'm still thinking about that security guard, to tell you the truth. We got to get on that when we get back, but the next thing I'm thinking is we need something to tie our friend Carl to the shells from those guns, and the third thing I'm thinking is we're not going to get it unless it somehow comes from him or Cissy."

"So what does that mean? A search warrant? Do we have enough for that? And even if we do, what are the chances he didn't throw them in the Potomac a long time ago?"

"I know," Wallace said. "And we're going to have to show probable cause for a tap too, so I'm not real sure what we got from her was worth the trip." He looked out the window and took in the flat countryside. "Two hundred miles from home and still in the same damn place."

Trainum stayed focused on the road, then reached for the car phone on the console. He punched in the numbers and put it on speaker before laying it back in its cradle. Wallace cocked his head. "God got a hot line?"

"I told Garrett I'd let him know what Joannie told us. Maybe he's got some ideas."

In a few clicks, they heard "Jim? What's up?"

Trainum brought him up to speed and they waited for Garrett to tell them what he thought. "Well, that's some good shit on the cop," he finally said, "but I'm not too sure it helps us much on Starbucks."

"Hey, Brad, this is Tom. That's pretty much where we come down on it too, sorry to say."

Garrett was quiet for a while before he spoke again. "I'm just thinking out loud here, okay, but tell me more about what she said about the robberies."

"They were all in Maryland, all over," Trainum said. "Carl and Man and sometimes the barber did the dirty work, she drove the car."

114

"And did she say how many they did?"

"She didn't, but her prison file listed a whole bunch of them, more than a dozen, and maybe fifty stolen cars. I stopped counting."

"Well, that's interesting," Garrett said. Trainum and Wallace threw each other the same look of confusion. "Why's that?" Wallace asked.

"Ever hear of the Racketeering Influenced and Corrupt Organizations Act, a.k.a. RICO?" Garrett answered.

"Yeah, sure," Wallace said. "We've used it in big drug cases. Rayful Edmond's doing a lot of time on RICO charges."

"Well, I think what you've got here qualifies for a RICO prosecution."

"Not to be a buzzkill," Trainum said, "but where's the corrupt organization here? This is three or four people riding around in a car."

"That's good enough for RICO," Garrett said. "All it requires – I know it by heart – is quote 'any group of individuals associated in fact although not a legal entity' unquote. It was always the three of them plus Leon sometimes?"

"Yeah."

"And over how long a time did they do all this shit?"

"Years," Trainum said.

"Okay, Garrett said, "then what you've got definitely squares up with the statute's definition of a pattern of criminal activities too, so, my friends, I think RICO may be your golden ticket to tap your boy's phone."

"But you said a judge still needs to approve it, right?" Wallace asked.

"He does, and, in this kind of case, you're going to have to get the FBI Director *and* the AG to sign off on it, so I can't just click my fingers and get a tap on our buddy's phone overnight, but I can at least get started on it today, if you want me to. So that's my final question: Do you want me to?"

Wallace looked out the windshield at the sun lowering in the west. He checked his watch. 4:33 p.m. He pinched the back of his hand and felt the pain, then looked over to see Trainum wondering what he was waiting for. *This* is *the real world*, he assured himself. *It's not a dream.*

"Hell, yes," he said.

15

By Friday, Ramsey and Mueller okayed the request to apply for a tap on Cooper's phone, a Lojack on his car, clones of his pager and Cissy's, and a camera pointed at his front door. The next Monday, FBI Director Freeh signed off, and on Tuesday, the head of the Justice Department's Organized Crime and Racketeering Section authorized asking the Federal District Court in D.C. to approve it. On Wednesday, Assistant United States Attorney Ken Wainstein called Garrett to let him know the court had okayed it, and a little after 11 on Thursday, Garrett let Wallace know everything was in place. At 1 that afternoon, Wallace and Trainum walked into the FBI field office data center and saw Garrett jump out of his chair beaming a smile that Wallace had never seen before. They shook hands all around.

"Brad," Wallace said, "we can't thank you enough."

"Don't thank me," he said. "Thank Congress. They made the rules. We just follow them." He took his seat, spun to face a computer screen, and motioned them over. They pulled up chairs just behind him and peered over his shoulders at a greenish picture of the front of a two-story brick house attached to another one to the left. A square window on the wall to the right of the door sat below a bigger rectangular one on the second floor. At the right of the screen, corrugated overhangs projected from the side of the house.

"That is Mr. Cooper's place of abode," Garrett said.

"Where's the camera?" Trainum asked.

"We got lucky there," Garrett said, "unbelievably lucky. The house is across from a huge park, which is really just a field of grass with nowhere to hook up anything – except one telephone pole right across the street from what you're looking at. Boys put the camera up there yesterday when the tap and the Lojack told us he and Cissy were gone. If grandma or the kid saw anything, we figured they wouldn't have a clue we were doing anything but fixing something, so that's where we are, and it's a good place to be."

"Hear anything interesting yet?" Wallace asked. Garrett shook his head. "Just chitter chat mostly, and most of that was grandma. Let's give it a few days. If we don't hear anything interesting over the weekend, we can start tickling the wire a little."

"Tickling the wire?" Trainum asked.

"Maybe do a few things to get some conversation going about what we're interested in."

"Like?"

"Like maybe visit a few folks who might pick up the phone and let Carl know we were there, see how he reacts, who he calls, where he goes afterwards."

Wallace thought back to how meticulous and prepared Joannie Lee said Carl was. "The lady we visited up in Pennsylvania said he was one cool cat. May be tough to spook."

"Maybe," Garrett said, "but now that he knows someone's suddenly paying attention to him for *something* – maybe the PG cop, maybe Starbucks, maybe something else we don't know – he may take us someplace we haven't been yet, at least till he figures out we're listening. Make sense?"

"My question is how long do we have all this stuff for?" Trainum asked. "Can the court shut us down if we're not getting anything?" Garrett riffled through a folder lying next to the computer until he found what he was looking for. Wallace watched his eyes quickly dart through a few pages before his eyebrows raised.

"Annnd he bought it," he said. "The order says we, quote, established probable cause to believe that additional communications of the same type will occur thereafter, unquote, which means there's no time limit and we can keep everything going as long as we need to." He offered the page to Wallace and Trainum, but when they shook him off, he dropped the papers on the desk and smiled again.

"God, I love that law," he said. "Give me a call Monday morning if you don't hear from me first, and we'll see what we can do about tickling his fanny."

When the weekend came and went without hearing from him, Wallace called him and put it on speaker when Trainum took a seat at the other side of the desk a little after 9 on Monday morning. "So, nothing?" he asked when Garrett picked up.

"No. The most exciting thing was him giving a pizza place hell on Saturday night because they screwed up his delivery."

"Noted. So what's the plan?" Wallace asked.

"You tell me," Garrett said.

"Maybe we get Robbie to chat him up, get him to confide in her."

"I thought of that too," Trainum said, "but they've been chatting for years and he hasn't fessed up, so I'm not sure we can make him do it now. But, I think I might have another way to go. When I was looking through my files to see if I had anything worth tickling him with, I came across the gun record where Cissy bought a nine millimeter back in '96."

"But that didn't connect with the shell calibers from Starbucks, right?" Garrett said.

"No, but bear with me a second. When I looked at the record, the address she put down for herself wasn't Gallatin Street, it was 4114

Delaware Street, in College Park. And when I looked up who lived there, it was one Cornelia Joiner, who turns out to be the mother of Selene, aka Cissy, Joiner. Maybe we could run over there, ask her if we could talk to Cissy, see where that takes us. If not to Starbucks, maybe to the PG cop shooting."

"Sounds good to me," Garrett said. "Tom, what do you think?"

"I think I'll grab us a car and head on over. We'll let you know how it goes."

A little less than an hour later, Trainum pulled to the curb just in front of a small white clapboard house with a dirt yard. They walked past an aging green VW Rabbit in the driveway and knocked on the door. When a curious gray-haired woman's face appeared in the small window across from him, Wallace greeted her with his MPD ID held high. Her eyes crossed to Trainum who only had time to smile before the door creaked open just a little.

"Yes?" she said to Wallace.

"Hello, ma'am. Are you by any chance Cornelia Joiner?" "Maybe," she said, keeping the door right where it was. "Who're you?"

"I'm Detective Tom Wallace with the Metropolitan Police Department in Washington and this is Detective Jim Trainum, but please don't worry, you haven't done anything wrong. We're just trying to see if you might be able to help us out with some information on a couple of cases we're working on."

"What kind of cases?"

"Ma'am, with all due respect, it'd be a lot easier and quicker for all of us if you could let us in for just a couple of minutes. Again, this has absolutely nothing to do with you, I promise."

Her gaze held steady and so did the door until she pulled it back far enough to let them in. She closed and locked it behind them, then led them over to take their seats around a card table in front of a naugahyde sofa facing a TV with rabbit ears on a black metal stand against the wall. She was a thin woman, probably in her fifties, with a scraggle of gray and black hair framing her face, and glasses hanging around her neck.

"So what're these cases?" she asked. "Somethin' in D.C., I take it?"

"One of them is, ma'am. But the first one we want to talk to you about it is a police officer who got shot in a park not too far from here a few years ago."

"I don't remember nothin' about that. What's the other one?"

"We'll get to that in a minute, Mrs. Joiner, and it doesn't matter if you don't remember this one." He nodded to Trainum, who reached into his shirt pocket, unfolded a piece of paper, and handed it to her. She lifted her glasses to her eyes with a shaky hand and started reading.

"That's the receipt we got from a gun shop where your daughter Selene bought a handgun a little before that officer got shot," Trainum said, then told the story they'd concocted on the way over. "We think we have the gun that fired the shot, but it seems that whoever did it tried to erase the serial numbers off it beforehand so that it couldn't be traced back to him. What we're doing now is going to all the people who bought guns with the numbers we can read, to see if we can figure out who might be connected to it, just by process of elimination."

She yanked her glasses down so she could give him her full glare unfiltered. "My daughter wouldn't've had nothin' to do with something like that!"

121

"I'm sure you are absolutely right, Mrs. Joiner," Wallace said, "and we hate to even bother you with this. We were actually hoping that she might be here – "

"She don't live here no more. I don't even see her hardly at all. We had a falling out."

"Over what?"

"Her taste in men, let's just leave it at that."

"Are you talking about Carl Cooper?" Wallace asked and watched her face flush in an instant.

"That's exactly who I'm talking about!" she said. "That man is bad business."

"How do you mean?" She tried to compose herself and they waited for her. After she blew out a deep inhale, she asked "So you said there's another case, in D.C. What's that one?"

Wallace looked at Trainum who held out his hand to give him the honor, then back at her. "Do you remember the Starbucks murders last –?"

"What!" she exploded. "Starbucks? Now why on earth would you think I know anything about that?"

"Again, Mrs. Joiner, we're not accusing –" Wallace got out before she slapped one hand to her chest and pushed back from the table with the other. "Oh my Lord, I need air!"

Trainum tried to salvage the situation. "Ma'am, again. We don't think you had anything to do with either of these shootings. We were just hoping that your daughter –". She lifted her trembling hands and waved them at him.

"Oh, no, we done here and you can kindly leave my house. Now."
She held the paper out for Trainum to take and he tucked it back in
his pocket. When he pulled his hand back out, a business card was
in it and he laid it on the card table.

"Mrs. Joiner, if anything does come to mind, that's my card. You
can call me any –"

"Ain't gonna be no calls," she said, walking quickly past him and
pulling open the door. "Now I'm askin' you to leave!" She turned
to Wallace. "Both of you!"

Wallace nodded and followed Trainum to the door. Trainum kept
walking, but Wallace turned back to her before he left.

"Mrs. Joiner, I am so sorry we troubled you about this today, but if
you do talk to your –". She glared back at him.

"I ain't going to talk to her now, or never. I don't even know where
she is, but all I can tell you is you're just barkin' up the wrong tree
with her – and me – okay?"

"Thank you, ma'am. Again, I'm so sorry we troubled you." He
pulled the door shut and headed down the walk to the car. When
they made a right at the next corner, Wallace pulled the clone of
Cooper's pager from his pocket and laid it on the console.

"And now," he said. "We wait."

Halfway back down the Baltimore-Washington Parkway, the pager
began to buzz and flash. By the time Wallace finished writing down
the number, it went dead again. He dialed Garrett up on the car
phone.

"Brad, you see that call?"

"I did. That was Cissy. She punched in 9-1-1 three times – that's pager lingo for emergency – then hung up. I take it you already saw momma."

"Yeah, we're on our way back. She said she barely knows anything about her these days."

"Yeah, well, Cissy's pager went off about ten minutes ago from a 301 area code call and she gave Carl the 911 about two minutes later, so it looks like she somehow managed to find her pretty damn fast. How soon can you get here?"

"Twenty minutes?"

"I'll let the security folks know you're coming. See you soon."

Half an hour later, they pulled up chairs next to Garrett in front of a cassette recorder.

"Okay," he said, "this is Cissy talking on the phone to a woman at Leon Ellis' house. Maybe his wife, his girlfriend, I don't know. They hung up a few minutes ago. I cued it up to where Cissy just told her two D.C. cops just left her mother's place. Listen."

He pushed the Play button and they heard a woman's voice say "About what? Something you did?" "That's Leon's lady," Garrett said.

"No" came over the tape. Garrett punched the Stop button. "That's Cissy," he said, "and it sounds like she started getting real careful because you-know-who might come in wherever she was." He pushed Play again.

"Something Carl did?"

"Maybe."

"Dealing drugs?"

124

"Uh uh."

"Stole something?

"No."

"Car theft?"

"No, uh-uh."

"Rob some store?"

"Yeah, sort of," Cissy said. There was a pause before the woman continued. "And somebody saw him?"

"Not really."

"Oh, somebody trying to say that it happened."

"Mm-hmm."

"The bank thing?"

"No."

"The park?"

"No. Hey, drink your milk before you get up." "I'm guessing that's to the kid," Garrett said quickly. "Now listen."

"Georgetown," Cornelia said.

"Georgetown? Oh, Starbucks!"

"Mm-hmm." After another pause, Cissy whispered "Listen, I know in my heart that Carl and them ain't had nothing to do with that, because they would have got the money, you know?" Her voice grew louder. "Okay, I'm comin! I got to go now. Be talkin' with you. Bye."

Garrett stopped the recorder and looked to Trainum. "You had a good idea," he said. "You had a real good idea."

16

Monday morning, Garrett called Wallace. "Just thought you'd want to know Cissy told Carl that you fellas visited her momma."

"How do you know?"

"We heard him tell a friend of his last night – and he also told him he had nothing to do with Starbucks. Said, and I quote 'They all be shooting around in the dark'."

"Good to know," Wallace said. "Keep me posted."

Ten minutes later, he heard a knock on his door frame and looked up to see Melvin Ruffin, a notepad in his hand and a shitfaced smile spread across his face. "Guess who I just got off the phone with?" he said. "Carl Cooper, and he was fucking berserk."

"What'd he say?"

"He was calling to talk to Trainum, but he was on another line, so I asked if I could help him, and the dude just went off, screaming about the two of you visiting his mother-in-law, invading her privacy, invading his privacy, just on and on. Did you talk to her about a gun?"

"Yeah, why?" Ruffin looked at his pad. "Said she didn't have it, but that he'd be more than happy to go get it and have you come by and see it."

Wallace tilted his head. "Did that sound like what I think it sounds like, 'cause I'm not too eager to find out the hard –". The phone rang and Wallace picked it up. Garrett was back on the other end.

"You may know this already," he said, "but our boy Carl just had a meltdown about you and Trainum talking to Cornelia."

"Melvin Ruffin was just filling me in. He took the call."

127

"Yeah, well, the call may not do justice to the whole performance." Wallace put the call on speaker. "What do you mean?"

"I mean the camera outside caught the whole thing and it was a show. He started out sitting on his stoop with no shirt on and screaming into the phone, then got up and stomped around kicking up dirt like he was Earl Weaver, you know, the guy who managed the Orioles? The guy was on fire! It was fucking hysterical."

"I'm not laughing, man," Wallace said. "You heard what he said about us coming over there to look at the gun, right? What'd that sound like to you?"

"I take your point." Garrett was quiet a few seconds, then said "Maybe Cissy can give you a better idea of how he meant it. She left about fifteen minutes before Carl put on his show, probably heading to the job at Best Buy." Wallace looked over to Trainum.

"You know, I've been thinking of getting one of them big screen TVs. This might be a good time to check 'em out."

An hour later, he flipped the price tag on a Sony 37-incher. "Jesus! Thirty-eight hundred bucks? On sale? I'll stick with my Sharp."

"Here comes our man," Trainum said and Wallace turned to see the security guard they met at the door wave to them. They followed him to an empty paneled office with a desk, a small round table circled by four aluminum chairs, and a large window half-covered by a venetian blind.

"Her boss went to get her," the guard said. "Need anything else?"

"Can you pull down the blind?" Wallace asked. The guard left when he was done, and Cissy was in the doorway a minute later. They made their introductions and asked her to join them at the table. No one spoke until Trainum closed the door.

128

"So, what do you want with me?" she asked. She was small, attractive, maybe in her early thirties, Wallace guessed. From the creases furrowing her forehead, he didn't have to guess she was worried about his answer.

"We visited your mother yesterday, trying to get some information on a gun you bought," he said. She looked back at him with what he could swear was genuine surprise if he didn't know better.

"And why would you all think she'd know anything about that?"

"We didn't. We were looking for you, at the address you put on the receipt, but she was the only one there and she said she didn't have any idea where you might be."

"She seriously told you that or you just bullshitting me?"

"That's what she told us," Wallace said. When she looked at Trainum, he raised his hand to God. She shook her head. "I don't know what to say," Cissy said, "'cept she probably thought whatever you wanted to talk to her about had somethin' to do with Carl and that probably freaked her out because she ain't exactly his biggest fan to begin with."

"And why is that?" Wallace said. Cissy shrugged. "You'll have to ask her."

"We did, but she didn't give us anything specific. You want to fill us in?" She lowered her head and shook it before she answered. "Well, you tell me first, *does* it have something to do with him?"

Trainum gave her his rap about the missing serial numbers on the gun that shot Officer Howard in PG, and asked if she still had it. She took her time answering.

"*I* don't have it, I can tell you that, and I have no idea if Carl has it or doesn't have it."

"Did you buy it for yourself or for him?" She squeezed her hands tight before she laid them on the table and asked Wallace "Do I need to get myself a lawyer? What's really goin' on here?"

"Of all the people who have the numbers we can make out on the gun, your husband is the only one who's a convicted felon, and used a gun to pull off the crime. We've got no reason to believe you had anything to do with anything we're looking at – other than your name on the gun papers."

"But just to lay it all out for you," Trainum said, "if we get the feeling you're not being straight with us, it's just going to make us dig a little deeper, into both of you."

Unless she was an Oscar-winning actress moonlighting at Best Buy, all the tears Wallace watched fill her eyes and spill down her cheeks were real. He waited for an answer until he knew none would be coming without a little more prodding.

"Cissy, are you afraid of him doing something to you if you talk to us?"

She shook her head and choked her words out between sobs. "It's not like that. It's just – I've tried everything to keep him on the straight and narrow, you know? I married him, I had his baby, I've stayed with him through everything, but, I just –". Her voice broke and she covered her face with her hands until she could talk again. "I just never know myself whether he's doing right or wrong. I just pray on it and hope, you know. That's all I can do."

"Do you know he called us this morning?" Wallace asked. Her eyes grew wide. "No, what did he say?"

"He said he'd be more than happy to go get the gun and have us come by and see it, but we don't know if that's a promise or a threat. What do you think?"

She rubbed the back of her hand across her eyes and tried to get herself together before she answered. "I can tell you this. If he told you to come to the house to see it, he doesn't mean you any harm. He would never do anything to put me or our boy in any kind of danger. He's a good father and a good husband that way."

"Okay," Wallace said. "Then how do you suggest we go about it?" When she lifted wet eyes to him, he got up and picked a box of tissues off the desk and handed them to her. After she finished dabbing her eyes and wiping her nose, she said "The gun's at my grandfather's apartment, in Mount Rainier. I can go get it on my way home tonight and you can come by tomorrow night, sometime after dinner time. How's that?"

17

The next morning, Wallace and Trainum were discussing the protocol of bringing dessert to a sitdown with a triple murder suspect when Wallace's phone rang. Trainum heard him say "Yes sir, be right there," then watched him put down the phone and point to him. "Chief just got a call from Cooper." In his conference room a minute later, Ramsey threw a small ringed note pad on the table like it'd been burning his hands. "That is one pissed-off brother," he said.

"We've noticed that," Wallace said. "What got him going this time?"

Ramsey stretched to bring the pad back in front of him. "Well, first and foremost, he was extremely agitated with you, Detective Trainum, for bringing up his criminal past with Cissy. Said 'Your officer slandered me in the presence of my wife.' Exclamation point! I added that."

"It's not slander if it's true, right?" Trainum asked. Ramsey kept reading. "'I'll be happy to give them 'Bamas my gun tonight or whenever they want it, and they can do a ballistics test on it or whatever they want because I didn't kill nobody with it.' Exclamation point! Then he hung up with an exclamation point too."

Trainum looked at Wallace, jutted out his chin, and raised a clenched fist. "Congratulations on joining the 'Bama brotherhood, Commander. Good to know we're finally an equal opportunity employer."

"Him bringing a gun to this get-together was already giving me heartburn, Chief," Wallace said.

"I get that. What's your FBI friend say?"

"We haven't run it past him yet."

"Then let's do that," Ramsey said. When Garrett picked up, he put him on speaker and waited for Wallace to lay it all out before he asked "So what do you think, Agent Garrett? Can we trust him to behave?"

"There's all kinds of reasons not to," Garrett said. "His record, his batshit psycho personality, and, oh yeah, how he treats his wife."

"What's that mean?" Wallace asked.

"It means he smacked the shit out of her last night when he found out she talked to you guys. I was about to call you but you beat me to it."

"How do you know that?" Ramsey asked.

"We heard Cissy tell her mom about it, on the phone."

Trainum spoke first. "I got a bad feeling about this. It's like we're getting invited to our own funeral."

"What if we told him we want to meet here?" Ramsey asked. Wallace shook his head. "That'd probably give him the same feeling we got, like we're setting him up to arrest him without the wife and kid around."

"Then how about some kind of neutral site? Like Cissy's mom's place?"

Trainum shook his head first this time. "She's already thrown us out once. I'm not sure she's going to be a whole lot more hospitable next time around either."

"There is another player on the scene," Wallace said. "She said her grandfather has the gun at his place in Mount Rainier. Maybe we could meet there."

133

"No harm in asking," Garrett said. Wallace exchanged glances with Trainum and Ramsey. When Trainum nodded his okay, Ramsey said "Okay then. Agent Garrett, you free to join these folks tomorrow night if we can work this out?"

"I am."

"Either of you gentlemen know how to conference Mr. Cooper into this call?" Ramsey asked. Trainum jumped up and pushed a few buttons until they heard a dial tone. Ramsey looked at his pad, dialed a number, put the phone on speaker, and pushed it to the middle of the table. A man's voice said "Hello?"

"Mr. Cooper. This is Chief Ramsey again. How are you?"

"Same as I was a half hour ago. So your boys comin' or aren't they?"

"They're coming, along with an FBI agent who we'd like to see the gun too. Is that all right?"

"FBI?" Cooper said with sour hack of a laugh. "Who am I now, Al Capone? Jesus Christ, man!"

"And," Ramsey said, "we'd like to meet somewhere else than your house. You can understand I don't want my men to take any chances they don't have to –"

"Really, man? Really? You think I'm gonna start shootin' up my house with my wife and my boy in it? Who *do* you think I am, man, huh?"

"We don't want to put them in any kind of danger either, I assure you, Mr. Cooper. Your wife told us the gun was at her grandfather's house in Mt. Rainier. Is it still there?"

"Yeah."

134

"Then how about if our people meet the two of you there tomorrow night? Her grandfather doesn't have to be there, or your son either. What do you think?"

They heard muffled talk on the other end before Cooper came back on the phone. "All right," he said, "that'll work, after dinner."

"Seven-thirty okay?"

"Yeah, fine. We done now?" Ramsey took a quick look around the table. "We're done, Mr. Cooper. They'll see you there. Do you want the names of the people who –"

"Trainum going to be there?"

"Yes – "

"That's all I need to know." Cooper said and ended the call with another exclamation point.

"I can't say that gave me a warm and fuzzy feeling," Trainum said.

"That made me a little antsy too," Garrett said. "Tom, what do you think?"

"I'm thinking his gun shouldn't be the only one in the room."

"Agreed," Ramsey said, "but is there another way to go about this that'd minimize the risk he'd do something crazy?"

"He's always liable to do something crazy, no matter where he is," Trainum said. "He's ready to meet us there, so let's do it." Ramsey nodded.

"Okay then," he said. "We'll stake out the area with plainclothes in civilian cars, and I'll call PG to see if they want to tag along, seeing as how that's where we're going," he said, then leaned into the

135

phone. "Anything you all can do would be greatly appreciated too, Agent Garrett."

"I can get a couple agents there too – and I'll wear a wire so if anything does go sideways, they can get there in a hurry."

"Okay," Ramsey said, "and you'll coordinate with Commander Wallace about who's going to be where, so if the shit does hit the fan, no good guys get hurt, okay?"

"I will."

"Ten-four, and thanks." Ramsey hung up the phone and looked at Trainum. "You sure you're good with this?" he asked.

Trainum slapped his hands on the table. "What'd the guy in Ghostbusters say? I'm excited about this plan. Let's do it!" He looked at Wallace, who shrugged his acceptance, and tried but failed to stop Schein and Eric Butera's dead bodies from flitting across his brain.

18

At 7:28, Trainum guided the black jeep to the curb in front of a three-story red brick apartment building on the 3000 block of Arundel Road. From the passenger seat, Wallace asked "What's the apartment number?"

"Don't think you'll need it," Garrett said from the back seat. Wallace turned to see a short thin black man in a Redskins jacket emerge from the door and saunter his way down the walk like he was coming to collect a bet.

"Everyone check in? We all good out there?" Wallace asked before he opened the door. "We're good," Trainum and Garrett said at the same time. Wallace nodded, got out, and headed up the walk. When he got to where it branched off towards another building in the complex, he waited for Cooper and held out his hand to greet him. Cooper kept his hands in his jacket pockets.

"I want you to know I've expressed my disappointment to your boss about how unhappy I am that you went to my wife's workplace."

"You want to file a complaint about that, feel free," Wallace said. "Our business is with your wife, not you." When Trainum came to his shoulder, Wallace watched Cooper scan him up and down. "Of course, you brought your 'Bama boy with you," he said, then nodded at Garrett behind them. "Who's the suit?"

"That's FBI Agent Garrett." Garrett did not nod back.

Cooper shook his head and headed back up the walkway. They followed him through the door, up two sets of stairs reeking of stale air and sweat, then through another door and down the hall to a door numbered 303. Cooper pushed it open, called out "Your friends are here, Cissy!" and disappeared around a corner to the right. Wallace looked across the room to see two heads turn from Pat Sajak to him.

One was a thin black man maybe in his seventies, the other Wallace guessed was his great-grandson, maybe eight or nine.

"Good evening," he smiled. "Please don't mind us. We're just here to see Selene." The older man put his arm around the boy's shoulder and turned back to the screen. The boy strained to keep them in sight until Cissy appeared in the hallway. They made their introductions and she led them down the hall to a small mahogany dinner table that filled an alcove across from the kitchen. She gestured to Wallace to take a seat on the far side and Trainum followed him around the table. She took a seat across from them and waited for Garrett to take the one next to her, but he was looking down the hallway at Cooper coming towards him carrying a dark wooden box in both hands. He hooked his right thumb into his belt below the bulge the Glock 22 made under his sport coat.

Cooper held Garrett's gaze till he passed him and laid the box in the middle of the table, then caught eyes with Trainum. He leaned across the table and pointed a trembling finger at him, barely a foot from his face.

"*You* are not taking this gun! *You* are not *touching* this gun! I don't even know why I agreed to let you come into my house and even *look* at this gun. You have disrespected my wife and you have disrespected me!"

Trainum returned Cooper's stare before he turned to Cissy. "May I open it?" She nodded a nervous yes. He opened the lid and looked down at a black Astra A-100 9mm handgun.

Cooper banged his fist on the table. "You came here to check the serial number, right? So you go ahead and you do that and then you put that gun back in the box and you leave it right here and then you leave – all of you, okay, am I clear?"

Trainum reached into his jacket pocket, pulled out Cissy's Atlantic Guns receipt, and held it in front of Cooper's face at point-blank range. "Sir, that is not your weapon. You have no say about what happens to it."

"It is my wife's weapon, and we are telling you that you cannot take it." Trainum looked at Cissy's face, now stiff with fear, and pulled the gun box to him. "Ms. Joiner, I'm taking this weapon because it's going to be possible evidence in a murder case."

A man's voice from the hallway said "You need to call your lawyer, boy." They all turned to see Cissy's grandfather, his great-grandson's arms wrapped around his leg.

"I need to do somethin'," Cooper said and walked briskly past them.

"Oh Lord, oh Lord," Cissy moaned and motioned her son to come to her. He squeezed onto her lap and she wrapped him in her arms.

Wallace and Trainum looked at each other and read each other's mind: *He's coming back with another gun and it's not going to be in a box.* Garrett's back was to them waiting and watching for Cooper to appear out of the darkness at the end of the hall. Wallace saw his coat flap move and heard his holster unsnap. At the sound of a door slapping against a wall and a flash of light in the hallway, Wallace looked past him to see Cooper striding down the hall, his face blocked by a video camera.

"Shut that thing off," Garrett said. "Now!"

"This is our house!" Cooper said, pointing the camera at Garrett, then at the table. "And I am ordering you to leave. Now!"

"We are law enforcement officers, Mr. Cooper," Garrett said. "We have a right to be here and a right to inspect this gun, and to take it if we see fit. And I am telling you for the last time to turn that thing off."

Cissy's son started bawling and buried his head in her shoulder. Eyes full of tears, she cried out "Stop it, Carl! Stop it!" and held him tight. Wallace heard the front door open and turned to see a white man in a dark blue suit turn the corner holding a gleaming gold badge high. A black police officer appeared at his shoulder.

"FBI, sir," the man in the suit said. "Please turn the camera off." Cooper didn't. "Well, ain't that some shit?" he said. "Now we got two FBI men and *three* D.C. cops here telling me what to do at my own house in Maryland!"

The policeman stepped forward. "Sir, I'm with Prince Georges County, not D.C." Cooper lowered the camera, his eyes filled with amazement.

"Really, man? You gonna let these buzzards get away with this shit? Come into a Maryland residence without a warrant and take a gun from a taxpaying citizen of this county? How is that possibly legal?"

"Put down the camera, Mr. Cooper," Garrett said. Cooper gritted his teeth, raised the camera back to his eye, and took one long sweep from the PG cop past Garrett to the table where Cissy and his son clung to each other before he clicked it off and turned to the policeman.

"How can this be, my brother? How can these peckerwoods come into my house in Maryland and take this gun out of here? This is still America, isn't it?"

"Yes, sir, it is. But we're all working together on this shooting under an agreement that allows them to come in here and us to go into D.C. to get evidence, talk to people, whatever. Happens all the time."

Wallace didn't wait to hear anything more. He stood up, picked up the box, slapped the lid shut, and looked across the table to Cissy.

140

"We have no more business here, Ms. Joiner. Thank you for your cooperation."

Trainum got up and walked past Cooper followed by Wallace, hard looks all around. Garrett followed them down the hallway and held the door for the other agent and the PG cop, his hand still under his coat and his eyes trained on Cooper. He pulled the door shut behind him and met them all at the curb by the car. They exchanged handshakes all around. When Wallace was back in his seat, he took a look up to the third floor and watched a silhouette of a man holding a video camera in one hand make a gun with his other hand and point it at the car as it drove away.

19

Two days later, Wallace called Trainum to tell him to meet him back in Ramsey's conference room asap. By the time they got there, Ramsey and a middle-aged white man in a suit who Wallace didn't recognize were already at the table. Ramsey introduced him.

"Gentlemen, this is Richard Hepburn. He's with the firearms examination section and just got done looking at the gun you brought back here the other night. Mr. Hepburn, I'll let you fill them in."

Hepburn waited till they took their seats to begin. "Well, like I told the Chief, I have some good news and I have some bad news."

"Of course you do," Wallace said. "Let's get the bad news out of the way first."

Hepburn pulled his glasses out of a case on the table, flipped open the folder in front of him, and started reading. "A ballistics test on the Astra A-100 9-mm handgun delivered to this office at 2105 on 15 September 1998 was performed by –"

"Mr. Hepburn," Ramsey said, "you don't have to read it. Just cut to the chase." Hepburn took off his glasses and looked at Wallace.

"The bad news is that the grooves on the bullet we fired from the gun you brought us did not match the grooves on the bullet fired into Mr. Howard, the Prince George's police officer."

"And there's still good news?" Trainum asked.

"Yes," Hepburn said. "Oftentimes that's not dispositive, I mean, it doesn't always resolve the question of whether a gun is, in fact, the gun that actually fired the bullets, and that is because sometimes a gun user, especially a shrewd one, someone who has had a lot of experience with firearms, if you will, will take out the barrel and

142

replace it with another one in order to hide the fact that the gun did actually fire the bullet in question. If we would just look at the barrel and the bullet, we would say 'Oh no, this gun could not have fired that bullet'. That's why –"

"But you didn't just look at the barrel, correct?" Ramsey led the witness.

"No. Sometimes, like here, where we don't have a bullet to examine but we do recover shell casings, we also look at the marks that the gun's firing pin and ejector left on the casings." Ramsey's look was enough to speed him up this time. "And, in this case, the marks on the casings that were found at the scene did, in fact, completely match up with the marks on the test bullet we fired."

"No doubt about that?" Wallace asked.

"None. They were a perfect match. I would estimate the chances of a match like the one here to be, oh, I don't know –"

"Gentlemen, any more questions?" Ramsey asked. Not waiting to hear the answer, he got to his feet and threw Hepburn a salute. "Thank you so much, sir. We greatly appreciate your help." He waited for him to leave before he took his seat. "So, it seems we got enough to tie our friend Carl to shooting the P.G. cop. Should I tell them to pick him up?"

"Let's play that out," Wallace said. "If they grab him and throw him in jail, where does that leave us on Starbucks?"

"If he's in custody," Ramsey said, "we can talk to him any time we want, and hopefully get him to crack sooner or later."

"Yeah," Trainum said. "But then there's no way anyone else is going to talk to him, much less get him to talk about Starbucks."

143

"And what's he going to crack about?" Wallace said. "Admitting to Howard? Admitting to Vontae Kincaid? That's small change compared to Starbucks. I agree with Jim. We need to goose him more on that – tickle the wire on his phones, get him talking to someone wearing a wire, whatever. If he's locked up, we lose all that."

"Okay, and I'm just playing devil's advocate here," Ramsey said, "but what if after P.G. busts him, he gets out on bail? Then we can still do everything you just said, right?"

"But what are the chances a judge puts him on the street for shooting a cop," Wallace said, "especially an elected judge like they got out there? Chief, will all due respect, if he goes in, we risk losing everything."

"I just wanted to get it all out there," Ramsey said. "Which means there's one more thing you should know. The word on Cooper doing Starbucks is getting out to the press too, and they're starting to ask why we haven't picked him up."

"Are you serious?" Wallace asked before he caught himself. "Of course you are. This place is a fucking sieve, always has been."

"How did they land on Cooper?" Trainum asked.

"The guy who called me didn't say, just said a little bird told him that the guy who did Starbucks also killed a P.G. cop a few years back. When I asked him if the bird was a blue bird, he wouldn't tell me, but I have no doubts on that score either, Commander. Chicago PD was leaky too, a goddamn colander."

"So what'd you tell him?" Wallace asked.

"I told him 'You publish that, it's gonna tip him off and queer the whole investigation and you don't want that now, do you?' He said of course not, but he kept pressing me, so I offered him a deal he

144

couldn't refuse. I said 'If you hold off, I'll give you the exclusive if and when we arrest him. What do you say?' He said give me a little time to think on it which probably meant he called someone on the Chicago Tribune or the Sun-Times to see if this dude can be trusted, but he called me back in fifteen minutes and said deal, so if you see a guy you don't recognize with a camera and a microphone on that glorious day, that will be one" – he looked at his sheet of paper – "Dave Statter, WUSA TV and WTOP radio." He stood up and saluted them. "Keep up the pressure on our friend and let me know what you hear – and see."

When the door closed behind him, Wallace shook his head. "You know this shit is going to keep leaking and one day someone's going to put it out there without calling him first, and then we'll be totally screwed."

Trainum got up and held the door for him, then walked with him to the stairs. "Maybe, but if we can get him on Vontae and Howard, especially with what this guy told us about the gun, maybe not. I got to run, Tom. Keep the faith!" He bolted down the steps and Wallace walked to the elevator and pressed Down, then felt a tap on his shoulder and turned to see a young white man in a suit and tie smiling at him.

"Hi!" he said. "Detective Wallace?"

"Yeah, who are –?" The man slid a thick manila envelope from under his arm and pressed it to Wallace's chest. "You've been served," he said. "Have a good day!"

He was gone down the stairwell before Wallace looked down to see he was holding the envelope with both hands. He undid the clip on the back and pulled out a binder-clipped sheaf of papers. He read United State District Court at the top of the first sheet and got as far as "Notice Of A Lawsuit" just below it before he folded it back and tried to take in the words spilling across the next page. The only ones that registered before he dropped everything were Plaintiff Terry Butera, Defendant Thomas Wallace, and $15,000,000.

20

They kept the pressure on. Trainum enjoyed getting in Cooper's face so much, he drove down Gallatin Street daily and parked in front of his house often enough to bait him into showing it, and his middle finger almost every time. Garrett called him or Wallace at least once a day to report exactly how Cooper was bitching about them – but mostly Trainum – on calls with Leon and his other pals.

Garrett gave also gave Trainum the double secret code that let him see what the camera across the street from Cooper's house was seeing. He downloaded the photos of whoever he saw coming or going so that he and Wallace could try to track them down and chat them up. Even when they didn't get anything they could use, they still looked forward to hearing Garrett's word-by-word account of how Cooper went off when a guy called to let him know some cop was asking about him.

When Wallace saw a note on his desk after lunch one day saying he got a call from a Sgt. Joe McCann at the Prince Georges Police Department, his mind jumped back to Trainum's account of the anonymous PG cop who reported the anonymous call about Cooper shooting the off-duty cop out there. He wadded it up and started to flip it into the trash can before he remembered that Officer Anonymous also gave him Joannie Lee Green's name and that another unnamed PG cop helped save their asses at grandpa's house in Mount Rainier. He put his skepticism on hold, dialed him up, and heard "McCann" on the other end.

"Hey, this is Tom Wallace from MPD, returning your call."

"Great. I was told you were the right guy to talk to about Carl Cooper. Is that right?"

"It is. What's up?"

"A couple things. First, I just want to give you a heads up that Cooper told us you guys can expect a call from his lawyer."

"I didn't know he had one, but, okay, about what?"

"About surveilling him."

"And how do you know this?"

"Because he told us the same thing."

Wallace was lost. "You've got him under surveillance? For what?"

"The cop shooting out here a few years back, Bruce Howard?"

"But why now? One of your colleagues" – *maybe you?* he wondered – "told us that was pretty much a dead case."

"Yeah, it was," McCann said, "until we saw you were looking at him for Starbucks." Wallace took it all back about PG.

"Thanks for letting me know, Sergeant. Where are you surveilling him?"

"Just trailing him out here, not in D.C., don't worry about that."

"And where's he go?"

"He's got a few buddies he likes to visit pretty regularly, sometimes where they live or sometimes where they work, like this guy who works at a hair place out in Bladensburg."

"Leon Ellis, right?" Wallace knew that was where 234 and Robbie's brother said he worked. He never did get that haircut.

"Right. One of our undercovers met him at his car after work last night and said he wanted to talk to him about a few robberies that had the same M.O. as some of the ones he'd served time for. At least that's what he told him."

148

"And what'd he say?"

"That was all in his past, of course. He's been straight for years. All he wants to do now is cut hair, stay away from trouble, blah, blah, blah, but when our guy asked him if he knew Carl Cooper, it got a lot more interesting. We brought him in for more questioning so if you want a crack at him, you've got it, at least for another eight hours. If we don't charge him by then, we've got to let him go. I can fax the guy's notes over if you want to look at them."

"Absolutely," Wallace said and gave him the number. He clicked off the phone, then called Ruffin to ask him to run down anything Ellis might've been involved in in the District asap, and Trainum to tell him to stop by in about ten minutes. By the time he got there, a copy of the barber's statement was in front of his chair and Wallace was about halfway through his. When he filled Trainum in on the call, he dug right in and didn't come up for air until he was done.

"So?" Wallace asked. "What do you think?"

"I think he's got some interesting things to say about what Carl told him about Officer Howard."

"He does," Wallace agreed. "Too bad he doesn't have more to say about Starbucks." He flipped back and read it out loud. "Carl talked to him about helping him out with Starbucks 1-2 months before it happened but didn't hear any more about it till after he saw it on TV. Figured he did it on his own and something bad went down. Swears he had nothing to do with it." He lowered the pad.

"We need to talk to Ellis – *and* PG to make sure they don't decide to charge him for anything. He's gonna be worth a hell of a lot more to us out than in."

21

Less than an hour later, they pulled into the parking lot of the PG police station in Landover. A minute after Wallace introduced themselves at the front desk, two men, one in a uniform, one in a blue blazer, came through the door behind the desk and headed their way. The name tag on the uniform read McCann. He introduced them to Detective Richard Fulginiti.

"But call me Rich," he said with a smile. He was about six feet tall with a full head of gray hair belying his youthful face. McCann was about the same height with dark black hair and a little more heft. "Let's go on back and chat a little." They followed them back to a room with a long walnut-stained metal table and took the two plastic chairs opposite theirs.

"So did you have a chance to read what I sent?" McCann asked.

"We did," Wallace said. "He say anything since then?"

"No. We were holding off till you got here."

"Do you have enough to hold him?" McCann shook his head and Wallace resumed breathing. "No more than we had before we picked him up. If we took it to the State's Attorney, they'd tell us to let him go in a heartbeat. I've had plenty of better cases bounce back."

"But," Fulginiti said, "he doesn't know that. So if you guys let him know you've got some stuff on him and Cooper, that might motivate him to play ball." The look on Trainum's face told Wallace they were thinking the same thing.

"How soon can he be available?"

"He's just down the hall. I'll bring him back, then we'll set up camp next door," McCann said, pointing to a dark glass rectangle on the wall facing Wallace and Trainum. "We'll see and hear everything. When you're done with him, just pick up the phone on the wall and punch 1-1, and we'll come get him. I'll be right back."

"Good luck," Fulginiti said and left with him.

By the time they opened their folders, McCann was back with a stocky black man who looked just like the mug shot in their files except for a thinner mustache, a thicker beard, and a thin smile on his face. He nodded to them, then sat surprisingly lightly in a seat across from them and opened his arms wide.

"Gentlemen, what can I do for you?"

You must get a hell of a lot of tips, Wallace thought before he said "Mr. Ellis, we'd like to talk to you about Carl Cooper."

"If that means Starbucks, I already told these fellas all I know, which ain't much."

"We'll get to that, but first, tell me how you two got to know each other."

Ellis shrugged. "He came in for a haircut one day, we got to talking, hit it off, that's all."

"What'd you talk about?" Trainum asked.

"Nothin' much. The usual bullshit, you know, 'Skins, Wizards."

"That was it? No business you might help each other out with?"

"No, nothin' like that." Wallace nodded and shuffled through the papers in his folder, then stopped to read one long enough for Ellis to see his upside-down face scowling back at him in a small photo clipped to what looked like a rap sheet. "That was a long time ago," he said. "I ain't that guy anymore."

151

"Wasn't that long ago," Wallace said, flipping the page to show a list of raps filling the next sheet. "1992, 1993, another 1993, 19 –"

"Man, I did my time. Changed me, dude, for real. I ain't going back. I got a wife, two kids, steady job." He jabbed a finger at the folder, his air of cool all but evaporated now. "You all looked at me for all that shit then and didn't come after me, okay? There's nothing I done since that would give you any cause to start up with me now, I swear to God."

"Except stay in touch with Carl Cooper," Wallace said.

"About Starbucks," Trainum added. Ellis smacked the table with both hands.

"I told the guy I had nothing to do with that! Jesus Christ!"

Wallace took his time turning to another paper in the folder before he looked back at Ellis. "You're married to Chantay Ellis?"

"Yeah. What's that gotta do with anything?"

"She friendly with Selene Cooper, maybe you know her as Cissy?" Ellis pointed a thick finger at him.

"Man, you leave my wife outta all this. She got nothing to do with it!"

"She will if you go to prison, my man," Trainum said and got a glare back worthy of Cooper.

"Leon, we got two informants who say you did Starbucks with Carl," Wallace said, and laid his hand on the folder. "And when I read what you had to say about it to the PG fellas? Honestly, man, it just sounds like so much bullshit."

"It ain't bullshit, man! It's the fucking truth! He talked to me about robbing Starbucks one time, just one time! And I figured that was

152

just him, you know, blowin' smoke, makin' noise, whatever, and I totally forgot about it 'til they asked me about it, I swear. He never ever brought it up to me again or told me he was plannin' to do it, I'm telling you!"

"So you turn on the TV one day and you see someone killed three people there, and that didn't ring a bell, didn't make you think 'Wow, what a weird coincidence. Carl Cooper told me he was planning to rob the very same place. Maybe I ought to tell somebody'?"

"No, man, of course, I figured he *probably* done it, but I didn't *know* he did it. Maybe he told somebody else about it and they decided to beat him to it, I don't know. The one thing I do know is I had nothing to do with whoever did it! How many different ways can I tell you that before you believe me?"

"Leon," Trainum said, lifting his folder, "you been around the block enough to figure this out. Now that you know some of what we know, you think that if we take this to a judge, he's going to believe you over these very reliable informants, especially when we tell him your past and your admission that you and Cooper talked about Starbucks? C'm'on, man. Get real."

Leon was wide-eyed and tongue-tied. Before he could recover the power of speech, Wallace leaned toward him. "But you have the power to do somethin' about that, Leon. You help us nail Carl, all of your troubles go away."

Leon shook his head. "Naw, man, no. And how am I supposed to do that anyway? I already told you everything I know. I got nothin' more to tell you, I swear to God!"

"But that doesn't mean you can't get more," Wallace said. Leon sat up straight.

153

"And what's that mean? You want me to lie, make stuff up? That shit ain't right."

"You still talk to Carl, don't you?"

"A little, once in a while."

"Well, that's all we want you to do: Keep talkin' to him. We'll hook you up with a wire –"

"A wire!? No fucking way!"

"Leon, hear me out. You get him to talk about Starbucks however you want to do it. Over the phone, face to face, today, tomorrow, a month from now, it doesn't matter." He pointed to his folder. "If he gives you enough to help us put him away, your worries are over."

Leon drummed his fingers on the table, lost in thought. When Trainum cleared his throat, then did it again, louder, Wallace turned to see him tip his head towards the door.

"Okay," Wallace said to Leon and stood up. "You keep thinkin' on what I just told you. We'll be back in a little bit." Leon gave no sign he heard him, and they walked into the observation room. Fulginiti pointed to the glass and they all watched Leon sitting forward with his head on his hands, sobbing.

"It looks like you got his attention," he said. Wallace nodded at Trainum.

"So what're you thinking?"

"I'm thinking this might be a good time to mention Cooper whacking that security guard in D.C. with him having a front row seat in the car."

"Wow! What?" McCann said. Trainum gave him the short version of what Joannie Lee had told them at Muncy, then pointed to his

154

folder a foot from Leon's head. "I brought my notes, just in case we needed them."

"I think we need them," Wallace said. "Good job."

"You want us to just give him to you so you can sweat him back in DC?" Fulginiti asked.

"I might take you up on that," Wallace said, "but let's see what he does when we read it to him. I don't want to lock him up nearly as much as I want him on the street and talking to Carl. We got no corroborating evidence here, there, or anywhere on him. The way I look at it, we're going to have to get it from his own mouth, and Leon's the best way we got to make that happen."

"Sounds right to me," Fulginiti said. "You ready to go back?"

"Why don't you take his temperature first, see if he needs anything?"

"Will do," Fulginiti said and walked back down the hall. He was back in thirty seconds. "Said the only thing he wants is to go home."

"That's a good start," Wallace said to Trainum and they walked out into the hallway. Trainum turned to Wallace at the door to the conference room.

"Can I take the first shot?"

Wallace opened the door for him. "After you," he smiled, "if there's anything left."

They took their chairs across from Ellis, who was staring vacantly at the black glass, his eyes bloodshot and wet.

"So, Mr. Ellis," Trainum said, "now that you've had a little time to think about it, do you think you can help us out with Mr. Cooper?"

"I want to help you, man, I do, but wearin' a wire? No, man, I can't do that. I just can't."

Trainum pushed his folder in front of Ellis.

"I want you to take a look at this. Open it up."

"What is it?" Ellis asked.

"I don't want to spoil the surprise," Trainum said. "Open it." Ellis flipped open the top page. Trainum watched him read for a minute, then saw the blood drain from his face.

"I did not kill that guy, man! I was in the car the whole time."

"Are you familiar with the felony-murder rule, Leon?" The look on his face told Trainum he wasn't. "What it says is if you're an accomplice to someone who carries out a felony, like, say, murder, you're as responsible for that murder just as much as the guy who pulled the trigger."

"I had no idea he was going to waste that guy, man!"

Trainum shook his head. "Sorry, Leon. Under the law, none of that matters. If Carl was doing something that was part of carrying out a robbery that both of you planned, and he shot that poor bastard as part of carrying it out, you are as guilty of murdering him as he is."

Ellis sat back in his chair and stared at the ceiling tiles until new streaks of tears started rolling down his cheeks. He brought a hand up to wipe them away but when they kept coming, he brought both hands up to his face and started sobbing hard into them. Wallace crossed his arms on the table and leaned in.

"Leon, it's the best thing. For you, your family, the families who lost people at Star –"

156

"Stop. Just stop, man," they heard from behind his hands, "I'll fucking do it. Just stop."

22

Two days later, Trainum and Ruffin taped a bug to Leon's chest and turned him loose at Georgetown Park Mall to see how it worked. They were happy to hear everything loud and clear from every vantage point. The next day, they watched him strap it on himself before they drove him out to Pentagon City Mall in Virginia. When it checked out perfectly again, they left happy again, Leon most of all because if he couldn't see or feel it under his shirt, neither would Cooper. They left it to him to decide when he'd start talking to him, but Wallace made it crystal clear that if he ever talked to Carl in person, on the phone, or any other way without letting one of them know first, their new and final plan was to put his ass in jail for the longest amount of time a judge would let them.

When his phone rang early the next morning, Wallace hoped it was Leon, but it was someone he didn't know from an office he didn't know either.

"Detective Wallace," she said, "this is Christine Gallagher from the D.C. Corporation Counsel's Office. How are you today?"

"Fine, I guess, but it's still early. What can I do for you?"

"I believe you know you've been named a defendant in a wrongful death action brought by Ms. Terry Butera, the mother of a gentleman named Eric Butera?" Wallace sunk back in his chair.

"I do know that."

"I wouldn't blame you if you haven't waded through her very long complaint, but she's seeking a lot of money from D.C., as well as from you and four other defendants personally."

"I know that too. It's hard to forget being on the wrong end of a fifteen-million-dollar lawsuit."

"Well, I'm calling just to introduce myself and to let you know that I'll be back in touch with you shortly to arrange a preliminary meeting of all the individual defendants to let you know what to expect as the case moves forward."

"Okay, is there anything I should start doing? Change my name? Move my money to the Cayman Islands? Move myself to the Cayman Islands?"

Gallagher laughed. "No, you just might want to start pulling your files regarding Mr. Butera together for now. That's all I —"

"Hey, can I ask you a few questions that've been building up in my mind?"

"Sure. Shoot."

"You're representing MPD, right?"

"Yes, of course."

"And each of us individual defendants too, right?"

"Yes."

"So what happens if our stories don't jive with each other, or one of us individuals starts pointing the finger at one of the other individuals? How do you handle that?"

"If there's a serious conflict, we'd eliminate it by getting one of you a separate attorney, someone in private practice."

"Okay, and who pays for that?"

"The District does, almost always."

"'Almost always'. When wouldn't it pay?"

"Detective, we're getting way ahead of ourselves here. I think it would be a lot better if we waited till our meeting –"

"Trust me, it would be a lot better for me if you told me now." Gallagher sighed.

"If it gets to the point where we believe that a defendant committed an intentional tort, regardless of whether he's pointing the finger at any other defendant, he may be asked to pay for his own counsel out of his own pocket, but I assure you that it's very rare for us to conclude that a government defendant has committed an intentional tort. First –"

But Wallace had stopped listening. He tucked the receiver against his neck and started leafing through his Rolodex to the Ks.

23

After Katz told him he was free for dinner, Wallace called to make a reservation at their old stomping ground Marrocco's, but when he asked if Eddie Marrocco would be there to greet them and they told him he'd retired last year, he hung up and called Georgia Brown's on 15th St. He had no idea if Katz liked soul food, but he knew he did, so he made a reservation for 6:30.

He was already at the table when he saw what looked like an older model Jake Katz stroll in. Still short, still trim, but grayer on top with a matching mustache he never saw before. He threw him a wave, then got up so they could give each other an honest-to-goodness hug. A lot of memories flooded through his brain before he sat down and judging from the smile plastered across Katz' face, he knew they were filling his too.

"You look great, Tom," he said. "Haven't aged a day."

"Does that mean I gotta lie to you too?" Wallace laughed. "But seriously, man, you do look good. Still running?"

"Hell no," Katz said. "Too many pulls and tears. Now I take the elevator down to the gym on the ground floor of my building, get on the elliptical just long enough to crack a sweat, then elevate back up and reward myself with a doughnut."

"Building? You used to be in a duplex somewhere out East Capitol, didn't you?"

"Yep, but when I saw how much I could get for it last year, I sold it and rented a one-bedroom at the Lansburgh just to give myself some time to decide where I really want to go."

"That's on 7th Street, right? Like two blocks from where you work? If you still work there."

"I do," Katz smiled. "Still three staircases up in the heart of 5th Street's most coveted block if, and only if, you're a starving criminal defense lawyer."

A busboy dropped off their waters and a basket of biscuits and cornbread, then cleared out to reveal a young black waitress smiling at them. "Greetings, gentlemen," she said. "Have you dined with us before?"

"I have," Wallace said. "I don't know about him."

"I have not," Katz said, and took a menu from her. "We have a few specials today," she said, "both of them shrimp because the chef got a whole big fresh bunch of 'em in just today. The first one is a Shrimp Perloo with bacon, basmati rice, white wine, and red and green bell peppers, and the other is Shrimp and Cheese Grits."

"You better bring him a grit just to see if he likes it," Wallace said. Her mouth opened but nothing came out.

"I believe he's just making a little fun of me," Katz said, "but I'll have you both know I've enjoyed each and every grit I've ever eaten." She squinted at him before she decided to just stick to the script. "Okay then. Can I get you something else to drink while you're looking over the menus?"

"Whatever you have that's clear and fizzy," Wallace said. Katz said he'd stick with the water for now and watched her leave in a hurry before he looked back at Wallace. "So you're still off the booze?"

"I am. Liquor has not crossed these lips since – hey, what day is it?" When Katz told him September 30, Wallace raised his glass to him. "Since ten years ago yesterday. And there's no one else I'd rather celebrate with."

"Me either," Katz said, then clinked his glass and took a sip. "So everything okay at MPD these days? How's your new Chief?"

162

"You know, he's actually pretty damn good. Anybody'd be better than Soulsby, but this guy seems to be the real deal."

"That's great. You working on anything interesting?" Wallace rolled his eyes. "Starbucks case? Remember that?"

It took a second for Katz' face to show that he did. "Wow! I just saw a thing on 'America's Most Wanted' on that."

"Yeah, Ramsey asked them to do it to try and goose things along. The last time we did it, all it gave us was a lot of dead ends so I'm not gettin' my hopes up."

"You getting anywhere on it?"

"Maybe, maybe not, it's hard to tell. But it does have something to do with why I called you."

"Someone need a lawyer?"

"Yeah," Wallace said. "Me."

Katz looked more confused than the waitress did. "Are we still talking about Starbucks?"

"Yeah," Wallace said and gave him the two-minute recap of what happened to Eric Butera at Greenleaf Gardens. "So a few weeks ago, his mom filed a fifteen-million-dollar lawsuit saying he's dead because of everything we did and didn't do."

"Holy fucking shit!" Katz said just as the waitress reappeared, pad in hand. Neither wasted time on apologies. Wallace said he'd have the Shrimp Perloo and Katz said he'd have the same, hold the bacon. She grabbed the menus and left in another hurry.

"So I take it you're named as a defendant."

"I am."

"And did someone at the D.C. Corporation Counsel's Office tell you that you needed to find your own lawyer?"

"She said not yet, but maybe down the road, and that's when I decided to call you." Katz laughed.

"Okay, so I can tell you from being on every side of these things – cop, prosecutor, defense – the normal thing in cases like this is that they will represent you, period. You'd have to be a war criminal before they cut you loose, and probably not even then. Even if it was something that never should have happened, that's a long way from an intentional tort, which basically means they have to prove that you intended to do something you were sure would hurt Butera. Negligence isn't enough, and gross negligence usually isn't either."

"'Usually' is not helping."

"Tom, unless you tipped off the bad guys that he'd be there and you knew they were going to kill him or even just beat him up, you did not commit an intentional tort, okay? Did you do anything like that?"

"No, but –"

"So if it's not an intentional tort, the government's going to have to pay whatever the jury awards – not you – and your attorney's fees too, I should add."

"But Jake, c'mon, man, not even you know what a jury's going to do, especially after her lawyer gets done spinnin' everything."

"Who's her lawyer?" Wallace reached down to open a satchel at his feet and handed him the complaint. "Lawyers. There's three of them on there."

Katz looked through the first few pages, then drummed his fingers on the table a little while before he said "Okay, how about this? You give me the name of who you talked to at the Corporation Counsel's office and I'll call her and tell her I'm your personal attorney and get her take on if I need to be involved. No matter what she tells me, I'll do a little research to see if there are any cases where they didn't represent someone, and find out why. Then I'll let you know what I find, good or bad, all at no cost to you. How's that sound?"

"That sounds good, man, real good. I really appreciate it, Jake."

The waitress brought the perloos and they dug in until Katz lifted his head first. "This is unbelievably good. Excellent choice, sir. So, did you ever catch whoever killed him, Butera?"

"Yeah, three guys. Two of 'em pleaded, but the other one said he wants a trial, which means I'm going to have to testify."

"I get it," Katz said, "and not to make it any grimmer, but keep in mind Mrs. Butera's lawyers can and will use whatever you say there to impeach you in her trial."

"The fun never stops," Wallace said and found some solace in the shrimp for a while before he found a way to ask Katz what he'd wanted to ask ever since he called him: Whether he ever heard from, or better yet, laid eyes or anything else on Cleo Smythe, the gorgeous client he represented – and slept with – while she was cooperating with the government against Rayful Edmond a few years back.

"So hey, you remember what you told me about how the Bar people let you off easy on your thing with Cleo?"

"Refresh my recollection."

"You said 'I got a slap on the dick.'"

Katz laughed and shook his head. "Thanks for reminding me, at least about that part of it. Yeah, I got an 'oral admonishment,' which

165

isn't what you're thinking. They just called me into the Bar office and shook their finger at me. I was a first-time offender, they'd just put in new rules, the bottom line was I caught a break."

"And you been a good boy ever since?"

"Yeah, with clients and everyone else for that matter."

"That was one fine-looking woman," Wallace said. "Ever find out what happened to her?"

"No, and never tried to either. You're still the only person who knows why I left her."

Wallace did know and would never forget it. By some dark, churning whirlpool of fate, the woman Katz fell in love with was responsible for murdering Schein, his best friend from college. The crew she ran for Edmond slaughtered him for being a snitch and Wallace got sucked into the vortex because he was the one who had to tell Katz that after a long time of not telling him. He was still amazed their friendship had survived and promised himself one more time it always would. He nodded and changed the subject.

"And how's business?"

"If you're using money to keep score, it's okay, but if you mean do I look forward to going to work every day, or do I get any satisfaction out of making one more plea bargain, it sucks."

"So you going to stick with it or look for something else?"

Katz wiped a napkin across his mouth, pushed his chair back, and crossed his legs. "I ask myself that every day. And every time I try to come up with an answer, I keep thinking about what would make me as happy as I was when I was at MPD."

Wallace threw him a look. "Really? You sure about that? You didn't seem all that happy to me. I seem to remember you going through a divorce and bangin' heads with some of your fellow officers – like, for example, me – and almost getting yourself killed at the Coliseum, not to mention the Howard."

The waitress came by and looked at their empty plates. "Well, I guess you enjoyed the perloo. Got room for dessert?"

"I'm stuffed, Tom," Katz said, "but I'm happy to watch you eat." Wallace waved him off and told her to just bring the check. When she left, Katz said "I don't think about any of that stuff when I think about my time there. I think about what it was like to have a sense of mission, something that got me up in the morning and motivated me all day every day. I don't have that now. Any day."

"Are you talking about doing what you're doing, or about being a lawyer altogether?"

"I haven't figured that out either. All I know is I want to do something that'll feed my soul as much as, or even more than my belly."

"Like what?"

Katz pulled his chair back to the table. "Like something I started getting into a few months ago. There's this thing called the Lawyers Committee for Civil Rights Under Law that started back when Kennedy was President. What they do is bring lawyers to people who really need them but could never afford one. It could be bringing civil cases to stop someone from stepping on their rights, or mediating things to keep something out of court, or filing briefs, a lot of stuff. I haven't done too much of any of it yet, but that's the kind of thing I'm talking about, something to get my juices flowing like when I was a cop, you know? I never knew what was coming my way on any given day, but whatever it was, I knew I was on the side of the good guys. That's what I miss and that's what I'm looking for, not just waking up every day knowing I'm going to work out a plea deal for someone who might, may be, could be, a good guy, but hardly ever is. It's burning me out, man."

"I hear you, Jake, but don't get your hopes up. As someone who's been a cop a lot longer than you were, I'm here to tell you it's been a long time since I got out of bed looking forward to the joys of whatever was waiting for me."

"I know that, and I'm not looking to get back with MPD in any way, shape, or form. I'm just looking for something that'll give me the motivation I had then and don't have now."

Wallace started to ask himself what was motivating him to get up and find whoever did Starbucks before he answered it with another question: *What the hell difference does it make anyhow?* He was trying to find a polite way to say that when Katz started talking again.

"You know, when it comes to work, I'm a very analytical person, emphasis on the anal, always looking into every possibility of what would happen if this, if that. But in my personal life, I've never been analytical, just impulsive – not often, but almost always when some crisis is smack in my face. Then I have this moment of clarity, I call it. I remember like it was yesterday the first time it hit me, when I knew I had to divorce Lisa. It was the same thing when I left MPD and the same thing when I walked out on Cleo. My brain, the world, the cosmos, whatever it was, just left me no choice. It had to be that way. I had to do it."

To Wallace, solving Starbucks was exactly that -- something he had to do, but the only way he'd have his moment of clarity was to earn it, the hard way: Find the clues. Put them all together. See where they led. Put the right guy behind bars. That was what motivated him to be a Detective when he studied with Tilman O'Bryant and

168

that was what motivated him to be one again when Hamaas Khaalis and Rabe and Katz gave him a second chance. But he didn't see the point of sharing any of that, so he just said "Sounds like you got a split personality, my man."

"No, it's all part of the same one. I'll give you an example. You know all these homeless guys on the street everywhere? I feel compelled to give every one of them money. That's my gut instinct. I don't know why. Because they break my heart? Because it's the right thing to do, what the Jews call a mitzvah? I don't know and it doesn't matter, I just feel the compulsion to do it, okay? But – and here's where the other side comes in – it can't be just any homeless guy, oh, no, he's got to meet my standards."

"Standards," Wallace said. "What's that mean? You give 'em a test?"

"No." Katz started counting on his fingers. "No young guys, no one I think is conning me, no begging, no signs that are so pitiful they make me think it's just an act. I can go on."

Wallace shook his head. "You already eliminated every homeless guy I've ever seen. What's on the plus side?"

Katz started ticking off a new list. "Selling the street paper – Street Sense? – because then I know he's at least trying. If he wrote something that's in Street Sense, that's a double plus." He threw up his hands. "I got a heart of gold and a tight sphincter, what can I say?"

"I say you need to get out more, man, at least outside your head. You're thinking too much."

"Listen, I'd be happy if I could just find some way of making a living that would give me enough time to spend on doing something that would motivate me. The Lawyer's Committee, the ACLU, the

169

Southern Poverty Law Center, whatever. I'm going to keep trying to figure it out until I do."

The waitress dropped off the check and Wallace picked it up. "How much do I owe you?" Katz asked.

"Nothing. Let me pick it up while I can still afford it. If I lose this lawsuit, I'll be looking for you out on the street. Hope I pass."

24

When 5:00 Friday rolled around and Wallace hadn't heard anything from Katz about whether he was on the hook for lawyer fees, or Garrett about whether Leon Ellis had got Cooper to say anything that would finally give them probable cause to arrest him, he was disappointed but not surprised. He scribbled a note to call them both on Monday morning and was two steps down the hall when the ring of the phone sent him hustling back to get it. When he said "Hello," he was surprised to hear a female voice he thought he knew but couldn't place until she said "This is Robbie Rawlins. Remember me?"

"Of course I do. How're you doing?"

"'Bout the same as when you saw me. Still ain't got no job, but we can talk about that some other time. I just got off the phone with Carl Cooper and thought you oughta know what he said."

Wallace pulled his pad over. "Tell me."

"First of all, you need to know that motherfucker is about to snap. He went on and on about how you all were listenin' in on his phone calls and followin' him every time he went somewhere."

Wallace wrote "Tell PG C made them". "He say how he knew that?" he asked.

"Nothin' that made any sense, other than he thinks Man or Leon or someone sold him out, but he was talkin' a hundred miles an hour, so I definitely coulda missed something. It was all was just jibber jabber to me, but that's not why I'm calling you either," she said. "It was what he said after. He finally shut up for a second, then he said he knew what he wanted to do but wouldn't, 'cause he was worried about what would happen to his son if he did."

"What did he want to do?"

171

"I wrote it down to make sure I got it just the way he said it. He said 'Shoot the three motherfuckers who're torturing me'." Wallace's grip on the phone tightened. "I thought you should know that, but trust me, that weak-assed pussy ain't got the balls to shoot anybody. Like with Vontae, he'd get somebody else to do it for him, but now if he thinks Man's turning on him, who's he got to do his dirty work? I'd just take it as so much bullshit if I was you, but I wanted you to at least know he said it."

Wallace didn't have Robbie's confidence that Cooper was just talk. Three dead bodies at Starbucks, Bruce Howard, and too many other people told him otherwise, but he was grateful for the heads-up. "Thanks, I think," he said. "He say anything else I ought to know?"

"I don't think so," Robbie said, "other than he's outta work now too."

"Why?"

"Dumb shit got fired for ripping off whoever he was working for – Wang? Is that the name?"

"What did he do?"

"Stole shit from his own office. How fucking dumb can you be?"

Arrogant maybe, but not dumb, Wallace thought. *Probably just one more thing he thought he could get away with.* He hoped he'd prove him wrong about Starbucks but focused on what he had to do next.

"Robbie, thanks a lot for letting me know all this. Soon as we hang up, I'm going to let the other guys know what's on his mind so we can figure out what to do about it."

"You know, you been on my mind, Detective. Maybe you can come by some day and we can figure out what to do about that too."

She didn't wait for his answer. He stared at his door a good while before he hung up the phone and refocused again. A minute later, he had Trainum and Garrett conferenced in.

"I just got off the phone with Robbie Rawlins," he told them, then summarized what she said about Cooper knowing PG was tailing him and losing his job before reciting exactly what she told him about the three motherfuckers torturing him.

"Ha!" Trainum said. "That almost makes him torturing us worthwhile. Almost."

"She got more out of him in one phone call than we got from Leon Ellis in a week," Garrett said.

"Got any ideas about how to help him get Carl to open up?" Wallace asked. Silence filled the line until Trainum asked "What's Leon wearing?"

"A miniature Nagra," Garrett said.

"And it's working okay?"

"We're hearing everything clear enough."

"Is he maybe not turning it on when he ought to be?" Wallace asked.

"Everything seems to be working fine but him," Garrett said. "He's not real good about getting Carl to talk about what we want him to talk about. Most of it's just everyday bullshit, the Redskins, their jobs – or former jobs now that Carl's got shit-canned. Maybe now that he needs the money, Leon can get him talking about doing some business together and that'll give him an opening to bring up Starbucks."

"Maybe," Trainum said, "but I got the same feeling you got, Brad. Every time I listen to them, I always hear something that would give him a good reason to bring it up, but he never does. I think we're going to have to come up with some way to have him go straight to Starbucks without getting Carl suspicious about why."

"Maybe he could say he saw something about it on America's Most Wanted," Wallace said.

"That'd be good," Trainum said, "but I got zero confidence he'll figure out how to follow up on it the way we want."

"Okay," Wallace said, "then how about we tell him how to follow up on it? We can write down what we want him to get Carl to talk about – and if they're on the phone, he can even just read it off a piece of paper."

"I like that better," Trainum said.

"Let me just put another idea out there," Garrett said. "They do get together, in person, from time to time. We've seen Leon get out of his car and go into Carl's place, and we've heard them at Leon's place. Maybe the next time they're at Leon's, he can pop a tape of AMW into his VCR and have Carl watch it with him. He won't have to do much to lead him – the show'll do that – and then we just listen – and hope."

"That sounds like Plan A to me," Wallace said. "What do you think, Jim?"

"I like it."

"Okay then. Seeing as how it's close of business, why don't we give him the weekend to make something happen before we make any changes? Let me know on Monday how things went one way or the other."

When he clicked off, Wallace shut off the lights and took his time heading down the hall. It didn't take long for him to start thinking about Robbie's parting remark again. He still had a lot to figure out.

25

After Garrett let them know Monday morning that Leon talked to Carl on Saturday with the same nothing to show for it, Leon called them that afternoon from a pay phone per Garrett's instructions.

"What's up?" he asked. "Everything okay?"

"Everything but getting anything we can use out of Carl," Wallace said.

"Man, I'm doin' the best I can."

"It's not good enough, Mr. Ellis," Garrett said.

"I'm trying to help you all out, but I don't want to get his suspicions up either. I know what the dude can do."

"Here's the deal, Leon, bottom line." Wallace said. "You got two choices. The first one is you figure out a way to get him to talk about Starbucks real soon. The second one is you don't and we just get on with the business of sending you away for as long as a judge will let us. So you tell me, what's it going to be?"

"Come on, man, I just need to do it in my own way, that's all. I'll make it work, I swear. Just give me a little time."

"We're now officially out of time, Leon. It's now or never," Wallace said.

"Shit, man, what do you want me to do? I'm doing the best I can."

"You got a VCR, Leon?" Garrett asked.

"Yeah. Why?"

"You know the show 'America's Most Wanted'?"

"Yeah, I see it sometimes."

"Did you watch it last week?"

"No."

"They ran a thing on Starbucks and how it's still an open case. We want you to invite Carl over and watch it with him."

"And how'm I supposed to do that, man? I didn't tape it."

"We'll burn you a tape. You watch it with him, we can hear what he says through your wire."

"So what, I ask him over and I just happen to pop in a tape that's got something on Starbucks? If that sounds like a set-up to me, man, it's gonna sound like a set-up to him, I guarantee you. And I'm sittin' right there with him? No man, uh-uh. You got to do better than that."

"Leon," Trainum said, "it doesn't have to be like that. You can tell him you were watching the show last week and all of a sudden this thing about Starbucks came on and you taped it just so you could show it to him next time he came over."

"I don't know, man."

"We can start the tape right after they said Starbucks'll be on," Garrett said. "That'll give you cover."

"Jesus Christ," Ellis muttered.

"I'm taking that as a yes," Wallace said. "Call me back when you have a time and a place I can meet you to hand over the tape. If I don't hear from you by nine tomorrow morning, I'll see you at the shop with some of PG's finest and nobody's going to be there to get a haircut. Am I clear?'

Leon invoked the name of his Lord and Savior one more time before banging down the phone. Fifteen minutes later, he gave him a time

177

and a place. Wallace scribbled down what he said, hung up, and got Trainum and Garrett back on the line.

"Just got off the phone with Leon. He wants me to meet him at a PG library out 450 past Kenilworth around 6:15 tomorrow night. Brad, can you get me the tape by then?"

"No problem. You'll get it today."

"Tom," Trainum said, "any chance he's setting you up, letting Carl know where one of us motherfuckers is going to be?"

Wallace thought about that, then said "Why don't you call McCann and ask them to get some folks out there just in case. In the meantime, I'll set up how we're going to work the handoff and let you know so you can tell them what to expect."

"Ten-four that. And good luck."

A little before six the next night, Wallace pulled his civilian Ford into the library parking lot and found a space near the back door. He grabbed a Popeyes Chicken bag off the passenger seat and opened it, spreading the napkins around to cover the tape before he rolled it back up and walked to the door. He nodded to McCann in the foyer, got a nod back, and went in. He strolled through the stacks for a few minutes before he wandered over to the Children's section and put his bag down on a little red table surrounded by little red chairs. He thumbed through a few books, then made his way down the carrels to the periodicals, where he pulled a dowel with the *Washington Post* off the rack and took a seat at a long table facing the kiddie books.

Ten minutes later, Leon came through the same door he did and headed for the Children's section. He walked past the little round table, then pulled a book off a shelf and opened it, but his eyes were scanning the room. He turned, but not far enough to see Wallace,

178

then turned the other way and put the book back on the shelf before he picked up the bag and left the way he came in.

Wallace waited a few minutes before he put the *Post* back on its rack and headed for the same door. When he got to the foyer, McCann said "All clear back here. Hope this works." Wallace crossed his fingers and tried to keep hope alive until his faith was rewarded a little after 4 on Friday. Garrett was on the line.

"Looks like we're on for tonight, Tom. Carl's bringing some food and beers over to Leon's around 7:30. Trainum's coming over here around 7 with pretty much the same thing. You want to join the party?"

Wallace and Trainum were led into the Bureau's data center about quarter after. A laptop screen showing the front of Cooper's house sat next to a small speaker buzzing quietly. Garrett handed him a plastic plate and slid him a bowl of pretzels and a can of Budweiser. Wallace reached for the pretzels but slid back the beer.

"Been on the wagon ten years, Brad, so thanks but no thanks."

"Good for you," Garrett said. "There's some water in the fridge over there." Wallace grabbed a Dasani and brought it back to the table.

"No news?" he asked.

"Nothing," Trainum said and glanced at his watch. "He should be there in about ten min – ". He stopped at the sound of a faint knock on a door coming over the speaker, followed by a creak and Carl's voice.

"Hey, man, there was no line so I figured I'd just come over."

"That's all right, man," Leon said. "Just take it on over there. I'll get us some plates."

179

"You thinking what I'm thinking?" Wallace said, remembering what Robbie told him about Carl being paranoid about them doing exactly what they were doing. "He come over early just to see if he could catch Leon settin' him up somehow?"

"Crossed my mind too," Trainum said. Garrett started to stay something but stopped at the sound of Carl's voice.

"Shit, man, I was glad to hear from you, I'm telling you. Sittin' around the house all day's drivin' me fucking crazy."

"I bet, man," Leon said. "What happened there anyhow?"

"Just bullshit, man. They were lookin' for a reason to get rid of me and made up a story, that's all."

"You gonna fight it?"

"Nah, for what they were payin' me, it ain't worth it. I can do a lot better on my own."

"What's Cissy say about that?"

"The fuck difference that make, man? She got her job, I'll take care of my end. I ain't worried."

They heard bottles open, then nothing for a while before Leon said "So hey, man, you watch that show 'America's Most Wanted'?" Wallace froze in mid-bite. The room went dead quiet.

"I seen it."

"You watch it last week?"

"No."

"Well, I did and I started taping it as soon as I heard them say they was about to do a thing on Starbucks."

"You fucking kidding me?"

"No, man, and I freaked out when they showed this picture of some 'Bama cop I swear I seen sittin' in a car on my street. Watch this."

The sound of the show came over the speaker, but Wallace couldn't make out what anyone was saying until Cooper said "That's them, man! That's the FBI fucker, that's the Tom workin' for DC, and that's the fucking 'Bama."

"That's the same fucking guy I saw in the car!" Leon said.

Wallace heard sirens, music, and garbled talk, then only silence before Leon said "Those bastards ain't found who did it yet, they ain't ever going to. That's what I'm thinkin'."

The next thing he heard was someone hitting something hard, then Cooper saying "No, man, that Starbucks shit, I ain't sayin' nothin'."

Wallace thought of what Leon could say to draw him out. *Why, man, what's up? What, you think they're lookin' at you? You know who mighta done it?* What he heard was "I hear you, man. You see those goddamned Wizards against the Heat the other night? Alonzo Mourning musta got a hundred rebounds."

"Fuckers need to learn to box out," Cooper said.

The next thing Wallace heard was Trainum's fist cracking his plate.

26

Forty-five minutes later, they heard the door close, then Leon say "He's gone."

Wallace dialed him up, put it on speaker, and said "That was some weak shit, my man" before Leon could even say hello. "I tried, man," he said. "You heard me."

"Yeah, I heard you all right. You could've kept him talking about Starbucks a million ways, but no, you went on and on about the Wizards, and Alonzo Mourning killin' 'em on the boards, and Chris Webber coming back and beatin' 'em and blah, blah, blah till I just stopped listening, man. Jesus, George Michael don't talk basketball as much as you did."

"I was just tryin' to get him comfortable, man, let him talk about what he wanted to talk about."

"You know what, Leon?" Trainum said. "I don't think you're cut out for this job. You want us to pick you up at home tomorrow or at the shop? Or should we just pick you up now and get this over with?"

"No, c'mon man, I want to do this, I do. While he was going on, I started thinkin' about another way I could go about it better."

"We're listening," Wallace said.

"I was thinkin' I could call him in a few days all frantic like and tell him that you guys pulled up alongside me while I was drivin' and we got into it and one thing led to the other and we started shootin' at each other and I took off and got away, but now I need a place where I can hide out a little while, so could he put me up? That way, you know, we could spend some more time together and he'd maybe relax and start talking more about what you all want him to talk about."

Trainum and Wallace exchanged eye rolls, but Garrett held up a hand. Wallace put his over the receiver and mouthed "What?"

"Tell him you'll call him back in a little bit."

"Hey, give us some time to think on it," Wallace said into the receiver. "I'll get back to you." He clicked off and turned to Garrett. "So what're you thinking?"

"I'm thinking that's a fucking joke. All spending more time with him would do is make Cooper more suspicious – and more likely to find the bug – but I do kind of like the idea of him running into us and letting Carl know it freaked him out, just without the part about us going all Jackie Chan on him."

"I agree with that." Trainum said, "and also with us having some time to think about it." Garrett turned to Wallace.

"Why don't you call him back and tell him we need a day or two to work it out? There's a way to do this right. We just gotta find it."

A day or two turned into seven to come up with the plan, then another seven before Leon got the balls to put it in play. Finally, late one Friday afternoon at the end of February, they heard him tell Carl they had to talk – in person – asap.

"Why, what's up?" Cooper asked.

"Them Bamas again. But this time they talked to me."

"What'd they say?"

"Uh-uh, not on the phone. How's about I pick you up and we talk about it face to face." After a pause, Cooper said "Give me an hour." An hour later, Wallace, Trainum, and Garrett watched Leon's black Toyota Corolla pull to a stop in front of the camera on Gallatin Street.

"Where's the bug?" Wallace asked.

"Under the driver's seat," Garrett said. "Long as he sticks with the plan, we're good. They get out, all we got is Leon's word and that ain't good."

"Here he comes," they heard Leon say and watched Cooper come slowly down the walk, his hands tucked in his jacket pockets, his face indistinct but clear enough to see he was not smiling. When the passenger door closed, Leon pulled away from the curb. They drove long enough without a word being passed that Wallace turned to Garrett to ask if the bug was working before they heard Cooper's voice.

"All right, so what they say?"

"I was walking to my car when they stopped me on the street and said they wanted to talk about some racketeering shit I did with you."

"First of all, who's 'they'? You recognize 'em?"

"Yeah, the Bamas sittin' on my street I told you about, the white motherfucker and the Tom."

"Shit, we just did some robberies, man. That ain't no racketeering."

"I know that, man, but they were comin' out of the woodwork with a whole list of shit we did together, some of 'em I didn't even remember, but they say all that makes us a 'racketeering organization'. That part I remember."

"That is bullshit, man. They were tellin' you a fuckin' story to mess with your mind."

184

"And there's another thing. They say they could link Cissy's gun, the nine, to Starbucks. They puttin' the Georgetown deal on us, man!"

They heard nothing but quiet again until Cooper said "Naw, man, if they had any leads comin' out of that nine that'd hold up in court, then how come I'm out? They're fuckin' with you."

"But why would they link either one of us to the Starbucks thing?"

"I don't know and I don't care, man. Hand to God, on my father's grave, on my son's life, I had nothin' to do with that shit."

"Man, I hear you, but listen, the motherfuckers told me they had your fingerprints in there!"

Wallace turned to Trainum. "You tell him to say that? I didn't tell him to say that."

"Hell, no," Trainum said and they both looked at Garrett, who shook his head and looked to the heavens. *Shit, man,* Wallace thought, *don't start freelancing now.*

"That's a place of business," Cooper said. "I done been *in* the motherfucker."

"But you called me about robbing the place that night, man."

"Ain't no crime to think about shit, man. I. Didn't. Do. It."

"Fuckers sayin' we had a conspiracy or some shit."

"There ain't no conspiracy – you gotta go through the motions about actually doin' something for there to be a conspiracy. So, hey, take that jackoff honky Trainum. Say I want to kill him, okay? They can't arrest me just 'cause I *want* to. I haven't gone down to headquarters, okay? I haven't followed him to his house. Bottom line is they can't prove that I did shit. The only way they can get me

185

is by me admitting it, sayin' 'Yeah, I did it.' That's the only way they can ever get me for anything, and I ain't ever gonna say it, bank on it."

No one said a thing on either end of the bug. Time stood still until Cooper started talking again.

"And I actually feel for them, you know, the families. But doin' that shit ain't my style, you know that. Let me put it to you like this, man. I'm married, dog. I got a beautiful almost four-year-old son. I am now a decent law-abiding citizen, okay?"

"The bastard know he's on a wire?" Trainum said.

"I've lived my life of crime. I done my dirt. I'm trying my hand at being right. I'll be a'right once I get a new job, I ain't worried."

"It's hard to know what goes on in his head," Wallace said.

"But I tell you," Cooper went on, "that FBI guy, nothin' ever come out of his mouth wrong to me. That 'Bama been quiet the whole time. Okay, he may be a tricky motherfucker, but he ain't never disrespected me or my wife. I actually kinda like him. Cuz cool. I actually followed him one day when he was walkin' across a parking lot. He ain't see me and I didn't do a thing – but if it was that asshole Trainum? He is on my shit list. That man has shown a blatant disrespect for me and my family and I am going to take care of him one way or the other. I can understand why Bennie Lee Lawson did what he did, truly."

They all knew exactly what he was talking about. About five years ago, Lawson walked into MPD headquarters, pulled a handgun out of his waistband, and killed a policeman and two FBI agents before killing himself with one of the agents' gun.

"If I were a petty person, man, I would come inside Trainum's house and kill his fucking family, then just wait there for him to come home. 'Hey honey I'm home' and pow pow pow. Ain't nothin' that motherfucker can do for me 'cept die, slow."

That hung in the air for a minute until they heard Leon say "All right, man. Here good or you want me to take you 'round front?"

"This is good. Stay cool, bro." They heard a door open and close.

"We need to grab him and start talkin' to him. Now." Wallace said. He got no argument.

27

Now turned into Monday night by the time they figured out who, how, and for what they should arrest him. At 7:05, Garrett and Robert Oxley, another FBI agent, watched Cooper park his car at the curb just past his house on Gallatin Street. His son got out the passenger side and ran past them up the sidewalk before Cooper got out, saw them, and froze. Oxley kept an eye on him while Garrett watched the boy run into the house. When he saw the door close behind him, he turned to Cooper, reached inside his sport coat for his badge, and held it up at chest level.

"Mr. Cooper," he said, "I have a warrant for your arrest for the shooting of Prince Georges County Police Officer Bruce Howard on August 12, 1996. We don't need to make a big production out of this. Our car's just up the street. If you wait where you are, Mr. Oxley here will put the cuffs on you and we'll just walk you up there with us and drive away, no muss, no fuss, okay?"

He slid the badge back into his jacket. Cooper dropped his head, nodded, and waited for Oxley to cuff him and walk him back to the sidewalk. Garrett pointed to the black Mercury four cars up and they all casually walked to it. When Oxley pulled the rear door open, Cooper ducked to get in, but stopped when he saw a Channel 9 camera and crew across the street. He looked at Garrett, his eyes asking "What the fuck?"

"Not our doing, Mr. Cooper. The quicker you get in, the quicker we get you out of here." He did and they did. No one said a word for ten minutes until Cooper said "Thank you for not making a big deal out of that." He didn't say another word until he spat out "Oh Jesus Christ!" when he saw Trainum and Wallace waiting for him.in the interview room at the Bureau's Washington Field Office. Oxley pulled out a seat for him across from them, then he and Garrett took seats across from each other. Garrett spelled out all the particulars of why he was arrested and told him that they were going to ask a D.C. judge to extradite him to Maryland after they were done interviewing him.

"Do you have any questions, Mr. Cooper?"

"I know what you're talking about, but I didn't do it."

"Okay, so noted," Garrett said, "and we also want to talk to you about the Starbucks murders. Is that okay?"

"Okay," Cooper said, throwing his arms open, "but I didn't do that either, so knock yourself out."

Garrett read him his rights and pushed a waiver form to him. "If you want a lawyer, we'll hold off till he gets here. If you don't, sign at the bottom and we'll get started." Cooper shrugged and signed.

"So you deny you had anything to do with the Starbucks killings, is that correct?" Garrett asked.

"Killing someone is not my style," he said, then pushed his chair back from the table and crossed his legs. "Now back in the day, when I was robbing people, I mighta, you know, hit somebody upside the head if they bucked, but killing 'em, naw. I read the article that said the Starbucks girl had the keys in her hand. Man, she didn't have to be shot. Maybe you'd'a had to whack her in the head a few times, break some skin, you know, so after a while her head starts to hurt and she gives up the money, okay? But killing her? No way. Not my thing."

"You may or may not know this, Mr. Cooper, but your name keeps popping up in our investigation. You have any idea why that is?"

"'Cause some people got it in for me, that's why. I was a very bad boy once upon a time, I admit it. I used to go hard when I robbed people, I ain't denyin' it, but that was back when I was smokin'

189

weed and sellin' drugs, man. Whatever, I got a reputation, and that's why some people are out to get me, okay? People tryin' to cut a deal with you-all, or people who just see a pile of money at the end of the rainbow if they help you out, but, man, I ain't done that shit in eight years. They just thinkin' 'Cooper can't be doing right and making money, oh, no, he must be doin' *somethin'*,' you know? And like I said, I would never kill nobody. The only way I would kill you is if – one – you are about to take my life or – two – you fuck with my family."

Wallace didn't have to look at Trainum to know they were both thinking he made the cut.

"Far as Starbucks goes," Cooper went on, "that ain't the way I woulda gone about it. Never mind shootin' no-damn-body, you would've needed at least two people to take the money and keep those three people at bay while you're doin' it. I'd'a never done it alone."

"So, hypothetically, what would you have done if, say, the woman started screaming?"

"The bodies were found in the back of the store, right?" Garrett nodded. "Well then, ain't nobody going to hear 'em screamin'. Just pepper spray 'em. I done that. Quiets 'em down quick."

"Have you ever been in that Starbucks store?" Wallace asked.

"Yeah, I'm a coffee drinker, actually more a cappuccino drinker, but I been there plenty of times, usually after I drop my mother off at church at Shiloh Baptist, over at 9th and P? I take my wife and my kids over to walk around Georgetown till she's done."

"How often was that?"

"I don't know, maybe six times, ten times, over maybe like the last six months or so? Every time we go, me and Cissy, my wife, get

190

something to drink and my son gets a cookie and we sit down, usually by the front window although one time we did sit upstairs, like all the way in the back."

"Ever go behind the counter?"

"No, never."

"Did you go there the week of the murders?" Cooper appeared to give that some heavy thought.

"No, I don't think so. I mean, you know, if I did, I'd'a thought like 'Oh shit, that coulda been me lyin' there dead,' but I didn't, so I seriously doubt it."

"How about after the murders?"

"Maybe about two weeks after. We took flowers down there and put 'em in that memorial window they had, but I ain't been back since because too many people were coming up to me saying I did it! I didn't want anyone to think I was one of those criminals returnin' to the scene of the crime, you know, so I just stopped goin'."

"You've done these kinds of things, Carl," Garrett said. "Why would someone have picked that store to rob?"

"It was a bad move to pick *any*thing in Georgetown, man. That place is hot, police all over the place even when the stores are closed. Plus the location is wrong. You need something on a side street, not Wisconsin goddamned Avenue. Too much lighting too. I never did the jump-out spontaneous shit like Vontae Kincaid or some other guys I used to run with – and I would never, ever go into a place I was going to rob beforehand. Then they see your face, you know?" Vontae Kincaid made Wallace's mind flash on Robbie's face before he made himself focus on Garrett's again.

"Do you know anyone who works for Starbucks, or used to work for them?" Cooper shook his head.

"Honestly man, I'll be real with you, most of the people I know don't have no job. No one I know would work there when they could be out doin' shit that'd make 'em some real money, so no I don't. And these people, and even people I don't know, they know where I live, and they come talk to me about all this kind of shit because they know my reputation. I get respect, you know, even though it's been so long since I did anything. And like tonight, with you all being at my house, that just boosted my reputation, so I thank you for that – and I thank you again for low-keyin' the whole thing. That was much appreciated."

Wallace raised a finger and Garrett nodded to him. "Did you ever talk to anyone about doing that Starbucks?" he asked.

"If I did, I would'a said what I already told you all: It's too hot. You need to pick another spot. And, like I say, people listen to me."

"Any people in particular you remember talking about that Starbucks?"

"Somebody might'a mentioned it to me in June at my house – no, wait a minute, it was *two* people at the rec center on Michigan Avenue, two people I didn't know but who, like I said, knew my reputation and wanted my opinion on hittin' it. It wasn't like they had a plan or anything, you know, it was just like general conversation. I think I talked 'em out of it, so I bet they didn't do it – but, maybe they said I did after I talked them out of doing it themselves, you know, just trying to keep people from thinking *they* did it. You just don't know, man, when guys are criminals, you just don't know."

"And just to be clear, you didn't know these people?" Oxley asked. "They weren't friends of yours?"

192

"I don't have friends. I only got associates. And these guys, they were just wanting to do one of these takeover type robberies, you know, like Vontae, runnin' in, yelling 'Get down! Get down!' Shit, man, someone could get hurt in one of them things who don't need to be."

"Did you ever do one of those?"

"Yeah, one time with him, and just the one time. Little kid almost got himself shot. That fucked me up, I tell you. Messed with my mind, you know? 'This shit ain't cool,' I said to myself. 'You got to slow down, brother.'"

"You think one of your associates might've flipped on you and called us?" Wallace asked.

"It's possible. I done my dirt – but shootin' someone, that's not my thing." Trainum apparently had had enough and jumped in.

"So, I just want to make sure I'm getting this right. These two people at the rec center just come up to you and start asking about Starbucks out of nowhere? Is that what you're telling us?"

Cooper gave him the hard stare before he answered "Yeah, that's what I said. If you hard of hearing, I'll speak up."

"Oh, I heard you," Trainum said, "and I heard all the razzamatazz b.s. you said about why they might or might not've done it. Just tell me straight up, do you think they did it?"

"I got no idea and I wouldn't tell you all if I did, especially you." He took a second to compose himself. "Listen, I ain't never been a snitch and I ain't going to start now. People know where I live, where I go, when I go, and when I come home. You all know I got a family, and I live in a neighborhood where guys have no problem shootin' somebody for snitchin'. I don't want to be a statistic, so no thank you, I ain't telling you shit."

193

But that didn't keep them from firing more questions at him, for hours. Cooper would get frustrated with each of them in turn, always saving his best bile for Trainum, but around 10:00, he asked to take a break and they had to send Oxley to fetch him out of the toilet ten minutes later. A half an hour after that, he wanted some water and they brought him some popcorn too, but a half hour after that, he said he had to use the head again. A little before 1:30, right after Garrett asked him to run through exactly what he did with who, back when he was a criminal, Cooper cracked. He waved him off, stood up, then sat back down, and started sobbing into his hands.

"I'm ready to go, man. I'm ready to get this over with, honest to Christ! Take me back to PG, please, please! I just don't care anymore. Just take me out, I'm beggin' you."

"Are you willing to take a polygraph?" Garrett asked.

"I just want to go back. I'm in it for life. I'm in dirt. Every time somethin' goes down, I'm in it. I'm destined to do dirt. I quit. I know what I've done. I'm constantly trying to defend myself, defend my name. I may as well go out and do all these fuckin' things people think I'm doin'. I didn't shoot that cop. I didn't do this Starbucks shit, but it keeps poppin' up on me, so just lock me up, okay? I ain't got a job. My reputation is no longer in good standing, and talkin' to you ain't going to help me out. I'm tired, tired, tired of this bullshit! I can't do right. I did not do any of this shit, but it don't matter. You're gonna take my family away from me anyhow."

"What would it take for you to tell us what you did do in the last few years, Mr. Cooper?" Garrett asked. Cooper stared at the wall behind him a while, then squared his shoulders, took a deep breath, and looked him in the eye.

"I didn't do Starbucks. I didn't do it and I'm going to beat it. You're gonna charge me with PG, but I didn't do that either and I'm

194

going to beat that too." His eyes filled with tears again and he shook his head. "I know I should've never said a thing about those two guys at the rec center. Even when I try to do right, it comes right back on me, never fails. And that's why I'm a very careful, a very cautious individual. Other people talk, man, so when I do shit, I do it by my fucking self. That way, I don't have to worry about people tellin' on me."

"Let's get back to the polygraph," Garrett said, but Cooper wasn't done. "You people can't do anything for me even though I haven't participated in any of this shit. I'm here only because people are trying to get back at me. I talked two people *out of* doing a robbery there and now I'm in the shit, and if there's a fingerprint of mine in that store, I guarantee you it ain't behind a counter or any shit like that."

"Okay, Carl, so while you think about whether you're going to strap in and give us some answers we can believe, let's go back to the robberies you were talking about when we first started here. Are you telling us you did those alone?"

"Yep, the ones I did, all of 'em were alone."

"Did you ever rob a pizza place?" "I did. Alone."

"A massage parlor?" "No. Never robbed no massage parlor."

"A bank?" "No. Banks weren't my thing. That's a Federal rap and I didn't need to get one of those guideline sentences that'd fuck me up. But that didn't stop some people I know."

"Like Teddy Thigpen, 'Man'?" Garrett asked.

"Like him, exactly, and his girlfriend Joannie Lee, I forget her last name. I never did anything with them, mostly 'cause I didn't trust her, and I only know about the bank job because Man told me about it when the two of 'em was staying at my house one night and they

195

started arguing about something that happened and finally I cut in and said 'You robbed a bank?' and when they said yes, I threw 'em the fuck out. But, like I say, that was the old days. I'm a new man now."

"Just so you know," Wallace said, "we've received information that you were in on every one of those jobs. You want to think about them a little more?" Cooper coughed out a laugh.

"Information from who? Man? Joannie fucking Lee? No, man, don't you see? Don't you get it? They're just trying to get out from under. Shit!" He shook his head and pursed his lips before turning back to Garrett. "Okay, you want to know what happened to that PG cop? Here's what really happened. *They* robbed him and *they* shot him, because he pulled a gun on 'em. Shot him in the head, I think they told me, and Man said he took off 'cause he thought he killed him, but turns out he didn't. Anyhow, I rolled up to Pennsylvania with him for two, three days so the brother could lie low, but here's the shit: I saw a composite picture of the guy the cops did, and it looked like *me*, not him! I'm telling you, man, the shit always comes back to me whether I did it or not, and I did not do that!"

"Do you know someone named Leon Ellis?" Trainum asked.

"Yeah."

"Do you know if he had anything to do with shooting Officer Howard?"

"I just told you who did it. Now, Ellis did do some lookout shit for Man way back, but they ain't got along for a good while and no, I don't know why. It got nothin' to do with me, so I don't want to know either."

"And you didn't do anything with Man or Joannie Lee up in Pennsylvania?" Wallace asked.

"Shit, man, no. That's too far away anyhow."

"Mr. Cooper," Garrett said, "you still haven't answered my question about taking the polygraph, and this is the last time I'm going to ask you."

"You know, I was willing to help you out when you brought me in here, okay, but now? I'm not taking it. I mean, why should I help you now, man, huh? All these other people are trying to set me up, and I'm going to let you help them do it? Uh-uh. Listen, man, this is all you need to know: I don't kill. It's not my thing. I know about some these things you're asking me about, but what now, because I didn't come forward and tell you 'bout 'em earlier, I'm gonna pay for it? That shit ain't gonna happen. Look, man, if I did it, I'd say 'You got me. Let's work out a deal', okay? But I'm not gonna make a deal for something I didn't do."

Garrett watched Oxley finish writing that up, then asked "So again, hypothetically, what would you ask for if you were to make a deal?"

Cooper stared at him a while before he answered. "I'd ask to not be put to death."

Garrett turned to Wallace and Trainum, his eyes asking if either of them had anything else. Trainum slowly shook his head no. Wallace looked over his notes, saw a few items still unchecked, then checked his watch. 2:48 a.m. "It can wait," he said.

Garrett flipped his folder shut and got to his feet. "Then I'll go get Mr. Wainstein."

They sat in silence waiting for him to come back. When he appeared at the door, he held his arm up to let a handsome, immaculately coiffed brown-haired man in an unwrinkled dark blue suit, starched white shirt, and tightly knotted blue-and-gray-striped tie come in before him. Wallace rechecked his watch, especially the a.m. part.

197

"Mr. Cooper," Garrett said, "this is Kenneth Wainstein, an Assistant United States Attorney in D.C. who's going to tell you exactly what you're being charged with. Once he's done and answered all your questions, we're going to let you get some sleep, then bring you before a Commissioner tomorrow morning and extradite you back to Maryland." He didn't wait for Cooper to say anything before he gestured Wainstein to take the chair he'd been in. "Mr. Wainstein, Mr. Cooper."

Wainstein took his seat and slid a manila folder to Cooper.

"Mr. Cooper, this is an indictment that a Maryland grand jury has issued, charging you with seven crimes that I'm going to walk you through. Please open the folder and follow along with me. If you have any questions, I'd be happy to answer them at the end." Cooper opened the folder.

"First of all, as you'll note here on the first page, all of these crimes were committed in connection with your assault on, and robbery of, Prince Georges County Police Officer Bruce Howard on August 12, 1996. The first paragraph charges you with armed robbery."

Wainstein watched Cooper read the count before he went on, pausing just a second or two between each count. "The second paragraph charges you with assault in aid of racketeering activity, and the third charges you with attempted murder, also in aid of racketeering activity. The fourth paragraph charges you with use of a firearm during a crime of violence. The fifth paragraph charges you with carrying a pistol without a license. The sixth paragraph charges you with unlawful possession of a firearm by a convicted felon, and the seventh paragraph charges you with unlawful possession of ammunition by a convicted felon."

He waited for Cooper to finish reading the document and look up at him. "Do you have any questions about the indictment or what's going to happen next?" he asked.

Cooper rubbed his chin for a few seconds before answering. "Yeah, a few. Am I going to get a lawyer?"

"You are free to find your own lawyer. If you don't, the court will appoint one to represent you."

"Okay, and is knowledge of the crimes after the fact a crime?"

"No," Wainstein said. Cooper closed the folder and pushed it to him. "Okay," he said, "then you got nothing on me."

Wainstein retrieved the folder and put it in his briefcase. "I just have one other question, Mr. Cooper. Have they asked you if you'd take a polygraph?" Cooper laughed.

"You guys don't quit, do you? Yeah, they asked and I answered: No. And you want to know something, I'm not going to do it now just out of spite. How do you like that? Because what am I going to get out of it? Nothing, that's what! It's my reputation that has me sitting here and people running their mouths even though they don't know shit about what they're talking about. That's what got me locked up in the Youth Center with Vontae Kincaid and I know better now. So, no. No fucking way."

Wainstein snapped the hasps on his briefcase shut and turned to Garrett. "Are you done?"

"For now."

Wainstein looked at his watch. "Unless you have another idea, Agent Garrett, I don't think it's worth waking up a Commissioner to extradite him now. Why don't we all get some shuteye and do it a little later this morning, like say 11?"

"Sounds good to me," Wallace said. "I'll get some uniforms to transport him to MPD to process him." He stood up and looked at Cooper. "I will see you there."

199

"You might see me," he said, "but you ain't gonna hear another word out of me until I talk to a lawyer." He turned to Wainstein. "I want one. Now. A good one."

28

A few minutes before eleven, Wallace walked into the Hearing Commissioner courtroom and joined Wainstein and Trainum at the prosecutor's table. The defense table was empty.

"He show up?" Wallace asked.

"He did," Wainstein said. "Thanks again for finding someone who knows what he's doing so quick." Trainum looked confused. "Who are we talking about?"

"Cooper's lawyer," Wainstein said. "Tom told me last night he might be able to get Jake Katz to come over here this morning to represent him, and they're back there now talking. Good job, Tom."

"Who's Jake Katz?" Trainum asked.

"He used to be one of us," Wallace said and pointed at Wainstein. "And them too. Now he's one of those guys on Fifth Street. When we broke up last night, I told Ken I might be able to get him to show up to represent Cooper at this thing and he told me to give it a shot. I'm glad it worked out."

"Me too," Wainstein said. "Jim was just telling me that the PG guys called him about a half hour ago to say they were just leaving, so everything seems to be on track."

A door behind the bench swung open and two uniforms led Cooper and Katz to their table. They talked quietly for a few seconds before Katz stepped to the prosecutors' table and shook Wainstein's hand.

"I'm not shaking your hand," he told Wallace. "None of us need him asking for a new lawyer just yet."

"Pleased to meet you too," Wallace said.

"I'm happy you're here though. I have a few questions about what happened last night."

"And I'll be pleased to answer –". A bailiff came through the door Katz and Cooper had just come through.

"Oyez, oyez, oyez," he said. "This court is now in session, the Honorable Evelyn Coburn presiding."

Katz returned to his table and they all stood until she sat.

"The matter before me is the extradition of Carl Derek Havord Cooper to Prince Georges County, Maryland for the shooting of police officer Bruce Howard on August 12, 1996. Mr. Wainstein, would you like to be heard?"

"Just briefly, Your Honor. I think the extradition papers spell everything out. We've arranged for the Prince Georges Police Department to transport Mr. Cooper to Maryland and expect their presence momentarily. If they are not here by the time this hearing concludes, we request that Mr. Cooper be held in MPD's Central Cell Block until they arrive."

"All right," Judge Coburn said. "Mr. Katz, do you wish to be heard?"

"I do, Your Honor" he said, rising. "I see that Detective Wallace is here today. My client has advised me that he was one of the men who interviewed him last night, so I'd like to him a few questions, if I may."

"You may." Wallace took the witness stand.

"Detective," Katz said, "I understand from my client that MPD detectives and FBI agents questioned Mr. Cooper from about seven o'clock last night until about three o'clock this morning. Is that correct?"

"It is," Wallace said.

"Was he given any food during this time?"

"He was. He was given water and popcorn."

"That's it?"

"He was offered food and beverages on several occasions but declined it."

"And was he given any breaks from the questioning at any time?"

"He was, repeatedly. Whenever he said he needed some time to use the bathroom or for any other reason, we gave him the time he needed until he said he was ready to talk again."

"Was the focus of your interrogation solely the shooting of Officer Howard?"

"Largely, but not solely."

"And did he request an attorney to be present at any time?"

"Only for this morning's hearing. He was asked if he wanted a lawyer present last night, and he signed a waiver saying he did not." Katz turned to the judge.

"Your Honor, for the record, my client will not consent to any further interviews by MPD or the FBI or the Prince Georges Police or any other law enforcement agency without his lawyer present."

"It's now in the record, Mr. Katz."

"With that stipulation, Mr. Cooper waives his right to challenge his extradition to Prince Georges County."

"So ordered," Judge Coburn said. Wallace watched the uniforms lead Cooper from the courtroom and waited for her to declare the proceedings adjourned before he and Wainstein walked over to Katz.

"Will you shake my hand now?"

"Gladly," Katz said.

"Thanks for helping us out today, Jake," Wainstein said. "Much appreciated."

"Always glad to help out old friends."

"Are you going to represent him in Maryland?"

"I'm going to have to think about that, starting with whether I'm still a member of the bar there. I can't even remember where the PG courthouse is."

"Well, I've got to let Mueller know how things went," Wainstein said. "Tom, I'm sure we'll be in touch soon. Jake, thanks again." They watched him leave through a side door and take the steps down.

"You heading back to your office?" Wallace asked.

"I am."

"Good. I'll walk with you."

The second they hit the main hallway, they had company immediately, a horde of reporters with mikes, cameras, and pads in hand, surging toward them, their voices a babble of unintelligible questions. In the second it took Wallace to realize they were all for Katz, he patted him on the shoulder, squeezed out of the pack, and hustled for the elevator. He heard someone yell "Detective! Detective!" but didn't turn around until he had the pleasure of hearing the door clank shut behind him.

In five minutes, he was back at headquarters and a minute after that, down in Central Cell Block looking for the PG cops. When Trainum waved to him from behind the counter, he saw Fulginiti and McCann turn his way.

"Well, it's your turn now," he said, shaking their hands.

"We're ready for him," McCann said.

"They said we could sit in the peanut gallery and watch if we wanted," Trainum said. "I took the liberty of telling him we wanted."

Wallace nodded his approval. "When do you think you'll get started?" McCann looked at the clock behind the counter. "Assuming we get him in the next ten minutes and we get there in twenty, thirty minutes, maybe one o'clock?" Wallace turned to Trainum.

"I got something I need to take care of before I go, so don't wait for me. I'll catch up with you and Brad when I get there."

"Sounds good, but Brad won't be there. He's on vacation."

"Vacation? When did that happen?"

"This morning. Skiing. In Colorado. With the girlfriend."

"He couldn't get out of it?"

"If it was up to him, no problem, but it wasn't, so he's in the air as we speak. I told him we'd keep him up to speed."

Cooper came out of the cell block, his hands manacled behind him, a uniform holding each arm. McCann and Fulginiti took their places and Trainum followed them to the elevator. Wallace watched the doors close before he grabbed the next one up. Back behind his desk, he riffled through his Rolodex and dialed the number.

"Hello?" Robbie said.

"Robbie, this is Detective Wallace, with the Washington Metro –"

"I know who you are," she said a little more brightly. "I was hopin' I might hear from you one of these days."

"I'm calling because I think I might have some good news for you."

"That mean you're coming over?"

"It means we arrested Carl Cooper last night."

"Oh, my good God sweet Jesus Christ almighty! For what?"

"For shooting a cop in PG a few years ago."

"Huh. How 'bout for Starbucks?"

"That's next."

"Well, praise the Lord," Robbie said. "I never thought I'd see the day."

"I knew you'd want to know," Wallace said.

"So what happens next?"

"He's on his way out to PG now for more questioning. As soon as we hang up, I'm going out there myself."

"Is that right?" Robbie asked. "So where you gonna be, Upper Marlboro?"

"Yeah."

"Well, that ain't too far from here. Why don't you stop by when you're done? Might be a good time for that piece of cake we talked about, you know?"

Wallace thought he knew what she was talking about, but just to make sure they were on the same piece, he said "I don't want to keep Albertha up." Robbie laughed.

"That's real considerate of you, Detective, but that's somethin' you don't have to worry about. She's been laid up out at the hospital in Cheverly since she fell down and fractured her hip last week. They say she'll be okay but they got to keep her and rehab her a little bit so it'll just be the two of us whenever you get here, okay?"

"Okay."

"Okay, then, I will see you later – oh, and why don't you stop and pick up somethin' for us to wash down all that cake with too?" He fumbled for an answer until he heard the dial tone.

29

Wallace's head reeled with so many good questions and bad answers. *Was she really talking about cake?* He didn't know. *And if it was, what was he going to wash it down with? Captain Morgan and Jack Daniels were off the menu now, so what? Coke? Dr. Pepper? That shit didn't go with any kind of cake.* He took his time clearing his thoughts in the men's room before he dialed the PG police station and asked to talk to Trainum. By the time he got on the line, his head was back on Cooper.

"So what's the story?" he asked.

"Nothing yet, so you can take your time getting over here. They just started processing him."

"He say anything on the way over?"

"Don't know. I took my own car."

"All right," Wallace said, "I'm leaving now." A half hour later, he was led back to an interview room where Trainum and McCann were sitting across from each other at a long laminated wood table, an empty writing pad and a full cup of coffee in front of each of them.

"Join the party," McCann said and gestured to a coffee pot sitting on a counter at the far end of the room. Wallace waved him off and took the seat next to Trainum.

"So where is he?"

"Takin' a dump," McCann said. "Fulginiti's running off a statement he just made about shooting Howard. We're all going to look it over before we talk to him."

"He talk on the way out here?"

"Oh, yeah," McCann said. "Couldn't shut him up. He's not exactly a big fan of you guys, but you probably know that. Wanted to know if he could take a polygraph on Starbucks out here, but I told him that wasn't our case, so no. Then Fulginiti took him over to do a polygraph on the Howard thing and that's the last I know." On cue, Fulginiti came in and handed each of them a stapled sheaf of papers.

"Good to see you, Detective," he said. "They're going to keep him back in the holding cell till we call for him, so we can take our time reading this."

"How'd he come to write it?" Wallace asked.

"I was going to give him a polygraph on Officer Howard that Sergeant McCann said he asked to take."

Trainum turned to Wallace. "He likes them."

"But," McCann said, "all he wanted to talk about was Starbucks. Then he started getting agitated about that – and you guys, again, of course – and then he started rambling about the Howard thing, so I just told him 'Hey, you know what? Put it down in writing so we all can read it and we'll take it from there, okay?', which he did. I haven't read it yet either, so let's all take a look, then we can talk about it."

Wallace read Cooper's very neat printing in all caps.

"I, Carl Cooper, was taking a short-cut home when I noticed a parked car up in the woods. I approached it and saw two people having sex in the car. Then I noticed the man's wallet so I decided to try and steal it unnoticed but was seen by the woman who started to scream. The man started yelling 'Take the money. Don't hurt us.' That's when I pulled out my gun. The man started going crazy, so I repeatedly said 'I'm not going to hurt you, I just want the money' over and over. I continued to say this in an effort to calm them down. The woman was very calm but I was afraid that the man would go into convulsions or something. He was sooooo panicky that I was getting ready to just leave. He finally agreed to give it to me and reached down for his pants which were down around his ankles.

'As I leaned into the car across the lady who was now sitting up on the passenger side, he punched me dead in the mouth. I was caught off guard and off balance. He was somehow able to turn the gun around while it was still in my hand. By overpowering me, he was able to take a shot at me. The bullet missed me, but shattering glass cut the back of my head. I was somehow able to get the gun back from him, because he was still sitting down and I stood up scared, amazed, and just plain shocked like hell. I let the lady get out of the car and that's when the man jumped across the seats and starts beating the shit out of me and tries to take the gun again. I tried to get up and run because this guy is twice my size and he's all over me again, trying to take the gun a third time. That's when it goes off again and he falls to the ground yelling 'You shot me! You shot me!' Then he got up looking at himself to see where he got shot and that right there told me he was alright so I took off running into the woods heading for my house.

"I wanted to call 911 for him but before I could make it home, there were police cars zooming up and down my street. The very next day is when I found out that the man in the park was a police officer. I was glad to know he was okay and was able to call for a backup because I was worried he might have lost a lot of blood. I'm sorry for what happened and I never meant to hurt anyone. I want to take responsibility and show good faith. I am sorry."

When they had all finished, Trainum was the first to talk. "So this happened, what, three years ago? He's either got a really good memory or he's told himself a really good story so many times he really believes it now."

210

"Any suggestions about what I ought to follow up on?" Fulginiti asked.

"Try to pin him down on the specifics," Wallace said, "dates, times, what else was going on in the park, what kind of gun he used so maybe we can track it down. Just see if you can trip him up on anything."

Fulginiti nodded and turned to McCann, who tipped a thumb to Wallace. "What he said."

Wallace pointed to the long mirror behind Fulginiti. "That an observation room?"

"Yeah," McCann said. "When we're ready for him, the three of us'll go back there, let Rich keep talking to him." He looked at Fulginiti. "Check back with us before you let him go, just in case someone got a good idea." Fulginiti stood up.

"I'll give you a minute to get yourselves together back there, then go get him."

In two minutes, Cooper came back into the room, followed by Fulginiti, who sat at the short end of the table and pointed to Cooper to take the seat nearest him on the long side, facing the mirrored wall. Fulginiti flipped open his pad and clicked his ballpoint black pen.

"Okay, Carl, I've read your statement and I want to ask you a few questions, all right?"

"All right."

"Before I start, do you wish to have an attorney present?"

Carl shook his head. "Nope, I told you exactly how it went down. I'm not hiding anything."

211

"When we're done here," Fulginiti said, writing in his pad, "I want you to go over everything I write down about what you said. If I got it right, I want you to put your initials after it. If I didn't, I want you to correct it to whatever you think you said, then initial it, all right?"

"All right."

"Okay, so first, do you recall the date this incident happened?"

"No."

"What time of day was it?"

"Late, like sometime between like midnight and four in the morning."

"Were you on foot or had you been in a car?"

"I had been in a car, but I parked it and was walking home."

"Were you with anybody?"

"In the car, yeah, but, you know, I'd rather not say who. The person dropped me off and I was walking home. That person had nothin' to with this."

Fulginiti finished writing that down. "How many cars were in the park?"

"Just the one. It was parked in the cut over by the racquetball wall. I've been over that way for target practice and I was surprised when I saw it."

"When you looked into the car, where was the wallet?"

"They were laying in the front passenger seat and his pants were down, okay?, so it looked like it was in his back pocket."

"Did you reach for the wallet?"

"I didn't have a chance to. The lady started screamin' when she saw me and he rolled offa her into the driver's seat and started goin' crazy. He kept sayin' 'I'll give you the money! Don't hurt us! Just take the money!'" So I took out the gun and said 'Okay, give me the money.'"

"What gun did you have?"

"My wife's gun, a nine-millimeter."

"Was this the same gun the D.C. police obtained from your wife's grandfather's home?"

"Yes."

"How much money did you get from the man?" Cooper snorted a laugh. "Shit, I didn't get any fucking money."

"When the gun fired the first time, what window broke?"

"I don't know. I wasn't thinkin' 'bout that. I just stood the hell up and let the lady out'a the car."

"Why didn't you run away?"

"I don't know. I should've, but I was scared and I was checking to see if the lady was all right. When I let her out the passenger door, the guy like lunges across the seat and grabs me around the waist. I went down to the ground and the guy's beating me on the face! Then he goes for the gun and we're fighting for it, then we get up, we're still fighting for it, and it goes off! He falls to the ground and starts yellin' 'You shot me! You shot me!'"

Fulginiti got it all down before he asked "Did the man ever tell you he was a police officer?"

"No, not once."

213

"Did you ever see the man or the lady with a weapon?"

"Other than mine? No."

"Did you ever give him or her any commands to do anything?"

"No."

"Did you ever tell them you needed the money because you had a drug or alcohol problem?"

"No, because I don't."

"How did you get home?"

"I ran, man."

"Who did you ever tell about the incident?"

"I told a bunch'a people, actually. Leon Ellis, and a lady named Joannie Lee somethin' who's Teddy Thigpen's common law wife, and I told some people up on 14th Street Northwest too. I was scared, man, so I was talking to a lot of people about what should I do? Should I turn myself in? That kinda stuff."

Fulginiti finished writing that down, then flipped back to the first page and read his notes before he spoke again. "Okay, let's go back to the incident for a minute. How many shots were fired?"

"Two."

"Did your wife know you had her gun?"

"Uh-uh, no. I snuck it out the trunk of her car."

Fulginiti looked through the rest of his notes, then up at Carl. "Do you have anything you'd like to add to this statement?"

"No."

"Were you advised of your rights?" "Yes."

"Did you understand your rights?" "Yes."

"Have you been treated fairly by me?" "Yes."

Fulginiti picked up his pad and got to his feet. "Give me a minute to check with Sergeant McCann and the MPD guys to see if they've got anything else before we break and get you some dinner. Sit tight." He left and went into the observation room.

"So, anything I missed?"

"Sounded good to me," Wallace said. Trainum gave him a thumbs up.

"I'd still like him to take that polygraph," McCann said, "but it can wait. Let's get him settled in and fed, then take it from there."

Wallace got to his feet and stretched. "I think we'll head on out then," he said and handed McCann his card. "My home and office numbers are on there. Give me a call when you're ready to go again." Trainum gave him his card too and they headed for the parking lot. Wallace walked him to his car.

"You want to grab some dinner?" Trainum asked.

"Not tonight, man. I'm beat. You hear from them first, let me know, and I'll do the same. If neither one of us hears anything by morning, I'll call 'em bright and early and we'll see what's up."

"Sounds like a plan. At least he's talking. That's something. See you tomorrow or whenever." They shook hands and Wallace headed for his car. He watched Trainum pull out, then picked up his police phone and called Robbie. She answered before the first ring finished.

"Hello?"

215

"Hi, Robbie. It's Detective Wallace."

"Your card says you're Thomas Wallace. Or is Detective really your first name?"

He laughed. "No, it's Thomas. You can call me Tom."

"Okay, Tom. So did that motherfucker confess yet?"

"No, we're just getting started, and the PG guys are more interested in him shooting that cop I told you about, so we haven't even gotten to Starbucks yet."

"Well, whatever's going to put that fucker away or, better yet, fry him, is good enough for me. So what're you doing now?"

"Talking to you. What're you doing now?"

"Well, now I guess I'm waitin' on you to come on over. Maybe bring us a little dinner?"

"I can do that. What would you like?"

"I'm okay with anything. There's a bunch of joints out Bladensburg. Wings would be good, or burgers, I don't really care. And, hey, why don't you make another little pit stop too, at one of them liquor stores out there? I know there's one about a mile or two past the KFC headin' into the city."

"I'll see what I can find," Wallace said, hoping he'd think of a good reason he came up empty by the time he saw her.

"All right then. I will see you soon."

He picked up a bucket of wings and fries at the KFC drive-thru, then pulled to a stop at Bladensburg Road. Right would take him to Robbie's, left to the liquor store. He played out how he'd tell her he never saw one, but it seemed lame even to him, and might kill the

216

vibe too, so he made the left. When he hadn't seen the store within a mile, he started conjuring up a whole new line of excuses, but before he got comfortable with any of them, he saw the sign for Syd's Liquor just ahead on the right. He stopped thinking and pulled into the lot.

A geyser of memories shot through his brain the split second he heard the bell tinkle over the door when he pushed through. He'd never been to Syd's, but the hundreds, maybe thousands of trips he'd made to liquor stores, ABC stores, wine stores, and anywhere else that sold booze rushed to the surface like they were just lying in wait for this moment to come. He walked through the place like an alcoholic homing pigeon finally come home to roost.

"Can I help you, sir?" a friendly young black clerk asked from behind the register.

"No thanks," Wallace said. "I'm just going to need a little time to decide."

"Got you," the clerk said. "And just so you know, we got some good stuff on sale right around the corner, on the other side of the fridge. Some great bargains over there."

"I will check them out. Thank you."

Wallace strolled around the corner as casually as he could and checked out the SALE! shelves. It was all swill, so he ambled over to the Rum section and saw his old friend Captain Morgan leering back at him in a black and yellow buccaneer outfit. *She'd like that,* he convinced himself, and pulled it off the shelf, then headed back to the counter, but stopped when he felt a cold sweat coat his forehead. He reached out for the fridge to steady himself and closed his eyes. When he opened them, he was looking at a six pack of Bud Light. *It's a sign,* he told himself. He could give her the Captain and suck down a Bud that didn't have enough alcohol to make an ant drunk and everyone would be happy. He grabbed the two-liter Coke sitting next to it and headed to the register. He didn't know if it was karma, kismet, or kidding himself, but whatever it was put a bounce back in his step.

Twenty minutes later, the Syd's bag hanging heavy from the hand cradling the bucket, he knocked on the door to 1-C. Robbie pulled it open, wearing a black V-neck sweater over jeans and smelling great.

"Dinner has arrived," he said with a smile, and let her take the bag before she closed the door and led him to the kitchen. She put the bag on the table, took the bucket from him and set it down, then held his face in both her soft hands and stared into his eyes. "And even better, you have too." She planted a kiss on him that was more passionate than any kiss he could remember and he returned it with a passion he couldn't remember either, until their lips separated what seemed like minutes later, their arms still encircling each other.

"Wow," he said. "You treat all your delivery boys like that?" She smiled and pressed her cheek to his chest, then let a hand slip down to cradle the hardening bulge behind his fly. He felt a smile lift her cheek. "Seems you brought somethin' else to the party too," she said and rubbed him lightly until he had to lift her hand and lay it against his neck.

"You keep doin' that and it's goin' to be over before it starts." She laughed and pushed herself away from him, then backed away until she was leaning against the stove. "This better?" she said.

"No, but it's safer," he said. She nodded to the bag.

"So what'd you bring us?"

He reached into the bag, brought out the Captain, and held him out to her. Her eyes lit up.

"Now, how did you know I love that shit?" He stifled *'Cause I remember how much I loved it* and said "Who doesn't? You got something to pour this in or you want to just take it straight from the bottle? I brought some Coke too if that helps you make up your mind."

She turned around, pulled a tall glass from the cupboard behind her, and held it out to him with a broad smile. He carried the bottle over to her, remembering the heft of a full bottle that never lasted long in his hands, and the sweet heavy taste going down. "Say when," he said. She let it fill more than halfway up before she said "When. For now."

He reached behind her for another glass, walked back to the table, and pulled the six-pack out of the bag. She nearly choked on the rum. "That's it?" she finally got out. "That's how you party? Bud Light?"

He yanked a can out of the plastic and stared at it, then lifted his eyes to hers, still looking at him in disbelief.

"There's something I need to tell you, Robbie. I used to drink a lot of this – and what you've got in your hand and pretty much anything else that wound up in my hand – but I haven't swallowed a drop of any of it for ten years. Plain and simple, I'm an alcoholic."

She stared at him, then shook her head. "Ten years? No, baby, that shit is out of your system by now, and whatever made you drink it is long gone too. Am I right?"

Whatever made you drink it covered a lot of ground, but his brain wheeled through all of it in a split second. His father, dead and gone long ago. All the partying with the big hero running back after every high school and college game. Shooting and killing Marcus. Getting busted from Detective for going to Memphis without

219

authorization to try and find whoever killed Brenda Queen on the Howard stage.

"Yeah," he said, "and no," his eyes fixed on the Bud Light in his hand.

"Well, shit, baby, c'm'on!" she said, throwing her arms wide open and looking at him like he couldn't possibly be serious. "We got something to celebrate tonight, I mean we got a *lot* to celebrate. If not now, when then, huh? Answer me that!"

Wallace lifted his eyes to her and took in that gorgeous smile, then put the can back on the table.

"You got another glass?" he asked.

30

Wallace woke up with a start and turned to see that the sound at the foot of the bed was coming from a small color TV sitting on what looked like a fold-out serving tray against the wall. He squinted his eyes to see two cops picking their way through some clutter in a basement somewhere. One of them looked like the fat cop who used to be on Hill Street and the other one used to be a kid actor. The names didn't come to him, but *NYPD Blue* did. When he fell back on the pillow, he tried to remember where he was and why he was there.

The sound of light snoring to his left solved both mysteries. He turned his head to see Robbie, still smelling so nice, but with a hint of alcohol that wasn't there before. A cascade of images and sensations swept through his brain. A swig from a glass. The taste of rum down his gullet and on her lips. Her leading him back here, where the images got sharper and sweeter. He remembered every detail of her unbuckling his belt. pulling down his zipper, yanking down his pants, smiling that smile, mounting him, and feeling himself explode into her soft sweet warmth.

He was happy he remembered it not just because the memory was making him hard again, but because he could remember it at all. He twisted his head to the nightstand next to him and saw the Captain Morgan bottle. He reached over and lifted it. Empty, but he dropped his eyes to the floor to see if there were any more down there. When he saw just one, he fell back onto the pillow, feeling almost as satisfied as he did when they came together. But when was that? His pulse jumped when his watch told him it was 10:49. *His phone was in the car and Trainum had no idea where he was. What if he was trying to reach him?*

He grabbed his boxers off the floor, tiptoed out into the hallway, pulled the door almost shut so the sound of the latch wouldn't wake her, and slid them on. He found the light switch in the kitchen and saw a Princess phone on the wall behind the sink. He dialed Trainum's home number and drummed his fingers on the counter until he heard a groggy "Yeah?" come over the line.

"Hey, Jim, it's me. I'm sorry to call so late but I got caught up in some stuff and didn't know if you were tryin' to get me."

"No, I wasn't, though I did get a call from them, sometime. What time is it?"

"A little before eleven. What'd they want?" he said.

"They said they were calling me because they couldn't get a hold of you. They wanted to let us know what they were going to talk to him about later, just in case we wanted to be there, but when none of it had anything to do with Starbucks, I told them to go ahead, we'd catch up tomorrow. I wasn't going to chase you down about any of that, but now you know."

"What are they going to talk to him about?"

"Hold on a minute. I wrote it down. Okay, it was really just the small shit he did out there and in Pennsylvania, nothing in D.C. at all – holdin' up the pizza place, the massage parlor, some other small –"

"Hey," Wallace heard behind him, "who're you talking to?" He put his hand over the phone and turned back to see Robbie naked in the doorway of the bedroom, backlit by the TV.

"I'm just checking in to see what's up with Cooper. I'll be right there." She disappeared back into the bedroom.

"Sorry about that," Wallace said into the phone.

"Who were you talking –" Trainum started to ask, but stopped. "You know what, never mind. Call me back when you're ready to

222

go in the morning." The click spared Wallace from trying to b.s. him, something he knew he'd never get away with anyhow. He turned off the light and headed back down the hallway. When he came through the door, he saw Robbie, sidelit now, sitting on the side of the bed, still naked.

"What was that about?" she asked.

"I called Trainum to see if the PG guys'd started talking to him about Starbucks."

"And did they?"

"No, but they said they'll be getting to it tomorrow, bright and early."

"Hallelujah!" she cried out and raised her hands to the Lord, then looked back down to see something else was rising too. "Aw, bring that bad boy over here," she said and he did as he was told. He watched her slide his shorts down to the floor, stepped out of them, then indulged himself in watching her stroke him to the full and upright position before he closed his eyes and felt her tongue caress him. He realized in less than a second that only one thing could make the moment better, and backed away from her. He held a finger up to her puzzled face, and stepped over to the TV to slap off the sound of – *Sipowicz*, that was it! – bitching somebody out, then stepped back and immersed himself in the soft sweetness he hadn't felt for a very long time.

31

A little after 8 the next morning, he headed down the hallway, freshly showered, dressed for the day, and pleasantly surprised to feel no lingering effects from the beers. Robbie was sitting at the table facing away from him, head down, a newspaper spread out in front of her, a cup of coffee next to it. He tiptoed to her and kissed her neck.

"Well good morning," she said. "Have a good night's sleep?"

"Excellent," he said. "Thank you for that too." He poured himself a black coffee, took the seat across from her, and watched her run her finger down a column of want ads.

"What're you looking for?"

"Pretty much anything. I need to start workin' again, like yesterday."

"You could save a little money by dropping your subscription to the Post, you know." She rolled her eyes.

"This ain't mine. I fished it out of the trash room. It's, let's see, Monday's. What day is today?"

"Wednesday. I think. What was your last job?"

"Waitin' tables at this pizza place on Bladensburg. But I'll take anything anywhere. I ain't picky. Obviously." She stopped her finger scan abruptly. "Okay, here's one. 'Warehouse stock person'. I could do that. 'Fortune 500 company seeks person to log in, identify, and locate items in Laurel warehouse'. Aw shit!"

"What's wrong with that?"

"'High school diploma or GED required', that's what's wrong with it. Goddamn it!" She knocked the paper onto the floor, then grabbed her coffee cup with trembling hands and took a long swallow before she smacked it down on the table and stared at him, tears dousing the flames in her eyes. "I ain't got either one, if you ain't figured that out already."

He reached over to hold her hands in his. "It shouldn't take too long to get a GED. I can help you make ends meet in the meantime and I'll help you study too. We can do this."

"No. We can't."

"Why?"

"You don't want to know."

"Try me," Wallace said. She lifted her hands to wipe her eyes, then looked hard into his.

"Okay, fine, I'm gonna tell you, but I don't want no pity or boo-hooin', all right?"

"All right. I promise." She blew out a long breath

"I ever tell you anything about my mother?"

"Just that she named you for Roberta Flack."

"First of many disappointments, both ways – though actually mine came first, before I was even born. I was a heroin baby. You know what that is?"

"Oh, Robbie, I'm so sorry," he said. She held up a hand.

"I told you. No pity, okay?" He held up both hands. "Later on, years later, after it was clear even to me that I was fucked up, she told me she knew she was on that shit when I was inside her, but she wanted a baby so bad, she thought Jesus would work a miracle, make everything come out all right." She shook her head and

225

coughed up a bitter laugh. "That's the first reason I stopped going to church. I knew I was different from as early as I can remember anyone talkin' about me. 'It ain't the poor child's fault, she just, you know, slow, that's all'. Shit, pity's all I heard growin' up. That's why I don't want to hear it ever again."

"Did you – I don't even know the right way to say this – did you get over it the older you got?"

"It ain't like booze, Tom, you don't piss it outta your system. It's there *forever*, man. Some shit's worse than the rest. I got" – she made quote marks with her fingers – "'learning disabilities', which means I have serious trouble payin' attention and figuring out how to do simple shit most people do, like addin' up a bill when somebody buys a pizza, okay? That's why I got fired. Cost 'em too much money, cost *me* too much money! You know people will only deal with that kind of shit for so long before they think 'You gotta go, child, be someone else's problem'. That's one thing I have learned."

"Robbie, you seem as normal to me as anyone else I know, and that's the truth." She cocked her head and winced.

"I maybe get along okay most days if I take my meds and keep it mellow, don't get too high or too low, you know, but if I do, like, get agitated over something, that's when I get mad. And worked up. And stubborn. 'Obsessed,' they call it."

"I haven't seen that," Wallace said. *Except maybe about wanting Cooper to fry,* he thought, *but you don't have to be obsessed to want that.*

"You'll know it when you do, I promise you that." She sighed and took a long sip of her coffee. "So that's my story. Still want to stick around?"

"I do, but let's get back to the GED. You really sure you don't want to try one more time? I think I can help." She shook her head from the time he asked till the time he stopped.

"No sir, no way. Learnin', studyin', school, they ain't my thing."

"How far did you get?"

"Eleventh grade. They should 'a thrown me out way before then, but it just was easier for 'em to carry me from grade to grade, you know, until I started – what do they call it? – acting out. Then I went to juvie and that solved everyone's problems, except, you know, *mine.*"

"How'd that happen?"

"The shit I did with Vontae, to tell you the truth. We met in the eighth grade and he wasn't like anyone else I knew – except me. He was just, you know, kind of buggy and spur of the moment, not a lot of thinkin' or carin' how a thing might turn out." Wallace remembered Cooper talking about Kincaid the same way, doing his 'jump-out spontaneous shit'.

"We bought some weed, sold some weed, stole some penny ante shit. We weren't even old enough to drive, so how much stuff could we take? But after a while, the state said we needed to be reformed, so they sent him to Cheltenham and I went to Waxter over in Laurel so I didn't see him for a while, but when we turned 18, they let us both go about the same time and we started up again, only a little less boy and girl and a lot more man and woman, all right?" She started to mist up again and looked out the small window over the sink. "And that's when he started running with that runt Cooper, and – well, you know the rest. I ain't going to go over that again, ain't going to *obsess* over it, okay?"

"How'd you support yourself when you got out?"

227

"Are you asking me if I was helping them hold up 7-11s and pizza joints and shit? No, I wasn't. I was trying to play it straight, keep my ass out of jail and get that motherfucking GED. Didn't make it through the first time, and even tried it a second time – but that was the last time, so don't even start with me on that again. I've lived off chicken shit jobs, welfare, and – yes – some of the penny ante shit Vontae brought back from the jobs he did with that punk ass, but none of it amounted to crap, and here I am again, looking for shit jobs in the want ads."

She looked down at the papers strewn across the floor, then walked across them to where a fifth of something dark sat on the counter and pulled a juice glass out of the cabinet before she turned back to Wallace. "You want somethin' serious to drink?" He waved her off.

"No, I got to get to back to DC, then hopefully back to PG to watch them start on Cooper."

She poured herself half a glass and sat back down. "All right, so now you know all about me. Tell me about you."

He gave her the headlines. Football in high school got him into college, then he came to D.C. for the money. "It took me some time to get this job, longer than it should've for a lot of reasons, but it was all worth it. I think."

"I want to hear about the reasons."

He gave her a quick run through the back story. Accidentally killing Marcus, the booze, the demotions. When he was through, she said "I guess we've both had our share, huh," and lifted her glass to him. "Glad one of us has landed on their feet."

He finished the last of his coffee, put the cup in the sink, and came back to give her a soft kiss on the lips that turned harder, longer, and wetter before he gently pushed himself away.

228

"I gotta go," he said.

He called PG from the car and asked for McCann, but Fulginiti picked up.

"Good morning," Wallace said. "I was just checking to see what the plan was for today."

"Hard to tell yet. McCann's not here yet and Cooper's still sleeping."

"How long you going to let him sleep?"

"No point in getting him up if McCann and you guys aren't here, plus the State's Attorney's Office always wants us to treat our guests with kid gloves, so their lawyers can't say we coerced them, blah, blah, blah. The bottom line is I'm not going to know anything for a while, so feel free to cool your jets until I do. Soon as I know, you'll know, okay?"

"Okay," Wallace said. "I'll talk to you later."

When he got to his office, he saw his answering machine light blinking and hit Play. A mechanical voice said "Nine-oh-nine. A.M." before a beep. The next voice he heard was Katz'.

"Good morning, Detective Wallace. I just looked at the Metro section in this morning's Post and read right there on the very first page that one Carl Cooper had been – I'm quoting here – "questioned by authorities" – unquote -- last night. It doesn't say exactly who questioned him or where, but none of that really matters because I distinctly remember telling her honor yesterday that he wouldn't consent to any further interviews with anyone without his lawyer present. Maybe I wasn't clear enough, or maybe, you know, someone – like maybe the someone I've known for about thirty years who got me into this thing – might've let me know before I

229

read about it in the funny papers. Please give me a call back, sooner than later. Thank you oh so much."

Wallace waited for the sarcasm to finish dripping off the call before he hit Delete and called him back. Katz picked up right away.

"I gather you got my message."

"I did and, you're right, I should'a given you a head's up, but my time hasn't been my own since the second I left that hearing. I apologize and I'll try to do better next time, I promise."

"Apology accepted and completely understood, but that doesn't answer the question. Did someone talk to him without his lawyer present?"

"The PG police did, and I watched them do it." A long pause passed before Katz said "And what? You just sat there and let 'em do it?" Wallace was starting to resent the tone.

"Jake, they asked him 'Do you want a lawyer?' before and after every session, and he said 'No', every time. I watched that part too."

"'Every session'? How many are we talking about?"

"I'm not getting into that. He testified voluntarily, he was Mirandaed up the ass, he was well fed, he got a lot of sleep. The guy was not coerced or abused by any stretch of the imagination, and I'd say the same thing under oath in a court of law to you, a judge, or anyone else who asks. End of statement. Period."

"I guarantee you you'll have that opportunity."

"Assuming you're a member of the Maryland Bar, right?" *Two can play this horseshit game*, Wallace thought.

"I'm not, but it turns out I don't have to be. Someone who is can move the court to waive me in to help him out, so as soon as I hang up with you, I'm going to go through my Rolodex and find me a Maryland lawyer who'll do just that."

"Okay, then. Good luck with all that."

"One more thing. If I haven't overstayed my welcome, can you tell me the next time they're going to talk to him or are they already doing it?" Wallace sighed.

"They're waiting for him to wake up and, even then, they're going to wait for me to get out there before they start. They're doing it by the book, Jake, I promise you. I wouldn't let them do it any other way. You know that."

"I do, but I also know you have absolutely no say over how they do things in PG. Thanks for getting back to me, Tom, but I gotta go make a few calls."

Wallace clicked off. When he saw the light was still blinking, he hit it and heard Trainum's message from 9:28.

"Hey Tom, I just got off the phone with Fulginiti. He said the only thing that happened since he talked to you was McCann had come in. Cooper's still sleeping. I'm here so give me a buzz when you get in." Wallace buzzed him.

"It's me," he said. "They still letting him sleep?

"That's what he told me."

"Which means they still don't know when they'll start."

"Correct. He said that even if he got up now, by the time he gets himself cleaned up and they get done feeding him, it's probably going to be sometime after noon before he even sits down to write his statement."

"About Starbucks, right? That's still first on the agenda?"

231

"That's what he said. You ready to talk to the Chief? He wants to hear everything about everything. I told him we'd be up soon as you got in."

Once they finished filling him in on every detail, Ramsey looked at his watch, which made Wallace look at his. 10:01.

"When was the last time either of you talked to them?"

"About ten minutes before we came up here," Trainum said. Ramsey nodded and pointed at the phone.

"That's long enough. Give 'em a call." Wallace called and McCann answered.

"Hey, Sergeant. Wallace here. We filled Chief Ramsey in on what happened with Cooper last night. Anything happen since I talked to Sergeant Fulginiti maybe 45 minutes ago?" He put the phone on speaker.

"He's up and in the shower now."

"This is Chief Ramsey, Sergeant. So what's on tap next?"

"Like we told your guys, we're gonna start in with him on Starbucks today. Once he's eaten and ready to go, we'll ask him to write out a statement like he did yesterday about the thing with Officer Howard, then we'll read it over and start asking him questions about it. My guess is that's still going to be 12-12:30, so don't feel any need to come over right away."

"He talk about anything yet today?" Ramsey asked.

McCann snorted. "Well, he threw a new name into the mix when we were taking him to the crapper."

"What'd he say?"

"Said he squared himself with God last night and he's going to come clean about Starbucks."

"So he's going to confess?" Wallace asked.

"Shit, no. He said it was all – hold on, let me get the name right – Alton Wesley's doing."

They looked at each other curiously before Trainum said what they were all thinking.

"Who the fuck is Alton Wesley?"

32

When Trainum said he'd run Wesley through the databases, Wallace found himself back in his office with time to kill for the first time in a long time. His mind immediately drifted to Robbie. In a minute, he was looking at the records under her name on the criminal justice information database that D.C. shared with Maryland. Everything she'd told him showed up, but so did a few other things. Charged with accessory to robbery once. Charged with possession of cocaine twice. Pleaded guilty to the second one and did 90 days in '96 at the Maryland Correction Institution for Women in Jessup. He read the psychological report in her intake folder from that August.

> With regard to Inmate Rawlins' claim that she was pre-
> natally addicted to heroin, my examination of her and a
> review of the literature indicates behaviors consistent with
> that condition. As indicated in the appended test results, she
> manifests a variety of cerebral impairments, including
> language delays, significant motor and memory skills delay,
> impulsivity, and hyperactivity. She also exhibits behavioral
> and cognitive problems, i.e., poor perceptual, memory, and
> verbal skills; hyperactivity; unrealistic expectations; poor
> self-esteem and sense of worth; and a heightened sensitivity
> to drug triggers.

He printed it out, slid it into his desk drawer, and took off for PG, trying hard all the way out not to think about how many of those behaviors he had to look forward to. By the time he stopped not thinking about them, he was pulling into the PD parking lot. He parked next to a car with MPD plates and remembered Trainum's puzzled look when he told him they should take two cars. His hopes that he'd forgotten about it by now were rewarded by the look on his face in the lobby that told him that whatever he'd moved on to was seriously pissing him off.

"Are they talking to him yet?" Wallace asked.

"Oh, they're talking to him, all right, but not about Starbucks. They're still giving him the third degree about the penny ante shit he told us and Garrett about. I listened to it for about twenty minutes, then just gave up and left."

"They know you're out here?"

"Not unless they heard me slam the door on my way out, which is a distinct possibility."

"So exactly what penny ante shit're they talking about?" Trainum opened the folder in his hand.

"They were still going over the pizza thing from last night, the place that him, Man, and Joannie Lee held up on New Hampshire Avenue? Then they moved to the bank job he told us he didn't do, by the way, and when they started on the massage parlor up in fucking Pennsylvania, I bailed, man." He slapped the folder shut. "Couldn't take it anymore. Sorry."

"How long ago was that?"

"Ten, fifteen minutes? I don't real –"

Wallace saw a door open behind Trainum and they both turned to watch Fulginiti and McCann head their way. Fulginiti gestured to Trainum.

"I thought you were behind the window."

"I was until I realized Starbucks still wasn't on the agenda for some reason."

"Hey, shit happens, okay? When he started writing his statement this morning, he says 'Is it okay if I get some of that other shit off my chest first?' What was I supposed to say? 'No, please don't

235

confess to crimes you did right here'? It's next, I promise you. He's writing it up now."

"Did he say anything about it?" Wallace asked.

"Yeah," McCann said, "he said he hopes we believe him because he's going to tell us the God's honest truth about how it all went down." Trainum hacked a laugh.

"Then we know it's a lie already."

"I got to hit the head," McCann said. "I'm with you," Fulginiti said. "Make yourselves comfortable. Hopefully, he's not gonna write a novel."

Wallace pulled the observation room door open and followed Trainum in. They mixed their coffees and sat down to watch Cooper write. Every time he stopped to read what he wrote, Trainum supplied the inner dialogue.

"Hmm. Let me see. Did I spread the bullshit too thick there?"

"Who can I say really pulled the trigger?"

"Remorse, Carl! Remember, show some remorse here!"

Wallace's attention drifted to what looked like two computers with monitors sitting on them on a desk in the far corner of the room. "What's all that?" he asked Trainum, who took a quick glance up before resuming his stare at Cooper. "I got no idea," he said.

They watched Cooper fill three pages and part of a fourth before he did a quick scan of each of them and threw the pad on the table. "I'll go get 'em," Trainum said. Two minutes later, he was back and Wallace watched Fulginiti step into the interview room.

"You done?" he asked. Carl reached for the pad and handed it to him without a word.

236

"All right," Fulginiti said, "give me a couple minutes to look it over, then we'll go over it. You need anything? Want anything?" Cooper held up an empty water bottle.

"Another one of these'd be good. And I probably oughta go to the shitter before you all come back too."

"I'll get someone to take you," Fulginiti said and went out of the interview room and into the observation room a few seconds later, trailed by McCann. He made four copies of Cooper's statement, handed them out, and headed out the door to get him an escort to the men's room. Wallace pulled out his pen and started to read.

"Alton Wesley was my cellmate when I was locked up. He came to me with a proposition of robbing the Starbucks in Georgetown because his friend worked there. He came to me because he knew I knew about robberies, I was excellent behind the wheel of a car, and I could keep my mouth closed.

"The only reason I was interested was because it was an inside job and he told me, by it being a weekend, they would have a lot of money in the safe. I told him that I would do it. All I had to do was sit in the getaway car and blow the horn if anybody was coming. There was no need for me to go inside because his friend would unlock the door and let him in. He would play the victim and get the other employees to cooperate. Alton would get the money, jump in the car, and we'd be off. The friend would get his share later. It sounded like a good plan to me. This was about a month before the robbery happened. I talked to Leon Ellis a little about it but after remembering how Alton is and how he didn't know Leon, I decided it was a stupid move and I never brought it up with him again.

"The Sunday morning of the actual robbery, I went to the store just to check it out, not knowing it was actually going to go down that night. Around 7 or 8 p.m., Alton came knocking at my door, telling me it was time. I was already dressed in black so I went with him.

237

He was dressed in dark blue sweat pants, boots, and a plaid shirt/jacket. There was no need for me to bring a gun because this was an inside job. He stated that we had to hurry up and get down there, so I ended up driving my car. That is the reason we parked up the street from Starbucks, because my car is so noticeable. Once we got there, we started shooting the breeze about old times, guessing how much money we'd make, and what would we do with our share. Not once did I see him with a mask and a gun.

"He told me to start looking out, start up the engine, he'll be back in a minute. He got out of the car, walked down to Starbucks, and walked right in. I waited for what seemed like FOREVER. Alton finally comes running out of the store, jumps in my car, and starts yelling 'Go, go, pull off, pull off!' As I speed down Wisconsin to make the left on P, I start asking him 'What happened? Where's the money?' He looked at me with a frowned up face and said he couldn't get it. I dropped him off by Archbishop Carroll High School and went home. Monday, I started hearing about the murders. I never heard any gun shots and I never asked Alton what happened. I was too afraid to ask any questions because he knows where I live with my wife, my toddler son, and my elderly mother, and he and his crowd are known for their violence and drug dealings, so I kept this to myself. I feared for my life, but especially for the lives of my family."

When he finished, Wallace pulled a folder out of his briefcase and flipped through it until he found the statement Cooper gave him, Trainum, and Garrett at the FBI. He glanced at Trainum, who held up a copy of the same statement to shield his face from McCann and mouthed "The guy is a fucking liar."

Wallace made a few notes until he heard Fulginiti come back in and ask if everyone was done. When they all nodded they were, Wallace said "Let me ask you a question first," the memory of his call with

Katz flitting through his head. "Did you ask him if he wanted a lawyer again?"

"I did. Said he's got nothing to hide, he doesn't need one."

"Okay, let's get that in writing." He held up Cooper's FBI statement. "He also said some things to you that don't square with what he told us and the FBI."

"Okay," Fulginiti said, "like?"

"Like he told us 'I didn't do this Starbucks shit.'"

Fulginiti wrote that down. "Okay, what else?"

"He also told you he didn't go there the week of the murders," Trainum said, pointing at and reciting the statement. "'I would never go into a place I was going to rob beforehand, they see your face'. But he told us he went there a lot on Sunday mornings, after he'd drop his mother off at church."

"And," Wallace said, "he just wrote 'The Sunday morning of the actual robbery, I went to the store just to check it out, not knowing it was actually going to go down that night.' Well, which is it? Were you never there, there a lot, or just scoping it out that morning?"

Fulginiti kept writing. "Anything else?" he asked, head still down. Trainum and Wallace looked at each other before Wallace shook his head no and Trainum shook his head in frustration.

"Let's just recap here a second," he said. "We got a couple of tips that he did it from an unknown source and a useless source. We got Leon Ellis, who ain't exactly a choir boy, telling us he did it, but when push came to shove, he couldn't get anything out of him. We got Cooper telling us why his prints could have been there – even though we don't have any of his prints there – or any other evidence of any kind for that matter, so, unless he somehow tells us the truth

239

out of his own mouth, we got nothing. Am I missing something, Detective?" Wallace shook his head no again.

"You're not," he said. "That's the sad truth."

Fulginiti and McCann stood up, but Wallace had one more question. He pointed to the desktop full of equipment in the interview room. "Before you go, what are those?"

"The one on the left's a computer that's hooked up to the thing on the right," Fulginiti said, "which is a Computer Voice Stress Analyzer, or a CVSA. You got one of these in D.C.?"

"No," Wallace said. "I never heard of it. What's it supposed to do?"

"It's basically a polygraph, but there's no wires to the guy you're analyzing, just a microphone that analyzes his responses in some way I do not pretend to understand, but basically every time he talks, the computer on the right shows his voice pattern, gives it a number, and saves it. They told us the thing knows when a guy's lying because there's some kind of involuntary thing your brain does that jacks up something in your voice that we can't hear, but this CVSA thing can. Whoever makes it gave the Department a big discount to be their guinea pig, so the brass is pushing us to use it."

"Does it work?"

Fulginiti threw his hands up and McCann rolled his eyes. "We're not the right guys to ask, okay?" he said. "We just plug it in and watch them wheel it out. As long as it doesn't set me on fire, I could shit care less what it does."

"Are you going to use it on him?" Wallace asked.

"We're using it," Fulginiti said. "It's been on the whole time I've been talking to him."

240

"He agreed to that?"

"He did."

"In writing?"

"No, but I'll get it. He started talking on the car ride over here yesterday about how he wanted to take a lie detector test to prove he didn't do Starbucks. I said we didn't use that anymore, we use the CVSA, and I gave him the ten-second story on what it did, and he said, fine, then I'll do that. 'I just want to clear my name' unquote."

"Is it saying he's telling the truth?"

"There's a whole process we got to go through to answer that, Detective," Fulginiti said, walking to the door, "but right now, it's show time. Anything else? Last call."

"Yeah," Wallace said, "I'd like to hear him talk a little more about his buddy Alton, see if he trips himself up or gives us anything more on that. We never heard of the guy in the however many months, years, we've been on this thing."

"I'd like to hear him say exactly what he told Leon and when," Trainum said, "so we can see if Leon backs him up – or not."

Fulginiti finished writing on his pad. "Got it," he said.

"Before you wind things up out there," Wallace said, "why don't you come back and see if we heard anything else we might want you to follow up on."

"Will do. Enjoy the show." He and McCann left and took their seats across from Cooper.

"When did Mr. Wesley first propose the idea of robbing the Starbucks?" Fulginiti asked. McCann flipped to the last page of Cooper's statement and started writing the Q and A.

"About a month before."

"Tell me how it happened."

"I was at the Michigan Park Rec Center and he came over to me and started saying he had a boy that worked at that Starbucks and he could set it up where we could hit them."

"What does 'hit them' mean?"

"Rob them."

"What else was said?"

"He said his boy said there was a lot of money there on the weekends and that he would let him in and get everyone to comply with his demands and instructions. He said he wanted me there because I steal cars and I'm good behind the wheel."

"Did you agree to participate in the robbery with Alton?"

"Yeah. I said I would drive the car."

"Did you and Alton discuss this any further?"

"No, not until the night of the actual robbery attempt."

"Did you tell anyone else about this plan?"

"Yeah, Leon Ellis."

"When did you tell Leon?"

"The same day Alton and I discussed it."

"What did you tell him?"

"I just told him I was thinking about hitting Starbucks. I never told him about Alton because I didn't think Alton would roll with it if he knew Leon knew about it. I knew it was an easy payday and I didn't want to fuck it up."

"When was the next time Alton talked to you about the robbery?"

"The day of the robbery. He came over my house around seven or eight p.m. and said 'It's time to do this'."

"Why did he choose that time?"

"He picked Sunday because there would be weekend money in there and he picked the time because it would be closed."

"Okay, then what happened?"

"The two of us got in my mother's car and we rode around looking for a car to steal, but he was nervous and anxious, and said we had to go, so I said we can use her car, but I got to park it up the street. Originally, the plan was to be for a stolen car to be double parked out front."

"Describe your mother's car."

"1994 Eagle Summit, blue, four-door sedan, tinted windows, DC tags."

"What happened next?"

"I drove over there and parked about a half a block up Wisconsin on the same side as Starbucks. At first, we talked about being locked up together and how much money we thought we were going to get and what we were going to do with it."

"Did you have a gun?"

"No."

"What type of gun did Alton have?"

"I didn't see a gun, or a mask."

"What happened next?"

"Alton said it was time. He told me to start my car up and look out. He said he'd be back in ten minutes."

"What do you mean, 'look out'?"

"Watch for the police. If I saw them, I'd beep the horn."

"How long was he gone?"

"It seemed like a hour but it could have been anywhere from five minutes to a half hour."

"Did you see him go in the store?"

"Yeah, I didn't think the door was locked."

"Have you ever been in that Starbucks?"

"Yeah, the Sunday morning it happened."

"Is that the only time you've been in that Starbucks?"

"Yes."

"You're lyin' to someone, dickhead," Trainum muttered, then called out "Pick your feet up, guys! The shit's startin' to rise."

"Why did you go inside Starbucks that morning?"

"Oh, wait, I forgot to tell you something. Alton came by my house that Saturday, asking if I was still interested in going in with him on the robbery. I asked him if he was sure there'd be money in there like he was saying. He said 'Yeah, check it our yourself,' so that's what I did. I wanted to make sure they was pulling money like what we was talking about. I didn't want to waste my time."

"Fucker makes it up as he goes along," Trainum said.

"Did you hear any shots after Alton went inside the Starbucks?"

"No."

"Okay, then what happened?"

"Alton came running out and jumped in the car and said 'Go, go, pull off, pull off'."

"What did he tell you happened inside the Starbucks?"

"He said she wouldn't give up the keys. I didn't know anybody got shot until the next day."

"Who is 'she'?"

"He didn't say. He just said 'she'."

"What keys was he talking about?"

"Keys to the safe."

"How'd he know the safe needed keys?" Wallace said.

"Did he ever tell you he shot anybody?"

"No."

"How did you learn that people had been killed during the robbery?"

"I saw it on the news the next day."

"Have you spoken to Alton at all since these homicides?"

"No."

"Okay, where did you and Alton go after the robbery?"

"I dropped him off by Carroll."

245

"Do you know where the gun, or guns, are that Alton used during the robbery?"

"No."

"Does anyone else know about what happened at the Starbucks?"

"No." McCann's beeper buzzed on the table and he looked over to read it.

"Why have you lied about this incident in the past?"

Cooper sat up straight, then looked to the mirrored wall at his left. Trainum waved to him.

"Those 'Bamas back there?" Cooper asked.

"Just answer my question, please, Mr. Cooper."

"Because I was afraid for my family."

"Yeah, right," Trainum said.

"Is what you told us today about Starbucks the truth?"

"Yes."

"Were you treated fairly today?"

"Yes."

"Did you understand your rights?" Fulginiti asked.

"Yes."

"Did you waive your rights?"

"Yes."

"Explain them to me please."

"I have the right to remain silent. Anything I say may be held against me. I have the right to an attorney and to have him present during questioning."

"That's impressive," Trainum said. "Guess he's heard it enough."

"Were you ever denied access to a lawyer?"

"No." *Could've asked that a little better,* Wallace thought, *but good enough,* he hoped.

"Were you denied any requests?"

"No."

"Have you been given food and drink?"

"Yes."

"Have you used the bathroom?"

"Yes."

"Describe your treatment by the Prince Georges County Police."

"I've been treated fairly. I don't have any problems or complaints."

"Do you want to add anything?"

"I'm sorry for the deaths of the three people."

"Why did you give this statement?"

"I wanted to clear my heart and the truth had to be known."

"I'm going to throw up," Trainum said. Fulginiti closed his folder and stood up. "Sit tight for a minute." In a few seconds, he was back in the observation room.

"So, anybody got anything else?"

"I got one," Trainum said. "When we talked to him at the FBI, he said that if someone did talk to him about doing Starbucks, he'd've told him don't do it, it's too hot. Guess he didn't tell Alton that."

"If there even is an Alton," Wallace said. "He also said he told some guys, plural, *not* to do Starbucks. They must not've been Alton either."

"You're making some good points," McCann said, "but can I just suggest we wait till we talk to Alton and let the CVSA do its thing on him, because," he held up his beeper, "he really does exist. He's got a robbery record and a Landover address. Units are headed there now."

33

Fulginiti went back in to tell Cooper they were bringing Alton Wesley in and asked him if he wanted to change his story before they talked to him. Cooper didn't hesitate. "No," he said, "I told you the truth."

"In for a dime, in for a dollar," Trainum said. "This fucking guy has brass balls."

"And I want to get a couple of other things off my chest too," Cooper said. "How I wound up killing a security guard at a building in D.C. five, six years ago is one."

Trainum turned to Wallace. "That's the guy Joannie Lee told us about – "

"And the other one's a guy I used to deal drugs with out here named Vontae Kincaid." Wallace froze. McCann sighed.

"Guys," he said, "I'm guessing that means we're not going to get to Starbucks till tomorrow."

Wallace managed to slow the planet's spin long enough to hear "if you want to stick around for this stuff, or just read the statements in the morning, it's your call," but flat-lined again until he saw Trainum looking at him and jerking a thumb to the door.

"Yeah, go, Jim," he said, "I'll stick around long enough to handle the D.C. one, no problem."

Trainum wasted no time getting up and saluted them both. "Then I will see you both bright and early." He left and held the door open for Fulginiti on his way out.

"You know about that security guard thing, Detective?" McCann asked.

"I do," Wallace said and watched Cooper stand and stretch before he realized he had something he needed to do. "I'll be right back."

He walked down the hallway back into the lobby and paused at the door to make sure Trainum's car was gone before he went to his and punched up Robbie.

"Hey! You done already? I thought you'd be comin' over a lot later."

"No, I'm still going to be here a while, but I just heard something I thought you'd want to know."

"What's that?"

"He's going to give us a statement on Vontae."

"Oh my God! What kind of statement? A confession statement?"

"I don't know yet, but he's got another one to do first, which means it could be a very late night here tonight, so don't wait up."

"Listen here, Detective. I been waitin' five years for this, okay?, so here's what I'm going to do. I'm going to leave the door unlocked and if you come in and I'm sleepin'?, you wake me up so I can hear all about it, okay?"

"Okay, but –"

"Ain't no ifs, buts, or ands about it. Praise Jesus! This is a miracle!"

"All right then, I will see you later."

With a final "Hallelujah!," she was off.

Wallace went back into the building, hit the head, grabbed a ham and cheese and a Ding Dong out of a vending machine, and headed for the observation room. Fulginiti was coming the other way out of the interview room and held up a hand to stay right where he was, then led him back out to the lobby.

"It's going to be a few minutes till we get started. McCann's doing a cold call on his Starbucks answers."

"What's that mean?"

"I did a first read on the CVSA analysis of his responses, and he's doing a second read without talking to me or watching him answer, just so there's two independent judgments."

"And what was your judgment?"

"He was lying."

"About everything?"

"No, just the stuff we care about. 'Did you shoot the people at Starbucks?' and 'Do you know who shot the people at Starbucks?'"

Wallace still didn't know if the machine was reporting the truth or making up some jive mumbo jumbo, but now he didn't care. *If it gets him to finally tell us the real story, that's all that counts*, he thought. "So what happens if McCann says he was telling the truth?" he asked.

"We toss it out. But, if he agrees, then we can tell Carl we know he's not telling the truth."

And pray he believes the thing has the magic they hope it does, Wallace thought. "And when would you do that?" Fulginiti shrugged.

"Let's wait for McCann's call, then we'll figure that out. In the meantime, take another ten or so. I'll come get you when he's done."

251

Wallace went back to the lobby and fell into a seat. His mind went back to reeling about Robbie and Vontae Kincaid so he distracted himself by digging into the Ding Dong until the churning in his stomach got more of his attention than the swirling in his head. He stopped in the men's room before heading for the observation room.

Cooper's statement on the security guard was on the table in front of his chair when he got back. He looked into the interview room and saw McCann asking Cooper his same litany of questions about wanting a lawyer and how he was treated, and getting the same answers. The statement in front of him mattered a lot less to him than the one Cooper was about to write, but because it was a D.C. crime, he made himself do a quick read.

He and Leon went to an apartment building near his mother's church to steal a gun from the security guard. Nothing about why. They went down the side of the building to a door where they could see the guard on the phone, sitting behind the front desk. Cooper went in, pointed a gun at him, and said "Nigga, don't move. All I want is the gun," but the guard reached into his holster and cocked it. Cooper started screaming 'Don't move! Don't move!' but the guard stood up and pulled his gun out. Cooper was 'scared for his life' and shot him. The guard fell back into his chair and the gun fell to the floor. Cooper picked it up and ran 'shitless back to the car with Leon in tow.' End of statement.

He flipped back to the front page and looked up to see Fulginiti looking at him, shaking his head.

"Shot and killed the guy for what? One more fucking gun? Makes no sense," he said.

"And why's he owning up to it now?" Wallace asked. "If I didn't know he was the lying bullshit artist he is, I'd say he was trying to get himself right with God."

"I don't buy that either," Fulginiti said. "Maybe he thinks if we think he did it in self-defense, we'll go easier on him, except that it wasn't self-defense. He said he had his gun out first."

"No telling what goes through his head," Wallace said. "Maybe he's feeling the pressure – or maybe he's throwing us these bones so we'll think he's telling the truth about Starbucks too."

"That's gonna depend on what Mr. Wesley has to say about it when he gets here. If the CVSA says he's telling the truth, but Mr. Cooper isn't, he's deeper in the shit than ever."

"So what's the plan?" Wallace asked. "You going to question him about this first, then have him write out his statement on Kincaid?"

"No," Fulginiti said, pointing to Cooper writing, "that's what he's writing out now. The idea is to get both of them on paper now and question him about them after he writes his Starbucks statement fresh and early tomorrow morning, I'm sure you'll be happy to hear."

"I am, but when's Alton going to talk about what Cooper said?"

"As soon as he's done with this thing, we'll talk to Alton, then we'll compare notes – and readouts – to see who's telling a story and who isn't. If Cooper's the one lying, we'll tell him that straightaway – and we'll make sure he sees his old buddy's on the premises before he goes night-night, just to give him something else to think about. If he's lying and knows Alton told us the truth, it should make tomorrow go down a whole lot quicker."

Wallace started to say *Sounds too good to be true*, but kept it to himself and watched Cooper spin his latest tale. In twenty minutes, he was reading it.

"Teddy Thigpen shot and killed Vontae Kincaid. Me, Vontae, and George Lewis were riding around drinking and bullshitting when I

253

received a page on my pager. I had robbed a drug dealer and was trying to sell the coke that I had obtained. I had paged a guy I knew had some money and would buy it off me and he was calling back. George and Vontae overheard my conversation about how much coke I had, how much I wanted for it, and what time he should meet me at my house. I dropped George off at his house across from Bertie Backus Junior High School and Vontae at his house on Sargent Road in Northeast D.C. I went home to chill out and wait for the guy.

"The guy comes up to my house a few hours later, banging on the door saying I set him up. He told me that two guys were waiting for him in front of my house and asked if he had the specified amount of money that him and I had discussed. He gave them the money, because he recognized them from being with me, but they ran off with it. To clear my name, I had to give him the amount of money that was taken, plus the coke. I did and we have never had dealings again.

"But now George and Vontae owe me money. I split the bill right down the middle, each was to give me half. Vontae gave me his half, minus fifty dollars. George never gave me so much as a penny, so I decided to have Teddy Thigpen whip both their asses for me. He really didn't know them that well but said it wouldn't be a problem. All he was supposed to do was just beat them up. The morning that Vontae wound up getting killed, he came to my house and told me that some guys up in Riggs Park had taken his car and he wanted help getting it back. I told him once I got home from work, I would help him.

"But when I came home that night from work, everyone was asking me did I hear about what happened to Vontae, he was dead. I asked Teddy if he killed him and he said they were fighting and things got out of hand. I didn't know that Teddy was taking a gun with him. I told him to get rid of the gun, bury it. He said he placed it in a

254

plastic bag and buried it somewhere under a tree in Avondale Park. The gun that was used was the one I'd taken off the security guard in the D.C. homicide. In a previous statement I said that I had sold that weapon to three guys in Riggs Park, but that was not true. I gave it to Teddy because I didn't want it and he said he would use it to do robberies. He was never supposed to kill Vontae, just talk to him, get his attention, you know, beat him up a little if he had to."

Wallace slumped back in his seat. *Man killed Vontae over fifty dollars!,* he thought, *unless Cooper's lying about all of that too.* He focused on McCann finishing up his notes across the table from Cooper before he looked up at him. "Are you ready to answer a few questions?" Cooper nodded.

"How long have you known Teddy Thigpen?"

"A long time, around fifteen years. His nickname is Man."

"How did he know where to find Vontae Kincaid that day?"

"As soon as Vontae left, I called Teddy and told him that Vontae was just walking away from my house and to catch up with him."

"What did Teddy tell you happened?"

"Just that him and Vontae were fighting and it got out of hand."

"Who else knows about this?"

"I almost told Leon, but I didn't, so no one knows about it."

"Who was the drug dealer that wanted to buy the drugs from you? The one that Vontae and George stole from?"

"His name was Boones, or Bones, something like that. He drove a black two-door Saab."

"How much money did you owe him?"

255

"I don't remember exactly. It was less than fifteen hundred dollars as I recall."

McCann took one last look at his notes, saw he had nothing more to ask, then went through his closing questions and got the same answers he'd gotten every time before. When he heard the last of them, he flipped his folder shut. "I think we're done for the day, Carl," he said. "Let's get you some dinner and let you get a good night's sleep before we start in on Starbucks tomorrow."

"No, man, let's get started now," Cooper said. "You're here, I'm here, I'm ready, let's just do it." Wallace leaned in, not sure he really heard what he just heard.

"Why are you so anxious to talk about it?" McCann asked. Cooper buried his head in his hands and wiped his eyes hard before he raised it. *This is a new part of the act*, Wallace thought, even as he hoped it wasn't.

"I just can't keep it inside anymore, man. I was inside that place, man, and I been waiting to tell somebody that for a long time. I need to talk about it." He looked like he was in serious pain. McCann looked at the observation room and Fulginiti jumped out of his seat and went out the door. Wallace heard a knock on the interview room door and watched McCann step into the hallway and shut the door behind him. Wallace turned to see Cooper fold his arms on the desk, then lay his head down, shaking and moaning low. Fulginiti came back into the observation room in a minute.

"Here we go, Detective, hang on," he said and they both watched McCann go back into the interview room and take his seat. Except for the trembling, Carl didn't move.

"Carl," McCann said, "I want to go over the CVSA results of your Starbucks statement with you. Are you ready to hear them or do you want to take a break? It's totally up to you." Carl lifted his head and pushed himself back in his seat, his eyes red and wet. He wiped them with both hands before he answered.

"No, let's do it," he said. "Let's get this over with." McCann nodded and fanned out a pack of charts with jagged red lines running across them.

"Detective Fulginiti and I each looked over these over independently and we each came to the same conclusion that you were not telling the truth with respect to certain questions."

"What questions?"

"'Did you shoot the people at Starbucks?' and 'Do you know who shot the people at Starbucks?'"

Carl started breathing heavy and raised his arms like he didn't know what to do with them. He stood up, unbuttoned his shirt, and started to take it off, then pulled it back in place and took a seat in front of the desk where the CVSA sat. He put his hands over his face and muttered into them, then pulled them down and sat motionless, his face wan and vacant for a good minute before McCann spoke again, his voice low and flat.

"We also thought it was kind of odd that you just happened to be friends with someone in Maryland who knew someone who worked at the Starbucks in Georgetown."

Cooper nodded, licked his lips, and took his time re-buttoning his shirt before he got up and took his usual seat across from McCann.

"I didn't kill nobody," he said. "It was all Alton, man, all him."

"Do you want to change your story about what happened?" McCann asked. Cooper took a deep breath before he turned and looked at him.

"I was inside, man, but I didn't do no shooting. I was just the lookout and the driver. That was it."

McCann looked up at the mirror separating them from the observation room. Fulginiti looked at Wallace. "You okay with this? You want to talk to McCann?" Wallace shook his head.

"I been waiting a long time too," he said. "Let him put it down on paper first." He watched McCann riffle through his papers, waiting for the knock that wasn't coming, before he clicked his ballpoint and looked at Cooper.

"Carl, did I attempt to question you about any crimes before you initiated talking about Starbucks?"

"No. I just need to talk about it."

"Okay, and have I advised you of your Miranda rights?"

"You did, a couple times."

"Do you still understand your rights as I explained them to you?"

"I do."

"Do you want to have anything to eat or drink before we start?"

"No, man. I'm too upset to eat."

"Okay. Now you just admitted that you were inside the Starbucks when the shooting occurred, is that right?"

"It is."

"All right, then, I'm going to ask you to do this just the same way we've been doing it." He pushed a pad and pencil to him and stood up. "Write up your statement and after you're done, I'll ask you some questions and make sure I got everything right."

"All right," Cooper said and started writing before McCann left the room. Wallace started to get up to call Trainum before he realized he'd never get back in time to add anything to the questions he'd have anyhow, and sat back down. In fifteen minutes, he was reading Cooper's statement.

"Everything up until Alton and I sitting in my mother's car a few doors down from the Starbucks in Georgetown are consistent. I did have a gun which I had stolen from my wife. It is an Astra A-100 9mm handgun which is now in police custody. I did also enter Starbucks with Alton. We walked up and knocked on the door and Alton's boy let us in. He then began to play the victim, telling the two white employees to do what we wanted. We corralled everyone into the back where Alton watched everyone. It was my job to check the store to make sure there was no one else in there.

"When I came back downstairs from their rooftop place, Alton and the girl were back out by the counter and I was told to watch the door. Alton's boy's job was to keep the other employee in the back by basically telling him to stay calm, let them take the money and go. Alton and the girl start arguing because she doesn't want to give up the keys. Alton starts yelling and they get into a shouting match. I start looking out the windows checking the street. I was afraid that if anyone out there heard them arguing, we would have to run. That's when I heard two to three shots fired. I turn around and don't see the girl anymore. Alton's boy comes running out from the back, I guess to see what happened, then Alton took him back there and that's when I heard three or four more shots fired. Then Alton comes running out from the back and I just bolted out the door with Alton right behind me. I was scared to death.

"We got in my mother's car and took off. Then I start thinking Am I going to be next because I'm a witness? I kept both hands on the wheel and just looked straight ahead. We drove back around the neighborhood and I dropped Alton off in front of Carroll. I just

259

knew that he was going to shoot me before he got out of the car. Not one word was said while we were in the car. It was strict tension. I just tried to remain calm. I didn't want him to snap. There was blood on him in little spots so I was scared that there would be blood in my mother's car. As soon as I pulled away from him, I headed to a gas station on University Boulevard in Takoma Park that had an all-night self-serve car wash. I never found any blood in my mother's car but I vacuumed the inside out and washed the outside anyway.

"I went home, took a shower, and decided that I couldn't take this anymore. I have a wife and a child and am going to start doing right. I found a good paying job and have been doing the right thing ever since. I just can't do this type of lifestyle anymore. I've done my dirt, but violence was not my way. I've wanted to get this off my chest for the longest time, but then anybody I told would be at risk. I really am sorry for the deaths of those people. He didn't have to kill them. There was nothing I could do for them."

"What do you think?" McCann asked Wallace.

"I'm thinking the fucker has told so many stories, even he doesn't know what the truth is anymore. Get him talking about exactly he did in there and exactly what Alton supposedly did, step by step. He may say 'Alton did this' and 'Alton did that' but he might really be tellin' us exactly what he did all by himself."

"Ten-four," McCann said and picked up his folder. "All right, here we go. Again."

After one more exchange of the usual questions and answers, he asked Cooper "What kind of gun did Alton have?"

"He had two guns on him. Both of them were in his dip, his waist."

"How many guns did you actually see?"

260

"Both of them. One was definitely an automatic. The other, I'm not sure of. I just saw the butt of it stickin' out the front of his pants."

"Do you know the name of the person who worked at Starbucks that was involved?"

"No, he just always called him 'his boy'. I didn't want to know, to tell you the truth."

"How was the robbery announced?"

"Alton's guy unlocked the door, then turned around. Alton took out his automatic and put it to the guy's head."

"Did Alton have the other gun out at that time?

"No, I never saw him take it out."

"What was said when you entered the Starbucks?"

"I was behind Alton. There was just two of them out in the open, standing in the customer area. Alton said 'You know what time it is! Everybody get in the back!' and he started walking them to the back. He looked over at me and told me to check the store for any more people."

"What did you do next?"

"I went straight upstairs to this patio place they had and scanned around for anybody, then went back downstairs."

"What happened next?"

"When I got back, Alton and the girl were back out by the front. He told me to go look out, so I walked over to the front of the store by the door to the right."

"Why weren't you watching the other two employees?"

"That wasn't my job. His boy was supposed to keep the other employees calm."

"What happened next between Alton and the female employee?"

"They started arguing, I don't know why, but it was getting pretty loud. She was like real confrontational, acting like 'Fuck you! I ain't gonna give you shit!' That type attitude."

"How long did the argument last?"

"A minute or two. He was screamin' at her to give him the keys, and she was movin' away from him every time he would reach for them."

"Then what happened?"

"I started lookin' out the window because they were gettin' real loud and I was worried someone would hear."

"What happened next?"

"That was when I heard the shots. I looked over and didn't see her no more. Everything started moving real slow after that, like a dream or something."

"How many shots did you hear when Alton shot her?"

"Two, maybe three. They were one right after the other, real fast."

"Did the female employee say anything before she was shot?"

"They were still arguing when Alton shot her."

"Then what happened?"

"Alton's boy came out from the back room and they went back there together."

"Did you have your gun out during the robbery?"

"Yes."

"Was it loaded?"

"Yes, seventeen in the clip and one in the chamber."

"Did you fire your gun inside the Starbucks?"

Wallace heard a knock on the door of the observation room and turned to see a uniform give a thumbs-up to Fulginiti. "I'll be right back," he said. "Take good notes." Wallace watched them head up the hallway, then turned back to hear Cooper say "I don't even think I had my finger on the trigger."

"What happened after Alton and his buddy walked into the back room?" McCann asked.

"I'm not sure. They were gone a minute or two."

"Were any shots fired during that time?"

Cooper nodded. "Three, maybe four, real fast."

"Did you hear either of the two male employees say anything?"

"No."

"Can you describe the three employees?"

"Caucasian female, kinda cute. I never really got a good look at her, but she wasn't fat, she was more like solid. She was shorter than Alton, but I couldn't tell if she was taller than me. I don't remember what she was wearing. She was in her late teens to early twenties. The guy who wasn't Alton's boy was a Caucasian male, maybe late teens, early twenties. He was kind of tall, maybe six feet, about the same size as Alton's boy, who was a black male, same age range."

263

"Did you ever go to the back area of the Starbucks?"

"No. I only got as far as the stairs."

"So how'd you know what the white guy looked like?" Wallace asked out loud.

"Good question, Detective'" Fulginiti said.

"Did you or Alton ever try to locate any money before or after the shootings?" McCann asked. Cooper shook his head.

"No. Alton tried twice to get the keys to the safe off the girl before all the shooting started, then we just ran out."

"Have you spoken to Alton since this incident?"

"No."

"Have you told anyone else about it?"

"I almost told Leon, but decided not to."

"Do you know what Alton did with the guns?"

"No. He still had them on him when he got out of the car when I dropped him off."

"How have I treated you?"

"Fairly. Much better than I expected, actually."

"How long did you sleep last night?"

"Nine or ten hours."

"Have you been denied any food, drink, or bathroom breaks?"

"No."

McCann finished writing and stood up. "You want anything now?"

"Another water'd be good. Maybe a popcorn too?"

"I'll get someone to get it for you. Just sit tight till I talk to the others and see if they have any questions."

"I know the drill."

McCann was just about to open the door to the observation room when he saw Fulginiti coming quickly down the hall in his direction.

"What's up?" McCann said.

"We need to get him out of there and put someone else in."

"Who?"

"Alton Wesley. He's here."

34

Wallace, Fulginiti, and McCann watched a line of headlights and beacons curl off Suitland Parkway before they saw five cars snake into the parking lot. Two PG cruisers and two sedans with Federal plates rolled past before the last cruiser pulled to a stop right in front of them. The cop in the passenger seat got out and swung the rear door open to let a handcuffed thin black man with a pencil mustache out, then led him into the building, McCann and Fulginiti trailing just behind. Wallace watched a herd of Feebies exit the Federal cars before he spotted Trainum heading his way with one of them. When they drew near, he was surprised to see it was Garrett.

"Welcome back," he said, shaking his hand. "I thought you were skiing somewhere."

"I was, until this guy called and told me our friend was starting to talk. I jumped on the first plane out and joined the herd picking up Mr. Wesley. What's the latest out of Carl?"

"Now he says he *was* inside the place when the shots were fired – all, of course, by Wesley. I also don't know if anyone filled you in on this CVSA thing they use out here as some kind of super-duper lie detector, but they had it on while Cooper was talking and they're going to have it on when they talk to Wesley so they can compare the readouts and see who's telling the truth and who isn't – supposedly. That's where we are. Anything happen when you picked him up?"

"Not a lot," Trainum said. "The PG guys busted him on a gun charge. Unless someone brought it up on the way over, Starbucks didn't come up. That's it."

Wallace led them into the building and down the hall to the observation room. Garrett did a quick look around until he spotted the coffee pot and headed for it. Wallace glanced at his watch. 7:55. P.M.

"That stuff's been out since this morning, Brad –". Garrett held up a hand while he emptied the remains of the day into a cup. "Doesn't matter. My brain's got no idea what time it is anyway."

They took seats facing the interview room and watched McCann fiddle around with the computers for a minute or two before Fulginiti brought Wesley into the room, took off his handcuffs, and told him to take the seat facing them. McCann explained what the CVSA was all about and read him his rights.

"Before we get started, Mr. Wesley, do you want anything to eat or drink?"

"No."

"Use the restroom?"

"The only thing I want to know is why it took nine of you fucking guys to bring me in on, what'd you say, a felony gun charge? Somethin' ain't right about that."

"We do want to talk to you about another matter," Fulginiti said. "You've been implicated in the Starbucks murders in Georgetown back in '97." Wallace saw the veins in Wesley's head throb from twenty feet away.

"What!?" Wesley said, looking at Fulginiti as if he really hadn't heard what he said. "Say what now? Starbucks? That is a fucking lie!" He slapped the table and started to stand up before Fulginiti got up first and held up a heavy hand.

"Relax, Mr. Wesley," he said. "We brought you in to hear what you want to say about it."

"I don't have anything to say about it! I don't know nothin' about it except what I heard on the TV and the radio. Nothing!"

"Mr. Wesley, let us just –"

"And who 'implicated' me anyhow, huh? What's the fucker's name? Tell me that!" Fulginiti nodded to McCann.

"Carl Cooper, Mr. Wesley. Do you know him?" Wesley went wide-eyed and shook his head slowly.

"I do know Carl Cooper, but I have no idea why that little fucking shit said I had anything to do with that Starbucks thing. I had nothin' to do with it!" He fell back in his chair, breathing hard, grasping for words or air, then pointed to the CVSA. "Is that thing a lie detector? Is that what you were telling me?"

"It is," McCann said.

"And was it on when you talked to Carl fucking Cooper?"

"Yes."

"And what did it say? Did it say he was telling the truth about me doin' that shit?"

"Mr. Wesley, I can't get into that with you. You just need to answer our questions truthfully, okay?"

"Goddamn!" Wesley slapped the table again, then pushed himself back, still steaming. "Okay, then, go ahead, ask me your questions."

"Do you want to take a short break first," McCann asked, "get yourself –"

"Hell no! Go ahead and ask me your goddamned questions."

"All right. You said you know Carl Cooper. How do you know him?"

"Me and him grew up together in Northeast, North Michigan Park."

"Were you friends?"

"No, not really. The only thing I remember doin' with him is playin' basketball at the rec center. He looked up to me, you know. I was, I think, three years older than him and he was just this little skinny dude who talked fast and laughed at everything. He was always wavin' to me and talkin' to me, you know, but I'd just nod at him and keep on goin'. Everyone knew him as 'L'il Cooper'".

"How about since you were kids? Did you see each other later? Hang out together?"

"Shit, no. I know he got in trouble with you-all and did some time, and he got married, had a kid, I think, but that's it, man. We definitely do not hang out."

"You weren't buddies in high school?" Fulginiti asked.

"No. I dropped out of high school before Cooper even got there, I think. I went back and got my GED so I could get into a medical assistant program." McCann opened a folder and looked at it.

"You've had some problems with the law, haven't you? Here and in DC?"

"Yeah, I had 'em. But I don't kill people, okay? You don't see that in there, do you? If I killed 'em, I'd say I killed them, but that's not me. I'm not a saint, man, but I'm not going to go out and kill people. No way."

"Did you know someone named Emory Evans?"

"I did know him. He got killed in that Starbucks thing, right?"

269

"That's right. He lived in your apartment building, didn't he?"

"Did you know that?" Wallace asked Trainum. Trainum shook his head.

"Yeah, he did," Wesley said, "and that's how I knew him, but that's all I knew about the dude, I swear. I'd see him in a hallway or in the parking lot and nod or say 'Hi' or somethin', but that was it. Did Cooper say somethin' else?"

"Again, Mr. Wesley, let's just stick to my questions." Wesley pounded a fist on the table.

"Jesus fucking Christ! I know Cooper and I knew who Emory Evans, but that was it, man! A lot of people knew both of 'em but that don't mean they did Starbucks, c'm'on, man." Wesley watched McCann look through his folder, shaking his head until something lit up his face. "Hey, when was that Starbucks thing?" he asked.

"July 1997."

"Okay, then I need to show you something," he said and turned to Fulginiti. "I gotta stand up though, okay?"

"Why? What for?" Fulginiti said.

"I got something to show you." He stood up and Fulginiti did too. Wesley pulled his blue denim shirt out of his pants and lifted the left side high enough to show the top of a thin plastic white bag protruding from behind his belt. He undid the belt and dropped his jeans to show the bottom of the bag somehow clinging to him over his boxers. Wallace thought he saw organs pressing against what looked like plastic skin grafted onto his stomach and focused hard on Wesley's face to stop thinking about them.

"You see that? That's a colostomy bag, man. In October, '95, I got shot five times right here," Wesley said, pointing to his right side. "I

270

mighta weighed one fifty, one fifty-five when I got shot and I'm probably back up to about one thirty now, but in July '97, shit, I was lucky if I was one twenty. I couldn't even stand up next to my bed for more than ten seconds, and I'm supposed to have shot three people in Georgetown? That is total fucking lying bullshit!"

"Do you have any medical records that will –" McCann started to ask.

"Shit, yes, I got a suitcase full of 'em," Wesley said. "Got the doctors' names, my momma, they'll all tell you what I'm telling you is true. There ain't no way on this earth I coulda done anything at that Starbucks, hand to God."

Fulginiti took one more look at the pouch before he turned to McCann. "You got anything else you need to ask him right now?" "No," McCann said, looking as shell-shocked as Wallace felt. Fulginiti turned to Wesley.

"Okay, get yourself back together and Sergeant McNabb will take you somewhere you can freshen up and eat something while I talk to my colleagues and figure out what we're going to do next, okay?" Wesley picked up his pants.

"I did not have a goddamned thing to do with that Starbucks deal. The one thing I do know is that that little bastard is telling you a fucking story to save his own ass. That, I'm goddamned sure of!"

Wallace, Trainum, and Garrett were silently watching Wesley tuck his shirt in and mutter dark thoughts when McCann came into the observation room. "So what do you think?" he asked.

"Not that I think we need it," Wallace said, gesturing at the CVSA, "but how long will it take you to get that thing to tell us who's tellin' the truth?"

271

"Here's what I've been thinking," Fulginiti said. "I think Joe and I ought to bring Carl back and tell him that Alton's here and gave us a different story than what he just said, and ask him if he wants to change anything he said. If he does, we hear him out. If he doesn't, that's fine too. Either way, we'll compare the readout of his last statement with Wesley's and take it from there."

Wallace exchanged looks with Trainum and Garrett. "Can you make some fresh coffee?" he asked.

35

A few minutes later, they watched Cooper and McCann take their usual seats in the interview room.

"So, Carl," Fulginiti said, "after we finished up with you, we talked to Alton Wesley." That got Cooper's attention.

"Where? Here?"

"Right where you're sitting," McCann said. "And he denied everything you told us about him being involved, so can you shed some light on that for us?"

Cooper hung his head for a moment, then looked back at McCann. "All right, Joe, let me tell you. I went to do it myself. Alton wasn't ever involved. I'd planned it with Leon about a month or so before, like I told you, but I couldn't reach him the day I was going to do it, so I decided to do it myself. I drove up and parked where I told you but when I walked up to the door and looked in, I saw somebody else was robbing it! I couldn't believe it so I just ran back to my car and got out of there as quick as I could."

"What the fuck?" Trainum said. Wallace nearly choked on his coffee and Garrett pounded him on the back, his wide-open eyes still trained on Cooper. Fulginiti and McCann were also looking at him in amazement.

"Carl," Fulginiti said, "don't you think that's an unbelievable coincidence?" Cooper shrugged.

"I guess, but it's the truth. That's what you want, right?" Fulginiti got up and headed for a phone on the wall next to the door.

"Yeah, listen, this is Fulginiti," he said. "Tell Mr. Wesley he can go. Right. Release him. Now, okay? Ten-four."

273

Back in his seat, he said "Carl, I now believe that you intended to do Starbucks all by yourself because you just told me that. But the fact that the exact time you happened to go rob it, it was miraculously being robbed already? I'm sorry, that I can't believe. No one would believe it."

Cooper looked to McCann. When his face told him the same thing, he dipped his head and stared at the tabletop for a few seconds before squinting his eyes shut. When he opened them, he took a deep sigh and looked at the ceiling before lowering them to Fulginiti. "Honestly," he said, "all I remember is shooting the girl. She wouldn't give up the keys and I shot her. Everything after that is just a blank."

Wallace jumped to his feet and raised two fists to the sky. "Yes! Yes! Yes!" he cried. Trainum and Garrett reached behind him to slap each other's hands. Fulginiti looked into the mirror and let a small smile crease his face for a split-second.

"All right, Carl," he said. "I'm going to ask you the usual questions. If you give me the usual answers, we'll leave you alone to write your statement about what really happened that night, then we'll come back to collect it and ask you any questions we might have, just like every time before, okay?" Cooper nodded his head. Two minutes later, Fulginiti and McCann were back in the interview room, trading hugs, backslaps, and whoops with everyone.

"Man, this calls for a celebration!" Trainum said. "I cannot tell you how long I've been waiting to hear those words come out of his mouth!" Before Wallace could start concocting a reason why he couldn't go, Garrett beat him to it with a real one.

"Honestly, I can't even tell you what day it is, guys. You'll have to give me a rain check."

274

"All right, listen," Fulginiti said, "let's see what he writes first before we do any celebrating. We've been down this road before with him. A lot. If he finally gives us the straight scoop, there'll be plenty to celebrate tomorrow too. And the next day and the next day. Let's just keep our fingers crossed."

Cooper laid his pen down in less than fifteen minutes. McCann picked up his statement and ran copies for everyone. Wallace never read anything with more anticipation.

"I had planned to rob the Starbucks in Georgetown for about a month prior. I had mentioned my plans to Leon Ellis but didn't go into details. On the Sunday of the murders, which were not planned, I went and checked the place out to make sure that they were doing a lot of business. Businesses that are open on Sundays rarely deposit their cash until that following Monday. Everything was set but when I tried to reach Leon, I was unable to contact him. It was getting late and I was afraid I'd miss my window of opportunity, so I went alone.

"I parked one street over behind the Starbucks and walked to it. The front door was unlocked. I drew my .380 and .38 and announced that this was a robbery. I asked who was the manager and the girl identified herself. I forced everyone into the back office where the safe was. The girl didn't want to comply and I didn't want the other two employees, two males, one black, one white, to try anything, so I fired a warning shot from the revolver into the ceiling. That's when the girl took off running. I caught her right outside the door. I kept telling her to give me the keys but she kept fighting me. I kept reaching for the keys and then she went for the .380, it went off, and everything else is like a dream. It's me, but it isn't me doing these things. I just start shooting. The white boy gets up and tries to run and there's more shooting. When everything's over with, everybody's dead except for the black boy. He's hurt but he's not going to make it. He's in so much pain it has to end, I had to stop

275

the pain. I leave empty handed, I'm not thinking about the money anymore, I'm starting to realize what has just happened, I have to get out of there, I have to leave, the money's not worth it. I put the guns in a plastic bag and buried them in the woods across from Saint Anne's Infant Home."

When he was done reading his copy, Fulginiti got up and looked at them all one by one.

"Okay," he said, "anyone got any hopefully last words of wisdom?" Wallace tried to think like Katz.

"Just go over everything again," he said, "the who, the where, the why, everything. We don't want his lawyer to have a field day because we use stuff he said that we know now is a lie. Let's tie everything up nice and neat with a bow."

"That's good," Fulginiti said. "Anything else?" When he heard nothing, he turned to McCann and nodded to the door.

After he and Cooper finished their usual preliminaries, he asked "Was Alton Wesley involved in this incident in any manner?"

"No."

"Did you act alone?"

"Yes."

"Why have you lied about the circumstances of this incident up to this point?"

"I don't want to go to jail."

"Have you consistently agreed to remain here at the Prince Georges County Criminal Investigation Division in order to assist us with this case?"

276

"Yes."

"Why?"

"Because I need help. I'm sorry for the deaths. I need closure."

"Why did you pick the Starbucks in Georgetown to rob?"

"Starbucks was the place in Georgetown that everybody went to. I knew they would have money on Sunday because they wouldn't make deposits."

"When did you decide to rob the Starbucks?"

"I began to plan it about a month before."

"How many times have you been into the Starbucks?"

"Twice. Once when I cased it and then when the attempted robbery and murder happened."

"When did you case Starbucks?"

"The morning of the murders. I went in and acted as a customer. I bought a cookie."

"What did you take note of once you were inside the Starbucks that morning?"

"I actually just wanted to see if they were busy."

"And were they busy?"

"Yeah."

"Who did you tell about your plan to rob Starbucks?"

"Leon Ellis."

"Did you want Mr. Ellis to participate in the robbery with you?"

277

"Yes."

"When did you tell him about your plan to rob Starbucks?"

"About a month before."

"What guns did you use in the robbery?"

"A .380 caliber black automatic and a .38 caliber chrome snubnose."

"What vehicle did you use during the robbery?"

"My mother's 1994 Eagle Summit."

"Where did you get the guns?"

"Actually, you know what? I really don't remember where I got them from."

"Tell me about what you did the Sunday of the robbery."

"I got up, took my mother to church, then went to the Starbucks. That evening, I paged Leon but he didn't return my call, so I decided to do it myself."

"Describe what happened at the Starbucks."

"I parked the car behind Starbucks one street over. I walked around to the front entrance and went right in. I saw a Caucasian female, a Caucasian male, and a black male. The girl was on the customer side of the counter. The guys were by the steps that lead upstairs."

"What happened next?"

"I announced the robbery, something like 'You all know what time it is?' I'm sure I said something ghetto, something stupid. I had pulled the guns out, the .380 was in my left hand, the .38 was in my right. I asked who was the manager and the girl identified herself right off the bat."

278

"Then what happened?"

"I took them back to the office on the left down the hallway. I was trying to get her to unlock the safe, but she was refusing. I started getting kind of worried because if she was bucking, the two guys might buck, so I fired one shot from the .38 into the ceiling. I didn't want them to do something stupid. Then she took off and ran out of the office into the hallway."

"What happened then?"

"I chased her and caught her. She had the keys in her right hand. I was trying to get them, but she was backing up and pulling away from me. I put the .38 in my waist. I reached for the keys and went to put my .380 in my left hand and the gun goes off."

"Where was she shot?"

"I don't know. Once it went off, I just started shooting her two or three times with the .380, then I pulled the .38 back out and shot her with that gun. At this point, the white boy comes out of the office. I turn around and the white guy backs back into it. As soon as I get to the doorway, I start shooting the guns again."

"Where did you shoot the white guy?"

"I don't know."

"Where did you shoot the black male?"

"I remember he was already shot somewhere. He was on the floor, he was hurting, he was crying, so I shot him twice in the head to put him out of his misery."

"Did you take anything?"

"No, I didn't want money at that point, I just wanted to run."

"What happened next?"

"I ran out of the store, went back to my car, and drove. I went into my house. I got a plastic bag and put the guns in it. I got a tool from the window ledge in the kitchen, walked to St. Anne's, and buried the guns in the woods."

"What were you wearing?"

"Black jeans, black T-shirt with a white design of a person's face, white gym socks, no gloves, no mask, black Timberland boots."

"Did you get blood on your clothes?"

"I don't know, but I tasted the girl's blood in my mouth, so I washed my clothes to be safe."

"Did you also clean your car?"

"Yeah, the next day at the car place on University Boulevard past Langley Park. It's a gas station before Flower Avenue."

"Where did you buy the ammunition for the guns?"

"At the K-Mart off Sargent Road."

"Did you ever try to move the guns?"

"Yes, when I lost my job at Wang, I went back and tried to dig them up, but I couldn't find them."

"Why did you try to retrieve the guns?"

"I was thinking about doing robberies again to make money."

"Have you told the truth?"

"Yes."

"How do you feel?"

280

"Worried."

"Why?"

"Because I've killed three people and I'm afraid of jail."

"How are you physically?"

"Alert, rested. I slept six, seven hours and more than ten hours the day before."

"Describe your relationship with me and Sergeant McCann."

"I have a lot of respect for you both. You've fed me and treated me with respect. I've wanted to admit this ever since it happened. It had to be known. I wanted to talk, but every time I tried to talk to Detective Trainum, he treated me like shit and harassed my family. If he would have shown me an ounce of respect, this would have been over for more than a year."

"Yeah, right," Trainum said. "And respect for what, by the way?"

"I put Alton Wesley's name into it just to get back at him. If he would've shown me he respected me as a person like you did, this would have been over a long time ago."

"Wow, hang three murder charges on a guy with a colostomy bag to spite *me*? That's showing me!"

"Were you ever denied a lawyer?"

"No."

"Did you ever ask for a lawyer?"

"No."

"How many times have you been advised of your right to have a lawyer with you?"

281

"Numerous occasions."

"Were you beaten?"

"No."

"Were you threatened?"

"No."

"Were you ever made any promises in exchange for this statement?"

"No."

"Do you want to add anything?"

"I'm really sorry for the deaths."

"No," Trainum said, "you're really sorry you got caught for the deaths."

"Do you have any questions?"

"No."

"Anything else?" Fulginiti asked McCann.

"Nothing. Let me check if anyone else does." Back in the observation room, he asked "So, anything else?"

"Yeah," Trainum said, "ask him if he'd like us to bring Wesley back so he could tell him he framed him to his face."

"Anything other than that?" McCann asked.

"Nothing, man," Wallace said. "You guys did a great job. Congratulations."

"All right then. Why don't you call tomorrow morning so we can figure out where to go from here? It's been a pleasure, gentlemen."

They waited until Cooper was led out of the room in cuffs before they headed for the parking lot. Trainum said he'd take Garrett back to the city, Wallace said he'd see them sometime tomorrow. They gave each other high fives and left.

Twenty minutes later, he let himself into Robbie's apartment and locked the door behind him. The clock on the stove said 11:03. The open door to her bedroom let a faint glow of light from the TV and a few gunshots escape. He took his jacket and shoes off and padded his way down the hallway until he could see the bed. She was turned away from him, sleeping soundly. He pulled the door nearly shut and went to the kitchen. He turned on the little light over the sink and pulled Captain Morgan out of where he remembered her putting him, then poured himself half a paper cupful. One sip brought back a flood of memories, most of them blurry, but all of them happy. *I must've forgot the bad ones* he thought, and savored another sip until he heard another sound from the bedroom.

"Hey, is that you?"

"It is," he called back. "Give me one second." He downed the rest of the rum, poured two cups, and carried them down the hallway. She was sitting up in bed and took one with a wary look on her face.

"Are we still celebratin' something?" she asked.

"We are," he said and laid down next to her.

"Oh my Lord, for real? I'm not dreamin'?" she asked. He reached his cup to her and she touched it with hers.

"For real," Wallace said. "We got a whole lot to talk about." He watched her drink, then wrapped an arm around her shoulder and drew her to his chest. Her tears wet his shirt before her warm breath grew fainter and deeper. He took the cup from her hands and put in

283

on the nightstand. When he turned back to kiss her cheek, he felt the stirrings of something he never felt before and was afraid to name.

36

The next morning, he showered, got into his clothes, packed his bag, and put up a pot of coffee before she teetered up the hall, still half asleep.

"What's the hurry?" she asked. "And where you goin' anyhow? I thought he confessed to everything."

"I have to go back to D.C., brief the Chief, get an arrest warrant – but, hey, you know what? I don't even want to think about all that. Come here." He opened his arms and she wrapped hers around him and held him as tight as he held her. "Believe me, I would much rather stay here." They kissed each other a passionate good morning before he made himself push her away and pointed to a folder on the table.

"If you want to read it, there's his statement on Vontae. I'm just warn –". She flipped the folder open, pulled up a chair, and started to read, silently at first. It didn't last long.

"'Teddy Thigpen shot and killed Vontae Kincaid'," she said. "Yeah, and who told him to do it, asshole?" She kept reading, her fingers tightening on the sheaf of paper. "Oh, here we go," she said a minute later. "'So I decided to have Teddy Thigpen whip their asses for me.' Wallace waited for the explosion and got it.

"What the *fuck*? For fifty fucking dollars!" She kept reading, even more wide-eyed. 'I didn't know Teddy was taking a gun with him'? Are you shittin' me?" She skimmed through the rest, then slammed the last page face down on the desk and pointed at it, her finger trembling. "'He was never supposed to kill Vontae'" she read out very loud, "just talk to him, get his attention, you know, rough him up a little if he had to.' You don't believe that shit, do you?"

"Robbie, I don't know what to believe with him," he said. "I lost track of how many stories he told us about Starbucks before he finally came clean."

"So what are you going to do about it?" Wallace saw his chance and took it. He came to her side and kissed the top of her head.

"I'm going to give PG any help I can to put him away for killing Vontae, I promise you, but first, I gotta take care of him and Starbucks. When they bring him to a grand jury on Vontae, that's when all the truth will come out, I promise you." She looked back down at the statement staring back at her and shook her head.

"I so want that fucker to get the chair, and I don't give a shit what for. I want him fried crispy black." She saw Wallace lift his bag and came back to the here and now. "So, what? You goin' home now?"

"I am," he smiled, "to get some clean skivvies, socks, and whatever else I'm gonna need if you'll have me back." She got up and pressed herself to him.

"Oh, I'll have you back all right," she said. When she felt he was paying sufficient attention, she sealed the deal with a deep soul kiss, then walked him to the door. "Hurry back now."

He stepped into the hall before he turned around. "I might be late again tonight too. We didn't get a chance to celebrate last night, so last I heard, the plan is to do it tonight."

"Uh huh," she said, "well, 'less there's somethin' about you I don't know, you're gonna like our celebration a whole lot more, I promise you that. Don't be too late now." She blew him a kiss and closed the door. He called Trainum from the car.

"How're things going over there?"

"Brad and I just picked up the warrant at the courthouse and we're heading back to headquarters now. And just so you know, they're about to start a press conference out front on Carl confessing, so I leave it to you if you want to hurry over to see it or take your sweet time and miss it."

"Who's doing it?"

"Ramsey's all I heard, but we're stopping to get some coffee just to make sure we're not any part of it."

"I'll look for you in the crowd," Wallace said. He took New York Avenue rather than 295 to slow the trip, and parked far enough away from the building to make sure he could add a five-minute walk, but when he turned off 4th Street onto Indiana, the crowd on the sidewalk told him he was still somehow right on time. He stood in the street behind them until he heard a whistle to his right and saw Trainum waving at him. He made his way over to him and Garrett, each holding a tall cup of Firehook Bakery coffee. Wallace squinted at the podium and saw Ramsey approach it, Fulginiti, McCann, and Melvin Ruffin standing behind him.

"I am pleased to announce," Ramsey said, "that the individual responsible for the murder of three people at the Starbucks on Wisconsin Avenue on July 6, 1997 is going to be brought to justice. We have filed charges this morning against Carl Derek Havord Cooper, a resident of the District of Columbia.

"I know Mr. Cooper's arrest doesn't completely relieve the families, but hopefully it will give them some peace of mind. This case took a lot longer than anybody standing here would have liked, but it was just one of those cases that had to take this long. Obviously, we would love to be able to solve every homicide within two minutes after it occurs, but it just doesn't always work out that way. This is one that proved to be very complicated, but it also demonstrates the resolve that our detectives had to bring it to a successful conclusion. They simply never gave up.

"The Prince Georges County Police Department has also arrested Mr. Cooper for the assault of their police officer Bruce Howard in August 1996. I'm pleased to have here with me Detective Richard Fulginiti and Sergeant Joseph McCann, who conducted the interrogation of Mr. Cooper in Prince Georges County that led to his arrests, as well as Detective Melvin Ruffin of MPD, who got the original tip on this case and helped our primary investigators, Detective Commander Thomas Wallace and Detective James Trainum, bring Mr. Cooper to justice. I also want to recognize Special Agent Brad Garrett of the FBI, whose assistance was indispensable. Those three gentlemen worked late into the night last night, which is why they're unable to be up here this morning. We salute them all for their efforts."

He turned to the ones who were up there. "Gentlemen, would any of you like to add anything?" Fulginiti and McCann shook their heads no. Ruffin stepped to Ramsey's side.

"I'd just like to say on behalf of Detectives Wallace and Trainum that this was one of the most difficult cases any of us ever handled. It was one of those things that we knew was going to take time to prove, but I always knew it would be closed. I'm just glad it's finally over."

"With that, I'll take a few questions," Ramsey said and pointed to a raised hand. Wallace couldn't hear the question, but figured it out from the answer.

"Mr. Cooper has been a suspect in the Prince George's case since last summer and in the Starbucks slayings since the November after they occurred. Yes sir." Another unintelligible question followed.

288

"I'm not going to describe the evidence we have against Mr. Cooper," Ramsey said, "but I can assure you that we have the right man based on the totality of all the evidence we have." He listened to the next question, then said "At this point, it appears that he was the only gunman. Thank you all. We'll be providing more information as events warrant."

Wallace and Trainum said their goodbyes to Garrett and headed back to the building. They walked past Ruffin holding forth to a gaggle of reporters around him and took the elevator up to four. "Want me to check in with McCann, see what the schedule is?" Trainum asked. Wallace nodded, walked to his office, took a deep breath contemplating all the crap that would be waiting for him on his desk, and pushed the door open. He exhaled when he saw only a pile of pink phone slips on his desk and nothing above the lip of his in-box. He dialed the top slip.

"Mr. Wainstein, please," he said.

"That's me," Wainstein said. "Congratulations, Detective," Wainstein said. "You got your man."

"Thank you. And thanks for all your help too. So what can I do for you?"

"I was calling mostly to congratulate you, but I also just want to give you a heads-up on what's coming."

"That'd be a grand jury, right?"

"Right, and we're going to convene one as soon as we can. I know you know this, but you will definitely be testifying there, probably pretty early on too."

"I figured as much. And you or someone from your shop will prep me, right?"

"We will.

"Sounds like business as usual then. I'll be ready."

"Well, your business will," Wainstein said, "but mine, maybe not so much."

"Why's that?"

"Because DOJ's making noises about going after the death penalty." That blindsided Wallace.

"Wait. What? D.C. doesn't have a death penalty."

"No, but the Feds do."

"So who decides that? The U.S. Attorney?"

"Nope. Janet Reno, the Attorney General of the United States of America."

"Holy shit! So when will that happen?"

"After the grand jury hands down its indictment, or indictments, I should say. There's going to be a slew of them." Before Wallace could let the wave of all that break over him, Wainstein said "You know what, I just got that news so it's all I'm thinking about. Please keep it to yourself, okay? At least till you see it make the Post, which it definitely will." Wallace had no doubt about that either. The only thing he had doubts about was whether he'd be able to keep it from Robbie.

The next slip on his pile was from Ramsey. For the first time in his MPD career, a Chief got on the line when he called, immediately no less.

290

"Detective! Congratulations! I just took your name in vain at a press conference not fifteen minutes ago. I'm sorry you weren't there to hear it."

"Actually, I was, and I greatly appreciate it. I came in a little late so I didn't –"

"I get it, believe me," Ramsey said. "I wouldn't've been up there either if it wasn't in the job description. So what's the plan? Are you going to bring him back here today?"

"You know, I don't know exactly when yet, but that is the plan. My next call is to PG to figure out how."

"Then don't let me hold you up. You did an outstanding job. I hope you're as proud of yourself as everyone else here is."

"I'm mostly exhausted, but I appreciate it, sir. I'll let you know what's going on when I do."

At Ramsey's "10-4," he pressed the button in the cradle to clear the line, but the phone rang in that split-second.

"Congratulations, Tom," a familiar voice said.

"Thanks, Jake."

"I watched the press conference on TV. Why weren't you up there?"

"Too much hoo-hah for me. I watched from the back row."

"But you were in PG for the *four days* my client was questioned, right?"

"Jake –"

"And do you remember seeing my client being given a chance to talk to his lawyer at any time after I first brought it to your attention, which, if you don't recall, was *three days* ago?"

"Jake, he was asked many, many times, and he declined every time. I saw them all, I can vouch for that."

"Uh huh. Well, fair warning, you may have to. And since it's going to come out anyhow, do you mind if I ask you exactly when you took him into custody?"

"Monday night."

"So that was March 1. Was it early Monday night, late Monday night?"

"Early, a little after 6."

"And this is Friday, and from what Ramsey said, it sounded like he was charged this morning, which my calendar says is March 5."

"Jake –"

"And when did you take him from PG to DC?"

"Yesterday," Wallace said. "Listen –"

"When yesterday? Hey, you know what? It really doesn't matter. Let's say he confessed bright and early, say, by noon, okay? That means – hold on, let's see if I can do this without an adding machine – that's 24 + 24 + 12. That's a zero. Carry the one. Okay, so I get that he was held in custody for sixty hours without talking to his lawyer. Check my math, though. I was a liberal arts major, so –"

"Add another twelve, Jake. And that's it. We're done."

"Tom, this is just business, okay?" Katz said. "Nothing personal."

Wallace remembered the last time he heard that. *The Godfather*. Right before a cop's brains were splattered all over the floor.

"Jake, you gotta do what you gotta do and I gotta do what I gotta do. I will see you in court. Did I say that right?"

He didn't wait for Katz to answer before he hung up and turned his attention to what was filling his in-box. He tossed a few reports back for later reading, threw some newsletters into the trash, then paused when he read the return address on a thin manila envelope addressed to him from Bode & Beckman, LLP.

He ran a finger under the seal, pulled out two stapled sheets, and turned them over. Under the heading United States District Court for the District of Columbia, he read "Terry E. Butera, Individually and as Personal and Legal Representative of the Estate of Eric Michael Butera, Plaintiff v. District of Columbia, et al., Defendants" followed by another heading: "Notice Of Taking Deposition" with a date and place named above an inscrutable signature. A note just below that "See Attached". The attachment told him he was required to bring with him a long list of documents that ended with "and any other documents, records, memoranda, and written materials related in any manner to the Metropolitan Police Department's relationship with Eric Michael Butera."

He was starting to envy that cop.

37

Wallace's mind started to uncloud, a dark swirl of faces spinning out of the haze, Trainum, McCann, Fulginiti, a few more he couldn't put a name to, whirling in time to a soundtrack, Britney Spears asking baby to hit her one more time, some guys whining about their heartache, then just a louder and louder babble of noise and laughs. The swirl finally slowed enough to let him see his hand holding a Maker's Mark high and remember someone saying *That fucker's going to fry!* before he remembered Robbie adding *crispy black*. But she wasn't there. His eyes popped open and watched a white stucco ceiling rotate to a slow stop until he had a flicker of clarity about where he was. He turned his head to the left but she wasn't there either. He looked for the clock and squinted to read it. The bright light knifing in between the curtains told him the 1:10 was p.m.

He fell back on the pillow and strained to remember something, anything, about how he got here. The best he could manage was someone pulling the door to her place open and someone else pushing him inside. He tried to roll back in time from there. That hazy party. Pulling into a parking lot of a strip mall. Calling Robbie from the car. Following a line of cars out of the PGPD parking lot. Ramsey telling him and Trainum to take the weekend off. Fulginiti telling him Cooper had to stay in PG till Monday for a hearing on Howard.

A squeak to his right was enough to shatter his fragile concentration. He turned to see Robbie lean against the door frame, wearing black jeans and a loose gray FUBU sweatshirt, and shake her head. "Wow!" she said. "Thank God. I thought I killed you, no lie."

Wallace groped to remember whatever she was talking about, but came up dry. "What? How?" She gave him the side-eye.

"You don't remember? For real?" The vacant look on his face, underlined by the bloodshot eyes and puffy lids, answered her question. "So let me ask you this. What *do* you remember about last night?" Wallace propped himself up on an elbow.

"I remember going to some club somewhere out here with a bunch of guys, McCann, Fulginiti Brad – ".

"Okay, I don't know none of those people. The only one I know was there was Trainer? Or Traynham or something?"

"Trainum. Right. How do you know that?"

"Because he dragged your ass in here."

"What? No. He doesn't know anything about you. You weren't here when we –"

"Whatever. He knows me now, I promise you that. Took both of us to get you back here and get your clothes off, well, most of 'em anyhow." Wallace lifted the blanket and saw all he was wearing were his shirt and socks.

"Where are my pants?" Robbie laughed and sat on the bed next to him. "Don't you worry about that. I took care'a those." She searched his face for some glimmering of understanding and didn't find it. "Man, you *don't* remember anything about last night, do you?"

He fell back on his pillow, covered his eyes with both hands, and shook his head. "Then you don't even know what a good time we had, especially you. I gave you the best blow job a man could ever have and you don't even remember it, what a pity." He felt his dick start to rise. "Well, at least he does," she said, patting the rising blanket before she got up. "Get yourself together," she said. "I'll make you some coffee."

In fifteen minutes, he had his face washed, his mind clearer, and his pants on. He went down the hall to the kitchen, but Robbie wasn't there either. He saw a note next to a coffee cup. 'Went out to grab us some lunch – breakfast?? Be back soon."

Wallace poured himself a tall black coffee and downed half of it before he knew what he had to do before she got back. He found his pager in the bag next to the door and sent Robbie's phone number to Trainum. In less than a minute, the phone rang and he picked it up. "Tom?" he heard. "Yeah," he answered.

"How are you, man? I'm mean, I've seen some shitfaced people, but I never saw you that shitfaced, or anyone else for that matter. I mean you were gone, man!"

"It's been a long time since I had any alcohol in my system, let's just leave it at that."

"Well, I tell you what, you made up for lost time, that's for sure. Is the girl there?"

"No. She told me you brought me here. How'd that happen?"

"I kept telling you that you were in no condition to drive, but you kept saying 'I got to get over to see Robbie, I got to get over to see Robbie'. It finally dawned on me that Robbie was Vontae Kincaid's old girlfriend and that she was living with his mother Albertha – which I remembered because it was a name you don't forget – so I called information to get her address and brought you over. How're you feeling?"

"I just got up, man. I'm still takin' inventory."

"I'm not surprised. You were out the second we dumped you in the bed. That was some show, my man." Wallace changed the subject.

"Anything going on with Cooper?"

"Wow," Trainum laughed. "Ramsey gave us three days off, but you won't let me have two minutes without thinking about him, will you?"

"I'm sorry, man. I –"

"I'm just giving you some shit, Tom. I called in to Melvin to ask him the same thing a few hours ago. You remember PG said he had to have a bond hearing out there on Monday? He said it's still on, which means we won't be able to extradite him back here till then, which means we might be able to actually enjoy the weekend off for a change, if you'll let me, that is."

"Shit, I'll let you," Wallace said. "I need the time too."

"Can I just say one more thing?" Trainum said and didn't wait for an answer. "I don't know what you got goin' on with this Robbie and I don't want to know but, from what I saw, you could use a day or two to just take it easy, you know, kind of pull yourself –"

"I appreciate it, Jim. I do, really, but I'll be fine. It's got nothing to do with her, okay? Have a great weekend. I'll see you Monday."

When he hung up, he downed the rest of the coffee in one swig. He appreciated Trainum's concern, but he could handle himself. He'd taken a daily 50-milligram dose of Naltrexone for years and been through AA and come out clean on the other side, thanks in large part to his sponsor. Years ago, Denny, an older white man with deep lines in his face and hardly any hair, handed him a folded-up piece of paper the last time they met, shook his hand, and told him "You ever need someone to talk to, you call that number, okay?" Wallace hadn't looked at it one time since then, but it didn't matter anyhow. He still remembered the number.

297

38

Over the next three days, his relationship with Robbie grew hotter, heavier, and wetter. For a long while, he didn't remember much of it at all, but when he started to sober up under a long cold shower Monday morning, he was dead for certain sure he'd never had that much booze and that much sex over that short a time. And he was even surer that no woman had ever enjoyed his company even that long either. Liquor was a constant companion of all the sex he had in the past, but, soon enough, violence was too. He'd slapped women, shoved them, even punched a few, but none of that was part of the deal with Robbie or, he promised himself, ever would be. He even let himself think that maybe that strange feeling he felt come over him last week had a name, but he wasn't ready to say it even to himself, much less out loud to her.

It wasn't just the sex, though he enjoyed every second of it. It was more that she needed him to heal the deepest wound in her life and he wanted to make it happen for her at least as much as he wanted to bring Cooper to justice for Starbucks. The simple pleasure of holding her hand watching TV or squeezing her tight just for the hell of it were joys he'd never experienced before. He'd had plenty of sex, but even that was bigger, richer, and deeper now too. He was grateful to her for finally letting him know how sweet being with a woman could be. He knew that the booze was exacting a high price for everything she was bringing him, but he was more than willing to pay it.

Stepping out of the shower, the only things he could clearly remember besides the feel of her, inside and out, were her leaving for the food store when he got in the shower and him yelling at her to tape Katz when he suddenly saw his face behind a cluster of mikes on the late news last night. He found the remote on the floor next to the bed and rewound to it.

"It's outrageous," Katz said, "and I don't care what spin anybody puts on it. I can't think of a set of circumstances where somebody is held for more than sixty hours and not allowed to talk to a lawyer."

PG's police chief came on the screen and said "Mr. Cooper was given steaks, hamburgers, whatever he wanted, and allowed to take breaks between sessions. He was sleeping for twenty of those hours and some of the time he was just waiting while we talked to another possible suspect who turned out not to be involved. I can assure you and Mr. Cooper's attorney that he was afforded all of his constitutional privileges. He was read his rights at least five times and waived his right to a lawyer every time."

A reporter asked why Cooper wasn't taken to a court commissioner within twenty-four hours after being arrested like the law required. Someone from the State's Attorney's office said "The statute does say that, but the case law is that if a defendant isn't taken to the commissioner within that time frame, that doesn't automatically mean the case has to be thrown out. It all depends on whether Mr. Cooper was afforded all of his legal rights and, as the Chief said, he was."

He flicked the TV off and threw the stick on the bed. He was just pulling his pants up when he heard the front door open. "Hey, you still here?" he heard.

"Yeah, just gettin' ready to go."

She sashayed down the hall to him, holding a Captain in each hand, and smiling that smile. "I made another stop. Sure you don't want one for the road?" He waited for her to draw closer before he reached out and pulled her close.

"One what?" he asked. She tossed the bottles behind him on the bed, then tugged his pants to the floor before she reached into his boxers and squeezed his already hard dick.

299

"You pick," she whispered.

"We can drink any time," he said.

39

When he fell into the car a little after ten, he pushed the radio button for the all-news station and waited to hear if they had anything to say about Cooper's bond hearing. As he crossed into the District, Dave Statter came on live from Upper Marlboro.

"Yes, Chas, the hearing just concluded. It was short and on a closed-circuit TV connection with Mr. Cooper at the County jail. He told Prince Georges District Court Judge Thurman Rhodes that there was no need to set a bond hearing for him because he'd also been charged for the Starbucks murders in the District of Columbia. His last words were 'I do apologize for wasting your time, Your Honor.' The judge ordered him held without bond and he's expected to be transferred back to face a bond hearing in the District on the Starbucks charges shortly. Back to you in the studio."

In his office twenty minutes later, he hoped to see a pink slip from someone in PG letting him know just when Cooper would be heading to D.C., but the only one was from Katz, with a note written by whoever took the call: 'Swears he has just 1 quick question.' He mulled his options, then punched up the number to avoid having to mull them again.

"Jake, you called?"

"I only have one question, I promise you."

"If it's got anything to do with PG questioning Cooper, you got less than one."

"It's not. I left a message with Wainstein about half an hour ago asking when Cooper was coming back here, and where he was going to be held when he was."

"That's two questions."

"It's one with a comma, but either way I haven't heard back. Do you know?"

"I don't," Wallace said, but that reminded him he had something to talk to Wainstein about too. "I'll get back to you if I hear anything." He hung up and called Wainstein, who picked up on the first ring. When they got past the niceties, Wallace got to his questions.

"First, do you know when Cooper's coming here, and where he's going to be held once he does? And full disclosure: Jake Katz asked me if I knew, and I told him I'd call you and find out, but if you don't want to tell me, or you don't want me to talk to him on the case at all, just let me know. You'll be doing me a favor if you say I shouldn't, believe me." Wainstein laughed.

"I saw Jake's message and it wasn't tops on my list to return. But I have no problem with you talking to him. It'd actually be nice to know what opposing counsel's thinking about."

"I know I don't have to say this, Ken, but I will anyhow: I have never given him any inside info on a case and I'm not going to start now. If you don't want him to know something, he won't, period."

"Never had a doubt in my mind. So let's just do what you're doing now, okay? You tell me what he wants to know and I'll either tell you or I won't. This is something I can tell you. He's going to be at the Northern Neck Regional Jail out in Virginia, and when he gets there depends on when PG processes him out, so Jake's going to have to take that up with them."

"Then that's what I'll tell him. And I have a couple of questions too. The first one is when do you think the grand jury's going to start?"

"Honestly, probably not for another six weeks and even that may be optimistic. You know better than anybody that we've got a boatload of stuff to go over and pull together, and then we've got to schedule

302

and prep the witnesses, so it's going to take a while, that's the best I can tell you."

"And I presume I'm going to be one of those witnesses, correct?"

"Not only one of them, Tom. The first one. I'll be in touch on that sooner than later, I hope."

"Thanks, Ken. I think."

"You're welcome," Wainstein said, "and keep me posted on all things Katz." Wallace called Katz back and gave him the Northern Neck news.

"Where in the hell is that?" Katz said.

"I have no idea," Wallace said, "but I bet a map of Virginia would." Katz groaned.

"I'm having déjà vu all over again. The last time I dug it out was when I had to figure out where Lorton was when Cleo was out there. What is it with the District? You'd think they'd want to keep the defendants close for everyone's sake."

But Wallace wasn't listening. Hearing Cleo Smythe's name for the first name in – what, ten years? – conjured up a vision of her that lingered long enough to make him lose track of whatever Katz was going on about. He caught up at the question mark to "Do you know where the hell that is?"

"Where's that again?" Wallace asked.

"The Spotsylvania exit off 95 – oh, wait, I see it. Good God! It's twice as far as Lorton. Is this some kind of plot to keep lawyers from talking to their clients? What's next, Richmond? North Carolina? All right, I gotta go. Jesus Christ!"

Cooper arrived at Northern Neck two days later, and for the next three weeks, Wallace's life returned to something near normal. He worked with Trainum and Wainstein to put together an affidavit for Cooper's first hearing in D.C. that ended with the same result as P.G.: No bail. Katz told the Commissioner that Cooper would have nothing to say to anyone without his lawyer present, but agreed to Wainstein's request for samples of his hair and blood. Wallace sat in the back in case one of them asked him to testify, but no one did and he left without even making eye contact with Katz.

He was indeed the kickoff witness at the grand jury in May and stuck to the script he and Wainstein wrote. The tears that welled up in every grand juror's eyes by the time he stepped down made him want to tell Katz he ought to think about entering a plea rather than going to trial, but he didn't. He also didn't tell him what Wainstein said Cissy told the grand jury about Carl saying his prints were in Starbucks because they went there after church: "We never went there". He also didn't share the strange coincidence that the amounts Carl stole from each of his robberies matched to the penny the amounts that his mother deposited in her account – and the checks she wrote to Carl – within the next day or two.

His personal life calmed down too. When Albertha went to rehab her fractured hip at an assisted living place and Robbie said there was no telling when – or if – she was coming back to her apartment, they started making her place theirs. He sprang for a new sofa, a new dining room table, and a bigger bed. Drinking was still part of the deal, but he told himself he was keeping it under control. He kept to a regimen of one drink every other day – except the weekend, which started on Friday – but persuaded himself every day that he had everything under control – until all hell really broke loose.

40

Over the next few months, Wallace was in a constant state of mounting pressure, squeezed daily by new twists of the vise, some expected, like the dates he was scheduled to testify, but most not, like groping to remember where he was when he went to sleep or woke up, and how he got there, but the source didn't matter. How he dealt with it did, and that was worse each time.

In early April, he was the leadoff witness at Renaldo Mathis' trial for murdering Eric Butera in the second degree. Wainstein led him step-by-step through why Butera was at 1015 Delaware Southwest that night, what MPD wanted him to do there, how Wallace found him on the sidewalk, and what Jerome McNally told him about what Mathis did to him there, all over the frequent objections of Mathis' lawyer Donald Dworsky, none of which were sustained by Judge Shuker. "Mr. Dworsky," she said more than once, "Detective Wallace is not on trial here."

But, Wallace thought every time, *I will be.* Per his agreement with the Corporation Counsel's Office, Wainstein stayed away from anything that would allow Dworsky to cross-examine him on how Butera managed to get murdered without anyone on his team seeing it or stopping it. The point was to keep Wallace from saying anything that could be used against him in Butera's mother's lawsuit, but Dworsky still pressed him on it to make the jury think Wallace was lying to cover up MPD's fuckups. Shuker wouldn't let him do that either, but every question gave Wallace a very bad feeling about what he could expect from Terry Butera's lawyers.

Seeing Katz in the gallery didn't make him feel any better. He'd called to let Wallace know he'd be there for moral support, but Wallace had seen Katz in action enough to know he could expect even worse from him when Cooper went to trial. He nodded at him and prayed for a plea bargain.

A few weeks later, he was the one nodding to Katz from the gallery. He wasn't there for moral support, but just in case Wainstein needed him to testify at a hearing in D.C. Superior Court about whether D.C. had a right to hold Cooper for the Starbucks murders. They met at the bar to the gallery and shook hands.

"I'd wish you good luck," Wallace said, "but you know I'd be lying so I won't." Katz laughed.

"Okay, then I'll be the gracious one. Congratulations on Renaldo Mathis. When's sentencing?" The jury had convicted him on Murder Two the week before.

"Sometime in June," Wallace said. "So, you going to tear us apart here?"

"You know I'll do my best. Let's catch up soon."

Wallace gave Katz an A for effort, challenging every aspect of PG's interrogation of Cooper, stressing the lack of any physical evidence linking him to the crime, and asking for bail for such a devoted family man, a long-time resident of the District of Columbia, and a former felon who had turned his life around. The Magistrate took it all under advisement, scheduled another hearing for August, and held him without bail till then.

In June, the Starbucks grand jury called him back to hear him tell them again why MPD was sure no one else was involved and how they knew the bullets came from Cooper's guns.

In July, Mrs. Butera's lawyer Monty Irving deposed him for six hours over two days, but what Wallace remembered most about it was the five-minute conversation Irving had with the Corporation Counsel's lawyer before it even began.

After all the introductions, Christine Gallagher of the Counsel's office picked up the complaint in the case and said "Mr. Irving, I just

306

want to say something before we go on the record. I am just – I don't even know the right word – staggered? amazed? mindblown? – by the amount of damages you're requesting in this case. Fifteen million dollars? Plus unspecified punitive damages against the District and each of the individual defendants? That is an outrageous sum of money, and it's not going to help anyone resolve this case any time soon."

"We're not here to settle the case, Ms. Gallagher," Irving said, "we're here to depose Detective Wallace for the trial we fully expect and want to happen."

"And the District of Columbia is fully prepared for that, but seeking punitive damages against Mr. Wallace and the other police officers you named is laughable. These men were just doing their jobs in a very hostile environment, as you know." Irving held a hand up, but Gallagher kept going. "Just think about this like someone who actually cares about law enforcement in the District of Columbia for a minute. What message does rendering police officers destitute send to everyone on the force, never mind all the young men and women who want to be members of the Metropolitan Police Department?" Irving kept his hand up.

"Are you finished?"

"Maybe. It depends on your answer."

"My answer is that you should save the histrionics for the jury and let us get to the business of what we're here for today: Getting Detective Wallace on the record." But Wallace wasn't thinking about the record. He was thinking about "punitive damages" and "destitute" and how he knew he'd stop thinking about them.

41

Just before noon on the first Monday of August, Wainstein gave him a call.

"Detective, I wanted you to be the first one to hear this."

"Oh, shit! What now?" Wainstein laughed.

"No, it's good news, very good news as a matter of fact. I'm pleased to tell you that the grand jury just voted unanimously to indict Cooper for the Starbucks murders."

"Oh, good Lord, that is good news. It's great news. Great job, Ken. You should be proud of yourself. I know it wasn't easy."

"Right back at you. Congratulations to all you guys." Wallace's mind raced ahead to who'd he tell first. Ramsey, Trainum, Robbie, of course, then Katz – until he remembered what he'd promised Wainstein: *I have never given him any inside info on a case and I'm not going to start now.*

"One thing, Ken, what's the protocol about telling Jake Katz? Does he just read about it in the papers like everyone else, or do you call him, or what?"

"Tom, if you'd like to be the one to tell him, I have no problem with that, but just hold off till you hear back from me. I'll let you know as soon as we're ready to announce it to the press, I promise. In the meantime, I'll send someone over with the indictment so you can see the results of what you've done. It's good reading."

When the messenger handed him a sealed unmarked large envelope a few hours later, Wallace was surprised at how heavy it was. When he opened it and read the indictment, he knew why. Starbucks was only part of it. There were 48 counts in all, including murder, racketeering, robberies, burglaries, kidnapping, weapons charges, and drug charges stretching back years. He didn't see anything specifically charging him with Vontae Kincaid's death, but there was more than enough in there to fry him crispy black if DOJ decided it would go for the death penalty, so Robbie would be happy about that. He hoped.

Wainstein gave him the all clear a little after 4 on Wednesday. "They're putting out the press release at 5 sharp, so if you call him now, you can tell him he's getting the early word with a straight face." Wallace called and heard a familiar voice say "Law offices of Jake Katz."

"You your own receptionist now?"

"And law clerk, and secretary. What's up?"

"I'm calling to let you know before the rest of the world does that your client Carl Cooper is about to be indicted for Starbucks and a whole lot of other shit."

"I am not shocked to hear that. What's the other shit?"

"If you subtract those three murders, forty-five counts of pretty much every other felony in the D.C. Code, plus a few Federal ones too."

"Jesus Christ! Can you send it over to me?"

"That I can't do, sorry. I had to get special dispensation just to call you. They're supposed to be putting the press release out at five."

"And will I also be reading that they're going for the death penalty?"

"That's above my pay grade, Jake. I have no idea."

"Who's the AUSA on the case? Can you tell me that?"

"Ken Wainstein, the guy you saw try Bruiser Mathis in the Eric Butera killing. He's a good guy."

"I will call him now. Appreciate the heads up."

He put down the phone and thought about how he'd give Robbie the news. After teasing out every possible answer to every possible question he could imagine her asking for a full ten minutes, he figured he'd spare himself the phone call and do it just once, face to face. At five-thirty, he detected a strange aroma as he came to her door. He looked at the number on the door to make sure he was at the right place before he went in.

"Hello!" he called. She spun around at the stove, then looked back at the clock.

"Why you here so early?"

He put his bag down next to the table and headed her way, but she held her hands up. "No, no, don't ruin my surprise!" He could place the smell now.

"Is that tomato sauce?" She smiled and moved to the side so he could see the stove top. She pointed to the pots. "That's the sauce, and that's the spaghetti, and I'm going to toast us up some garlic bread in the oven. Oh yeah," she pointed to the Chianti bottle on the countertop, "and I got us some wine."

"What's the occasion?" A big smile cracked her face and she threw her arms around his neck.

"I got me a job today!" He hugged her tight and she squeezed him back before stepping away to stir the sauce.

"That's great! I'm so happy for you! Tell me all about it."

"It's out at the CVS on East-West Highway, across from the mall. I'm a trainee stocker!"

"That's fantastic! How did you get it?"

"Saw a 'Now Hiring' sign on the door this morning, pulled it down, walked over to the lady at the cash register, and said 'I think I'm just what you're lookin' for'. She laughed, white lady named Grace, and we started talkin', and she told me I could start Monday! How do you like that?" He squeezed her again, then pulled back.

"And no GED or –".

"None. Guy named Ezra'll be training me, see if I can handle it. If I can, I'll be his assistant and he'll give me more shit to do over time, see how I do with that. I might be greetin' you at the door one day, ha!"

"And the pay?"

"Minimum wage to start, but that's fine. If things work out, I can start gettin' some benefits too, but all that's down the road. All I care about now is I finally got a job and some money comin' in and everything else don't matter."

"Well, I have some good news for you too." She looked at him curiously and watched him reach into his briefcase, slide a thick packet of papers from an envelope, and hand it to her. "Just got this and wanted you to be the first to see it. This is the indictment of Carl Cooper on forty-eight counts of murder, robbery, and all kinds of other crimes." She took it from him, wide-eyed, and started leafing through it. He cut to the chase. "I didn't see Vontae's name in there, but I haven't gone through it all yet. Either way, there's enough in there to fry him six times over."

"Does it say that? Are they going to kill him?"

"You're the second person who asked me that already" escaped his lips before he remembered that getting into or not getting into his friendship with Katz was one of the reasons he decided not to talk with her on the phone. He tried to nonchalant it and reached for the corkscrew. "And I'll tell you what I told him: I don't know. That's going to be up to the Justice Department."

"Who was it that asked you that?" she asked over her shoulder at the stove.

"Just a guy I know, Jake Katz."

"Who's he?"

"We used to work together at MPD before he decided to go to law school."

"And why were you talking to him about it so right away?" He felt the tightening grip of a new vise.

"The guy who's going to be prosecuting the case said it was okay if I did." She turned to him.

"No, but what was the reason you talked to him? He got something to do with Cooper?" Wallace jerked the cork out of the bottle, poured a tall glass, and handed it to her.

"He might be representing him in D.C. Right now, he's only working for him in Maryland, so I don't know –"

"So he's Cooper's lawyer? That's what you're sayin'?"

"Yes."

"Okay, I'm lost here. Why would a cop be talking to Cooper's lawyer about anything?"

312

Wallace reached over to clink his glass with her, but she wasn't clinking anything. He took a long sip, more like a gulp, before he answered.

"We've just stayed in touch over the years, and when I saw he was representing him, I thought I'd let him know we were both involved, that's all. It was just a courtesy thing." She sipped her wine and thought for a second, then shrugged.

"You know what, that's good. Maybe he'll do a favor for his old buddy, won't try so hard for that scumbag."

It doesn't work like that, Wallace thought. *He's duty bound to defend Cooper. That's his job.* But he said "There you go," raised his glass to her and enjoyed the feeling of a vise loosening for a change.

42

The next day, Cooper was arraigned and pleaded not guilty to every count. A month later, the case was assigned to Judge Joyce Hens Green, who appointed Katz Cooper's lawyer for death penalty proceedings if the government decided to go that route. The last day of September, she committed Cooper to Northern Neck pending trial and set a status hearing for the first week of November. But that break in the action didn't give Wallace any relief. On October 5, he took the stand in Terry Butera's civil trial.

After making it through the deposition, and the four hours Gallagher had prepped him over the last two days, Wallace felt comfortable and ready to go. He told Irving his name, rank, position, and history with MPD before he brought him to the night in question.

"Detective, were you in charge of the operation involving Mr. Butera that night?"

"I was."

"Can you elaborate on that? What did being in charge actually entail?"

"I was responsible for supervising the other detectives to assure that Mr. Butera entered and left the premises as planned."

"And how did that work out?"

Gallagher rose to her feet. "Objection! Your Honor," she said to Judge Coleen Kollar-Kotelly, "may we approach?" She waved them forward and Gallagher turned to Irving. "Cut the crap, counselor. There are sanctions for that kind of bullshit and you know it. Can we play by the rules, please?" Irving turned to the judge.

"I'll do my best, Your Honor, I promise."

"Please do, Mr. Irving. I know you can and I expect you will."

Back behind his table, Irving asked Wallace about MPD's plan that night and what Cimino and Ruffin were supposed to do, before he zeroed in on him.

"Detective, tell the jury where you were during the operation."

"I was parked about forty, fifty yards down Delaware, past K, facing towards 1015."

"Could you see the rear entrance of 1015 Delaware?"

"No. The building was set back from the street, with a courtyard between it and the sidewalk."

"Could you see the courtyard?"

"No, just the entrance to it off the sidewalk."

"Was Mr. Butera wearing a wire or any other device that enabled you to hear what he was saying and what others might say to him?"

"No, we were afraid that people inside the building might pat him down and we didn't want to take that risk."

"So your answer to my question is 'No,' correct?"

"Correct."

"Now once you parked, Detective, did you see Mr. Butera enter the back yard of the building?"

"I did."

"And did you see him after he entered the back yard?"

"No."

"Could Detectives Cimino or Ruffin see or hear Mr. Butera after he entered the back yard?"

"You'll have to ask them."

"You said you supervised the operation, didn't you, Detective?"

"Yes."

"Did you and the detectives have any occasion to discuss the murder of Mr. Butera afterwards?"

"Yes."

"And did they tell you in the course of any of those discussions whether or not they saw Mr. Butera after he entered the back yard?"

"Objection. Hearsay," Gallagher said. "Sustained."

"You planned this operation, didn't you, Detective Wallace?"

"In conjunction with other people at MPD, yes."

"Who were those people?"

"The detectives I've already mentioned, plus Detective James Trainum, and everything was run past the Chief and the Deputy Chief for their approval too."

"That's Chief Ramsey and Deputy Chief Proctor?"

"Yes."

"And did they approve your plan?"

"Objection, hearsay." "Overruled."

"They did."

"Did the plan they approved provide for observing Mr. Butera in the back yard?"

"No."

"At the door to the house?'

"No."

"Inside the house?"

"No."

"Did the plan they approved provide for listening to Mr. Butera in the yard, at the door to the house, or inside the house?"

"No."

"So, just so the record's clear, your plan, that the Chief and Deputy Chief approved, did not provide for observing or listening to Mr. Butera anywhere at all, at any time after you watched him enter the back yard, do I have that right?"

"Objection, asked and answered." "Sustained."

"Now, Detective Wallace, do you remember any particular conversations you had with Detective Cimino during one of your visits with him that night?" One did stick in Wallace's mind and thanks to Cimino, it made its way into the department's Internal Affairs Report on Butera's death, but he hadn't shared it with Gallagher or anyone else, and she never asked him about it either. He avoided looking at her and pretended to think on it a while before he said "No, not really, nothing specific, just, you know, a sense of uneasiness, I guess you'd call it, about the fact that he hadn't come out yet."

Irving reached across the plaintiff's table and pulled a clipped copy of a document to him. "'Uneasiness'. Is that what you said, Detective?"

"Yes," he said and watched Irving slowly look for the clip he finally found. Gallagher sighed loudly and drummed her fingers on the defense table. "Detective," Irving asked, "do you remember making a joke about what was going on that night?"

"Absolutely not." In for a dime, in for a dollar. Irving reached into his file, pulled out something on MPD stationery, and handed it to Gallagher.

"Your Honor, I've just given counsel a certified copy of Detective Cimino's statement to the Metropolitan Police Department's Internal Affairs Office about the incident that night and would like the court to receive it as plaintiff's exhibit 41." Wallace watched Gallagher look it over for the first time and imagined what she had to be thinking. When she said "No objection" and handed it back to Irving, he was grateful that he was too far away to be singed by the fire in her eyes.

"Let me refresh your memory, Detective," Irving said. "Detective Cimino said that on one of your drivebys, you motioned him to roll down his window, then made what he took to be a joke. Specifically, you said, and I quote, 'Why don't you keep the window down in case we hear any gun shots or screaming?' Is your recollection refreshed?" Gallagher got to her feet.

"Objection! Hearsay!" Irving held the report up.

"Your Honor, this is a record of an act that MPD maintains as part of its regularly conducted business, which makes it admissible as an exception to the hearsay rule under section 6(b) of Rule 803."

"I'll allow it. Overruled."

318

"I honestly do not remember saying that," Wallace said, "but if he said I did, I'm not going to argue about it. I'd just tell you that a joke like that wouldn't be anything out of the ordinary during a stakeout like that."

"So is it your testimony that was a joke, or did you mean it seriously?" Wallace weighed the advantage of answering one way or the other and found none.

"It was just typical cop humor, you know, just trying to take the edge off a tense situation."

"So tense that you had to wake up Detective Cimino during one of your circles around the building?"

"It had been a long day for all of us."

"Is that a yes?"

"Yes. That's a yes."

"And how did you come to wake him up?"

"I'd paged him a few times and didn't get a response, so I stopped by his car and saw he was sleeping. Again, you need to understand we were putting in long days on this case under a whole lot of pressure, Mr. Irving."

"So, Detective Cimino fell asleep because you were undermanned and overtired, is that your –"

"Objection. Argumentative. Asked and answered." "Sustained."

"Detective Wallace, I believe you said you arrived at 1015 Delaware at 9:20 and circled the block the first time at 9:30, is that correct?"

"Yes."

"Did you have occasion to make a second pass around the block?"

"I did, maybe another fifteen minutes later."

"And had anyone seen or heard anything by that time?"

"No."

"Had Detective Cimino followed your order?"

"What order?" Irving looked down at his notes. "'Keep the window down in case we hear any gun shots or screams'."

"Objection!" Gallagher said, but Wallace answered anyhow.

"I told you that wasn't an order. It was a joke." He followed Irving's eyes to the jury and didn't like what he saw. He disliked Irving's smirk even more.

"Withdraw the question," Irving said, then led Wallace through his surprise at seeing a police car arrive at the scene and his sprint into the courtyard. He asked him to describe what he saw there.

"I saw Mr. Butera on the ground being tended to a by a uniformed policeman."

"How did you know it was Mr. Butera?"

"I recognized him from our meeting to talk about him going to 1015 Delaware."

"Did Mr. Butera look like you remembered him?"

"Objection!" Gallagher called out. "The witness has no way of knowing what counsel's asking."

"Okay, I'll be more specific. Did Mr. Butera look like he had been injured?"

"Yes."

"In what way?" Wallace pulled up the crystal-clear vision of Butera's battered face that he'd never forget any more than he'd forget Schein's severed neck.

"His face was bruised and bleeding. His eyes were closed and his eyelids were puffed up with blood, all black and blue."

"Can you be more specific about where you saw him bleeding from?"

"It was hard to tell. Nose, ears, forehead, cheeks. Pretty much everywhere." Irving turned to the jury.

"'Pretty much everywhere,'" he repeated. "Was he breathing?"

"The officer attending to him said he was."

"Did you personally attend to him, Detective Wallace?"

"No." Irving turned to the jury again, but his question was for Wallace.

"Let me make sure I have this right, Detective. The man you sent to this crack house was lying bleeding and unrecognizable on the ground and you couldn't be bothered to tend to him?"

"Objection! Counsel is putting words in his mouth." "Sustained. Mr. Irving, please."

"I'll rephrase, Your Honor. Why didn't you offer Mr. Butera any assistance?"

"I left that to the professionals, the EMTs who arrived at the scene just after me."

"Did the EMTs remove Mr. Butera from the scene?"

321

"Yes."

"Was he alive when they removed him?"

"Yes. Barely." When Irving said he had no further questions, Wallace felt the same way.

Gallagher tried hard to resuscitate his testimony, but two weeks later the jury put the nail in his coffin. On October 18, she called to let him know they awarded Mrs. Butera $98,100,000 in damages for the loss of her son, $70,000,000 of it to come from Wallace, Cimino, and Ruffin as compensation for depriving them of their civil rights, plus another $530,000 thrown in as punitive damages just in case the $70 million wasn't punitive enough. The District was on the hook for the other $27,000,000 and change.

"You can rest assured the District's going to appeal, so this isn't over by a long shot, don't worry about that." He finished his calculations and read the number he'd circled at the bottom of the page.

"Believe me, I'm not, mostly because I've got another seventeen million, six hundred and thirty-two thousand, five hundred other things to worry about first. Who's going to pay that?"

"Detective, like I said, there's a long way to go –"

"It's staring me in the face right now, trust me. Is that supposed to come out of my pocket?" He could hear her sigh over the phone.

"I can't guarantee anything, but the usual practice, by far, is that the District will cover you for any compensatory damages." Wallace looked over his sheet.

"Including the punitive damages? I can't afford the one-thirty-two-five any more than I can afford the seventeen million."

"That's going to be a judgment call, I'm afraid, but, again, let's jump off that bridge when we come to it."

The jumping off the bridge part sounded like a pretty good option, but a better one was waiting for him at home. He said his goodbyes and in fifteen minutes, was pouring himself a full tumbler of Jack, neat. Halfway through it, he noticed a light flashing. It was from Robbie, asking if he was coming by. He called her back.

"Hey," she said. "I tried you at work but they said you left about an hour ago. Everything okay?"

"Actually, it's not," he said. "I got some bad news in the Butera case."

"Oh, no. How bad?"

"Like seventeen million bad."

"Oh, my Lord! Are you joking?"

"Not hardly."

"I am so sorry, Tom. How about if you come over and let me take your mind off it a while? That'd help, wouldn't it?"

"It would, but I don't think I'd be too good company tonight. Let me just take a little time to wrap my head around it a while, okay?" They both knew what meant, but before she could answer, another call clicked in and he excused himself to get it. It was Ramsey. He told Robbie he'd call her back and put down his drink.

"Detective," Ramsey said, "I just got the word about what the jury did in Butera. I want you to know that we're going to fight this all the way up the line. You know and I know that you ran a good operation that went south through no fault of your own. Rest assured, we've got your back."

323

"I know that, sir, and I appreciate the call. It's just a lot to take in. You don't pay me that kind of money, you know?" Ramsey laughed.

"Keep that sense of humor, Detective, and listen, seeing as how tomorrow's Friday, if you want to take the day off and take some time to regroup over the weekend, that's fine with me."

"Thanks, Chief. I'll take you up on that. See you Monday." He put down the phone and started to punch up Robbie's number until the half-full glass reminded him he had a better idea.

43

A tangled pile of bodies, black and white, male and female, arms and legs sprawled over one other, stretched away from him. He knelt down and separated the limbs before he sank to his knees next to the first body on the left, clutched the man's shoulders, and turned him over. He screamed at the sight of Marcus' dead face, the bullet hole from his gun where his left eye used to be, then watched in horror as his body rolled over a ledge and disappeared noiselessly into the darkness. He turned the second body over and screamed again as the head rolled away and Schein's face disappeared into the bottomless gorge. When he caught his breath, he crawled on his knees and somehow managed to gather up the next three forms at once and watched, weeping and wailing, as Caity, Baby, and Emory rolled past him into oblivion. He crawled dutifully to the next corpse and rolled it over to see Eric Butera's death mask stare vacantly back at him before his body plunged into the chasm. He waited for his heartbeat to slow before he turned to the only body left and saw the back of a thick black neck, and arms reaching away from him across dirt that was turning into mud before his eyes. He made himself reach down and roll him over, then screamed at the sight of his own face, bloated and vomiting, falling without a sound into the abyss.

His eyes sprung open and stared at the ceiling of a brightly lit room, his mind unsure if the echoes of terror rippling through it were real or imagined, and just as unsure about where he actually was. The sharp sunlight streaming through cracks in the shades forced him to close his eyes again and he swatted at the nightstand, hoping that his hand would find the Snooze button on his clock radio. When it came on, he threw his arm over his eyes, exhausted from waking up.

"Let's check in with Alexandra Steele on what we can expect for the rest of the day and tomorrow," he heard. "Alexandra, it looks nice and bright out there now. Has the rain gone for good?" He turned to the clock and saw 4:08 P.M. He struggled to remember the last thing he was sure was real. Nothing came to him after he hung up with Ramsey, so he leaned over the side of the bed to see if circumstantial evidence on the floor would jolt his memory. He saw the usual suspects – a tumbler, a tall glass, an array of bottles and cans – some standing, some not – and an empty Miller six-pack carton. He tried to convince himself that some of it been there for days, but he wouldn't swear to it.

He spun to see if Robbie was next to him and was happy to see she wasn't, but one grain of relief had no chance against the waves of pressure that rose yet again from the deepest caverns of his waking brain and pinned him to the bed. The $17 million-plus verdict was the first to crash down on him, followed immediately by the unabating torture of realizing that his own words made it so much easier for the jury to render it. The looming prospect of the Cooper trial dead ahead came next, then the consequences of his fucking up there: Would he walk? Would Robbie ever forgive him if he did, or would he lose her too? And would he ever be able to pull his life back together, with or without her? The vise had clamped tight long ago and he didn't have the words to describe the unremitting pressure he felt now, or the will to find them.

He pushed himself out of bed, got slowly to his feet, and waited for the world to stop spinning. When it wouldn't, he steadied himself with a hand against the wall until he made into the bathroom and stood under a cold shower that shocked his system enough to convince him that he had to pull himself together, just like it did every other time, until he didn't. He threw on his boxers and a sleeveless undershirt and put up a pot of coffee in the kitchen, then headed down the half-flight of steps to his living room to lay on the couch while it brewed. The blare of the phone blasted him back awake. He scooped it up and mumbled hello.

"Tom! Finally! This is Jim. Where you been, man?"

"Hey. Hold on one minute." He put the phone down, sat up, rubbed his face, and waited for a good answer to come to him. When it didn't, he picked the receiver back up and said "Yeah, I was out takin' a little walk for a change. It was great to get outside, get some fresh air, you know."

"Wow. That's good to hear, man. Especially since it was rainin' like a bitch downtown till like a half hour ago, but I'm glad to hear it's nice and bright all the way out there in Southwest."

Silence hung on the line until Wallace answered "Jim, I'm fine. Everything's good, man, seriously, okay?"

"Tom, I was just checking in to see how you were handling the Butera thing. I couldn't believe the fucking jury would do that, even in this city."

"It's rough, man, I'm not going to lie about it, but the lawyer and the Chief tell me it ain't over till it's over, so I'm just going to wait and see what happens. What else can I do?" Wallace knew Trainum had an idea about that and thought about how'd he reassure him he was taking care of himself until he heard him say "Nothin', man. That's all you can do, just hang in there, right?"

He uttered a silent thanks and said "I appreciate you checkin' in on me, Jim. I'll see you on Monday."

The coffee machine dinged it was ready for him and he got to his feet only to sit back down when he saw the answering machine light flashing. He clicked through two Trainum messages, then heard Robbie.

"Hey, darlin'," she said. "Just checkin' in on you to see how you're doin'. Give me a call when you're up to it. Miss you. 'Bye."

He lifted the receiver to call her back, then put it back down. He got himself dressed, packed a bag, and headed for the KFC on

Bladensburg. When Robbie pulled her door open an hour after he left, he dropped the suitcase and held up the paper bag. "Dinner," he said and lifted it higher till she freed him from her arms and cupped his face in her hands.

"Oh my Lord, you are a sight for sore eyes. I was so worried about you. You know I left a message, right?"

"I do, and when I heard it just a little while ago, I thought I'd surprise you rather than call you back."

"I am so glad you did," she said and pulled him by his free hand into the kitchen. "Sit yourself down and let me pour us something before we eat. What'll you have?" He stole a look at the Captain before he looked at her.

"You know what? I think I'll just have some water or a Coke if you got it." She threw him a look.

"What now? This shit scared you sober or what?"

"No, not yet, at least, but I'm thinking I ought to start cutting back a little, you know. Save the booze for when we have something to celebrate, not just to get me past feeling like I'm feelin' now, which is nothin' but rotten. But you go ahead, doesn't mean you can't have something." She thought about it a second before she opened the fridge, reached in, and pulled out half a half-liter of Dr. Pepper.

"This do? Been in there since Albertha left." He laughed for the first time in a long time.

"It'll be a good test. Pour me a tall one. With a lotta ice." She did and poured herself one too. When the ice stopped fizzing, she reached over to clink glasses with him.

"To Dr. Pepper," she said and watched him bolt a swallow down while she took a sip and crinkled her nose. "You like that shit?" she asked. "I can't tell what it's supposed to taste like, 'less it's cough medicine. Ugh."

He grimaced his agreement and slid the glass back to her. "Okay, now give me some water, like quick." She ran it straight from the tap and handed him the glass. He downed half of it before he pulled it down.

"You sure you don't want somethin' got a little kick to kill it?" she asked. He drained the rest of the glass and shook his head before heading to the sink for more. "I'll stick with this for now."

By seven o'clock, they finished the chicken. By eight, they'd finished each other. She lay in his arms and pulled strands of his chest hair straight until he swatted her hand away. She smiled and raised herself up on one elbow to look into his eyes.

"Can I tell you something?"

"As long as it's not more bad news, absolutely."

"I think I'm in love with you. Is that good enough?" He lifted his head to kiss her full on the lips.

"It sure is, for me at least, but you sure it's good news for you? You been payin' attention to what's going on with me, see the same mess I see in the mirror?" He fell onto his back and shook his head at the ceiling. "Hard for me to believe anyone'd have a good feeling at all about me these days, much less love. I don't even *like* myself." She snuggled in close.

"I think that may be why I love you. When we first took up, I was the needy one, I was the fucked-up one, I was the one feelin' like shit, and you bailed me out in all kinds of ways, made me actually feel good about myself for the first time in a long time. Hell, the reason I went out and looked for that job at CVS was 'cause you said you'd help me out with the GED. I ain't had no one say they'd do anything good for me since – I don't know, maybe Vontae – but even all his stuff was just talk and dreams. He couldn't do what you did for me, just that alone."

"I appreciate hearing that, Robbie, I do, but you don't need to compare me and him. You two were right for each other then. We're right for each other now." He rolled her onto her back and kissed her long and hard before he pulled his head back and said the words he'd never said to anyone before.

"I love you too." She laughed and reached for the cock making its presence felt down below. "And I can feel just how much."

It took him a little longer to finish this time, but it was worth every tickle, lick, suck, and thrust. Since she exploded three times before he did, it didn't seem to bother her too much either. She snuggled in his arms and fell asleep quickly, but he was still wide awake. Her clock told him it was only 8:48. He'd been up barely five hours, but they might've been the most important five hours of his life. If she meant what she said, and if he did too. Two more things to worry about.

Ten minutes later, he downed a shot of Jack at the sink to try to loosen that vice one more time.

44

A few weeks later, Katz called and asked if he wanted to meet him for dinner at the restaurant of his choice, which they both knew would be Georgia Brown's. At 7 o'clock that Thursday, they took their seats at a table in a quiet side room.

"As you requested, Mr. Katz," the waitress said. "And you're going to have it all to yourselves, gentlemen. I'll be right back."

"You asked for this?" Wallace asked.

"Not the alone part, but I wanted somewhere where we could hear each other talk."

"About something more than 'What're you doing for Thanksgiving?', I'm guessing."

"Just a little," Katz said. "We can get the business out of the way first, then spend the rest of the time catching up." The waitress popped back with some bread and water.

"Can I take your drink orders?" Katz opened his hand to Wallace. He'd prepared for this moment at least a dozen times, but felt his steely resolve melting now that it was actually here. He wasn't sure what he'd say until he opened his mouth and heard the words come out just as he rehearsed them.

"A club soda, please. Perrier if you've got it." She turned to Katz. "Johnny Walker Red on the rocks with a splash of water please." When she left, Katz gave Wallace his impressed face.

"So you're still hanging in there," he said. "That's great." Wallace stuck to the script, complete with shrug.

"Yeah, it's a struggle every day, you know, but I'm still doing what I got to do, man." Katz suddenly looked stricken.

"Hey, does it bother you that I ordered booze? I didn't even think about it. I can change –". Wallace held up his hand. That was off script but he knew the answer cold.

"Not at all. I'm the one with the problem, not you. Live your life, man. Enjoy yourself." Katz shook his head.

"'Enjoy' is not a word that leaps to mind these days."

"'Cause of Cooper?"

"Yeah, but before we get to that, I just want to tell you how sorry I am you got pasted with that judgment in Butera. I was amazed – and appalled."

"Appreciate the sympathy."

"You're not really going to be on the hook for that, are you? The District will cover you, right?" Wallace spread his hands wide.

"Remains to be seen, man. It's really going to fuck up my credit rating if they don't." Katz smiled.

"Seriously, though, if you need any legal help on that, let me know."

"I appreciate that too, Jake, but let's move on to something more pleasant, like your client facing life for triple murder." Katz nodded, but took his time before he said anything.

"Let me ask you something. Do you see the motions I file?" Wallace remembered just one that Wainstein showed him to give him a heads-up about what might be coming his way.

"The only one I saw said you were going to ask the judge to suppress Cooper's statements to PG, the wiretap stuff, and a lot of other stuff I gave up on reading. He's getting his money's worth out of you, I'll say that." Katz shrugged.

"It comes with the job. And that's why I wanted to talk with you before things got too far along. I'm assuming Mr. Wainstein has told you you're going to testify, right?"

"Jake, I can't talk to you about any of that, you know that."

"Fair enough, but just know that if he doesn't call you for some reason, I will, and either way, I'm going to have to come at you full throttle. That's part of the job too." Wallace flashed back to Irving roasting him on a spit.

"Will it cost me $17 million?"

"No."

"Then I'm already ahead of the game. Now let me ask you something. Did you read Cooper's statements to PG?"

"I did. All of them. More than once."

"Then you know they dotted every i and crossed every t. After a while, he was reciting his rights better than PG was asking about them."

"Let's save all that for the courtroom. I just want to make sure you knew what to expect and you'd be ready for it. Like Michael Corleone said–". Wallace didn't to hear that or see the cop's brains again. He held up his hands.

"I got it. Now I'm going to tell you something. You're going to have your hands full with this guy. You read what he said. He's a world class bullshit artist in addition to being a murderer. His version of the truth is whatever he thinks anyone will believe." Katz shrugged.

"But you believed his last story because that was the truth you wanted to believe, right?"

"Because it *was* the truth, and he only told it when he finally ran out of lies."

"Did you believe him when he said he was sorry about it?" Wallace laughed.

"Hell, no! And what does that matter anyhow? I didn't think 'sorry' was a defense."

"It's not, but it is a mitigating factor at sentencing."

"Little early to be worrying about sentencing, isn't it?"

"That list of motions you read? If you looked at the heading at the top, they were just if your side doesn't ask for the death penalty. If they do, you're going to see a whole shitload more." Wallace played dumb.

"The death penalty? Here? In D.C.?"

"That's the word on the street, at least Fifth Street."

"When was the last time that happened here? Never?"

"So close. Once, in 1957. A guy was electrocuted for killing an off-duty police officer. And you want to know the last time a Federal court ordered the death penalty? I looked it up. 1942. And that was by the military."

"You're making my point. There've been a lot of murders, even triple murders here since 1957. And even if they did ask for it, what're the chances a DC jury will give it to him?" Saying it out loud made him seriously doubt Robbie's fondest wish would ever come true.

"You're probably right, but I can't leave it to chance, so just be ready to be grilled, that's all I'm saying." Wallace threw him a salute.

"Message received. Do your worst." Katz lifted a glass to him and Wallace clinked it, then took a bubbly sip and looked away until Katz finished enjoying his.

"By the way, you know how they kill Federal prisoners?" Katz asked. *Stringing them up by the balls might satisfy Robbie,* Wallace thought, but he was pretty sure that wasn't on the list. "Enlighten me," he said

"It's in the DOJ regs. 'Intravenous injection of lethal substance or substances'."

"I look forward to seeing that, but even that's too good for this fucker for all the shit he's done."

"Allegedly. Anyhow, you might want to refresh your memory about him showing any remorse, contrition, whatever, because you will be asked about it if they do wind up trying to kill him."

Wallace remembered reading and hearing Cooper say "sorry" a whole bunch of times about what he did to Officer Howard and the people he slaughtered at Starbucks, but he didn't believe it once, even for a millisecond. Like Trainum said, the only thing he was sorry about was getting caught, but he decided to keep that to himself and save it for trial too.

"Noted. So you up for defending your first death case?"

"I'm not looking forward to it, but if I have to, I'll partner up with someone who has. That Lawyers' Committee for Civil Rights I was telling you about has a lot of lawyers from states where they try them all the time, so I'll find someone, don't worry about that." Wallace watched Katz bolt down the rest of his Johnny Walker and ask for another one when the waitress came by to see if they were ready to order. When she left two Perloo orders later, Katz must've decided he'd taken care of all his business.

335

"Let's change the subject," he said. "How're you handling all this?"

"All what? Cooper? I'm glad it's finally coming to a head, man. It's been pretty much all I've been thinking of for two years and, what, four months now? I'm ready for it to be over." Katz nodded, then leaned towards him, a look on his face that Wallace couldn't recall seeing before.

"I don't mean just Cooper, which'd be enough for anyone to have to handle that long. I'm talking about everything else that's been coming your way – Butera, trying to stay on the straight and narrow with the booze, never mind what I don't know about –".

"Gentlemen," the waitress said, "here are your Shrimp Perloos. Enjoy!" Wallace was never so happy to see a meal come and dug in right away. Katz must have got the point and enjoyed his with the same gusto. Wallace kept the dinner conversation to a minimum, partly because he didn't like where it was going, but mostly because the sooner they started, the sooner they'd finish and he could get his hands on a bottle of something a lot stronger than club soda. Katz came up for air first and didn't wait for Wallace to stop eating to pick up where he left off.

"But seriously, you ever talk to anybody about all the stuff you got goin' on?" The only face that flickered through Wallace's head was Denny's, his old AA sponsor, but he wasn't going to get into that.

"Who, like a shrink? That would be a no."

"Doesn't have to be a shrink. It could be just, I don't know, someone at the department, or the Police Benevolent Association, or a friend you really trust. I'd love to volunteer for the job, but seeing as how I'm going to go for your jugular sometime soon, I'm probably not the right guy." Wallace took another sip of his soda, and a chance.

336

"Well, you'll be happy to know I do have someone to talk to. I'm actually seeing someone, believe it or not – and no, I don't want to talk about her, either. I'm good, Jake, okay? I appreciate you worrying about me, but you don't have to. I'm good, man, really."

"'Someone' is good, Tom. I'm really happy to hear that." *You wouldn't be if you knew she thought Cooper would be getting off light with a lethal injection*, Wallace thought while Katz finished digesting a shrimp.

"Where'd you meet her?"

"Just around."

"She in D.C.?" *Nothing good is going come of this*, Wallace thought, and put his fork down.

"Jake, I'm glad you're interested and happy for me and all, but it's just a boyfriend-girlfriend kind of thing right now and I don't want to jinx it, okay? It's been a long time since I had even that, so I just want to be cool about it for a while. I'll invite you to the wedding if there ever is one, I promise. Till then, let's just chill."

Katz waited for the shrimp in his mouth to slide down, then nodded. "Absolutely," he said.

"Thank you. I appreciate it."

Katz downed a slug of scotch and waited for Wallace to fill his mouth with Perloo before he added "Sounds serious, though." When Wallace's laughter turned to choking, Katz hopped out of his seat and slapped him on the back, stopping only when Wallace waved him off. He fell back in his seat, laughing loudly.

"You fucker!" Wallace got out after the last of the debris cleared his throat. Katz stopped laughing long enough to tell him "Tom, I don't give a shit who she is. I'm just happy she's doing you some good."

The rest of the meal passed without incident and a little after 9, they came out the door and enjoyed watching a little whirlwind of a breeze stir the leaves in McPherson Square before it was joined by a light rain growing harder. Wallace pointed up 15th St.

"My car's up there a couple of blocks," he said. "I'll drive you home." They hustled up the walk and stopped for traffic at the corner of I where Wallace felt Katz nudge him, then followed his eyes to a homeless guy trying to get himself under a blanket outside Loeb's Deli across the street. Wallace dug into his wallet and waited for the last car to pass before he crossed the street and threw a buck into his hat. Katz kept walking.

"Excuse me," Wallace said, jogging to his side. "I thought you helped these guys out, man. "Didn't you give me a whole big rap on who you give to and who you don't? This guy didn't qualify?"

"He did not."

"And why is that?"

"Because I was giving so many of them money, I thought I'd go homeless myself trying to help 'em all out, so now I limit myself to two dollars a day – one to a Street Sense guy at lunch, James McNeil if I'm on his block –".

"Hold on. You know the names of the guys you give money to?"

"Just him. He's usually around 18th and K, so whenever I'm up that way, I buy it from him and we chat a while. He's a good guy. Then I give the second dollar to another guy who camps out in front of the MLK library on G Street."

"So you buy two copies of Street Sense?"

"No. He started yelling jokes at me whenever I got near him, so we've become buddies."

"What kind of jokes?"

"Puns mostly, horrible puns. The first time I saw him was when I was walking back from the July Fourth celebration on the mall and I gave the guy next to him a buck, and he says, 'May the Fourth be with you!' I wasn't sure I heard him right so I kept walking, then I hear 'No good deed goes unpunished!' *Pun*-ished, get it? So that was it. He's got a different one every night, so it's like I'm just paying a cover charge for the entertainment."

They jumped in Wallace's car and made a left on G. At the light at 10th Street, Wallace looked to his left at the square black metal and glass library running the length of the block to 9th. Right after he got the green, Katz pointed to a cluster of bodies up ahead camped out under the overhang that kept the entrance area in the middle of the block dry. Some were standing, some sitting, some stretched out for the night. He pulled the collar of his coat up.

"He's probably there," Katz said. "Pull over somewhere. I'll be back in a minute." Wallace pulled to the curb and laid a hand on Katz' arm before he got out, then dug another dollar bill out of his wallet and handed it to him.

"Maybe he'll give you an encore tonight." Katz took it and headed around the front of the car. Wallace watched him ask someone a question, then head towards the front doors. He tapped the back of a man standing in a crowd and shook hands with him when he turned around. They chatted for a few seconds before Katz handed him the two dollars and pointed to Wallace. They exchanged waves through the drizzle before the guy poked Katz in the chest and said something that made him laugh. Katz chatted with him another few seconds, then fist-bumped him and headed back to the car.

"So, did you get an encore?" Wallace asked.

"No, but when I told him you were a cop, he said he had a special one just for you."

"Okay. Let's hear it."

"Did you hear why the Energizer Bunny got arrested?"

"No, why?"

"Charged with battery."

Wallace rolled his eyes and pulled away from the curb. Two minutes later, he pulled to a stop across from the Lansburgh Building. Katz extended a hand and he shook it.

"Tom, it was a pleasure. I look forward to getting our business behind us and getting back to normal."

"Me too," Wallace said and watched him punch up a code and disappear through the doors before he popped his glove compartment, pulled out a plastic flask, and didn't wait a second longer to get back to normal.

45

He spent the holidays with Robbie, mostly at her place, but more and more at his, especially after Christmas, when he gave her a VISA gift card so she could buy some new clothes to keep in D.C. New Year's Eve morning, they stopped at the Maine Avenue Fish Market to pick up the night's dinner and cooked up a mess of fresh shrimp and crab jambalaya, washed down with two bottles of a chardonnay on sale at Schneider's, before they fell onto his couch and put on the tube a little before 11:30.

She stretched out with her head on his shoulder and watched him rapid-fire click from Billy Joel to a bunch of dancers stomping across a stage to Donald Trump talking to Tom Brokaw. Wallace stopped clicking when he heard him say Gladys Knight was going to perform at Mar-A-Lago. "I love her," he said.

"But, if you're thinking of running for President," Brokaw asked, "shouldn't you be up here in Times Square rather than Palm Beach?" Trump laughed.

"Well, we're looking at it seriously. I think I'd do a good job. We'll let you know probably in February."

"Jesus Fucking Christ! Really? Sorry, Gladys, next time," he said and squeezed the clicker faster. When he got to the Neville Brothers playing something with a snaky rhythm, Robbie squeezed his hand and he stopped.

Yellow moon, yellow moon, why you keep peeping in my window?
Do you know something I don't know?
Did you see my baby walking down the railroad tracks?
You can tell me if the girl's ever coming back.

When they finished, she threw her arm around his chest and snuggled in tighter.

"You don't have to worry about me comin' back, 'cause I ain't ever leavin'." Wallace kissed the top of her head.

"That's good to know," he said, "and I ain't either." When the song ended, she took the remote from his hand, muted the TV, sat up, and turned to him.

"Know what I been thinkin' about?" she asked, but didn't wait for his answer. "I been thinkin' about how we got together." He hadn't ever thought about it, but now that he did, he didn't think the FBI bugging her line was what she had in mind.

"Oh yeah?" he hedged.

"Don't you think it's weird that so many people had to die to bring us together? Vontae. Then the people at the Starbucks." *Or maybe just one person who's still alive, at least for now,* he thought. "I do," he said. "It is weird." She snuggled back in.

"'The Lord works in strange ways'," she said. "Isn't that what the preachers say? Maybe it was God's plan."

"That's a pretty cold-blooded God, isn't it?" Wallace said. "Maybe it was really just chance, you know? Two other guys came with me that night to see you, remember? Why didn't you fall in love with either of them?"

"I don't know, it's just nice to think something good might've come of all those murders, that's all I'm sayin'. So they didn't die for nothing, you know?" A career of investigating homicides had convinced Wallace long ago that nothing good ever came out of anyone's murder, but he didn't want to kill the buzz, so he said "It is. It's a good thought and you're a good person for thinking it."

She reached up and turned his face to hers and kissed him softly, then harder, before she reached down and let her hand linger on the bulge growing below his belt before she slid it up to undo the buckle.

342

When she rolled over on the remote, he heard Trump's voice again and felt Wallace's hardness start to wilt until he found it and killed the sound. Pulling his cock out, she revived it with a massage and smiled as it rose to the full and upright position. He slid on to his back and watched her love him until he lightly tugged on the back of her hair. She gave his dick one last kiss, then smiled and lifted herself up without a sound to take him in. They swayed together before the ride got rougher and stayed rough until it gradually slowed and finally came to a full stop.

When he opened his eyes, she was still up there, smiling sweetly, eyes closed, her hands clapped to his hips, her body rocking slowly in time to a song only she heard. When she opened her eyes and saw him smiling up at her, she put the words to the music.

The first time ever I saw your face
I thought the sun rose in your eyes
And the moon and the stars were the gifts you gave
To the dark and the endless skies

Wallace waited till she finished, then laid his hands on hers.

"Your mama was right," he said. "You can't sing for shit." Her jaw dropped and she smacked his stomach before he pulled her forward and down into a tight hug against his chest. They lay for a while breathing in sync until he asked "What time is it?" She spun her head to look at the TV.

"Ten minutes till the ball drops."

"You get yourself cleaned up. I'll mix us some drinks. What'll you have?"

"Whatever you're havin' – unless it's rum. I'm kinda off that. Surprise me," she said before she scampered up the steps to the bathroom. He got himself together and remembered he'd bought some champagne at Schneider's too. He poured it into two deep

343

goblets just before she made it back two minutes before midnight. They sat next to each other and heard Brokaw tell Katie Couric he hoped the Washington Monument didn't burn down because of the fireworks tied to the base of it.

"Ooh, let's watch that," Robbie said. "See if someone's got it on." He flicked the stations till he heard Dick Clark say the countdown was about to start. "Get close to someone you love!" he said and they squeezed together and raised their glasses watching a golden orb starting to come down in New York City. They joined Dick in screaming the numbers down from ten and watched Times Square disappear behind an avalanche of confetti before they clinked their glasses and drained them. The TV picture changed to the Monument aglow with red lights rising from the base to the tip that made it look like a rocket ship ready to take off.

"Oh wow!" Robbie said. "Look at that! DC did good!" They watched fireworks burst all around it until New York City came back onto the other side of the screen and Dick told them they were watching 3500 pounds of confetti blasted from cannons in 13 locations all across the City. Wallace's eyes roamed around his apartment.

"I'm just glad the lights stayed on. All this Millennium shit was freaking me out."

She reached for the champagne and refilled their glasses. "Let's make a toast."

"Okay," he said, tapping her glass with his. "To us." She clinked back and raised her glass high.

"And to burnin' Carl Cooper's ass and sendin' him straight to hell! Happy New Year, motherfucker!" That reminded Wallace of something he'd been telling himself not to worry about till after New Year's, but now that it was after, he started officially worrying. It must have shown on his face because Robbie was looking at him funny.

"You all right?" she asked. "Somethin' the matter?" He finished off the champagne before he told her.

"Did I tell you there's a hearing coming up in his case?" Her look turned to intense interest.

"No, what kind of hearing?"

"It's a preliminary hearing. Basically, it gives Cooper's lawyer a chance to ask questions about any legal problems in the case, how he was questioned, that kind of stuff."

"What kind of legal problems? He confessed, right?"

"Right, but any defense lawyer worth his salt's going to make sure we didn't beat it out of him or do anything else unconstitutional. It's standard operating procedure." Robbie thought on that a while.

"And his lawyer's the guy you told me you knew from when he was a cop?"

"Yeah," Wallace said. "Katz, Jake Katz."

"And he's his lawyer for real now, no 'maybe, could be' kind of thing."

"For real, and I've seen him in a courtroom. He'll do his best to carve me a new asshole, believe me."

"Even though you're buddy buddy from way back?" Wallace took a long swallow of his champagne.

"Even though. His job's to try his best to make the jury think we fucked his client over, and mine is to do my best to convince them

345

we didn't – which we didn't, by the way – but the truth doesn't always carry the day." Robbie snorted.

"Tell me about it. If it did, that runt Cooper'd already be in the ground for what happened to Vontae." Wallace got up and nodded to the champagne bottle. She nodded back and he refilled both their glasses before he sat back down next to her.

"The good thing is I'll get a practice round before I get up on the stand. The guy trying the case for the government is going to walk me through his questions and another guy from his shop'll do his best Katz impression so I can get ready for him too. I hope."

He thought back to his last dinner with Katz at Georgia Brown's for the umpteenth time since the hearing was scheduled, searching his brain for anything he might have said that Katz could beat him over the head with. He might've said something about Cooper knowing his rights better than PG did, but the passage of time and the amount of liquor that'd saturated his brain since then made him doubt his memory. He had no doubt about the biggest thing on his mind, though. That was what lay in store for him if DOJ decided to go for the death penalty. He'd never testified in a death case and he knew from Katz' history lesson that no one in the USA's Office had ever tried one either, so that leap into the great unknown was the most unsettling thing of all. He had a vague recollection of telling Katz to do his worst, but now he hoped he didn't or, with an even fainter hope, wouldn't do even worse himself.

46

Two Mondays later, a secretary escorted him into a conference room where Wainstein was chatting with a tall black man who looked to be in his early forties.

"Tom, good to see you again," Wainstein said and pointed to his companion. "This is Ellis McIntire, one of our senior litigators. He'll be playing the part of Jake Katz this afternoon."

"The resemblance is uncanny," Wallace said. After smiles and handshakes all around, Wainstein pointed him to the far side of a conference table. When they were seated, he said "So, we've all been through this a hundred times, but just to lay it out there and hear any questions or concerns you may have, Tom, this is just to prep you for what you can expect to hear from me and the real Jake Thursday morning. If there's anything we ought to know about what happened during Cooper's arrest, or his interrogation in PG, please tell us so we don't hear it for the first time from Mr. Katz. Stop us at any time and we'll figure out how to deal with whatever it is, okay?" Wallace turned to McIntire.

"Cooper's arrest was straight by the book, so I'd be surprised if you or real Jake will be able to make anything of that."

"Just to be sure, who else was there?" McIntire asked.

"Two FBI agents and one of my senior detectives from MPD. Oh, and a news crew from WUSA that filmed it off the TV, so that's probably even better proof that no one fucked with him."

"That's good as far as it goes," Wainstein said, "but Katz is going to be asking about what happened every second from the time you drove away until Cooper confessed, and Judge Green's probably going to give him wide berth to do it."

"Which Judge Green?" Wallace asked.

347

"Joyce, the redhead, the shorter one. June's the gray-haired one."
Wallace knew exactly who he was talking about. He still
remembered her from a case he testified in probably twenty-five
years ago when she was on the D.C. Superior Court. A black
policewoman named Gail Cobb got shot point-blank in the head by a
guy who was a member of something called The New Nation whose
mission was to rob banks to get money to buy weapons to overthrow
the government. She was the first policewoman, white or black, to
be killed in the line of duty in the country. Most of the Nation
wound up pleading, but the jury convicted the two Judge Green
tried. He had a lot of respect for her.

"Are you prepping Fulginiti and McCann too?"

"Oh, yeah," Wainstein said. "The six days Cooper spent with them
in PG's going to be the main event, no question. They're coming in
after lunch and probably going to be keeping us company till lunch
tomorrow, so why don't we get started and get you back to your
office as soon as we can?"

Back behind his desk two hours later, Wallace's head was still
spinning. He thought he did okay and they didn't tell him he didn't,
so he took some heart from that. Wainstein stopped him once to ask
him to clarify an answer and a couple more times to ask him to give
something a little more thought, but that was it. Nothing out of the
norm, but when Wallace woke up a little before 7:30 Thursday
morning, the thought that'd been nagging him since he left
Wainstein's conference room was still there, this time front and
center: McIntire was no Katz.

He changed into the jeans and sweatshirt he'd left in the bathroom to
keep from waking Robbie, took his suit and shoe bags off the hook
on the door, and tiptoed out to the kitchen. He saw a note on the
table and picked it up. "Good luck today! You'll do great. I love
you." he read, then tucked the note into his pocket and headed for his

348

car. By the time he got to MPD, showered in the gym, changed, and looked over Cooper's statements one more time, he still had 45 minutes to kill before the hearing started at 10, so he fixed himself another coffee and slow walked it to the courthouse to settle himself down.

Wainstein greeted him at the side door to Judge Green's courtroom. "Take a look inside," he said. "You're apparently very popular." Wallace peeked in and saw almost every seat taken. He caught eyes with Trainum sitting in the first row of the gallery and exchanged thumbs-ups with him.

"The PG guys here yet?"

Wainstein nodded to the lawyers' conference room across the hall. "McIntire's just wrapping it up with them. Anything we need to go over?" A favorite line of Katz' popped into his head for some not-so-odd reason.

"No," he said. "Ain't nothin' to it but to do it." Wainstein laughed and patted him on the shoulder.

"I like that," he said. "Good attitude. Why don't you find a seat in the reserved row and I'll see you in there."

At 10 sharp, Judge Green took the bench and at 10:02, Wallace took the stand. He didn't expect any surprises from Wainstein on direct and didn't get any. At 10:20, he sat down and Katz got up. By 10:22, he knew he was right to worry.

"Detective Wallace, did you participate in the arrest of Carl Cooper on the night of March 1?"

"I did not. The FBI handled that."

"Were you present during the FBI's questioning of Mr. Cooper at the FBI Washington Field Office later that night?"

"I was."

"Did you participate in the questioning of Mr. Cooper?"

"Yes."

"Who else participated in it?"

"Detective James Trainum from MPD and FBI Special Agent Brad Garrett."

"Anyone else?" Wallace seemed to remember Oxley being there too, but he couldn't be sure.

"Maybe Special Agent Oxley too?"

"Are you asking me or telling me, Detective?"

"I remember he was on the arrest but I can't remember if he was in the interview room. He may have been sitting behind me. I don't –
". Katz held up some papers to Judge Green.

"Your Honor. This is the FBI 302 on Mr. Cooper's interview that night. May I show it to Detective Wallace to refresh his recollection?" She waved him forward, scanned the document, and told him to proceed. Katz handed it to Wallace and pointed to the bottom of the first page.

"Does that refresh your memory, Detective?" Wallace saw "SA Robert A. Oxley" on the "Interview by" line right next to his own name.

"It does. Thank you, Mr. Katz."

"Now I see that the form uses the word 'interview' and you used the same word, Detective, but to my mind, an 'interview' is something Oprah Winfrey or David Letterman does. You and Detective

Trainum and Agent Garrett and Agent Oxley were conducting an interrogation of Mr. Cooper, isn't that right?"

"Objection!" Wainstein called out. "Sustained," Judge Green said. "Mr. Katz, we all know what an FBI interview is. Let's move on."

"Of course, Your Honor," Katz said.

"How long did this interview last, Detective?"

"Several hours." Katz looked at the top paper, then flicked to the last.

"On page one, it says you began at 'approximately 8:30 p.m.' and on the last page, it says 'the interview ended at approximately 3:24 a.m.'" He extended the packet to Wallace. "Would you like to double-check me on that?" Wallace shook his head no. "So that's about six minutes shy of seven hours in the dead of night, isn't it, Detective?"

"Like I said, it was several hours."

"Was Mr. Cooper arrested that night for the Starbucks murders?"

"He was not."

"What was he arrested for?"

"The shooting of a Prince Georges County police officer in 1996."

"Was he interrogated about that shooting for seven hours?"

"Part of it."

"How long a part of it?" *A very short part*, Wallace thought, but he said "I really don't recall." Katz flipped forward a few pages.

"Let me see if I can help you out. At the top of page three, his 302 says 'At approximately 9:00 p.m., Cooper was advised of his rights, and waived and signed an Advice of Rights Waiver form in the presence of you and FBI Special Agents Garrett and Oxley. Cooper was specifically asked about the Starbucks investigation.' Does that clear things up for you?"

"If that's what it says, that's what happened." Katz nodded and walked back behind his table, milking the moment for all it was worth. Wallace saw a door open at the back of the courtroom and froze when he saw Robbie come through and look for a seat. She edged along the back row until she found one and sat down, then beamed a smile at him but he didn't smile back, petrified by the prospect of not only being in Katz' crosshairs, but having her witness it.

"Detective?" he heard Katz say, "would you like me to repeat the question?" Wallace nodded, and struggled to hear it over the pounding in his brain.

"So, of the nearly seven hours that you and the FBI spent interrogating Mr. Cooper that night, only one half-hour was spent on the charge that he was actually arrested for, isn't that right?"

"Again, if that's what it says, that's what it says."

"And so the remaining six hours and twenty-four minutes were spent on a crime that he was not arrested for, isn't that correct?"

"Yes."

"And after that six hours and twenty-four minutes of questioning, did Mr. Cooper confess to the killings at Starbucks?"

"He did not."

"In fact, he repeatedly denied that he did the killings, didn't he?"

"He did."

"Detective Wallace, did you have any physical evidence at that time that tied Mr. Cooper to the killings?"

"No."

"So if you didn't have any physical evidence on him and he denied any participation in the matter, what reason did you have to interrogate him at all?" Wainstein jumped to his feet.

"Objection, Your Honor! Mr. Katz knows very well that the government does not have to disclose its evidence at this stage of the proceedings. Detective Wallace is not on trial, Your Honor, Mr. Cooper is." "Sustained." Katz picked a transcript off his table and held it up, cover page out.

"You were present at Mr. Cooper's extradition proceeding before Commissioner Coburn last March, correct, Detective? I can give you this if you need your recollection refreshed again."

"Objection, Your Honor!"

"Sustained. Mr. Katz, please."

"I apologize, Your Honor. Detective Wallace, would you like to see the transcript of the proceedings?"

"No, counselor," Wallace said. "I remember being there, thank you." Katz riffled to a clipped page.

"Do you remember me being there?" Wallace blazed a stare at Katz before he answered.

"Yes, Mr. Katz. You were Mr. Cooper's attorney."

"Excellent. And do you remember me asserting Mr. Cooper's Sixth Amendment rights at that hearing, specifically saying," he read, "'Your Honor, for the record, my client will not consent to any further interviews by MPD or the FBI or the Prince Georges Police or any other law enforcement agency without his lawyer present.'"

"I do."

"And yet, on March 1, you let the FBI question him without his lawyer present. Why did you do that, detective?"

"You read it from his 302. He signed a waiver." Katz flipped a page on his pad.

"Detective, I want to ask you some questions about the Prince Georges Police Department's interviews of Mr. Cooper, but first let me ask you if you accompanied Mr. Cooper and members of the PG police force on the ride from D.C. to the county police station."

"I did not."

"Did anyone from the PG Police Department tell you what Mr. Cooper might have said on the way over?"

"Objection. Hearsay." "Your Honor, this surely qualifies as a regularly conducted activity exception for law enforcement officers," Katz said.

"I'll allow it. You may answer, Detective."

"Not that I remember."

"Do you want to take a minute to think about it? Or would you like me to refresh your memory about that too?" Wallace took more time than he wanted to plumb the depths of a memory that even he was starting to question now, but he still couldn't locate any evidence of hearing anything about that from anyone at PG. Was Katz just screwing with him or was the booze or the passage of time keeping him from the truth? He took a chance that he actually did know what he was talking about this time.

"If you know something I don't know, counselor, please tell me, but I have no recollection of anyone at PG telling me anything Cooper said in the car." Katz stared at him hard, the look of doubt on his face telling the courtroom he did know something, but Wallace thought he saw a flicker of regret in his eyes before he dipped his head to read from his pad.

"Mr. Cooper told me that during the ride over, he asked Sergeant McCann if he could take a polygraph on Starbucks at the PG police station, but the sergeant told him he couldn't. Is it your testimony that Sergeant did not tell you that?"

Wallace cursed himself for remembering only now that McCann did tell him that, but he wasn't going to give Katz the pleasure of knowing it. "Sorry, counselor, I truly do not remember hearing that," he said and prayed that McCann wouldn't remember it either when Katz grilled him.

"Let's move on, Detective. You were present when the Prince Georges Police Department questioned Mr. Cooper, weren't you?"

"Not for all of it," he felt compelled to qualify, "but for most of it, yes."

"And you heard him answer their questions during the time you were present?"

"Yes."

"And it still didn't occur to you that you heard me assert his right to be silent?"

"I heard them ask him repeatedly if he wanted a lawyer and I heard him waive his right to one every time."

"With all due respect, that's not what I asked, Detective. Do you remember hearing me assert that right?"

355

"I do."

"Did you ever inform anyone at the Prince Georges Police Department that I did?"

"No."

"Not Detective Fulginiti?"

"No."

"Not Sergeant McCann?"

"No."

"Not anyone else with the Department?"

"No."

"Despite knowing from my statement in open court, in your presence, that I expressly said he was not waiving his rights." Wallace shrugged.

"I guess he changed his mind. He spoke freely and voluntarily to me and the FBI, and to the Prince Georges PD, after he was read his rights every single time he was interviewed by any of them."

Katz turned to Judge Green. "Your Honor, I intend to move that these statements be excluded from evidence."

"I'll be setting a briefing schedule for all of your motions, Mr. Katz. Continue, counselor."

"Detective, I've read Mr. Cooper's statements while he was in the custody of the PG Police. Have you read them?"

"I have."

"Is it fair to say that he gave several different accounts about what happened at Starbucks that night?" Wallace grunted a bitter laugh.

"Yeah, that's fair to say."

"Regardless of what he said his role was – or wasn't – at any particular time, do you recall him making statements of remorse about his role in the incident?"

"Maybe once or twice, but it was more him being remorseful about being caught, that's all."

"Really?" Katz said. "Let me read this to you from his statement on March 2: 'I'm sorry for the deaths of the three people. I want to take responsibility for my part and show God faith. I am sorry.' Do you recall that statement, Detective?"

"Yes, but you left out the part where he blamed the killings on Alton Wesley."

"And do you remember this from March 3? 'I really am sorry for the deaths of those people. He didn't have to kill them. There was nothing I could do for them.'"

"He's sorry Alton had to kill them, but he was the one who killed them. That's whatever the opposite of taking responsibility is."

"My question is do you remember him saying that?"

"Yes."

"Again on March 3: 'I'm really sorry for the deaths'. Do you remember him saying that?"

"What difference does it make? It was all part of him trying to cover up the fact that he murdered those people, not Alton Wesley or anyone else."

"You're missing my point, Detective Wallace. You told me that Mr. Cooper said he was sorry for his role 'maybe once or twice,' but now I've refreshed your recollection about him saying that three times." He shook his handful of statements at Wallace. "Would you like to hear more, Detective, because there's a lot more in here?"

"Objection, Your Honor!" Wainstein called out. "Counsel is badgering the witness!"

"Your Honor," Katz said, "I am trying to demonstrate that Detective Wallace is not a credible witness, either because he truly cannot remember statements that he did hear, or because he's willing to shade the truth to convict my client." Wallace grabbed the arms of his chair. He took a quick look at Robbie, her face aimed at Katz, taut with tension and rage.

"Mr. Katz," Judge Green said, "you've made your point. The objection's sustained. Please move on."

"Certainly, Your Honor. Detective Wallace, how long have you been a policeman with the Metropolitan Police Department?" Wallace took a second to do the math and was shocked to hear the answer that came out of his mouth.

"A little over forty years. I started in 1959."

"Were you at the Prince Georges Police Department when they used the Computer Voice Stress Analyzer, which you may know as the CVSA?"

"I was." Wainstein's furrowed brow made Wallace think that he may not have mentioned that ridiculous thing to him on Monday.

"Does the Metropolitan Police Department use the CVSA, Detective?"

"No, it does not."

"Did the FBI use it during its interrogation of Mr. Cooper?"

"It did not, to the best of my knowledge."

"Does the FBI ever use it –"

"Objection!"

"– to the best of your knowledge, Detective?"

"You may answer, Detective," Judge Green said.

"To the best of my knowledge, it does not. You'll have to ask them."

"Oh, don't worry, I will," Katz said. "So would it be fair to say that you have never been trained on its use?"

"Objection! Irrelevant." "Sustained."

"In your forty years of police experience, Detective Wallace, had you ever heard of the CVSA before you went to the Prince Georges Police Department?"

"No."

"Are you aware of any law enforcement agency – Federal, state, or local – that uses it or has used it other than Prince Georges County?"

"No."

"Do you know if its results are admissible in court?"

"I do not."

"Does the Metropolitan Police Department use a polygraph – a lie detector machine – in its investigations?" "Yes."

"Are you familiar with its use?" "Yes."

"Did you suggest they use it?" "No."

"Are polygraph results admissible in court, Detective?" "No."

"Why not?"

"Because there's no proof they're based on scientifically reliable principles."

"So, if polygraph results are not admissible in court, why would the CVSA's be? Are you aware of –"

"Objection, Your Honor! The witness has just said he has no knowledge of CVSAs."

"Sustained. Do you have any more questions about Detective Wallace's actual participation in Mr. Cooper's case, Mr. Katz?"

Katz walked back to his table to look through his notes. Wallace riveted his eyes on him to keep them from wandering to Robbie.

"I do," Katz said, "and I'll be brief. Detective Wallace, have you seen the written statements that the Prince Georges Police Department says are what my client told them?"

"Yes."

"And they include the time that each session started and finished, do they not?" "Yes."

"Do you have your copies of those statements with you?"

"I do not."

"I can give you copies if it'd make it easier for you to follow along."

"No, counselor, that's okay. *I* trust *you*," Wallace said pointedly. Katz recited the dates, times, and length of each interview on the

360

sheets in his hand before he laid the last one down and looked at his legal pad.

"By my count, that adds up to nine sessions totaling seventy-eight hours over a period of four days before my client allegedly confessed. Does that sound right to you, Detective, not in the moral sense, of course, which is for this court and a jury to decide, but does it sound correct to you?"

"I didn't follow every one of your calculations, counselor, but it sounds in the ballpark."

"And isn't it true that you stopped then only because he finally told you what you believed to be the truth from the very beginning?"

"Absolutely not."

"And is it still your testimony that he did not even ask for a lawyer until more than three days after he endured all the above?"

"Yes. I saw almost every hour of it, and I know what I saw."

"But do you remember it, Detective Wallace?" Wainstein jumped to his feet.

"Objection! Badgering the witness." "Sustained."

"No further questions," Katz said.

"Detective, you may step down," Judge Green said, but Wallace didn't hear her, the rage and humiliation filling his brain overtaken by fear when he stood up and turned to see Robbie's seat empty.

47

Wallace fell into his chair with a loud and heavy thud, his mind still recovering from the beating it took in the courtroom. Katz' cross was bad enough, but Robbie's coming, and especially her going, were worse, much worse. He flicked a glance at his desktop and saw what he expected: No pink note telling him she called. It didn't take him long to decide not to call her either, so he grabbed the pile of paper in his in-box and tried to concentrate on anything that would take his mind off what it couldn't stop thinking about. A knock on his door mercifully got his attention until he looked up and saw Trainum looking back at him, as sad as he'd ever seen him.

"Rough one in there," he said. Wallace motioned him to close the door and he did, then sat in the chair at the side of the desk.

"Yeah," Wallace said. "Why'd you leave? I thought the PG guys were up next."

"Fulginiti went up after you, but when I heard Wainstein take ten minutes to even get him in the car with Cooper, I took off. It'll probably take him longer to testify than the four days they actually talked to him. How you're doing?" Wallace shook his head in disgust.

"Not good, man. I fucked up."

"That guy Katz was good, man. You know him, right? From when he was one of us, or am I imagining you telling Wainstein that?" Now Wallace remembered that conversation right before the extradition hearing.

"I know him, and I knew he'd show me no mercy up there, but I didn't have to help him out so much either. I just fucked up, man. Bad."

362

"It wasn't that bad. Don't beat yourself up over it. We've all had some lawyer make mincemeat of us."

"You're a good friend and I thank you for that, but just forgetting McCann told us Cooper said he wanted to take a polygraph on Starbucks was bad enough. When he tells Katz he *did* tell me that, my credibility's shot."

"But it wasn't like you said it to a jury. The judge isn't going to do anything about it."

"Maybe not," Wallace said, "but it doesn't fill me with confidence I'll do any better in front of a jury, and I'll bet it fills Wainstein even less. Shit!" Trainum waited a while before he said anything.

"Tom, can I ask you something?"

"Anything. Shoot."

"Are you still drinking?" Wallace levelled his eyes at him and lied as convincingly as he could.

"No," he said. "I've been sober for ten years now. You know that." Trainum nodded and stared at his hands slowly rubbing each other.

"I'm just bringing it up because, you know, alcohol can sometime blur your memory." Wallace waited for him to look at him.

"You got something specific in your mind?" he asked. Trainum kept his eyes on his.

"I do. You remember that night we all went out and celebrated in PG after Cooper confessed?" Wallace sat up and leaned towards him, his arms folded on the desktop.

"That was a one-time thing."

"And the girl too? Was she a one-time thing?" Wallace strained to find some reason buried deep in his brain why Trainum would ask that but found none.

"What girl?" he challenged him. "There ain't no girl."

"There was that night. The girl who helped me get you out of your clothes and into bed at her place. That girl." Wallace sat back and did his best to impersonate a sober person who just remembered something he'd forgot. He smiled and wagged his finger at Trainum.

"Oh yeah, right," he said. "You got me, man. I'd forgotten all about her. That was a one-time deal too, no lie." Trainum rubbed his chin, then pointed at Wallace.

"You know who she reminded me of, man? It's probably been two years and I could be wrong, but she looked like Vontae Kincaid's girlfriend, what was her name – Roberta? – the one we talked to out there somewhere about him and Cooper? In my mind, you know, she looked just like her."

Wallace let that hang there a minute before he said "Man, I honestly have no idea what you're talking about. I know who you mean, but I have no idea what's going on with her, and that's the truth." *Especially now*, he thought, then stood up and reached out his hand. Trainum stood and shook it. "I appreciate your concern, Jim, really, but I'm fine and I've got to get back to work now, man. Keep me posted on what happens over there."

"I will." Trainum looked like he was groping for something else to say before he shrugged and said "Just take care of yourself, Tom, okay? That's all."

"No worries, man. Will do," Wallace said and watched Trainum close the door behind him before he sat back down. He tried to refocus on whatever he was looking at before, but couldn't, so he took a stroll to Popeyes to sit and have an early lunch, but he couldn't get through that either, so he put the rest in his bag, got to his car, and drove home, not sure if he hoped he'd find Robbie there or not. When he didn't, he steeled himself to call her in PG. Her answering machine clicked on and he hung up. Five minutes later, he screwed up the courage to leave his own message.

"Hey, I didn't see you leave," he said before he realized he had no idea what to say next. "Give me a call when you're back," he forced out before he hung up. He threw the Popeyes bag onto the coffee table and headed for the bedroom to change into something more comfortable, but stopped in the doorway. He thought it looked different than he remembered it this morning until he realized why. Robbie's bag and backpack were gone and so was everything hanging in the closet that wasn't his. He did a quick search for a note, then hustled back to the kitchen to look there too.

Nothing.

He kicked his shoes off and yanked off his tie before he went back to the coffee table and attacked the rest of his spicy chicken with red beans and rice with a newfound gusto, interrupted only by trying her line and hanging up when he got the message another three times. He dumped the bag and bones into the trash and took a seat on the john to clear his bowels, but it had no effect on his head. He started towards the steps to the living room until he had a better idea and turned around. He laid himself across his bed and pulled a pillow still smelling of Robbie over his face to block the sun streaming through his blinds. The events of the morning swirled through his head and Katz was asking him one more question he couldn't answer, this time about the capital of Nigeria, until he was saved by the bell. Only when he woke up still buried in his pillow did he realize the ringing was coming from the phone on the nightstand. He lunged for it, not sure he wanted to hear Robbie's voice on the other end or not. When he heard Wainstein's, he wished he'd never picked it up.

"Ken, I'm so sorry about this morning."

"We can talk about that, Tom, but not now. I'm calling to give you a heads up about a meeting I just came out of. You and me and Ellis have a meeting with the U.S. Attorney Monday morning."

"About what?"

"About the Department wanting the death penalty for Mr. Cooper:"

48

At eleven o'clock sharp on Monday, Wallace arrived at the office of Wilma A. Lewis, United States Attorney for the District of Columbia, to find Wainstein and McIntire already there, chatting in front of a black leather couch in the waiting room, briefcases at their feet.

"Tom, good to see you," Wainstein said, followed by smiles and handshakes all around.

"Anyone else coming?" Wallace asked. Wainstein shook his head.

"It's just us and Ms. Lewis this time around. Later today, she's going to lead Ellis and me into battle with the DOJ folks before we have the pleasure of seeing Jake again, probably Friday." He laid a hand on Wallace's chest before he could speak. "And don't worry about the other day. Just look at it like a good warmup for what you can expect at trial. We'll do a better job of prepping you then, too, I promise." Wallace appreciated the kindness, but it didn't stop him from asking what was still on his mind.

"So I take it McCann testified he *did* tell me about Cooper wanting to take a polygraph on Starbucks."

"He did." Wallace took himself to task for the thousand and first time. "I only remembered him saying it after I'd already said he didn't and I didn't want to give Katz the pleasure of telling me – and the judge – I was wrong. It was a rookie mistake. It won't happen again."

"I have no doubts, believe me. We'll cover every–". The door to Lewis' office swung open and Wallace turned to see a smiling, solidly built black woman, maybe in her early 40s, standing in the doorway, wearing a black skirt and jacket buttoned over a wide-collared white blouse.

367

"Gentlemen," she said. "Come on in." Wallace thought he detected a light accent he guessed was from somewhere in the Caribbean. When she took the job in the summer of '98, he remembered someone telling him she'd been an Assistant U.S. Attorney in D.C. a while back, but he couldn't remember handling a criminal case with her. He didn't need anyone to tell him she was the first black woman to ever serve as the USA in the District.

Lewis took the brown leather chair behind her desk and waited for them to take the wooden ones in front before she turned to Wallace.

"Detective, are you aware that the Justice Department's considering whether to ask for the death penalty for Carl Cooper?"

"Mr. Wainstein told me that."

"And did he tell you the process we'll be following for making the decision whether to seek it or not?"

"I know you're going to be meeting with DOJ and then with Mr. Cooper's lawyer, but that's about it." She nodded and put on the glasses hanging from her neck to scan the memo laying below her before she took them off again and looked back at him.

"Let me ask you something, Detective Wallace. How long have you been with the Metropolitan Police Department?" Wallace knew that one cold now.

"About forty years."

"And in all that time, do you remember anyone getting the death penalty in the District of Columbia?" When he said no, Lewis held up the document she'd skimmed. "Do you know the last time anyone was given the death penalty in the District of Columbia?" Wallace knew this one too, thanks to Katz, he was unhappy to remember.

"I think it was in 1957, to a guy who killed a cop?" Lewis looked impressed.

"That is correct. Very good. Robert Carter was electrocuted that year for killing an unarmed, off-duty police officer. Yet in the last five years, despite no one being put to death in this jurisdiction for forty-three years and despite the fact that the District of Columbia repealed its death penalty statute in 1981, Attorney General Reno has authorized it here – twice! May I assume you remember those instances too?"

"I remember the Jason White one," Wallace said, seeing Eric Butera's bloody swollen face flash through his mind one more time before he realized why. Right at the end of 1993, a guy named Donzell McCauley shot and killed White, an MPD cop, and would've killed his partner too if she hadn't been wearing a Kevlar vest. When they told McCauley they wanted to talk to him as he was going into a drug house, he turned around and put four bullets in White's face and two in his back for good measure. Eric Holder, the U.S. Attorney at the time, told the papers that, after conferring with Reno, they agreed that death was appropriate not only because he killed a cop, but because of how he did it too. Holder ultimately signed off on a plea bargain giving the scumbag life without parole.

"I'm sure all of you at MPD remember it," Lewis said, looking down at her memo, "but there was another one too, a few years earlier, where a man named Wayne Anthony Perry killed nine people as an enforcer, if you will, for a drug gang. The U.S. Attorney took a plea for life in that one too. So, in all that time since 1957, despite hundreds of heinous, wanton, multiple murders being perpetrated in this City every year, just like the one Mr. Cooper's accused of at the Starbucks, this office has not asked for the death penalty in any of them – until now. And why do you suppose that is, Detective?"

"That's above my pay grade, Ms. Lewis. I don't have a clue." She turned to Wainstein.

"Would you like to – quote, unquote – enlighten him, Mr. Wainstein?"

"Tom, are you familiar with the Federal Sentencing Guidelines?"

"Just that there are some."

"They came in sometime in the late '80s, and the idea was to have Federal defendants who committed the same crime sentenced to the same prison term, regardless of where they committed the crime, so that someone in Texas, say, wouldn't wind up serving a much longer term than someone who did the same thing in New York. From what we're hearing, the Attorney General's trying to bring the same approach to imposing the death penalty. If the facts warrant giving a guy the chair in South Carolina, the same facts should give him the chair in California – or D.C."

"Which sounds all very just and equitable," Lewis said, "but ignores the fact that fifty states and the District of Columbia each have their own reasons for doing many of the same things in different ways. The will of the people who live in those states – and the District – should mean something, so," she started counting on her fingers, "where no one's been put to death for forty-three years, the D.C. City Council expressly *repealed* the death penalty almost twenty years ago, and then the voters rejected reinstating it in a referendum just eight years ago, all that has to mean that we must be very judicious, very selective, about when we impose it."

Wallace wondered *If Cooper doesn't deserve it, who would?* before she told him.

"In fact, I have only recommended it once since I've been here. Are you familiar with the name Tommy Edelin?"

370

"Of course," Wallace said. Edelin was the leader of the 1-5 Gang, named for where he lived on 15th St. S.E. Like Rayful Edmond, he'd built an empire based on drugs, with a heavy side business of murder, thirteen of which he'd been charged with ordering. Edelin had been arrested over a year ago but hadn't been tried yet. Now he was starting to understand why.

"He is the only person I have ever recommended be put to death, because of the magnitude of the crimes his enterprise committed and the terror it caused in the city for years. His actions were far more reprehensible and on a much larger scale than Mr. Cooper's, but, I will tell you, I still lose sleep over recommending death even for him."

"Where does it stand now?"

"It's sitting on Ms. Reno's desk, awaiting her decision, but I have no doubt what it will be." She shook her head before she looked back at Wainstein. "Do you have any thoughts about what else we should bring up, pro or con?"

"I think there's one more con," he said. "In any state, this would just be another local case, one more murder – a terrible murder, to be sure – but it wouldn't be one that any local D.A. couldn't handle. He wouldn't want or need any help from the U.S. Attorney in his jurisdiction. So where's the compelling Federal interest in deciding the appropriate punishment in this one? Other than the geographical justification, there is absolutely no overarching substantive reason that this case demands the Federal government to seek the death penalty. If the same killings occurred in PG or Baltimore, would that make them any more important to the Feds? No. I'd definitely tell the AG that, with all due respect, there is absolutely no good reason that the United States should get involved in sentencing this defendant in this case." White finished writing before she pointed her pen at Wainstein.

"That is an excellent point, Mr. Wainstein, and one that I will make to the Attorney General too. Anything else from any of you?"

When she got nothing, she got to her feet.

"I think we're well armed for our meeting with Mr. Katz. Mr. Wainstein, Mr. McIntire, I'll let you know when it's scheduled. Gentlemen, thank you for your help." She held the door open for them and they trooped out to the elevator. Wainstein pushed the button, then turned to Wallace.

"Tom, I know you're brokenhearted you won't be in Reno's meeting with us and Katz and I am too. Given your history with him, you might be the only one who could keep him from bouncing off the walls."

That is *a shame*, Wallace thought. *I would really enjoy seeing that.*

49

Back in his office, Wallace toyed with the idea of calling Robbie to let her know the death penalty for Cooper was on the table. He knew by now she wouldn't pick up, but he hoped that news might be enough to finally get her to return the messages he'd been leaving further and further apart since the day he saw her, then didn't, at his pitiful appearance at the preliminary hearing. He picked up the phone and began to punch up her number but put it back down when he realized he really had nothing to say. Yet. He'd reassess after he heard back from Wainstein about the meeting with Reno.

He threw himself into thinning the herd of files, folders, and papers filling his in-box until he got the call late in the afternoon.

"So what'd I miss?"

"Well, we sure outnumbered him," Wainstein said. "It was Lewis, me, Ellis, a couple of other AUSAs, and our press guy on our side, and just Jake for Cooper. But he still managed to do most of the talking." Wallace wasn't surprised.

"And what did he say?"

"He really covered most of the points Lewis made in our meeting, and one she didn't. Do you remember a guy named Kenneth Marshall?"

Wallace did. He was a murder defendant back in the '90s in a case that was a lot like Starbucks, except for one critical difference that he was embarrassed he hadn't thought of before he realized why Katz did. Marshall herded four of his coworkers at a McDonald's in Southeast into a freezer room, left them there while he cleaned out the cash register and took the videotape out of the security camera, then went back to the freezer and killed them all because they could identify him. The similarity to Starbucks wasn't what got Wallace's attention though. It was the fact that everyone involved – the killer and the killed – were black. Marshall got 80 years in prison for what he did. Was Cooper's crime more worthy of the death penalty because the two white people he killed counted a lot more than the four black people Marshall killed? He wasn't sure if the bile rising in his throat was a product of coming face-to-face with the blatant bias still festering in the criminal justice system or his own failure to connect the dots.

"I do," Wallace said, "and I know why he brought him up."

"Yeah, and when Lewis asked us after the meeting if Katz was right about it, she was as appalled as he was."

"So is your meeting with Reno set yet?"

"Lewis is doing that now. I'll let you know when it is." Wallace still wasn't sure he could tell Robbie anything more than he could earlier, so he took a shot that Wainstein might be able to give him a good reason – or at least a good excuse – to give it one more try.

"Got a guess how it's going to go?"

"Honestly, Tom, your guess is as good as mine. You know how Lewis feels and nothing Jake said did anything but reinforce that – plus she also talked to a few other U.S. Attorneys who'd met with Reno on death penalty cases in their districts, and every one of them said she deferred to them. On the other hand, as you heard, she's authorized it twice here already in cases that, to me, warranted the death penalty even less than this one. I guess it's just going to come down to how she weighs everything."

"Here's hoping she does the right thing," Wallace said. "Let me know how it comes out." Wainstein had barely hung up before Wallace decided that was enough to try Robbie again. As he figured, it went to her voice mail, but this time he left a message.

374

"Hey, it's me again. Just wanted to let you know that the Justice Department's thinking of asking for the death penalty for Cooper and they're going to make up their minds in the next few days. Give me a call at the office if you want to know more." He paused, hoping that'd make her pick up. It didn't. "Okay, well, call me any time." Another pause. "Hope you're doing okay. Bye." One last pause. He hung up. And waited. Nothing.

The clock told him it was 3:45. When he looked at the thick pile still filling his in-box and heard his stomach remind him that he'd worked through lunch, he decided to visit the cafeteria before taking one last stab at it. A Ding-Dong and a Coke later, he made his way back to his seat and saw his message light flashing. The same hope that had flickered in his brain every time he saw it flash since the preliminary hearing flickered once again, but this time hope was rewarded.

"Hey," he heard Robbie's voice say cool and flat, "call me back. Bye." He got up to push his door shut, then dialed her up and didn't realize he was holding his breath until he exhaled when he heard "Hello?".

"Hey, it's me again. Thanks for calling me back."

"So what's goin' on?"

Wallace told her about the morning's meeting, leaving out where Lewis stood, and lingering on where Reno did. "So, if she sticks to what she's done before here, it looks like they're going to ask the judge to sentence him to death, and I thought you'd want to know that."

The lengthening silence on the other end made him wonder if he'd missed her click off.

"So when's she going to decide?"

"I'm not sure, but soon. They're going to meet with Katz to talk about everything first –"

"Talk to Katz first? Why? What's he got to do with what she does?"

"I don't know. It's just what they got to do under their rules, I guess."

"So that fucker's going to have two bites of the apple? One to talk them out of it and then another one to talk the judge out of it? That is bullshit, man!"

"I feel the same way, believe me," he made up on the spot. "I just figured you'd want to know they were actually thinking about it, and I wanted to be the one to tell you that before you heard something on the TV or the radio or somewhere."

Another long pause, then "Okay, then. I appreciate it." He decided he'd bring up the other thing he hoped would keep her on the line.

"Listen, Robbie. I just want to tell you I know I didn't have my shit together on the stand when you saw me and I'm really sorry about that, but I'm better now, honest. To tell you the truth, I finally realized it was all the booze that was affecting my memory and my judgment, so I've cut way back now and it really seems to be working." He hoped she bought that. "The bottom line is you won't see that from me again at the trial, I swear to God and Jesus Christ and anyone else you want me to swear to, I promise." Now she answered right away.

"Shit, it wasn't just that, Tom. I was pissed, I ain't goin' to lie, but I was embarrassed for you too, especially 'cause it was that fucker Katz who put you through all that. That's some friend you got, man. Wow!" Wallace didn't expect the wave of relief he felt sweep over him.

376

"Thank you, Robbie, seriously. I appreciate that."

"That boy needs to be taught a lesson, for real." He decided to press his luck.

"Well, once I hear what happens, maybe we can talk about it in person next time."

He wasn't sure he heard the click this time either until the dial tone confirmed it again.

The next four days felt like four weeks before Wainstein's voice made it feel like no time at all.

"Tom, we got a decision out of Reno today, but you've got to keep it to yourself until the Department announces it, okay?"

"Okay. What'd she say?"

"They're going to ask for the death penalty." Wallace mouthed a silent "Yes!"

"Katz must've been on fire," he said.

"She waited till he left the room to give us the word. He did a good job, though. He brought up Marshall again and basically made the case that what Cooper did didn't warrant a death sentence any more than the other 300-some killings in the District that year. I was leaning more his way than I was even before he started, to tell you the truth, but as soon as he was gone, Reno said go for it, so that's what we're doing, like it or not."

"There was no discussion?"

"There was, before Jake got there. Let me check my notes. She said she'd been hearing from a lot of victims' groups and the families of the people killed there that they wanted her to go for the death penalty, and then she said somebody on her staff had reminded her of a case out of Kansas where she went for it a few years ago. Seems this guy from Laos whose name I won't even try to pronounce killed a restaurant owner in Wichita during a robbery because, get this, she couldn't open the safe. Sound familiar? Anyhow, she said the fact that both this guy and Cooper planned their crimes and Cooper killed three people, not just one, made it easy for her to make the call. Jake did his best, but he really had no shot. Her mind was made up."

"So let me make sure I have this straight. If the jury finds him guilty, you're going to ask for the death penalty, no matter what, right?"

"That's right, with one asterisk. If he's convicted, Lewis still has the discretion to work out a plea bargain that would give him life. Anticipating your next question, I have no idea whether she would actually do that or not. You know where her head is now, but we're just going to have to see how the trial plays out." Wallace had one more question.

"When's the world going to know about this?"

"That's a good question," Wainstein said. "There are a couple of hearings coming up in the next few weeks. As soon as we can get our motion pulled together, Judge Green'll be the first to see it, so until then, keep it under your hat, okay?"

"No worries. Thanks for letting me know, Ken."

He pressed the button in the phone cradle, let it go, and was happy to hear the dial tone this time. After he punched in the numbers, he was even happier to hear Robbie's "Hello?"

378

50

Two weeks later, Wallace pulled to a stop on New York Avenue
N.E. without a red light even in sight. He looked at the clock on the
dash. 7:47, the same it was the last time he hit the brakes.

"It doesn't start till 9, right?" Robbie asked from the shotgun seat.

"Yeah, but at this rate, we won't get there by 10. I'm about one
more stop from throwing the flasher up on the roof."

"And do what? Drive on the other side of the road? Ain't no place
for anyone to move anyhow." Driving on the other side of the road
was exactly what he had in mind, but he pumped the brakes on that
idea too when the purple VW van blocking his view inched forward,
then actually accelerated to near-double digits. Robbie's hand on his
thigh got his attention.

"Did I ever tell you how glad I was you called me?" He smiled and
looked at her.

"No, but you let me know in your own way." She smiled and inched
her hand up until he batted it away.

"Hey, give him a rest, okay?" Wallace said. "My man needs to pace
himself." Her grin grew wider, but she folded her hands primly in
her lap.

"This better?"

"No," he laughed. "But it's safer."

It had been a wild two weeks though. They picked up right where
they left off, not just with the sex but the booze too. He told himself
he'd cut back for real once he knew when he'd have to testify, but
for now he was so happy to be back in her life and her arms and
everywhere else, that he wanted to please her any way he could. If

379

she wanted sex, who was he to say no? If she wanted to drink, he'd drink too. There was plenty of time to get himself together.

"All right," Robbie said, "so tell me what's going to happen today. I assume your shitbird buddy Katz'll be there."

"He will. You remember what I told you about what happened at the hearing last week?"

"I remember it was something good, but that's about it."

"The main thing was the judge saying that when the case goes to trial, the government can use everything Carl said to me and the FBI in D.C. – and all the stuff he said to the PG guys – because no one beat him or tricked him into saying anything."

"Okay. And today they're going to tell her they want him to get the chair, right?"

"I don't think that's how they'd kill him, but, yeah, they're letting her know they're going to ask for the death penalty."

"For Vontae too, or just the Starbucks people?"

"Just Starbucks. PG can still try him for killing Vontae, I guess, but I don't know if they'd do it if he already got the death penalty in D.C., and I don't know if Maryland even has a death penalty."

"Yeah, well, if they don't," Robbie said, "I know plenty of people out there'd love to kill him themselves. I'm one of 'em."

"Hang on," Wallace said. He made a quick right onto Florida, a left on P, and another left down North Capitol just as the light turned red. "All right, now we got plenty of time."

"Do Katz and him know they're going to ask for it today?"

"The death penalty? No – unless somebody leaked it, which is a definite possibility." She smiled a tight smile.

"I hope they didn't. I can't wait to see the look on their fucking faces."

He let her off outside the courthouse to avoid anyone asking questions about why the two of them came in together. By the time he parked at MPD, got back over, and took a look into the courtroom from the corridor, she was in a seat close to the far wall near the back. He looked for Wainstein in the lawyers' conference room before he saw the clock over the empty table said it was 8:55 and went back into the courtroom. He took the seat Trainum was holding for him in the Reserved row.

"Wasn't sure you were going to make it," Trainum said. "I was going to start taking bids on the chair."

"Where's Wainstein?" Trainum pointed to the door behind the bench.

"Back there. Giving Carl the bad news." Wallace looked at him curiously.

"So you know?"

"About the death penalty? Hell, yes. I think you're the only person who didn't tell me."

Katz came through the door first, looking more pissed than Wallace could remember.

"Looks like he knows now too," Trainum said. Wainstein came through next and, in a few seconds, the bailiff told them all to rise. When Judge Green climbed the steps to the bench and sat down, he told them to be seated. The judge got right down to business.

"Mr. Wainstein," she said. Wainstein got up and stepped to the podium below her.

"Your Honor, first and foremost, I would like to inform you, Mr. Cooper, and his counsel that the government believes that the circumstances of the capital offenses charged in counts 36, 39, and 42 of the indictment are such that, in the event of the defendant's conviction of one or more of them, a sentence of death is justified under Title 18 of the United States –." The rest of the sentence was buried under a collective gasp, a few cheers, and the noise the back row of reporters made getting out of their chairs, banging through the doors, and running for the phones. Judge Green rapped her gavel.

"Order please, we will have order in the court." Once she got it, she nodded to Wainstein.

"Specifically," he said, "the government will seek the sentence of death for each and all of the following offenses: The first-degree murders of Emory Allen Evans, Aaron David Goodrich, and Mary Caitrin Mahoney in the course of using a firearm during a crime of violence in violation of Title 18, United States Code, sections 924(c) and (j)."

Wallace took a quick look at the defense table. Katz looked like he was about to detonate, but Cooper's face was a blank, like Wainstein was talking about someone else. In the row behind him, Cissy's hands clenched the hand of the older woman next to her. Wallace bet it was his mother.

When Wainstein sat down, Katz didn't wait for Judge Green to invite him to the podium. Wallace couldn't see his face but the artery throbbing in his neck told him all he needed to know.

"Your Honor, this is an outrageous and unwarranted exercise of prosecutorial discretion. As the government well knows, no one has been given the death penalty in the District of Columbia for more than forty years, even for murders far more brutal and heinous than the ones my client is accused of. The citizens of the District, in fact, expressly rejected the availability of the death penalty in this jurisdiction nearly a decade ago, but yet the Attorney General of the United States has seen fit to usurp the discretion that properly belongs in the hands of the people and the United States Attorney for the District and ordered her to seek it if Mr. Cooper is ultimately convicted of these crimes.

"Your Honor, the defense intends to fully litigate both the constitutionality of the death penalty and the racial disparity of its imposition by the Justice Department. African-Americans make up twelve percent of the country's population, but two-thirds of the prisoners on death row for Federal crimes are black, more than five times their presence in the general population." Judge Green raised her hand.

"Mr. Katz, you will have every opportunity to brief these issues and submit them to the court, I promise you, but today I'd like to focus on setting a schedule so that we can consider all of the issues that you and the government will be raising in this trial in an orderly manner. Once we take care of that, both of you will have every opportunity to litigate this important matter fully and fairly, all right?"

"Certainly, Your Honor," Katz said. Wainstein stood and said "Of course, Your Honor," and Green waved them to both come forward. Wallace watched them for a minute before he looked back at Robbie, her eyes glistening, jaw clenched. He waited to see if she'd look his way, but when she didn't, he turned back to the bench and saw Katz and Wainstein return to their seats and wait for the judge to finish writing her notes.

"All right, back on the record, please," she said. "We'll have our next status hearing on February 22, two weeks from tomorrow, at which time we'll address jury issues, and I've set May 2 as the tentative trial date, which should give counsel for both sides adequate time to prepare their cases. Do either of you have anything else we need to address today?"

Neither of them did, and after she rapped her gavel one more time and disappeared through the rear door, Wallace told Trainum he'd be back in the office after he took care of some business with Wainstein. Trainum threw him a salute and Wallace counted to three after he watched him walk into the hallway before he turned to Robbie. When she caught his eye, he held up a hand and she stayed there until he made his way to her.

"So? What'd you think?" he asked. She shook her head.

"Your buddy made me sick goin' on about how poor little Carl doesn't deserve to die because so many other black folks're screwed over too. Even if we are, doesn't mean some of 'em don't deserve to die sometimes anyhow, does it? If not him, then who?"

"There's a long way to go," Wallace said. "Just be patient. He'll get what's comin' to him."

"Sorry, patience's not something I'm too good at." Wallace didn't need to be told that and didn't see a need to keep talking about Cooper either, so he changed the subject.

"You want me to drive you over to the CVS?"

"No, I told 'em I wasn't comin' in today. Maybe I'll just hang around D.C. a while, then take the bus back home. Stop's pretty close."

The room was empty now, so Wallace walked her into the hallway and down to the elevators. When the doors closed behind them, she

384

went to kiss him, but backed away when he pointed at the pinhole camera peeking at them from the corner. Out in the air on Constitution Avenue, he squeezed her hand.

"Give me a call if you decide you want a ride back." She gave him a quick peck on the cheek, then waved good-bye as she headed towards the Monument. He headed back to the office.

This time, he took a normal lunch and actually got the paperwork below the brim of the tray before the phone rang. He saw it was 2:30 and figured Robbie wanted a ride home after all. His sweet "Hello" curdled when he heard Katz on the other end.

"Counselor, how are you doing?"

"I've been better," Katz said.

"You sound better than you looked this morning."

"That's a low hurdle, Tom. I knew it was coming, but hearing it was a whole other thing. I just couldn't believe Reno would do that over Lewis' objections." Wallace didn't know if Katz was playing him or not, but either way, he wasn't telling him anything out of school.

"Do you know she objected for sure?"

"I know what I heard last week and I know what I read in the Post, so I'm pretty damn sure she did."

"Okay, so why the call?"

"I'm just checking to see if you might know something based on your investigation, off the record."

"Okay, I'll tell you if I can," Wallace said. "About what?"

"About who might've left me a threatening message – actually two threatening messages – on my answering machine in the last twenty-four hours." Robbie's grim face in the courtroom flitted through his synapses even before he remembered her telling him that she'd love to kill Cooper herself. *But that was just talk*, he thought. *Like she said, plenty of people want him dead.*

"Did it sound like the same person both times?"

"No. The first one was from a man, the second from a woman." Wallace took heart in realizing that plenty of men wanted Cooper dead too and reminded himself to think like a detective, not a paranoid boyfriend.

"They call today?"

"She did. His was last night." Wallace combed his brain for who the man might be.

"What'd he say?" he asked.

"Something like 'back off on Cooper if you know what's good for you.' I didn't write it down."

"And the woman?"

"That I wrote down. She was a little more to the point. 'Hey there, Mr. Katz. Let me just tell you something. If Carl Cooper don't get the death penalty, you will'. Anyone come to mind?"

Wallace wouldn't let himself think the unthinkable. This case was headline news. He knew dozens of people who had it in for Cooper and there were probably hundreds more he didn't know. It also could have been two totally unconnected people calling for two different reasons. And what man would have been as pissed as Robbie about Vontae? No one, he thought – until Jaysonn's face floated back into view for the first time since his first trip to Albertha's place. But still, what are the chances? He needed proof and this was wasn't nearly enough.

"No," he said, "but I'll keep my eyes and ears open, and let me know if you hear or see anything else from either of them, or anyone else for that matter."

"Thanks, Tom. I appreciate it."

"Thanks for letting me know, Jake. I'm on it."

After they hung up, Wallace ran through all the possibilities and unknowns one more time, then two more times, before he gave up trying to answer the two questions that wouldn't stop nagging him. The first was *Why would she be telling me, a DC cop, that she was going to kill Cooper and Katz if the Feds don't? No one's that crazy.* The second was *Or is she?*

51

Continually stumped by those questions, Wallace also found himself unable to answer any of the three bigger ones that crystallized over the next few weeks: What was best for him and Robbie? What was justice for Cooper? And what would save his friendship with Katz?

Every time he thought he had a clue about how to answer any of them, one of the other sharp angles of the Robbie-Cooper-Katz triangle would give him a serious pain in his neck, his heart, and/or his ass. The only two surefire sources of relief were her loving and alcohol, so almost every split decision went her way. But he never could bring himself to make a final call on anything. There was too much on the line and the game was still a long way from being over.

One good thing was that Katz never let him know about any other calls, probably because he was too busy to waste time telling him about them. Wainstein kept sending over every motion that he and Katz filed just to keep him up to speed, and every time Wallace picked up the phone to tell him *No mas!*, he always put it down because there was something worth reading every time.

Over the past month, Katz had filed dozens of different motions. Some were about what Wainstein called housekeeping issues like subpoenas, discovery, and jury questionnaires, but others raised more serious issues, like asking the government to tell him Lewis' recommendation to Reno or give him the aggravating evidence they planned to use at a capital sentencing hearing. Most importantly of all, he asked Judge Green to dismiss every count of the indictment. On the last day of February, she gave him the same answer to all of them: Motion denied.

The next week, Wainstein called to tell him they were going to start prepping him for the trial because he was not just the leadoff witness but, in his words, 'the witness di tutti witnesses."

"But no pressure, right?" Wallace laughed. Wainstein laughed back.

"Nothing you can't handle, right, Tom? You've been through this a thousand times."

"Yeah, but there haven't been this many chips on the table before. Helping a jury decide if someone should live or die – even Cooper – that's heavy stuff."

"No one knows as much about Starbucks and Cooper and what he did here and in PG than you do, okay? All you have to do is tell the jury what you know and you'll be fine." *And remember what you know and don't lie about it and don't make shit up and don't lose your cool* went unspoken, but Wallace heard all of them loud and clear anyhow.

"I'll start reviewing everything tonight, I promise," he said. "How long do I have?"

"How long do you need?"

"A week, maybe two. There's a lot to go over."

"Take three," Wainstein said. "That'll still leave us a month to get everything straight and make sure everyone's following the same playbook."

"Thanks, Ken. I'll do you proud, I promise," he hoped.

At 9 a.m. sharp on March 24, three weeks and two days later, Wallace took a high-backed, cushioned black leather seat in a makeshift mock courtroom on the fourth floor of the U.S. Attorney's office. There was no bench, no judge, and no jury, just Wainstein facing him from one end of a conference table and McIntire from the other. Trainum, Garrett, and Chief Ramsey sat behind them. Wallace felt loose and ready to go, mostly because Robbie relaxed him last night in a way that only she could, but also because they

389

both got lubricated in their usual recent fashion, Chivas Coolers, light on the ginger ale. Washing down half a dozen Altoids with a tall black coffee from 7-11 on the ride in boosted his confidence to the point that he really believed he was at the top of his game.

"Okay, Tom," Wainstein said. "Anything you want to go over before we start?"

"No, I'm ready. Let's do it." Wainstein nodded and turned to his gallery.

"Gentlemen, please take notes about anything you think I ought to ask, or not ask, or ask a different way. Ditto anything about Detective Wallace's answers, and anything we should expect from Mr. Katz that Ellis doesn't cover. None of us is going to be perfect this time around, but the whole point of this exercise – and however many more times we need to do this – is that by the time he takes the stand for real, we're as prepared as we can be for anything that will, should, could, or might maybe come up." Once he got nods all around, he turned back to Wallace, opened his three-ring notebook, and said "Then let's get started."

Just like at the preliminary hearing, Wallace easily handled Wainstein's softballs walking him through the highlights of the case without a hitch. McIntire, though, started throwing smoke right away.

"Detective, could you tell me again what date the murders occurred on?"

"July 6, 1997."

"And what date was Mr. Cooper arrested for those murders?" It was sometime in early '99 but Wallace wasn't sure he even knew it then. He tried to buy some time.

"It was a long time after that, but I don't remember the exact date right offhand." Out of the corner of his eye, he saw Wainstein scribble on his pad.

"You'd think you remember such an important day, wouldn't you, after all that time in such a big case?" Wainstein raised his hand.

"Let's not waste time on this. Tom, if Jake brings it up, it was March 1, 1999, a Monday."

"March 1. Got it. Won't be a problem," Wallace said and tried to ignore Trainum and Ramsey exchanging glances.

"So you were investigating the murders for just about twenty months before you finally arrested a suspect, is that correct?"

"I never did the math, but I'll take your word for it."

"Again, if Jake asks," Wainstein said, "Ellis is right. It was just about twenty months."

"And what led you to arrest Mr. Cooper on March 1, 1999?" McIntire asked.

"The accumulation of all the evidence we'd been collecting since the murders."

"But what specifically, Detective? Please tell the court the particular piece or pieces of evidence that gave you probable cause to arrest him that day." Wallace turned to Wainstein.

"Ken, can't you object to that? There was a shitload and it's all spelled out in the arrest warrant, isn't it?"

"Not all of it, Tom, and not in the detail that Judge Green's probably going to let Katz explore in a death case. I'll object, I promise, but we can't take the chance that she'll sustain it." Wallace's head started banging a loud, unrelenting rhythm that made it even harder to put together an answer.

"Okay then, let's see. The first suspects were people who'd worked at Starbucks with her."

"Hold on, Detective," McIntire said. "You were at the scene of the crime the next morning, weren't you?"

"Yes."

"In fact, you were in charge of investigating the scene that morning, weren't you?"

"Yes."

"Did you find any physical evidence in Starbucks that morning that implicated Carl Cooper in the murders of any of those people?"

"No, that morning we did not."

"Did you find any physical evidence in Starbucks at *any* time that implicated my client in those murders?" Wallace knew the answer to that one was a big fat 'No,' but he wrestled with the idea of trying to tie the shell casings of the gun Cooper used to shoot Officer Howard to the murders at Starbucks before even he realized that would only lead to a messy dead end anyhow.

"We did not."

"So, if there was no physical evidence implicating Mr. Cooper in those deaths, why did you believe he was implicated in the murders at all?"

Wallace thought about the two America's Most Wanted tips but couldn't clearly remember which one went first. Leon Ellis and Eric Butera and Robbie tumbled through his mind next, but he definitely did not want to talk about any of them, so he played it safe with

"There were a lot of leads that implicated Mr. Cooper over those twenty months, sir."

"Can you share those with us, Detective?" Wallace sighed.

"Two came in on him through America's Most Wanted, the television show. That's what started us looking at him but, like I say, it was a long time ago and I don't remember who said what when in any detail at this point. If you or Mr. Wainstein can refresh my recollection by showing me the files, I could definitely give you a better answer." Wainstein turned to Ramsey.

"Chief, can you provide Detective Wallace a full copy of the records?"

"I can," Ramsey said. Wallace was impressed by how even his face didn't give away that he already did, weeks ago.

"All right then, I'll skip over the AMW stuff until you have a chance to review the files, Detective. So, let's go back to your decision to arrest Mr. Cooper on March 1, 1999. Is it your testimony that you don't recall what specifically motivated you to do it on that particular day?"

"No. The driving factor to do it that day was that we got some disturbing information about what his intentions were concerning Detective Trainum." McIntire made a show of sifting through his papers before he looked back at Wallace.

"But I don't see anything in the arrest warrant about Detective Trainum. What do you mean by 'disturbing information'?"

"We overheard Mr. Cooper saying in so many words that he'd like to kill him."

"Do you remember his exact words?" Those Wallace couldn't forget.

"I do. He said he would come into his house and kill his fucking family, then wait for him to come home and 'pow, pow, pow,' kill hm too, and hope he died slow." McIntire looked like he was puzzled.

"I'm confused, Detective. Are you saying you really arrested Mr. Cooper for threatening Detective Trainum, even though nothing in the warrant says anything about that?"

"No, we arrested him for shooting Officer Howard."

"But nothing Mr. Cooper said about Mr. Trainum, as reprehensible as that may be, had anything to do with that, did it?"

"No, but –"

"Then, again, I ask why you picked that particular time to arrest Mr. Cooper?"

"Because we'd just learned he made that specific threat to kill Mr. Trainum and we decided to take him off the streets before he could make good on it, that's why."

"And that's all very noble, Detective, but it had nothing to do with what happened with Officer Howard, much less Starbucks, so I don't see any justification for making that the reason for his arrest."

"Objection," Wainstein said with a smile, "but good job, Ellis, I can actually hear Jake saying that. We'll have to work on how Tom can handle that better. Go on to your next point." McIntire flipped a few sheets in his notebook before he lifted his head.

"Detective, did you have occasion at any time to meet with a woman named Joannie Lee Green?"

"I did. Detective Trainum and I drove up to Pennsylvania to interview her."

"Do you remember when that was?"

"Sometime in 1998, the summer, but, again, I couldn't give you the date right off the top of my head." McIntire held up what looked like an MPD Witness Interview form.

"This says August 7, Detective. Does that sound right to you?" *If he knows the date*, Wallace thought, *he knows the place, and that's not good.* But he saw no way to bullshit around any of it.

"Again, I'll take your word for it."

"And where did this interview take place?"

"Muncy, Pennsylvania."

"And where exactly in Muncy, Pennsylvania, Detective?"

"At the Correctional Institution there." McIntire feigned surprise. *Katz would've been much cooler about it*, Wallace thought.

"Did Ms. Green work at the institution?" Wallace gave him a long stare before answering.

"No, Mr. McIntire. She was an inmate there."

"And do you know what she was incarcerated for, Detective?"

"I believe it was for some robberies she pulled off with an acquaintance of Mr. Cooper."

"Do you know if she was convicted of felonies for those robberies? *No, but I'm sure you do,* Wallace thought, and went peaceably.

"I believe she was, yes."

"Can you tell us what inmate Green told you about Mr. Cooper?"

"Yes. She said he'd used his wife's gun to shoot a policeman in Prince Georges County a few years back, and that he'd killed a security guard in D.C. a couple of years before that."

"And did Ms. Green tell you that she was providing you all of this information out of the goodness of her heart?"

"She said she was telling us the truth and it checked out."

"Let me be clearer, Detective. Did she want something in return for giving you this information?" Wallace looked at Wainstein, who gave him the universal gesture for 'Spill it'.

"Yes, she asked us to let the prison and the D.A. up there know that she'd given us the information so they might reduce her sentence, but that's just the way the game's played, as you well –"

"So, just to summarize, Detective," McIntire cut him off, "she told you what you wanted to hear because it would get her out of prison, do I have it right?"

"Okay," Wainstein said. "Let's not beat this to death. Tom, I assure you we'll object if Jake goes down this road. The judge has already ruled that nothing you and PG did during the investigation warrants throwing the case out, so it's irrelevant."

"So why would he even get to ask that?" Wallace asked. McIntire answered.

"Because Mr. Katz is going to try and plant any seed he can with the jury that Cooper's being railroaded, that we don't have any real evidence against him – except what he told you and PG out there – and that it took you fifty hours over six days to pull it out of him. He's going to focus on that like a laser beam, which is why we're doing what we're doing – to get you ready for it." Wainstein nodded to him to continue.

396

"Let me ask you this, Detective. By March 1, 1999, the pressure must've *really* been building up on MPD to find whoever murdered those three people, isn't that true?"

"There's always pressure to find a murderer, sir."

"Of course, but here, where you had a headline case that hadn't been solved for nearly two years, with multiple families of the victims crying out for justice, and the press and your bosses on your case, you really must've really felt the pressure to come up with somebody, anybody, didn't you, Detective? Be honest with us." Wallace honestly felt like jumping out of his chair and committing another murder until Wainstein got up first.

"Ellis, I'm impressed. You really have Jake down pat, but why don't we take a few minutes to go over our notes and see if we can shorten this up a bit for our observers. Tom, you can stand down for a while."

Wallace pushed himself out of his chair and made his way to the restroom. When he came out, Trainum and Ramsey were talking in front of the elevators. Trainum saw him coming first, then tapped Ramsey on the arm and disappeared down the stairwell. Ramsey waited for him before he pushed the down button.

"Mr. Wainstein excused us all from further duty, Tom. He'll let us know when we'll regroup. You heading back?"

"I am. Chief, I need you to know –" Ramsey held up a hand and they waited in silence for the elevator to ding. He let the Chief go in first and waited till they cleared the elevator and the peephole and were out the 4th Street side of the building before he started over.

"Chief, I just want you to know I'll do better, I promise you – and I want to thank you for covering for me too. I'm sorry you had to do it." Ramsey nodded.

"Tom, I need to head over to the District Building for a Council meeting and I'm sure I'll find it in my best interests to have lunch with the Chairman, so why don't we continue this conversation up in my office, say at 2:30, just to be on the safe side?"

At the appointed hour, Wallace took a seat across from the Chief's large walnut desk. No one else was in the room. Ramsey propped his elbows on the arms of his chair, clasped his hands, and touched his thumbs to his chin. The look on his face reminded Wallace of the looks he saw on too many teachers' faces too many times back in high school, somewhere between concerned and exasperated.

"So tell me, Tom, how're you doing these days?" Wallace tried to nonchalant it.

"I'll be honest with you, sir. I'm a little nervous about my testimony because there's a lot riding on it and I know that probably came across a little today, but it's only because I don't want to let you or Ken or anyone else down. I'll be fine when the bell rings, don't worry about that." Ramsey nodded, then folded his arms on his desk and leaned forward.

"Was that why you had trouble with your testimony at the preliminary hearing too?" Wallace wasn't expecting that.

"I don't remember having any trouble there."

"Ken told me you said that no one at the PG PD had told you that Cooper wanted to take a lie detector about Starbucks out there, but the next witness – a Sergeant McCann, I think it was – said he did tell you, in great detail."

"I just didn't remember that, sir. I'm sorry, I wish I did but there's been an awful lot to remember over the last – what? – almost *three* years now? It's a big case, sir." Ramsey nodded and leaned back, then pulled a legal pad to him and pointed at a line of his notes.

"And, of course, as you know, I sent you the files Mr. McIntire was asking about this morning over three weeks ago." Wallace felt his cheeks heat up.

"I know that, sir, and again, I greatly appreciate you covering for me, I do. I had no intent –" Ramsey lifted his hand.

"Tom, I understand, but just let me be frank. Your performance this morning did not inspire a lot of confidence in me – and, more importantly, Mr. Wainstein – that you'd spent much time actually reviewing those files. And there's one other thing that's been brought to my attention. A little birdie told me you might be drinking a little too much these days and I'm concerned that's having an impact on your testimony and maybe the rest of your job too." Wallace let the image of Trainum in canary feathers flutter by before he answered.

"Chief, I don't know if that birdie also told you that I was stone cold sober for ten years until I had a couple of drinks to celebrate the night we got Cooper to confess. I know I shouldn't've done it, but it was a one-time thing, I promise you. It's got nothing to do with what happened today or at the preliminary hearing, I swear." Ramsey didn't look convinced, but he stood up and reached his hand across the desk. Wallace shook it hard.

"I'm going to take you at your word, Tom, but if I still have doubts the closer we get, you need to know I'm going to ask Mr. Wainstein to start prepping Detective Trainum and Detective Ruffin and whoever else we need to put our best foot forward on this. The bottom line is that you're going to have to do better than what I saw today. Hit those files harder and do whatever else you need to do to get yourself together, but do it pronto okay?"

"I'll be ready for Mr. McIntire the next time around and I'll be ready for Mr. Katz too. You don't have anything to worry about with me, I guarantee you."

Ramsey saluted him and Wallace walked out the door and took the elevator to the garage, his mind filled with swirling images of Trainum, McIntire, and Katz until he raised his flask and washed them all away.

52

Over the next two weeks, Wallace kept his distance from Robbie and weaned himself from the bottle, even refilling his Naltrexone prescription and unfolding the yellow sheet with Denny's name and number on it and daring himself to call it more than once. He never did, but limited his intake to a quick congratulatory swallow – or two, if he thought he deserved an extra star on the fridge for effort – every time he made it through a file. When he was sure he had his answer down pat to something McIntire asked – or Katz would ask – he recorded it on his eight-track and played it back constantly. By the time he was done, he felt like he'd memorized a triple-album version of his own Greatest Hits.

At 4:30 Friday, he forced himself to go over his notes one last time to make sure he'd really earned the prize of seeing her. When he was done, he put his folders away, closed his eyes, and shuffled a short stack of index cards face down before turning the top one over and giving himself a final mental closed-book test on the five questions he'd written on it. This one was about Cooper's interrogations by the FBI and PG.

How many times was he interviewed? *Nine, one by the FBI and eight by PG.*

How long was he in custody? *Sixty-nine hours over four days, March 1st to 5th.*

How many hours was he interviewed? *Twenty.*

How many times was he given his rights? *Eleven, once by Garrett and ten times by PG – four on a form, five during the Q&A, and once voluntarily.*

What happened during the time he wasn't being interviewed? *He said he slept nine to ten hours one night, he'd been allowed to eat, drink, and go to the bathroom every time he was interviewed, and he was denied nothing.*

When he flipped the card over and saw he'd aced every one, he picked up the phone and hoped Robbie might want to stop missing him as much as he wanted to stop missing her.

"Well, hello," he heard. "Takin' a study break?"

"I actually think I might be done." Her skepticism oozed back over the line.

"Really? And why is that?"

"I think I got it all down cold."

"Everything? The whole three years?"

"Hold on a second," he said and pulled a pad and pencil to him. "So, July 6, 1999 was two years, and today's April 7, 2000, so that makes it two years, nine months, and one day which means, I hate to tell you, Robbie, you're three months off." He smiled when he heard her laugh.

"Okay, I'm impressed," she said. "So you calling me just to show off?"

"Yeah, a little, but mostly to see if you have any dinner plans tonight." He heard her fridge door creak open.

"Unless you mean scarfing down what's left in the KFC bucket, no, I don't."

"Want me to bring something in?"

"What you got in mind?"

"Let me think on it a little. I'll figure out something. I might stop for a little dessert too."

"You might stop for a little booze too. I'm back down to the Captain and he ain't been opened for months. I'm scared to touch it, never mind drink it."

"Well, we can talk about that when I get there, okay? I'll be there soon," he said and hung up before she could ask him *Talk about what?* He'd packed a travel bag betting on the come and threw the tape recorder and his file on Joannie Lee into his briefcase just to stay sharp. Just as he clicked the latch, the phone rang. He took a longing look at the door before he picked it up. It was Wainstein.

"Tom, I'm glad I caught you."

"Why? What's up?"

"I just got off a conference call with Jake and Lewis and thought I ought to let my leadoff witness know plans may be changing."

"How so?"

"We've been talking the last week or two about seeing if we can work out a plea bargain and it's starting to look like we just might."

"What kind of plea bargain?"

"Life. Without parole." The first face that crossed Wallace's mind was Robbie's and it wasn't happy. Neither was the second one.

"What about Reno? Is she going to go along with that?"

"We've been keeping her – or at least the Deputy – in the loop all the way and no one's told us to stop, so we're hoping she will. It might not be what he deserves, but when you factor in all the risks of a D.C. jury finding him guilty, then giving him a death sentence, I think she'll buy it." *But none of that's going to mean jack shit to Robbie,* Wallace thought.

"When're you going to find out?" he asked.

"We're meeting at ten on Monday," Wainstein said. "You'll be the first to know what she says right after I tell Jake. In the meantime, don't let your files get too far away from you, okay?"

"Okay," Wallace said, "good luck!"

He knew Robbie would have a very different idea about what that meant than he did, so he gave some thought to how he might get her in the right mood if and when he got the balls to bring it up. The next minute, he called in two carryout New York Strip platters from Bobby Van's and thirty minutes after that, he pulled out of the parking lot at Syd's Liquor with a Canada Dry and a Chivas that he promised himself was just for her, then stopped at a 7-11 for two Chocolate Chunk cookies before he knocked on her door. When she pulled it open, he handed her the Bobby Van bag and smiled.

"Your dinner has arrived."

"Bobby Van? Who's that?"

"He runs a top-notch steak house on 15th St, and he's a brother too, so what's not to like?" She laughed and led him back to the kitchen. Once he set the cookies and the bottles on the counter, she wrapped her arms around him.

"I am so glad to see you, Tom. Lord, I missed you." He tilted her head up and kissed her softly on the lips, then harder as they pulled each other tight.

When they finally broke, he told her "I don't know how I've lived without that. I love you. You still know that, right?" The tears welling in her eyes told him all he needed to know but she sealed the deal with another kiss that lasted even longer before she laid her head on his shoulder and whispered "I never loved anyone as much as you. *Anyone.* And that's the truth." He wrapped her in his arms and they rocked slowly back and forth until she laid a hand on his chest and looked him in the eyes.

"So. What's it going to be?" she asked. He followed her gaze to the Bobby Van bag, then felt her hand slide his zipper down and saw that smile cross her face. "Him or me?"

"Wow, that's a hard one," he said and felt her fingers stroke his fly and her teeth nip his earlobe before he surprised himself by stepping back, his hands on her shoulders.

"Let's not let the steaks get any colder," he smiled. "You can re-heat my meat a lot quicker."

She laughed and he helped her set the table, filling two tumblers, hers mostly Chivas, his mostly Canada Dry. Once they toasted and after she rolled her eyes in delight at the taste of the steak, he felt if any time was right to talk about what he didn't want to talk about over the phone, this was it.

"So you remember when you told me to pick up some booze and I told you I had something I wanted to talk about?"

"I remember the 'pick up the booze' part. What do you want to talk about?"

"And you remember how you said you were impressed with me saying it was two years, nine months, and a day from the murders till today?"

"Okay, yeah. Anything else I need to remember before you tell me what we're really talkin' about?"

405

"No, but the reason I knew that, and the reason I know – and remember – everything I didn't remember when you saw me screw up at the preliminary hearing is because I been cutting back on the booze the last few weeks." She squinted at his full glass.

"That's cuttin' back?" He shrugged.

"It's like four parts ginger ale to one part Chivas. And I haven't totally stopped, but I'm fixin' to."

"Stopped like for good, or just till you testify?"

"Like for good." She thought about that a second before she returned the shrug.

"Okay. You gotta do what's right for you – but I hope you're not expectin' me to quit. You might need to tighten up to do your job, but I could be shitfaced and do mine just fine."

"No, I'm not. This is just me trying to get myself together, one step at a time." After he lifted his glass and she touched hers to it, he savored a sip and watched her finish hers. When she speared a chunk of steak, he figured he couldn't put off what Wainstein told him any longer.

"So I got some more news," he said.

"I'm pretty sure you ain't givin' up sex, so what? You got a coke habit I don't know about?"

"No, it's not about me. It's about Cooper." She stopped her fork in mid-air and tilted her head.

"They gonna kill him or not?"

"Right now, it's still up in the air."

"Okay, ain't nothin' new about that."

"Yeah, but they're going to make a decision Monday morning." She put the fork down slowly but he saw the heat rise in her face a lot faster.

"And you got an idea what they're going to decide." Wallace nodded.

"Yeah. Wainstein – the prosecutor – called me to tell me that he and Katz are going to recommend a plea bargain to the Attorney General, who's going to make the final call on it."

"So what you're telling me is he ain't gonna die." He shook his head.

"They're recommending life without parole." She swept the plate off the table, sending it cracking into the wall.

"Goddamn motherfuckin' hell! They're going to let that miserable SOB keep breathin'? After what he did to them people, never mind Vontae?"

"The AG might not take it. It ain't over yet." Robbie shot to her feet and kicked her plastic chair, ricocheting it off the oven behind her.

"Don't even try it!" she snapped. "Ain't no way you woulda told me that if you weren't Goddamned sure that's exactly what was going to happen. C'm'on, man, don't fuck with me!" Wallace held up his hands.

"It's not me, Robbie. Wainstein and his boss are afraid a D.C. jury won't sentence a brother to death and that they'll wind up with a hung jury or a sentence that's less than life."

"And what do *you* think?"

"It doesn't matter what I think."

"It matters to me!" He took his time trying to find the words that would tell her what he thought without inflaming her even more.

"What I think is I can see how they got there. I've seen what a D.C. jury can –"

"So you're on their side. I got that right?"

"Robbie, I'm not taking sides. They're just looking at the best thing to do to make sure Cooper gets what he deserves."

"What that fucker deserves is death! Period!"

"But what if the jury says he's not guilty? All it takes is one of them to make 'em go through a retrial – assuming they do re-try him and not settle for a plea bargain that's even crappier than this one. Or what if they say he's guilty but they don't want to kill him and come back with just twenty or thirty years? Then there's no re-do at all. That's what they're thinking about!"

Robbie paced the hallway, her arms clenching herself tight, still fuming, until she stopped on her second lap back and pointed a shaking finger at him.

"You know what? You've been telling me for weeks now – *months* maybe – that everyone's against you, but me. Your buddy Trainum ratted you out to your Chief. The Chief said you had to get your act together or he'd find someone to take your place, and your old buddy Katz has already taken you up one side and down the other and made you look like a fucking fool." She smacked herself on the chest. "I'm the only one who's been on your side! And now, what? You going to bend over and let all them bastards let Cooper live? When you know more than anyone what he did to them people in the Starbucks and Vontae? You just trying to make it unanimous now huh? Get everyone against you?"

408

He lowered his head before he pushed himself out of his chair and started to come her way in peace, but she backed against the oven and waved him off.

"No, no," she said. "Kissy-face and talky-talk ain't going to do it. This shit is serious." She shook her head, staring somewhere far past him, until she levelled a very steady finger at him. "Somebody needs to have a talk with that Katz, tell him he needs to let that fucker fry."

"He can't do that, Robbie. He's got a legal duty to represent his client as best he can. That's his job." She locked eyes with him.

"Somebody needs to make him see right."

"And who's going to do that?"

"You! You're a cop. You've got a gun." He stared at her in disbelief, then shot a look at her empty tumbler.

"Robbie, you've had a lot to drink. Let's get you into bed. You can sleep it off and we'll talk about it tomorrow morning when –"

"So you ain't got the balls to do it?"

"Robbie! Yeah, I have the balls and I've got a gun, but let's circle back to that part about me being a cop – for forty years! I got – we got – a nice retirement to look forward to one of these days, if I'm not spending it in prison! There's no way I'm going to do that." That seemed to slow her down. For a second.

"Okay then. Here's all you need to do. You just talk to him, find out where he's going to be one night, and leave the rest to me."

"What's that mean? *You're* going to kill him? You are drunk, aren't you? Or you're crazy!" Her eyes lit up with fire.

"Don't call me crazy, man! That's the shit I used to hear all the time growin' up! Don't ever call me that again!" Wallace tried to take things down a notch or ten.

"Okay, fine, I won't ever again. But think about it just for a minute. There are a lot of lawyers out there. Killing Katz isn't going to change anything." Robbie put a hand on her chest.

"Who said I was going to kill him? I just want someone to, you know, get his attention, okay? That's all." She buried her face in her hands and shook her head before she looked back at him, red-eyed, face drawn, worn out. "Shit, you know I'm gonna go to bed. You do what you want. I'm fucking done."

He watched her head down the hall and close the door without a look back at him. He looked at his watch. 8:35, way too early for sleep, but he knew he'd be just as on edge at 9:35 or 3:35. He refilled his glass, this time with the mix he made for Robbie, fell onto the sofa, and stared at the vacant TV screen. He flipped it on in the hope it'd distract him, but muted it after he flicked the channel from one group of good-looking white girls talking to a good-looking group of white boys about some petty crisis in their petty lives, to another group of what looked like the same exact people.

He muted the second group and downed the glass in one gulp, hoping it'd mute the racket in his brain. It didn't. There were way too many unanswerable questions, but he couldn't keep from thinking about the last one she sent banging through his mind: *Where'd I hear 'get his attention' before?* He riffled back through everything he'd read and everything he'd lodged in his mind over the past few weeks until it hit him like an electric shock. That was what Cooper told Man about how to handle Vontae ripping him off. And how did that work out? He told himself he was overthinking it, but couldn't shake the feeling that she put it just that way for a reason.

He got to his feet and kept telling himself that was unthinkable. But if it was, why did he keep thinking about it? He had to get some fresh air. He tiptoed back to the front door and closed it quietly behind him before he walked down the concrete walk, pushed open the chain link gate, and walked slowly down the middle of the dark street disappearing into the woods to his right. He listened to his deep breaths and waited for a pathway that would show him the way out of the churning maze of hard and painful thoughts colliding in his head. He couldn't begin to ferret out why and how events brought him to this place, where he had to choose between Katz and Robbie, but he did know this: He had to get it right. One of them would be lost to him forever, whatever he did, but he didn't know who he could bear losing more.

Headlights from behind lit up the road in front of him and he hoped they'd show him the way, but when they passed, he was still in the dark. The chill was heading for cold, so he turned around but stopped, feeling something he'd never felt before, like some kind of a tractor beam pulling him, compelling him to go in the only direction he could take. He remembered Katz telling him there was a time he felt he had no choice but to take a certain road and let the chips fall where they may. Whatever it was, it was happening to him now. He could see the path. There would be consequences, serious consequences, but none of that mattered now. All that mattered was he knew what he had to do.

He jogged back to Robbie's, quietly pushed the door open, and made a beeline for his briefcase. He wrote "I'll let you know where and when" on the top sheet of his pad, left it on the table, and quietly let himself out.

53

On the way to the car, he thought about whether he should wait till morning to call Katz, but as soon as he roared through the first yellow, he knew the answer. He found a pay phone on Pennsylvania Avenue Southeast, parked in a handicap space, threw the 'Official Police Business' placard on the dash, and dialed him up. He heard a groggy "Hello?" over a crowd cheering on the other end.

"Hey. You sleepin'?"

"Wow, guess I was. I thought I was watching the O's." The cheers got louder. "Man, that Mussina can pitch. What's up?"

"I was wondering if you might have time for dinner sometime this weekend."

"I'm always delighted to have your company, Tom, but I need to put something together on Cooper first thing Monday –"

"Like the finishing touches on a plea bargain?" Wallace heard a sour chuckle.

"Of course you know that. Why wouldn't you? At least tell me you heard it from Wainstein."

"I did. And that's why I need to talk to you this weekend. I've got something that might help you help him convince the AG to take the deal." He had nothing, but hoped that was an offer Katz couldn't refuse.

"Can't you just tell me now?"

"No, it's got to be face to face." He nearly bit his tongue in half waiting for an answer.

"Okay, I'll make it work. The usual place? Sunday at seven?"

"I'll call 'em right now. See you then."

Wallace made the reservation at Georgia Brown's then headed for bed, but didn't conk out till he knocked down a Benadryl a little after midnight that got him through to seven. By eight, he was alone in the evidence room in the MPD basement, looking for a box from any one of his drug busts. In five minutes, he found one: Wilmer Florio, a wanna-be gangster in Northeast who was running a coke distribution operation made up of four parts grade school buddies and one part undercover detective. Wallace put the box on a table, undid the ties on each side, pulled off the lid, and saw what he wanted right on top. He wrapped the charger cord around the burner phone and slid them into his inside jacket pocket. Fifteen minutes later, it was powering up in his living room. Thirty minutes later, he saw the green light flick on and called Robbie.

"Good morning," he said at her 'Hello'. "How'd you sleep?"

"Not too good. When'd you leave?"

"Around 9:30. I didn't sleep too good either, but I did do some thinkin'."

"Oh yeah? About what?"

"About what we were talking about last night." She was quiet a few seconds.

"You think it's a good idea to talk about that now, on the phone?"

"Don't worry. It's a burner. Everything's cool. So I think I came up with a plan for how you can get his attention." Another few seconds went by before he heard "I'm listenin'."

"Okay. The first thing is I'm going to meet him at Georgia Brown's for dinner tomorrow night at 7 o'clock."

413

"Where's Georgia Brown's?"

"You don't have to worry about that. You know where the MLK library is downtown?"

"Kinda. It's near where the basketball team plays, right?"

"Right. It's runs the whole length of G between 9th and 10th. It's the big black and glass place."

"Okay then, I know it. What about it?"

"That's where Katz is going to be after we get done eating dinner tomorrow night."

"Why there?"

"That's the route he takes walking home and I know he takes it because I've done it with him. There's a homeless guy he gives money to there, so he'll probably stop for a minute to talk to him. That should help you out too, you know, give whoever's going to do whatever they're going to do a little more time to do it."

"You going to be there too?"

"No, but if you can get me a burner number for your man there, I'll call him when he leaves the restaurant, then I'll call him again when he's five minutes away. Tell him to let it ring three times both times, and I'll hang up so he'll know it's me."

"Okay, so when's he going to be there?"

"I'm not sure yet. My guess is we'll be done sometime around 8, which means he'll get there around 8:15, but whoever's going to be there ought to plan on getting there before 7:30 just in case. You getting all this?"

"I got it."

"Without writing it down, right?"

"Are you serious? Hell no!"

"All right, then give it back to me."

She did, perfectly.

"And you remember what he looks like so your man doesn't take care of the wrong guy?"

"Short, middle-aged, gray hair, stupid smart-ass look on his face all the time. That good enough? I got it all, believe me. And I appreciate it, believe that too."

"Just one last thing, well two. It goes without saying, but I'm saying it anyhow: Your man's got to ditch the burner afterwards. And you need to stay home right by your phone just in case too, okay? If anything changes, I need to get in touch with you right away."

"I'll be here, Tom. And listen, I appreciate you doin' all this, and there's a whole lotta other people gonna appreciate it too. You're a doll. I love you."

"I love you too," he said and hung up. He looked at his watch. Nine-thirty. Now he had nothing to do but wait.

54

At 5:50 Sunday afternoon, he couldn't wait any longer. He drove up to the 1st District station on M Street SW and made a right onto Delaware Avenue to find the most totally unremarkable unmarked car he could, which turned out to be an aged taupe Taurus that fit the bill so well he didn't notice it till the second pass. He parked down the block, then walked back and stooped down to yank the magnetic key box off the back of the driver's side front wheel. After he opened the door and pushed the manual handle at the side of the bench seat all the way back to give him just enough room to squeeze behind the steering wheel, he was even happier to find another handle that lifted the steering column just enough to let him breathe. He put the key in the ignition and prayed the engine would kick over. When it did, he adjusted the mirrors and made his way, slowly and unremarkably, to 15th Street NW.

He found a street full of empty spaces on a Sunday night and picked one about twenty yards up and across the street from Georgia Brown's. The clock on the dash said 1:43, so he checked his watch for the real time. 6:31. He flicked on the radio with another prayer that was answered and turned the dial to the all-news station at 1500 AM, catching the end of a story about how the Internet was proving handy to not just the demonstrators protesting at the World Bank, but also to MPD, which was tracking their every move. He fidgeted his way through a dry cleaner jingle and traffic and weather on the eights, waiting for the sports, where the lead story was the night's NCAA women's basketball championship between UConn and Tennessee. With hometown pride, the announcer noted that the Volunteers were led by freshman Kara Lawson, who went to high school at West Springfield in Northern Virginia. He looked at his watch again – 6:47 – and after another six interminable minutes, finally saw Katz coming out of McPherson Square about ten yards ahead of him. He slid down in the seat and stayed there until he saw the door close behind him at Georgia Brown's.

He waited through the headlines at the top of the hour, another round of commercials, and one more report on the traffic and weather before he punched in Katz's cell phone number on the burner. After three rings, he heard "Jake Katz" and realized Katz didn't recognize the number.

"Jake, it's me, Tom."

"Hey. You running late?"

"Worse. I'm not going to be able to make it. I got pulled into something in Southeast. I'm really sorry, man."

"That's all right. Shit happens. I'll just get something to go. We'll do it again."

"I look forward to it – and say hi to your man at the library for me." Katz laughed.

"I'll give you his latest, don't worry. And take care of yourself out there."

"You too, Jake," Wallace said and hung up. At 7:27, he saw Katz come out of the restaurant with a carry-out bag in his hand and watched him walk back into McPherson Square before he put the car in Drive and headed up 15th. He couldn't trail him because of the maze of one-way streets and diagonals that downtown D.C. inflicts on its drivers, so he made his way to G Street and pulled into a parking space close to 12th that would let him see Katz whether he came from behind or turned onto the street in front of him. He spent the next five minutes flicking his gaze from the windshield to the side rear view mirror before he saw him coming down G from 14th. He picked up the burner and let it ring three times twice before he punched it off and made his way back into the maze, coming out two

417

blocks further down G and pulling into a space in front of the gray stone Catholic Charities building across from where the library started filling the block between 10th and 9th.

He looked across the street and saw the same swarm of homeless men he saw the night he was there with Katz. He scanned the crowd for someone who looked like Jaysonn or any of the other characters whose faces he'd seen in the pages of Vontae's rap sheets, but the darkness and the size of the crowd made it impossible to make anyone out clearly, even Katz' pun buddy, so he gave up quickly, trained his eyes on his rear-view mirror, and waited for Katz to come out of the darkness behind him.

In a couple of minutes, he saw him cross 10th and start to scan the crowd. He stopped almost directly across the street from him, looking right, then left, before he tapped the shoulder of a black man sitting on the sidewalk wrapped in a gray blanket and asked him something. The man waved him down the block and Katz put a bill in his hand before walking a few more yards and squeezing himself into the crowd. Wallace lost him for a few seconds and felt his throat tighten until he found him again, his hand on the punster's shoulder, both of them grinning. The punner was doing the talking now, his finger in Katz' chest. Katz shook his head 'No' to whatever he asked, waited to hear the answer, then cracked up. When he reached in his pocket for another bill, Wallace was distracted by a tall young black man in a Redskins cap standing near the curb flipping open a phone and muttering something into it before he folded it up, put it in his right jacket pocket, and turned to stare in the direction of 10th Street.

Wallace looked back there too and saw a shorter young black man in a dark zipper jacket turn the corner onto G, both hands in the jacket pockets. The tall man raised his hand and waved at him, then turned and walked slowly towards 9th. Wallace held his breath when he saw Katz walking about twenty yards in front of him, heading in the same direction. When the short man caught up with the taller one, they both picked up the pace. Wallace cursed himself, knowing that whatever was about to happen was totally out of his control. He watched, hands frozen on the wheel, as they narrowed the gap to Katz. When they got within a few feet of him, the taller man quickened his stride to pass him on the right and pulled a gun from his pocket, but Wallace's attention was suddenly diverted by Ruffin sprinting down the block behind them.

"Stop right there! MPD!" he yelled. Wallace watched the men run past Katz until they saw two uniformed patrolmen running at them from 9th Street, the sirens and lights of two patrol cars turning the corner just behind them. The cop in front stopped and levelled his weapon at them.

"Drop the gun!" he yelled. "Now!"

The tall guy froze in his tracks, then bent and laid his gun on the sidewalk before slowly standing up and raising his arms as high as he could raise them. The short guy spun around and ran past Ruffin, darting in and out of the crowd and losing the hat as he booked it back to 10th. Ruffin couldn't keep up and the guy bolted into the street before he weaved to dodge a car door flying open right in front of him and felt Wallace's cross-body block crush him to the ground. Ruffin knelt on his back and cuffed him before he turned to look at Wallace sprawled out in the middle of the street.

"Detective! You okay?" he called out.

Wallace slowly rolled over and rubbed his right hip. "Been a long time since I laid anyone out like that. And I was wearin' pads then." He got to his knees and waited to feel if the pain was throbbing anywhere else before he tried to get up. He managed to bend his left leg and started to push himself up when he felt a hand on his back and looked up into the face of one of the patrolmen breathing heavy after running to him.

419

"You okay, sir?" Wallace held his hand up and the patrolman grabbed it and wrapped an arm around his back to help him up. His right knee held and he took a few cautious steps just to make sure before he nodded and the officer let him go. "Thanks. I'm good," he said and limped over to the car. He saw the burner staring back at him from the middle of the seat, and heard it taunting him, asking him if he was man enough to finish what he started. But courage hadn't mattered since he knew Friday night exactly what he had to do. Now he just had to finish it.

He sat down, picked up the phone and punched in Trainum's number. When he heard him pick up, he said "Where you at?"

"Right where you told me to be. Should we go get her?"

Wallace waited one last time for an answer to come to him besides the one he knew he had to give.

It didn't.

"Yeah," he said. "Bring her in."

"Ten-four. Your man Katz okay?"

"He's fine."

"How about you? You sound winded."

"I'll be fine," he said. *One day,* he thought. *Maybe.*

August 8, 2000

Wallace showed up at Georgia Brown's ten minutes early and ducked into the men's room to take a second dose of Naltrexone, just in case. When he came out, he was surprised to see Katz already at the table. He stood up and extended his hand with a smile.

"When you said dinner was on you, I just couldn't wait." They shook and Wallace shrugged.

"I bailed on you the last time we were supposed to be here, so I figured I owed you one." When they took their seats, Katz said "You know, that turned out be a very weird night." Wallace's demeanor didn't change.

"Really?" he asked. "How so?"

"So I was walking home past the library like usual and I talk to my man and he gives me his pun and I'm starting to head home when a cop runs up the sidewalk right at me, then stops and pulls out his gun!"

"No *shit*," Wallace figured was the appropriate response.

"I swear to God! And I thought he was pointing it at me but when he yells 'Drop the gun!,' I realize he must be talking to someone else, so I turn around and I see a guy laying his gun on the ground. Then this other guy just takes off running back to 10th Street and a cop starts chasing him, but it looks like he's going to get away – until he just gets fucking *nailed* by someone who jumps out of a parked car! They both go down and before the running guy can get up, a cop puts the cuffs on him and they put him and the other guy in patrol cars and take 'em both away. It was crazy!" Wallace sat back, shaking his head, his face the picture of awe.

"Wow!" he said. "That *is* crazy! Let me ask you something. The guy who took off running, was he a short black guy in a dark jacket?" Katz didn't have to think about it.

422

"Yeah, he was." Then he thought about it. "How'd you know that?"

"And the tall guy, was he wearing a 'Skins hat?"

"What the fuck?" Katz said, his face now searching for answers until he found a question. "Were you there?" Wallace couldn't stop the smile spreading across his face.

"I'm the guy who jumped out of the car." Katz' expression went from confused to bewildered to disbelieving in a matter of seconds.

"No, wait. You told me something came up at the last minute." Wallace shrugged again.

"Something did," he said, and pointed at him. "You."

Katz fell back in his seat as the waiter came to take their drink orders. "Johnny Walker Black," he said. "A double. Straight up."

"Any kind of fizzy water'll do," Wallace said.

Katz waited till the waiter left before he threw up his arms and told Wallace what his face had already told him. "Tom, I am totally lost. Enlighten me."

"We got word that someone wanted to, let's say, persuade you that agreeing to a plea deal for Cooper wasn't such a good idea."

"Really! What were they going to do?" Wallace shook his head.

"The lawyers and the courts'll figure that out, but since there were two of them and one of 'em had a gun, I think we can assume it was something more than just chit-chat." Katz tried to keep up.

"And why were you there in a car?"

"I was parked outside Georgia Brown's when I called to tell you I couldn't make it. I waited till you came out, then drove over to where I had a pretty good idea you were go–"

"But how did you know that? What if I went somewhere –". Wallace reached over and laid his hand on his. "You *told* me you were going there when I asked you to give my best to your pun buddy, remember?" He watched Katz pull their conversation up from the back channels of his brain and start nodding.

"And you knew that whatever was going to happen was going to happen at the library."

"I did. And don't ask me how. Let's just leave it at I knew."

The waiter dropped off the cornbread basket and turned to Wallace. "Do you know what you'd like to have, sir?" Wallace handed him the menu.

"The usual. Shrimp Perloo, thanks." The waiter jotted it down and turned to Katz.

"I believe I'd like the Carolina Gumbo," he said. When the waiter left, Wallace said "Well, that was impressive. Stretching out your tastes, I see."

"I ordered it to go that night. It looked interesting and I figured I could always toss it and fix myself a tuna sandwich if it didn't taste as good as it looked, but it did, and here I am back for more." Wallace raised his glass and clinked it with Katz'.

"To an old dog learning new tricks." They clinked and swallowed but by the time Katz laid his glass back on the tablecloth, he looked like he was still trying to figure out exactly what happened and why. Wallace decided to give him at least part of the answer.

424

"You remember what happened with Eric Butera?" he asked. "The guy who got murdered at a crack house in D.C. because we didn't have eyes on him every minute? I swore that was never going to happen to me again." *Especially with you* went unsaid. He waited for Katz to keep probing him in his usual anal way, but then saw his brow unfurrow and his hand lift his glass back up.

"You know what? I know all I need to know. Thanks, Tom. Here's to you, and Eric Butera." They clinked and swallowed again, then watched the waiter put down their plates and leave. After a couple of forkfuls and accompanying appreciative noises, Wallace pointed an empty fork at him.

"Did that freak you out about ever going back to the library?"

"No, but it freaked my pal out. I got the courage up to go back there a week or two later, but he wasn't there. One of the other guys told me he got a bad vibe about the place after that night and had started hanging outside Union Station, so I went over there and, sure enough, there he was."

"His puns get any better over there?"

"Still just as awesome. Want to hear the latest one?"

"No, but you're going to tell me anyway. Let's get it over with."

"Why couldn't the sesame seed leave the poker table?"

"I don't have a clue. Why?"

"He was on a roll". Wallace stared back at him blankly and shook his head.

"And you keep going back for more," he said. "That's the most amazing part."

They ate a little more before Katz stopped to draw a napkin across his mouth. "So unless there's something else I don't know, that's the second time you saved my ass, or maybe my neck." They both thought of Wallace scooping him up at the DC Coliseum all those years ago. "But the only reason you were in a position to save it this time was because you put me in the situation where it needed saving, so that should get an asterisk, if it even counts."

Wallace put a finger to his ear like he was trying to hear something far away. "Let's see what the judges say," he said, then shook his head and looked back at Katz. "Nope. Still two-nothing, me." Katz finished downing a spoonful of gumbo, shaking his head all the while.

"Hold on, man. I saved your career when I got you your Detective bars back at the B'nai B'rith during the Khaalis thing. You remember that, don't you? You'd still be filing parking tickets in the MPD basement if I hadn't told your Deputy Chief whoever to give you another shot back there."

"Fine. His name was Rabe, by the way, and I'll give you that one, which makes it two-to-one, but then we need to count me sparing you living with a woman who you didn't know killed your best friend. Three-one."

"Hold on. First of all, she didn't kill him. Second, that's kind of like this, isn't it? If you hadn't told me, I might still be with her, happy as a clam." Wallace wiped his face and waved his hands like the kick was no good.

"The judges have already ruled. But I do know you would've been happy waking up and seeing her next to you every day." Katz grew quiet and Wallace pretended not to notice the sudden weakness in his eyes before he got himself together enough to take a healthy taste of the JW Black. Wallace refilled his Perrier before he changed the subject.

"So where'd they put Cooper?"

"Beautiful downtown Sumterville, Florida. Coleman Penitentiary Number One to be exact."

"Are you in touch?"

"That would be a no, but he did leave me a message about two weeks after he got down there, saying he wanted to talk to me about appealing, getting a new trial. My guess is his new roommates put the bug in his ear."

"And what'd you say?" Katz shook his head.

"I never called him back. He was no longer my client so I just figured he'd be better off finding someone else who could at least complain about the ineffective assistance his trial lawyer gave him. And that plea bargain was even a better deal for him than just letting him live, by the way. I also got the Government to promise not to go after his wife for buying the gun he used in a bunch of robberies. Or his mother for laundering the proceeds."

Wallace picked his plate clean and sat back. Katz had a few spoonfuls of gumbo left in his bowl, but he was done too.

"Want to finish it for me? It's great, but I'm full."

"No, I'm good," Wallace said and waved to the waiter.

"Can I interest you in dessert?" he asked. "We have many –". Wallace held up a hand, shook his head, and pointed to Katz. "I'm out too," he said, "but I will take a decaf coffee." "Make it two," Wallace said. Katz looked at his watch and laughed.

"Two wild men," he said. "Decaf at 7:45."

Wallace snorted his laugh. "At least you can still handle your drinks." Katz shook his head.

427

"Just when I'm out somewhere, which is not often these days. So let's see, I'm 53. How old are you?"

"62 next month."

"62?! Why aren't you retired already? Doesn't MPD have one of those 20 years in, 50 years old retirement deals?"

"It does and I could, but what am I going to do in retirement? I got nowhere to go, no one to retire with. What's the point?" Katz squinted at him.

"Didn't you tell me you were seeing someone? I remember you saying something about inviting me to a wedding." Robbie's face popped back into Wallace's head, then popped back out just like it did every time he remembered why he hadn't seen it in the flesh for 130 days now and counting.

"Nah," he said. "There was someone I thought might be special, but that's been over for a while and I can't get motivated to try again. Maybe someday. How about you?" Katz grimaced.

"I'm too old now. I'm still up for the game if you catch my drift, but to do what it takes to get there – the phone calls, the dating, the going, the doing – that brings me right back down."

"Maybe you shouldn't've been too quick to let Cleo go," Wallace smiled. Katz actually seemed to think about that a second before he lifted his decaf and Wallace lifted his.

"To lost loves," Katz said, and they clinked.

* * *

Robbie pulled the cord next to the toilet and waited for the blare of the guard's voice to come back through the tinny speaker over her head.

428

"You need help?"

"Yeah, sorry. Just still a little weak, you know."

"Sit tight. I'll send someone over."

She hadn't been able to get off the can by herself since she had the baby three days ago – and six weeks early – and she hadn't held him or seen him since they took him away from her the morning after he dropped and put him in foster care. Unless she had a family member who could take care of him, that was 'policy,' they said. There was no way Albertha could take care of him and Jaysonn was in the D.C. Jail for the same reason she was here, so family wasn't happening.

As soon as she was healthy enough to walk a lap from one end of the treatment facility to the other, the only place she was going anyhow was back to Lorton because she couldn't make bail. The only lawyer she ever talked to one time was someone from the public defenders who told her point blank that she was a 'low priority' because what she did – 'conspiring to assault' was what he called it – wasn't a major felony. He said she'd be better off pleading but if she did that, she could kiss the CVS job goodbye and then how was she supposed to feed herself, never mind the baby? Jaysonn was supposed to have his lawyer call her, but the only other person she ever talked to on the phone was whatever guard was on toilet duty. She heard a knock on the door.

"Come on in," she said and was happy to see the round smiling face of the one guard who was nice to her. She was black, about her age, with processed blond hair tucked under her cap. Her name tag said 'Blair,' but she told her to call her 'Dolly'. "How you doin' today, sister?" she asked. Robbie grunted.

"I'll be good soon as I get my ass offa here and back in that bed." Dolly laughed.

429

"Well, come on now. I'll help you and then I got a little surprise for you."

"What? A hacksaw?"

"Girl, you are something. No, even better than that. Now give me your hands."

Dolly walked her back to the bed and helped her tuck herself in, then raised the head of the bed till Robbie told her to stop.

"You still expressin' the milk okay?"

"Yeah," Robbie said. "You know if he's takin' it okay?"

"As a matter of fact, I do. They were on my foster home run yesterday, so I got a chance to check up on him." Robbie's face shone.

"Aw, how's he doing?"

"He was chuggin' it down when I was there. He is one strong and hungry little man."

"Lord, I wish I could see him." Dolly shot her a sly smile and reached her hand inside her breast pocket.

"I was thinking you might want to, so I took a few Polaroids with their camera. Surprise!"

Robbie gasped and took them from her. His little face was hidden by the bottle in the first one, but it was clear as a bell in the other two. He was sleeping, with a little spit-up on his tiny cheek in the third one. Tears ran down her cheeks.

"Oh my God! He is *so* beautiful." Dolly grinned and came around behind her to look at his face.

"Who you think he looks like?" Robbie fanned out the pictures, then shook her head.

"Hard to tell. He's going to have to fill out a little more, I guess."

"He got a name now?" Robbie closed up the pictures and held them to her chest.

"He does," she said. "His daddy's name. Vontae."

POSTSCRIPT

Like my previous books about Tom Wallace and Jake Katz, this is a work of fiction. Although I changed several names to protect people's privacy, occasionally tweaked timelines, and supplied most of the dialogue, my depiction of all of the events relating to the Starbucks murders and their investigation is true. Over the two and a half years I worked on this book, I relied greatly on five people to help me make sure it was. For that, I am immensely grateful to:

Jim Trainum, who met with me, responded to dozens of my e-mails, and gave me access to his extensive personal materials on the case;

Ken Wainstein, for sharing his memories and insights about numerous facets of the prosecution of the case;

Brad Garrett, for his willingness to provide information and his memories of the case;

The ever-helpful Bryant Johnston, the Records Supervisor at the United States District Court for the District of Columbia, who, as is his custom, went above and beyond to give me ready access to the Court's archived records; and

My wife Sandy Tevelin for her unabating love, support, and encouragement, as well as her reviews, critiques, and recommendations.

A few of the statements Jake Katz made in the book were quotes or adaptation of quotes made by Mr. Cooper's actual defense attorneys that I found in newspapers or court records. I asked both lawyers to talk to me about their experience in the case, but both declined to do so.

I would also like to express my deep appreciation to:

Jeff Leen for his article "A Dance With Death" in the March 2, 2003 Washington Post Sunday Magazine (A Dance with Death - The

Washington Post), which was of invaluable help to me in organizing the story;

Tumbler.com for its September 4, 2017 story "Murder In Georgetown" and the photograph that appears on the cover of the book (So Give Me Coffee & TV, History - Murder In Upper Georgetown (tumblr.com));

Harry Jaffe for his article "Another Starbucks Murder" in Washington Magazine's April 1998 issue, which provided me a wealth of information about the murder of Eric Butera;

Courtland Milloy for his February 9, 2000 column in the Washington Post, "A Death-Penalty Study In Black and White" relating the story of the 1995 killings at McDonald's; and

Former Law Enforcement Assistance Administration Office of General Counsel colleagues Greg Brady and Charlie Lauer for reminding me of so many of the restaurants where we used to eat lunch – and avoid eating lunch – during our time together at 633 Indiana Avenue, N.W.

I would also like to note that, due to my interest in making the incredibly complex facts of the case clearer to the reader, the book does not recognize the key roles that two police officers played in investigating and solving the case, Tony Patterson from MPD and J.D. Harding from the PGPD.

Some details concerning MPD officers' actions before and at the scene of Eric Butera's death were also modified to make the event clearer and more readable. The essential details of Mr. Butera's death are, however, sadly true. On January 9, 2001, the $98.1 million verdict against the defendants in the suit brought by Terry Butera was reduced to a little more than $1 million, but still included the $570,000 punitive damages verdict against the four officers on the scene. *Butera v DC*, 235 F.3d 637 (DC Cir.).

At this writing, Carl Cooper continues to serve a life sentence at Coleman I Federal Penitentiary in Sumterville, Florida.